GUSTAVSON

TAMMY OUT OF TIME

Tammy Out of Time

A NOVEL

By

CID RICKETTS SUMNER

PEOPLES BOOK CLUB, CHICAGO

This is a special edition published exclusively for the members of the PEOPLES BOOK CLUB, P. O. BOX 6570A, Chicago, Illinois; in Canada, 228 Bloor Street, West, Toronto, Ontario. It was originally published by The Bobbs-Merrill Company.

TAMMY OUT OF TIME

1.

OLD DEADWOOD'S shanty boat had squatted all winter at the foot of the bluff in a tangle of bare willow trees like a hen on the nest, the skiff a lone chick behind. Now the Mississippi had begun to rise and the *Ellen B.* was rising too, among the willow branches, yellow-green with early spring. The big hackberry with the hawser chaffing at the trunk was lifting folded leaves against the sky and all the bluff was touched with tender promise.

Old Deadwood's granddaughter Tammy ran up the path that cut a slanting gash across the face of the bluff. Her blue dress flashed between the bushes like a jaybird's wing, her bare feet made no sound. But the little nanny goat she had trained to follow like a dog, was keen to hear, and came on a run, the thud of her hoofs fluttering hens from the way. Tammy stopped at the top of the bank and waited for her, swinging the empty water bucket at her side. The sun was slanting toward the far Louisiana shore, but there was time enough to go to the spring and back.

The path led straight along the crest of the bluff for a way, then the trees opened out to show the rippled shine of the river, curving back upon itself, cradling the swamp in the crook of its arm. "It's a fair sight, Nan," Tammy said. Nan nibbled grass and Tammy waited, looking up at a plane so high in the sky that it went easy and quiet as a buzzard, a silver buzzard, beelining it for New Orleans. Then she went on with Nan following close at her heels. They dropped down the wooded slope into a glen and crossed a still, black bayou by a fallen beech.

It was a long way to go for water when all the river was ready to

7

hand, but Tammy was going to wash her hair and it was no fun washing in water that was already so muddy the dirt didn't show. Grandma used to say the first of April was time enough to wash your hair but Tammy was not going to wait till then—her head was getting itchy and this was a fair, warm day even if it wasn't even February yet.

The spring water had a good taste to it, though Grandpa claimed he liked the river better. "A sight healthier for you," he'd say. "The mud's good for your constitution. Bet I got enough mud in my stummick to raise corn and I ain't never been sick a day in my life, if you don't count the rheumatiz." Grandpa was always talking like that.

The spring itself was a kind of mystery. On the far slope where the fern began, it came out from the roots of a sweet-gum tree and ran over lichen and leaf, clear and cold and no kin at all to river or bayou. Where had it come from; how was it made? Did the earth strain out the earth, creating something better than itself, making the unclean pure? Or was it a miracle, as when Moses smote the rock? Without a ripple it slid into the circle of a sunken barrel so old that it would be gone to staves and hoops but that the water pressed it outward, the earth pressed it inward and the sky was laid atop it.

The water in the barrel made a mirror. Looking in, Tammy could see herself fair and true. The blurry little looking glass on her wall put a crook in her cheek and warped her mouth this way and that as she moved, and set one eye higher than the other. "I wish I could see myself whole just once," she said, kneeling, leaning over, careful lest she frighten the water bugs to ripple her image. "Seventeen year old and I never seen myself altogether yet." Would she always have to have this wonder about herself? Would she never be able to gather into one the inward self that was known and the outward that was yet strange? "That's me, that one in there, me," she whispered, trying to link the two.

The water mirror teased her. When she bent down so that her

dark hair, falling loose and long, was just above the surface, her reflection came into shadow and she could see no more than the wide sweep of her forehead, the line of dark straight brows. She had to draw back to guess how gray her eyes were, how pointed her chin. Turning a little, she got a notion what her nose was like—too big, she was sure.

She sat back on her heels with a sigh. Maybe there was another kind of looking glass to know one's self by—made of things people said. Like Cap'n Joe on the fish boat, calling out to Grandpa, "Likely-looking gal you've got there, Deadwood. Looks like she could stand in a peck measure and shoulder a bushel of meal!" Then there were those ladies on the packet boat long ago, with a sign across the boat saying they were bound for the Pilgrimage at Natchez and New Orleans. "Quaint!" they had said, speaking right out as if she could not understand, looking down from the high deck as they passed close by, laughing at the line of clothes she was hanging on a fishing pole cane stuck out from the window, pointing to the stovepipe smoking its blue wood smoke right into their laughter. Grandpa, with his pipe in the shade of the tin roof, had paid them no mind. Not even when they said, all high and mighty, "How do they live, people like that?"

A kind of fury had possessed her then, made her free and daring. She had mounted the rail and stood balanced there. Her body swayed as the shanty boat rocked with the packet's churning and her bare toes curled over the flat toprail. "We live all right," she shouted into the noise of the packet's engine, into their frightened faces looking down, drawing away, going forever out of her ken.

"Quaint! I'll teach folks to call me quaint," she shouted. Then Grandpa had yanked her down to the deck before she had time to fall overboard.

"Spunky little devil, ain't you? But you needn't drown yourself sassing folks. Quaint's nothing bad. 'Tain't a thing to be ashamed of."

Tammy, on her knees by the spring, laughed to herself. Then

she picked up the bucket and, plunging it deep in the barrel, shattered her image and set the water bugs leaping and skimming. "I'm as good as the next one, I reckon," she said, setting the brimming bucket down on the ferns and shooing Nan back from sticking her nose in and slobbering all over it. Eddy and Gladys had said she was better than most. That was way back when she was no more than six or seven and they were tied up close to Natchez with lots of other shanty boats. Circus folks gone to seed, Grandpa had called them.

Tammy found a level spot and walked on her hands just to prove she had not forgotten. Eddy'd taught her that, and Gladys had showed her some dance steps and made her sing all the old songs Grandma had taught her, like "Last night I dreamt of my truelove," and "Old Rosin the Beau." They'd said, "That's a smart young un." They'd wanted to take her away with them, said she'd fit into their act. Goshamighty, she'd have been a top performer by now if Grandpa hadn't said such dancing and doings were sinful and the fire and brimstone would get her if she didn't lay off. What a whipping he'd given her about it! He'd give her another, big as she was, if he knew she still had that little jar of face paint Gladys gave her—kind of dried up, but holding its color still.

That whipping hadn't hurt half so bad as she hurt inside the morning the police came and got Eddy. She hadn't really known what it was all about then, though she'd seen Gladys taking on over that man who was always hanging round when Eddy was out of the way, cutting her eyes at him, snugging up to him. Then along in the middle of the night she'd heard her screaming bloody murder and hollering at Eddy not to kill him. But Eddy must have killed him, all right. Because they found the man next day floating downriver with a knife hole clean through him, and then they came and got Eddy and took him away. It still made her ache just thinking about how he looked with a man each side of him.

Tammy picked up the water bucket and set it on her head. It was

Gladys that had told her to put books on her head and it would teach her to walk like a queen. "You got to walk like a queen in the show business," she'd said. But all the books Tammy had on the *Ellen B.* were the Bible and the catalogue and some her mamma had in high school and the one a boy got mad and threw at her once. She thought she'd better save them for the inside of her head instead of the outside. Besides it was more fun with a bucket of water because she'd get a ducking if she didn't walk right. She'd got drenched many a time, but now she could walk across the beech log and up the slope without spilling a drop.

At the crest of the bluff Tammy stopped to look out over the river. She had come at just the right moment to see the sun sitting on top of the land, to watch the land bite a piece out of it and the shadow of the far willows creep across the river. A tugboat was chugging barges upstream, hugging the other side, too far off to wave or holler at. It put a veil of smoke across the sun and made it look like an orange the earth was eating.

Tammy looked away downstream. There was no sign yet of Grandpa coming back from wherever he'd gone. "You tend to your business and I'll tend to mine," he'd said when she asked him what-for he was going to the swamp all the time, instead of fishing like he used to do. She called, "Yoo-hoo" loud and long, patting the sound with the palm of her hand so it was broken like a hoot owl's cry. She cupped her ear to listen. There was no answer save a far-away cowbell down the river somewhere. The lonesomest sound in the world was a cowbell.

Tammy looked down at the *Ellen B.* nuzzling at the shore, red geraniums bright on the shelf and stovepipe thrusting out and up like a saucy wren's tail. A good boat, bigger than most, with two rooms and the tin roof jutting out to make a little porch. Good enough to go anywhere in. Only Grandpa—looked like he wasn't ever going to move far from this lonely neck of the woods. Grandma's grave in the little old graveyard along a bluff a way, was an anchor, holding him. Oh, he'd go a little piece up toward Vicksburg or down toward Natchez—he'd been doing that every now and then for the last ten years or so—but he'd never go back all the way to where there were folks.

It was lonely here without other boats drawn up alongside, the way she could remember it long ago. She could recollect clear as day how it was to shout back and forth with the washing waving on the line and all the other children running about and jumping across from deck to deck. There were big girls making their hair frizzy and their lips red and moving with that special motion that beckoned better than a finger, there were babies crying and dying and getting born with pain and struggle, and the old women talking their long talk about how to cook a gumbo proper and all the sicknesses their folks had died of and how they used to live in a house set steady on the ground with a real good salad patch and Cape jessamines at the door or oleanders, upriver somewhere or down in the French-speaking parts, back in the good old days that don't come back.

She could remember Grandpa preaching to all the river folks on deck or alongshore of a Sunday morning, the women silent for once and hushing their children, the men harking reluctantly to the Word of God and all joining in at the singing of the hymns, the sound spreading free across the water and going up like a waterspout to top the towering bank. Oh, Tammy sighed, that was living! Maybe Grandma had thought it was too much living. "'Tain't fitting for a young girl," she'd told Grandpa and, right after, they'd come on up the river to here and Grandma'd taken sick and died. Then the lonesome time began.

Tammy called once more and, getting no answer, went on down the slanting path singing to keep herself company:

> "Make me a cambric shirt
> Without a stitch of needlework,
> And you shall be a true lover of mine,
> Rosemary and thyme."

The sun was clean out of sight now and the air was saying it wasn't summer yet. She shooed the chickens back out of her way and crossed the plank that led from shore to deck. Time to feed them, time to milk Nan. Always something to do—and never anything happening. She did wish something would happen for a change. And by something she meant something sure enough, and not just the young preacher coming from ten miles or so down the big road and three miles through the swamp to tell Grandpa she ought to be going to school and learning how to live in the world. As if they didn't know anything, either of them. It made her mad just to think about it, even yet. Milking Nan, she played a quick sharp tune on the bottom of the can with the streams of milk. She didn't need any schooling. Why, she could read and write and she could figger faster than Grandpa and she knew the Bible backwards and forwards. And yet—if there was more, she'd like to know it.

The river still held light from the sky, but in the kitchen, which was Grandpa's bedroom too, it was time to get the lantern going. Tammy took a spill from the flowered china mug on the shelf, stuck it through a crack in the stove door till it blazed. Then she stood on a box to reach the lantern that hung down from the ceiling. The soft yellow light made the room cozy and welcoming. Grandma's crazy quilt that covered the bed had kept its colors in spite of many washings, and the curtains made of flour sacks and dyed with boiled-up juice from yellow clay still looked gold at night though by day the sun streaks showed.

Tammy got wood from the box beside the stove and built up the fire so her wet hair would dry. The collard greens were boiling on the back hole and she put the griddle with the hoecake in the oven to finish off and to make room for the skillet. While the catfish was frying she sat down in Grandma's rocker with the goatskin seat and leaned back, her feet on the footrest, her arms resting on the chair arms and her hair flung over the high back to air and dry as she rocked. It sure was a luxury, having a rocking chair. Pity Grandma never got to sit on it. She'd pestered Grandpa to make it for her ever since the old goat died and they tanned the hide. Then the day after Grandma was buried up on the bluff, Grandpa got out the hickory boards and started whittling on them. A kind of fury of grief had come over him and it looked like he couldn't rest till he got it done. Sometimes now when a boat went by and the waves rocked the *Ellen B.* and set the chair to rocking all by itself, he'd look at it like he saw Grandma sitting there. It gave him the lonesomest look in his eyes. That was a good kind of love for a man to have for a woman, Tammy reckoned. Lasting.

She rocked on with her eyes closed and her head leaning back on the slats of the high chair back. Love—nigh as she could figger out, there was more than one kind, not counting the love-your-neighbor kind in the Bible. One was fancy-spoken, like the lords and ladies in the *Idylls of the King* she had read the covers off of; one was fancy-pillowed like that frizzy-haired woman who left her cabin open on hot nights and Grandma said she might have the decency to shut it. Still, it was a good thing to know about, even if it had made Grandma say they had to get the *Ellen B.* amoving and find a place where they could raise a girl decent.

Tammy stood up to turn the fish and heard the rattle of Grandpa's oars. The lantern swayed as he stepped aboard and the boat rocked lightly with his weight. "Supper's ready, Grandpa," she called.

He came in grunting because of his rheumatism, a thin old man with a round head, skimpy-haired, a round ruddy face and a small, sparsely bearded chin. He hung his coat and battered felt hat on a nail on the wall, sat down on a box and leaned his arms on the bare pine table. "Dish it up honey. I ain't got much time." His blue eyes were round and sad when he was not talking, and they went over the room now the way they always did when he first came in, trying to find somebody that wasn't there and wouldn't be ever again.

Tammy said in wonder. "You've got all night, haven't you?"

He made her no answer nor did he speak again, except to say the blessing, till they both had cleaned their plates. "Anything happen today whilst I's gone?" He got his pipe from his pocket and started filling it.

"Cap'n Joe came by soon this morning. I got a sack of meal and some side meat from him like you said. He brought me seeds like I asked him for, and some extra flower seeds thrown in. Now if there'd just be some chicken wire come floating down, I could add on to the garden patch and——"

"You have enough fish to pay him?"

"Yes, I had a sight of them." She lighted a spill at the stove and held it to his pipe.

"Say anything special?"

"Wanted to know when you's going to start fishing again. Said fish's bringing a good price now."

"Humph. That all?"

Tammy had the dishes in the pan that was rigged up with a pipe to make a sink, and she waited till she had poured hot water over them. She looked round at him through the steam. "He brought you a word from the sheriff."

Grandpa's face closed up like a turtle drawing into himself. "The sheriff?"

"Yes. He said you'd remember how the Straker boys had a still somewheres in the swamp, they never found where."

"I've heard tell of it."

"Well, the sheriff says somebody's found it and set it going again, because there's sure liquor going out of the swamp like it was before they caught the Strakers and sent them up. The revenue men are looking, he says."

"What's it got to do with me?"

Tammy turned back to her dishes and rattled them all she had a mind to. She knew now that it was true, what she'd been thinking for a long time, ever since she saw the load of corn Grandpa rowed way up the river and got from some farmer over on the Louisiana side. He'd had it covered with his old coat and a gunny sack, but she'd seen it all right. "Sheriff wants you to be on the watch for any signs, he said."

Grandpa puffed on his pipe. "Next time you see Cap'n Joe, you tell him I'm much obliged and for him to tell the sheriff I'll sure keep an eye out. Now fetch me down the lantern from the shelf."

Tammy wiped her hands on the sides of her skirt and got the lantern. "Plenty of coal oil in it, but looks like the wick could do with a trimming."

Grandpa opened it up and turned the wick, pinching off the black. "Make me a pot of coffee, child. Leave it setting where it'll keep hot. I'll need it when I get home."

"What you going to do in the night, Grandpa?" Tammy set the plates on the shelf and put the knives and forks beside them.

"Got to see if there's any floaters come down."

Tammy sat down at the table, her arms resting on it, her gray eyes growing wide and dark as she thought of calamity come to someone. "What happened?"

"Fellow was telling me this morning. Airplane crashed smack down into the river a while back. Flew the water up like a fountain, he said. Broke itself to bits."

Tammy drew a long breath. Seemed like she could almost see the plane coming along fast and sure and high, with people sitting in it, talking about nothing more than this or that, thinking ahead in their minds about the next stopping place and how they'd just step out on the ground and go about their business. Not thinking about all the miles in between and the river and the swamp down below. People in a dream, they were. Then down, down, the dream breaking, the real world hitting them, so that if they knew anything, they knew there was more to going than just stepping aboard and stepping out when they got where they were going. "Did they—were they all kilt?"

"They rescued two, kind of banged up, and they got one out of the wreckage. Two they couldn't find, maybe three. Somebody claims the last minute before they took off from some place out

West, a man comes and hitches a ride. So they don't know what's his name. There'll be good reward money for the others, if I have any luck. Now give me a light. I got to get going."

Tammy put a flame to the wick. It burned bright and the tin reflector Grandpa had made threw the light out strong and clear in a half circle. "All the same," she said, "seems like you ought to wait for daylight."

"I got other things to do by daylight. Besides, it's time they was acoming down, near as I can calculate." He rose stiffly and reached down his old coat and hat from the nail. When he'd got them on, he pulled a bottle from his pocket and set it on the table. "Fill her up, honey. Maybe it'll keep the aching out of my joints."

Tammy took the jug from the shelf above the wood box and poured the bottle half-full of corn liquor. Grandma never would fill his bottle but half-full so she wouldn't either. It wasn't seemly for a preacher to drink more'n half a bottle at a time, she said, even if he was just a kind of off-and-on lay preacher.

Grandpa had knocked his pipe empty and now he cut himself a chew of tobacco. It filled out his cheek and gave him a one-sided plumpness. "Funny, how anybody gets drowned betwixt here and Vicksburg ends up floating in that big old whirlpool. I've got good money for fishing them out, and them that ain't claimed I've give a Christian burial up yonder atop the bluff."

Tammy put the jug back where it belonged. "I hope these are all claimed because we got no more green paint to paint the date on any more grave markers. I used the last on these shelves."

Grandpa chuckled. "I got better reason than that for hoping they get claimed. I could sure use some reward money right now." He picked up the lantern and went out.

Tammy put the coffee to boil and built up the fire. Then she buttoned on her old plaid jacket against the night air and went out on deck. She stood in the dark, on the blind side of the lantern, watching Grandpa make a neat coil of his rope. The lantern flung a fan of yellow light over him and across black water to the shore. It lighted up the hens, roosting on a limb of the hackberry tree, and they edged along, nudging one another, making little uneasy sounds. Grandpa's shadow danced about among the tree trunks, and the green of the leaves had a strange, unreal look, like the artificial flowers on Grandma's old straw hat. "Let me go with you, Grandpa," Tammy said.

He flung the coil of rope down into the skiff that was drawn up close to the side, and the grappling hook sent a shiver through it. "It'd turn your stomach, child, if I's to have any luck. You can hand me down the light when I get in." He braced himself against his aching and climbed down, grunting, into the skiff.

Tammy looked over her shoulder and saw the blackness of the river and the moonless sky, a thin mist dimming the stars. She heard the ripple of the current along the side and it seemed as if Grandpa was too feeble against the force of the river, too little and bent and old against the dark. She took up the lantern. "Get onto the stern, Grandpa," and her voice surprised her, sounding so like Grandma's. "Move on. My stomach's strong and my arms too, for rowing."

He sat motionless a moment, not looking at her, hearing the echo of Grandma, maybe, savoring it in his mind. Then he did as she said.

2.

IT WAS a steady pull upstream and a hard one, even though they followed the shore where the current took its time. The lantern shone in Tammy's eyes but she could sense the height of the bluff towering on her left and the wideness of the river on the other side where northern waters hurried along, not yet slowed by the lazy land. Nighttime everything was different, the water deeper for being black and its depths closer, all ready and waiting. The sky waited too and not a star would stir no matter what it saw. Now and then between strokes of the oar an owl's quavery cry came out of the woods. It was enough to give a body the shivers. A bad sign, for sure, folks said—a sign of dying. Maybe it was crying tonight for those they sought, for those already dead.

Grandpa leaned forward, squirting a stream of tobacco juice into the water, watching the water. "Pull hard now," he said with sharpness.

Under the floor of the boat there was a new movement, a tumble of waters struggling against one another. Tammy looked over the side and the sight of yellow foam in the lantern's yellow light made her heart beat faster. They were coming into the edge of the whirlpool and she had never been here before by night. She pulled on the oars with all her strength and had a pride in her muscles, that they were young and powerful against the river's might.

"Now ease your oars," Grandpa said. He turned his lantern on the dark wooded wall of the bluff, and here was a strangeness made doubly strange by night. Slowly they drew away from the land. They were caught by the curving current that bore them outward, upstream.

The worst of the rowing was over with now. The eddy's sweep and only a guiding oar would carry them where they would go. This was the lookingtime with the lantern held high so its light pushed back the darkness to show what floated with them in the whirlpool's outer arc and what moved faster in the swifter inner circles. "I declare, Grandpa," Tammy said, speaking because she had to show him she was not afeard of the dead, "I declare I wish I could see a good big bunch of chicken wire to fence us in a bigger garden place."

Grandpa took the bottle from his pocket and had a sip to warm his innards. "Look where the drift of logs goes all together, child. Never mind your chicken wire nor the boxes and boards. We're not out for them tonight."

No, Tammy thought, it would be something low-lying in the water, dark and given up to the way of the water. Not like the dead trees that went as if rebelling, with upflung branches, all rigid and resisting. Not like that great bare trunk of the forest with roots outspread before it, going proudly like something out of the past, high-prowed, in dignity—like a picture in one of her books. "See, Grandpa, that one. It's like the barge that was a bier that the princess floated on—Elaine the fair, Elaine the lovable, Elaine, the lily maid of Astolat."

"Leave off your fancies and look sharp."

There was no land now within the lantern's glow, only the dark river and the things that floated on it. Tammy looked up into the sky to rest her eyes from looking sharp. It was still above them, holding the far, pale stars. She reckoned you couldn't ever get away from the stars, not on land or water or even up in the air. Only down under the water, maybe there the sky was lost. Then she saw a brightening in the east and the shape of the bluff's tall trees standing out black and sharp against it. "The moon's coming over the bluff, Grandpa. It will help us."

Grandpa just kept on looking, leaning a little now as if he saw something. "What's that beyond the logs, all low and turning?"

The blood pounded hard in Tammy's ears and she stiffened herself against what she should see as her eyes followed the line of his pointing. "N-no, Grandpa," she said on a long breath, "that's only a barrel, that's all it is."

"M-m-m. Sight ain't as good as it used to be." But he must have seen something even as he spoke. He was holding it with his eyes while he kept the lantern high and reached down with one hand to fumble for the rope at his feet. "Pull in, child—there's something." His voice was a whisper, though the loudest speech could not disturb the thing he saw.

Tammy thrust in her oar. "Where, Grandpa, where? Show me——" Her breath gave out.

"The big log with the roots—there's something more, tied on, atop it."

"The barge—the bier," Tammy whispered. "I should have known——" The log was drifting closer, overtaking them because it was nearer the center of the eddy and faster moving. Now, beyond the outflung roots, she saw a shape that was not the shape of the log alone. There was something trailing in the water—a leg hanging down. There were arms too, clasped round the log in desperate embrace, the dark head hanging in a final giving up. Tammy, holding the oars in one hand, lifted the other to her lips, pressing back her cry of pity. For here was something worse than death. Here was struggle against death, here was a last defeat.

Grandpa set the lantern on the seat beside him and readied his rope. He cast out his hook, shaking the boat with the force of his casting. The grapple caught fast in the tangled mass of roots and he drew the rope taut. "Row out!" he cried with urgency.

Tammy gave her strength to the oars and kept her eyes on the floor of the boat, not wanting to see put to shame this one who had fought to live, who being hurt beyond swimming had found a log to fasten to, roots to hold on by. For such a one it would be a shame to be thus handled, dragged and grunted over, with swearing under the breath.

Grandpa, leaning, tipped the skiff and Tammy flung her weight against his. She kept her eyes on the wet floor boards, yet saw in spite of herself the flash of his knife as he slashed the strap, the cord or whatever it was that bound the body fast.

"God Almighty," Grandpa cried out of the midst of his hauling, "this one's alive! Help me, Tammy, quick!"

She was struck atremble but her hands could help, no matter if they shook. It was a struggle to tug, to lift and balance and shift the long weight of him with the head falling back all helpless, the arms hanging loose. Alive, alive—this one's alive, she kept saying to herself in wonder. They got him in at last with his legs thrust under the middle seat, Tammy sitting on the bottom with his head in her lap to keep it from the water. She shrugged off her jacket to wrap round his chest, she held him close to warm him.

Grandpa had the oars now, his feet planted wide astride the man's middle, the lantern set in the bow. "Here—" he took out his bottle and reached it down to her—"get some of this down him."

It was hard to make out where his mouth was but she found his lips with her fingers and tipped the bottle to moisten them. The drops ran down his chin in a pitiful way and were lost. He breathed on, light and silent with the least small motion of his chest. Her hand could scarcely feel it or the slow faint beating of his heart. "God, let it beat!" she prayed with fierceness. "God, keep him abreathing!" As she kept on praying, it seemed as if maybe his heart beat harder. Then she felt the shape of his face with her fingers and knew, by the feel of his cheek where the stubble of beard did not grow, that he was young. He had a long thin face, she thought, thinned down to the bone, a smooth young forehead. When she pushed back his hair, she felt a lump, a swelling. "He's had a blow on the head, Grandpa, a fearful blow."

"But he's aliving all right. He ain't easy to kill or he'd been dead afore this."

The skiff shot ahead with oar and current both to speed it now, for they were far out amidstream, going faster than the river. The moon spread silver on the water and the current broke it into a million dollars and dimes. Then slantwise they shot across into the shadow of the bluff where the light from the *Ellen B.* came out to meet them, warm and welcoming.

It was another struggle to get him out, dead weight, from skiff to deck and then to Grandpa's bed. Grandpa spoke sharp in excitement. "Build up the fire, fetch another blanket here quick as you can. Get Grandma's brick from the back of the closet and put it to heat for his feet."

Tammy jumped to do his bidding and she thought the flurry she made would surely stay the floater's soul for a minute if but to see what all the to-do was about. The pine knots with wood atop them caught with a roar that went clean up the stovepipe. Tammy flung open the closet door and knelt down, reaching back into a far corner for the brick. On her knees so, she could pray a powerful prayer, for the lower down one got, the higher the prayer went. "Don't let him die, God!" she prayed as hard as she could. "Don't let him die now! He's come this far safe—it wouldn't be sensible to take him now." Her cheek brushed Grandma's black wool dress that, being black, was too old for her, so she hadn't cut it down like all the rest. "Grandma, shoo his soul back if it gets that far, shoo it back, please ma'am!" Then her fingers found the brick and she crawled out and put it to heat in the fire.

Grandpa had got the wet clothes off and was piling the cover over him. "This here's something new to me," he was mumbling. "Getting home a live one is something I ain't ever looked for yet. Nothing like it afore in all my born days." He straightened up. "Nigh on to gone, but he ain't plumb gone."

Tammy poured coffee for them both. Grandpa drank his, standing by the bedside, looking down at the floater. "Funny, what a little space lies 'twixt the quick and the dead. So teeny it would take more than a mikerscope to see it, so weeny a cobweb couldn't catch it." He set his cup down in the dishpan.

"Want some more?" Tammy asked, drinking her coffee in small quick sips, keeping her back to the stove so her skirts would dry.

"I don't want nothing but to lie down in my bed and sleep." He searched through pockets of the floater's wet trousers and, finding naught, laid them on the rack beside the stove to steam and dry. "I want nothing but my bed, and the floater's got it away from me."

"Go lie on my bed, Grandpa. I'm not sleepy. I'll sit here and watch and doze a bit maybe in Grandma's chair."

He drew a long breath. "That's a good child, Tammy. You call me if there's need. I don't look for a change in him tonight. The great danger's pneumony—he's like to die of that, if we don't watch out." He looked back from the doorway at the still face on the pillow. "He comes of gentlefolk, whoever he is—you can tell that by the look of him."

"Can't we head off the pneumony somehow, Grandpa? Isn't there anything against it?"

"Just pray the Lord and keep him warm. I don't know no more than that except a onion poultice, and it ain't time for that yet." He hobbled away through the door by the foot of the bed. Tammy heard the creak of the springs, the thud of one shoe falling, then another and the long slow yielding of the sagged-out springs as he eased himself down to sleep with all his clothes on.

Now she would look at him good—the floater, Grandpa called him, as if he was dead. He wasn't dead and he wouldn't be if she could help it. She moved closer to the bed, bending sideways to get her shadow out of the way of her looking. Yes, he looked about the way she'd figgered from the feel of him—lean and hollow-eyed with a longish face. Get that dark stubble of whiskers off him, give him a little meat to his height and he'd come nigh to being a handsome man. His hair was black and one black brow had a kind of quirk at the corner as if he'd got cut there once. She wished she could read his life off his face the way Grandpa said some folks could look at rocks and hills and read the history of

the earth. She wished she could go into his mind and read the
thoughts that were sleeping there.

She turned away to get the brick from the fire. She wrapped it
in a piece of old blanket and placed it at his feet. That would
warm if anything could. Then she thought it might be he could
take corn liquor now. She poured some in a cup and fed it to him
with a spoon. He swallowed and choked and swallowed some
more. It might be he'd come to directly and talk to her. It would
sure be nice to have somebody talk to her, somebody young like
this. She'd been fair aching for somebody to talk back and forth
with.

As she watched, his hand moved. It came out from under the
covers and dropped limp, hanging down at the side of the bed.
Tammy set away her cup quickly and bent breathless over his hand.
He seemed all at once more real, more present, now that his hand
had stirred. It was strong and bony like all the rest of him, but the
strange thing was that he had a wide silver chain on his wrist. Why
should a man wear a bracelet? It gave her dismay to see it—was he
womanish? She bent lower till she could see the other side. A
watch! Of course. There was sense in a man's wearing a watch.
Did it tick? Grandma's that she used to pin on her front with a
gold pin never ticked. Tammy put her ear close and listened. Yes,
yes, there it was, just like a clock's tick only lighter, more secret
within itself, yet telling the time as good as if it spoke louder. It
broke time into small bits that one could hear, made it real and
urgent in each moment of its passing. How would it be to measure
one's life by such small pieces? How could one know how to live
by the minute and the hour? Time was large and wide as the sky,
one part slipping into the next, unbroken as the flowing of water.
She would not like it shattered so.

There was another thing to puzzle over as she sat rocking lightly
in Grandma's chair. A watch like that had to be wound up every
so often. Must be he had come to now and then, lying atop the log.

That was how he had had sense to know he must tie himself on so's he wouldn't fall off. She dozed a little, thinking about it.

Along past the middle of the night, his breathing woke her. She leaned forward, looking, seeing that his face had changed. It was more alive, with fever color in his cheeks. As she watched there was a faint small quiver of his eyelids, like the wind's first finger on the water. Then slowly his eyes opened, fever-bright black eyes that fastened on the lantern that was swaying a little as always with the movement of the water. The light seemed to put a spell on him and he could not come out of it, not any more than summer bugs could escape. She did not dare move or speak lest something snap, something delicate beyond all knowing.

His stillness and his fixity were thin and breakable, like Grandma's best little glass bowl the old woman gave her long ago because the young ones would just smash it and it was a rare one. His silence had an otherworldness in it, holy-seeming as the sound of the glass bowl when you struck it with a spoon. It must be that his spirit had been so far gone out into unmarked time everlasting that he had to draw it back with care and tenderness lest it snap away and be gone forever into the kind of time that made eternity. He would be lost-feeling, and afeard of that vastness, having the habit of small ticking time. Oh, it was better not to be accustomed to clocks, better to know only the dawn's blending with the sunrise and the day's slow sinking into dark! Then one might pass smoothly into the largeness of eternity.

At last his eyes moved to the window. It made her afeard to see them fixed on the deep darkness there, afeard lest he go forth into it and be lost to her forever. For he was something of her own, that she could not bear to lose. He seemed to her a thing she had made herself, one she had borned, warming him out of the river's cold and putting life into him.

Then, almost without moving, his eyes seemed to focus on the curtains, and the green-painted shelf with her glass jars of black-berry juice, her jellies—crab apple, dewberry and muscadine. It gave her pride that he should see first the things she had made, that he should have nice things to see with his first look.

After that his eyes came straight down to hers and they had a question in them, a concern. What could she say to make him sure that he was safe? She leaned forward, holding his eyes with her own. Her hands tightened on the arms of the chair, her breath came faster. What words were richest in comfort? Bible words, surely, and out of the Bible, they came to her. "Let not your heart be troubled," she said, smiling a little because the words had come to her.

They satisfied him. He closed his eyes and went back into his sleep.

3.

TAMMY came out on deck and smelled the early morning with surprise. It struck her sharp and pure as the redbird's whistle from the bluff. Five days and nights she had been busy fending off a dying the hoot owl had said was due; she'd wrestled with the fever and delirium as Jacob wrestled with the angel. She'd had no time to stop and look around and see there was anything outside, beyond what the shanty-boat walls contained. She had not even thought of doing the exercises she had promised Grandma to do, so she wouldn't get the lung fever like her mammy did. She started in on them now—rising on her toes, lifting her hands till they met overhead, pointing to the pale-blue sky, then bringing them down slowly, letting out the long breath. Ten times, breathing deep of the morning air, filling herself with refreshment while the first sun shone on the far green willows and spread itself on the water, driving back the dappled shadow of the bluff.

Spring had come while she was not noticing—and the floater was going to get well. Grandpa said it was sure, now. He hadn't died of the pneumony as Grandpa said he might. God had taken care of that, maybe because she had prayed so hard and fast, or maybe God would have done it anyway—it was hard to know for sure about God. Of course it might have been the onion poultices. She had cooked up meal and onions and filled two flour sacks with hot mush, changing them turn about on his chest so he had one hot all the time, night and day. That was what broke the fever.

He had come to himself after that and said his name—Peter Brent, mostly called Pete, he said. He lived over in the next county

28

and nobody would be missing him. That was all he'd said, even when able to say more, except for no, thank you and yes, please. He was a mannerly man, but one not given to speech.

Tammy finished her exercises and went round to the shore side to see what Grandpa was doing. She stopped by the window shelf and pinched off yellow leaves from the geraniums while she studied about Grandpa. He sat on a box, working with his jugs. "You going jugging, Grandpa?"

"No, I got other things on my mind. Been held back too long, what with nursing the living and hauling in the dead. Not that I'm grudging of either—the two dead ones brought me good reward money, and the live one—he may be bread cast on the waters, for all we know."

"The airplane was what cast him on the waters," Tammy said. "But I reckon it can work one way as well as the other, if the Lord takes the notion." She watched Grandpa as she spoke. He was not baiting the hooks. He was untying the lines from the jug handles and he was putting the jugs in a gunny sack as he freed them. "You going to the swamp?"

"Yes." He put a finish to the word so no other could follow. He lifted the last jug into the sack and began tying up its mouth with a piece of string.

"Grandpa?"

"What you want, child?"

Tammy stood motionless, looking down at the jug sack. "I know what-for you're going to the swamp. Grandpa—it ain't right. Long time ago I seen the men come and take a man off to jail and I sure would hate to see them come get you like that. We do all right without your making more money. I mean—" she shook back her hair and spoke out with boldness now—"I mean, hell's bells, Grandpa, we've always been decent, law-abiding folks and——"

Grandpa rose up so quick that, considering he had the rheumatism, it was downright scary. One eyebrow went up and the other down. "That's enough, young one. Of course we're decent folks.

Ain't none better—independent and God-fearing. But about this corn-liquor business—it's against the law in the state of Mississippi, I grant you that. But row across the river and the law don't say a word. Now if the running of a river is all the difference between what they call right and what they call wrong, then I say it's purely a man-made notion and a lot of tomfoolery. I got a good setup for making liquor on this side the river and I got the freedom to make it here—I don't care what the law says. Now. You got that straight in your head?

"Yes, Grandpa. Only just the same, wouldn't you go to jail if they caught you?"

"I don't aim to get caught. Besides, better men than me have gone to jail account of a moral principle and don't you forget it." He started dragging his sack along the deck.

Tammy wasn't ready to give up yet. "We got plenty of money just the way we are. What-for you have to be making money?"

He lowered the sack over the side into the skiff before he answered. Then he turned his deep-blue eyes on her with a sadness in them. "Honey, I got to get you some schooling."

"B-but—you didn't talk like that when the preacher come telling you—you said different to him."

"I told him a lot of things, because I'm not going to have anybody come here telling me my business. He's a mealymouth fellow I got no use for. But that ain't saying he ain't right about some things. Tell the truth, honey, the years kind of slipped up on me since your Grandma died. I kept on thinking you was just a mite of a thing I could take my time about schooling. But the preacher made me see. I got to hustle."

Tammy stared at him, wide-eyed. "You think I need to get more learning than I've got?"

Grandpa pushed back his hat and scratched his head. "Time was when all a girl needed to know was how to cook and sew and mind a baby and hold her tongue. Nowadays everything's different. Take preaching. Things have come to such a pass that it ain't enough for a man to know his Bible and feel the call. He's got to know the isms and ologies before he can preach the gospel. Honey, I got to send you to school somehow, and fix it so you can make out when you ain't got your old grandpa round to pester you."

"Oh, Grandpa, don't say that!" She flung her arms around him and hugged him tight. Then she drew back and looked into his round ruddy face, loving it, even to the prickly gray whiskers and the deep-cut lines around his eyes and the tobacco stain on his lip. The ache of her loving sharpened with the thought of a time to come when he wouldn't be here and she would have to make out without him. Then the making-out, the unknown ahead, the mystery and magic, dulled the ache and blurred its edges. "I ain't saying I wouldn't like to be going somewheres and learning something new, because I sure would." She let go her hold of him and stepped back. "So that's why you're going to the swamp."

"That's why. And I better be getting along."

Tammy stood watching while he got down into the skiff and paddled away. "God, don't let the revenuers or the sheriff or anybody get him! He ain't doing it for himself. It's for me. Amen."

When she came back to the kitchen door, she stopped short there with a little cry. Pete had put on his pants and his shirt that she had washed and ironed and readied against the day of his recovery. He was sitting on the edge of the bed, bent over with his head in his hands and his black hair hanging down over his fingers. When he heard her, he let his hands drop, then he let himself drop sideways, back on the pillows. He got one leg up on the bed but he seemed to have no power in the other. Tammy took hold and lifted for him.

"Not as strong—as I thought." He had to catch his breath between the words.

"You shouldn't have done it," Tammy scolded, marking the drops of sweat on his upper lip. "I reckon you need some spirits to stay you."

He drank the corn liquor at a gulp. "I was trying to look around. To see where I am."

"Nothing to see. Just my room there, no bigger than a minute.

Out here's the bluff, and through the door you can see what it's like yonder—just the river and way off, the Louisiana shore. Sometimes maybe a barge goes by, maybe a dredger. Fish in the river, buzzards in the sky, squirrels and varmints in the swamp. Not a human critter anywheres. It's a kind of lonesome spot, I reckon, that you floated down to."

"I'm damn lucky I floated at all. And lucky to fall into such hands. I've been a great deal of trouble to you, I know."

Tammy, sitting on the edge of Grandma's chair, shook her head. "No. It pleasured us no end, to have a live body to tend."

He studied her a long moment with a lightening of his face as if something pleased him. Then he said, "I don't even know your grandfather's name."

Tammy leaned back, rocking gently to and fro, hoping he would note the luxury of such a chair. "Well," she said, "there are some that call him Brother Dinwoodie because he used to be a preacher off and on, when he got the call. But mostly he goes by the name of Old Deadwood, account of his getting bodies out of the big whirlpool. He ain't ashamed of that name; he says deadwood keeps a sight of fires going, and it's what they trim out to make room for the young, and it's a good thing."

"What is it he calls you—Tammy?"

"Yes. My baptized name is Tambrey. My full name is Tambrey Tyree."

He repeated it slowly, making it sound better than it ever had before. "It's a new one to me—Tambrey."

"It came out of the book."

"What book?"

"I'll show you." She jumped up so fast the chair went on rocking high and fast till she came back from her room with the book in her hand. "Here. It's got Grandma's name—Ellen that the *Ellen B.* is named for—and Mamma's name that was Susannah, and mine—all named out of it." She gave him the book with pride.

It was an elegant book with stiff covers, with the shapes of flowers pressed into the cover, and there was still some gold left in the lettering. It looked tiny in Pete's long, bony hands. He read the words on the front of it—"Ladies' Names and their Significance together with their Floral Emblems."

"The colored pictures show the floral emblems. Not all, just seven. My name is on page twenty-two." She rocked back and forth, waiting while he read the first page where it said it was printed in Philadelphia in 1858. My, but it was nice, having somebody to look at things! When he turned the pages as if seeking her page, she bounded out of the chair to come and stand by the head of the bed and look with him. "There—see it?"

"Tambrey or Ambrey," he read. "Significance—immortal. Floral emblem—amaranth."

"I been wondering all my life what a amaranth was. Did you ever see one?"

"Some of them. It's the name of a species, a whole family of plants."

"Plants come in families?"

"Yes. Prince's-feathers belong to the amaranth family."

"Prince's-feathers—it has a noble sound."

He looked up at her then and smiled. The smile lighted up his face and gave it a kind of sweetness she didn't know could come into so grave a face. "It grows with little care, survives heat and drought alike. You must have seen it—stiff, bright red and ruffly. Nearly every litttle cabin in the country has some growing in the front yard."

Tammy turned from him and stood by the chair, not looking at him, feeling all at once her lack, her limitation. It rose up like a wall between them. "I . . . I haven't seen the country—not since I was big enough to remember." A sadness came over her, beyond comprehension, as if something not yet here had gathered dark around her. "I been living on the river. All my remembering days."

"On the river. Always." He rested the book on his chest, his fingers keeping the place.

Tammy sat down, taking comfort in his way of speaking, as if he

accepted her life, though with wonder. He was looking past her to
the river framed in the open door.

"It's not like the ocean. The land holds it, and yet it goes on its
way, in peace, bound and yet free. It would be good to live on the
river." His dark eyes came back to her, and then they went over
the room and back to her as if he were searching out her life.

"I'll tell you how it was," Tammy said. "My mamma died when
I was a little baby. It was in the hard times and my pappy went
away West, looking for work. He hitched a ride on a truck that
turned over and kilt him in the state of Colorado. His name was
Luther Tyree. I like to say it, because it's all I have. Then Grandma raised me, till she died. That's every bit of my life." She leaned
back in the chair, looking out the sink window to the pale green of
the hackberry tree on the bluff. "I mean, that's all the outside of
my life. I reckon it would take a million years of telling to tell
the inside of anybody's life."

"Yes," Pete said, and she felt his eyes upon her. "Yes, it would."

"I been wondering a heap about you, Pete—where you come
from, what-all you been doing all your life and how-come you said
there wouldn't be anybody missing you. Haven't you got any
folks?" She leaned toward him, elbows on knees.

"Yes, I have. Only they aren't looking for me back from my
trip West for another week or so. My father teaches at Longhaven
College, and there's my mother—she's busy running things generally. Then there's Aunt Renie. She lives at the plantation, where
I've been staying since I got out of the service. She paints. Maybe
she's a little queer. Only I'm used to her, so I don't mind."

"But you—what about you?"

"Me?" Pete waited, as if he wasn't so sure about himself. "I'm
twenty-four. I just grew up. Like everybody else around me, I
went to college and went into the service. Then I got out. I went
home and then to Aunt Renie's. It doesn't sound like much—I'm
still on terminal leave, and trying to decide what I'm going to do."

The book slipped out of his fingers. He clasped his hands under his head and stared up at the lantern that rocked gently as always with the movement of the water. "I went looking for something that wasn't there. Perhaps it isn't anywhere—a kind of certainty, peace. I had it in the middle of war and I lost it in the middle of peace."

"Sounds like a muddle to me," Tammy said, shaking her head. "Did you have a fight with somebody and have to clear out or was it just the peace-of-God peace you were looking for?"

Pete laughed and came out of his mulling spell. "You do say the damnedest things. How old are you, Tammy?"

Tammy bent and picked up the book that had slipped to the floor as he moved. He had given her a look into the inside of his life, and it was a muddle, no matter if he did laugh at her for saying so. It was a muddle and a mystery, closed off from her knowing. Did anyone ever come to know another clean through? Would loving the other open the door a little crack? It might. She didn't know about that.

"I'm seventeen and going on," she said. Her fingers moved over the covers of the name book. Then her eyes flashed and she shot her words at him. "And even if I do say the damnedest, I've got my name in a book. Not everybody has that."

Pete propped himself up on one elbow. "I didn't mean I didn't like what you said, Tammy. I do like it. I like it very much."

"Do you?" was all she said. She opened the book. "It's nice to turn the pages and come on yourself. Only sometimes it gives you a funny feeling. Like you was past and over and done with and put down and recorded. It gives you a start."

Pete dropped back on the pillow. "I'll say it does. I came on my name that way one time. I was down—as one of the missing."

Tammy leaned forward, her bare toes curling on the footrest of the chair. "Was that . . . when you couldn't get enough air?"

His face made a startled question.

"You talked, when you was out of your head. What did you keep knocking somebody out for?"

"Good Lord, did I go through with all that?"

Tammy nodded. "Wh-what was it?"

"We couldn't get off the bottom . . . submarine. I had to knock a man out because he wouldn't keep still."

Tammy drew a long breath. "It would be awful not to have air free and easy to come by. Even the children of Israel had free air when they come through the Red Sea on dry land." She waited for him to tell her more, but he was silent. Maybe he had talked too long. She would give him some soup and then let him rest. Another time they could talk. Time opened out before her, rich and wonderful.

4.

THE weather couldn't seem to make up its mind. Spring had gone to its head and unsettled it. One day there was blue sky with high white clouds blowing, light as milkweed down, then up from the south and the Gulf of Mexico came a darkness in the middle of the day. Lightning sprang from one cloud to another, nimbler than a squirrel, faster than a splinter cat, quicker than any human thing, excepting maybe a thought in a man's mind.

Today the rain came down as if it had forgotten how to stop. It cooled off the air to shivery coolness, it curtained the windows with silver streaks and played music on the roof of the *Ellen B.* It made the kitchen, with the wood fire going in the stove, a snug little square, safe and shut off from all the world. It made the three human beings there draw closer together in their talk.

Pete was able to be up and around. He liked Grandma's chair, said he'd a notion to make one like it himself sometime. A real native craft, he called it with admiration in his tone. He sat in it now, whittling on a cedar chain Grandpa'd told him how to cut. His long, bony fingers were wise at carving, and he said he'd done a lot of it, only he'd never made a cedar chain and he was bound to learn how to cut the links without a seam. Tammy sat on a box by the table, sewing some flour sacks together to make a pillow cover. Grandpa was over by the stove talking as if he'd been hungering to talk. Pete kept asking him about old times and listening with a homesick look on his face, as if he wished he had been living in those days. Why, if he'd been living then, he'd be dead now—so what was the sense in that?

"Yes," grandpa said, "I picked up the *Ellen B.* cheap in '31.

Tammy's little ma left a mite of insurance money and it looked like a good kind of open-air life for the child she left us to raise. Besides, it gave us a way to live."

"Did you preach a good many years before that?" Pete asked.

"Nigh on to forty year. Been all over the state about and some time in Louisiana. Never got much for it in the way of money because I don't hold with sects and creeds. But I preached the Word. That give me satisfaction above all earthly dignities. I reckon I was too free-spoken and independent to get anywheres with it—a man's got to play politics to get anywheres nowadays, even in the church. Politics is aruining the country."

Tammy bent over her sewing to hide her pride. Grandpa could talk men-talk as good as the next one, about corruption in high places and how somebody ought to do something about it. It was a wonder, how much he knew. But he liked best to talk about his preaching and it was not long before he worked round to that again.

"Yessir, I've preached a good sermon in my time. I'm one of them that early seen the coming of the scientific age, and how man has sot himself up to reason out and put down in figgers and such what the Lord's already made plain in His Word so that a wayfaring man though a fool could understand. But modern man's given up faith and hope and he's all for reason and knowledge, so I'm humoring him along, seeing he's bent on taking the long way round."

"Grandpa," Tammy said, "are you going to preach every bit of that sermon at Pete?"

They both laughed and Pete said, "Go ahead, it is very interesting to me—and that's more than I can say of a lot of sermons I've heard."

"Well, I don't aim to be preaching. But fact is, I been reconciling science and religion ever since I seen a incubator for hatching out chickens without having hens set on the eggs. Right now I'm working on a sermon about Sodom and Gomorrah and the atom bomb. I figger the Lord had a bomb with the kind of rays that would turn you to salt if they hit you in the face and that's what happened to Lot's wife. First sermon I ever preached was about the earth's being round. Got me into a peck of trouble, too."

"How was that?" Pete asked.

"Well, there was some of the bretheren who said the earth couldn't be round because the Bible told how four angels stood on the four corners of the earth—and so it does tell. But that's where I say you got to use common sense. You'd be surprised how many people don't believe in common sense."

"You wouldn't think there was anybody that much behind the times, even in those days," Pete said.

"Well, it was in one of them parts that's back'ards to this day, and most of them belonged to the Cover-to-Cover believers."

"What's that?"

"Oh, it's a kind of sect believes every word in the Bible, cover to cover. They just said, 'The earth ain't round, brother,' and they never let me preach there again."

Pete said, "Out in the Pacific where I've been the last three years, it's easy to see the world's round."

Tammy looked up with eagerness. "What does it look like there, Pete?" And after that she kept on asking him questions till she knew about the islands and what grew on them and what kind of fish swam in the waters. She was glad she had studied her mamma's geography book because now she knew what he meant when he spoke of Australia and Honolulu and strange places like that. It was educating to hear him.

"You didn't do like some of the boys and get you a wife off in those heathen places, did you?" Grandpa asked.

Pete shook his head.

"Got a girl home, I reckon."

"Well," Pete said slowly, "nothing's settled between us. She doesn't care much for the country; thinks I ought to keep off the land, get a job in town. I've been thinking it over."

Tammy dropped her sewing. "You got land?"

"Too much—we're land poor."

"Land poor! How can you be poor if you have land?"

"It's worn out."

Grandpa said, "All the land in this country's worn out. But you don't starve on the land. It's like the river that way."

"Goshamighty!" Tammy said. "If I had land I'd raise everything there is in the world."

"It's not so simple as that," Pete said. "Things aren't as they were back in slavery times, or even the way they were fifteen or twenty years ago. Yet it seems to me that on the land there is a measure of security, as you say—in an insecure world. One would have the feeling of being something more than just a consumer, one would be producing something."

"That's sound." Grandpa nodded. "That's good sense."

"Only—it's a hard life, away from town and excitement. The place is terribly run-down and shabby. It's too much to ask anybody to . . . to share such a life."

"Meaning a girl?" Tammy asked.

"Meaning a girl," Pete said.

"You wouldn't be thinking about a girl named Barbara, would you?"

Pete's knife slipped and he looked to see if he had made a miscut before he lifted startled eyes to Tammy. "What do you know about—?"

"You talked when you were out of your head. Seemed like you were arguing with this Barbara all day and all night."

"That's about what we do," Pete admitted.

"You couldn't take up with anybody of that name," Tammy said.

"Why not?"

'You know what it means?"

"What?"

"Barbarian. That's what the book says. I'd be afeard to——"

Grandpa chuckled. "I wouldn't set too much store by what a ladies' book like that says, honey."

Tammy turned her head away so her hair curtained her face from them. Grandpa ought not to be saying that, making her sound like a silly child, shaming her like that. She tied a hard knot and snapped the thread with a jerk.

But Pete answered her as if Grandpa had not spoken. "No, Tammy, she's no barbarian; she's more modern than anybody I know. She just wants to have things nice—clothes, conveniences, a decent car, the things you see advertised everywhere and that other people have. That's only natural."

"Well, hell's bells," Tammy said, "for all you know that's some new kind of barbarian ain't been discovered yet. I bet it is."

Then Grandpa asked him how he found things out West, and after a minute Tammy slipped out to stand under the tin roof of the porch where the rain couldn't reach her and nobody could see how mad she was, thinking about that Barbara, and her not being satisfied with a chance to get Pete and land besides. Goshamighty, she had more sense than that, herself. "I just naturally hate that Barbara. Sight unseen, I hate her," she whispered into the noise of the rain, knowing it was sinful and ungodly to hate, and trying to take it back. But the words had been spoken and they stayed hanging in the air. The rain could not wash them away. She stood watching the rain fall into the river, each drop striking a shower of sparks from the surface. "Some people!" she said. "Some people look like they have to have everything!" Then she went in and started cooking dinner.

There were other days when the sun shone and the new green leaves spread themselves to its warmth. Then Pete followed Tammy ashore to watch her milking Nan, or to see her digging in the little salad patch, wire-enclosed against the chickens and the rabbits and wild things. He sat on top of the chicken coop, smoking the corncob pipe Grandpa had made him, and it seemed as if he was trying to find out everything in the world about her, study-

ing, trying to make her out, asking her what she remembered about
other places they had lived, asking her what books she had read.
Seemed he was turning her over in his mind the way she was turning over the ground for planting here on the little ledge of the
bluff where Grandpa had cleared off the trees to make a garden
space. It gave her a new feeling, as if the warmth of the sun had
entered into her. Now she knew how the growing things felt when
spring set them stirring and unfolding. This was how the earth
awoke.

"You're kind of early with your turnips," Pete said.

"The bluff keeps the cold off. I planted long afore regular plant-
ingtime this year because winter went early. In another week I'll be
thinning out for greens and pot licker. You'll like that. Do you
good."

"I'd like it all right. But I'll have to be shoving off soon. My
folks'll be looking for me about now. They never expect to hear
from me when I'm away because they know I'm no letter writer,
but they look for me to turn up when I say I'm going to."

Tammy stood still, one hand holding tight to the hoe handle and
the other feeling for the cedar chain Pete had finished and put
around her neck, saying he'd made it for her. She had been dread-
ing to hear him speak of going, though she knew it was bound to
be, with the coming of his strength and good weather.

"Besides," Pete went on, "my tomatoes will be ready to come out
of the hotbeds by the time I get back. I've got a good man looking
after things for me, but there's nothing like seeing to it yourself.
It's going to be an early season and I mean to clean up on my
tomatoes."

Tammy swallowed down the choking in her throat. Pete's life
—it really was all away from here, inland, far from her. His time
on the *Ellen B.* was just a small time, set apart out of the whole
which was unbeknownst to her. "How does the road run to take
you home?" For if she knew that, then he wouldn't be just gone
off, into space, into the wholly strange, leaving her with nothing

but the cedar chain and what she kept hidden, deep in her heart.

Pete leaned over and took up a little stick. He drew a map on the ground and Tammy came out of the salad patch to sit on her heels and see how it went. He made a **Y** of the roads and another **Y** going off of that and curving round. Then he drew a little square. "That's the house, set back from the road. Brenton Hall is its name. There are two beech trees at the gate and the road goes in like this with live oaks on each side."

Tammy studied the map till she knew it by heart. The lines he had drawn made a tying-up and a linking between the *Ellen B.* and Pete's home, so it did not seem so far away. "There must be more than two rooms to your house," she said, remembering how he'd said his aunt lived there and that his father and mother came for vacations and for the Pilgrimage time.

"There's room enough. I want to keep up the old place, and the old tradition. It's all been neglected so long—no money for repairs. . . ." He fell silent.

Tammy sat back on her heels, looking up at him. "Looks like it ought to satisfy you, just having it. Ever since I was big enough to want anything I been wanting a house that stands on solid ground with space enough for planting and time for staying to pick what was planted—not going off to another mooring before the beans were big enough to eat, the way Grandpa always used to do." She was silent, thinking how she'd like a man in the house with her, sitting across from her at the fireplace, if it was a house that had a fire on the hearth. She'd like a man like Pete, and she'd have a raft of children, all the house would hold.

"What do you think about, Tammy, looking at me so?" Pete broke in on her thoughts.

Tammy turned her head, looking down at the map he had drawn. "How do you mean—so?"

"Like something out of the woods, wild and young and—and wise. Like a woods owl, maybe." His voice had a twinkle in it, a kind of condescension such as one uses with a child.

Tammy stood up with dignity, the way she rose with a bucket of water on her head, and for once, remembering how Grandpa said she spoke too free sometimes, she said only, "It wouldn't be seemly, I reckon, to tell you what I was thinking."

Pete laughed. "Seemly," he repeated. "I thought that word was buried with Queen Victoria. You know, Tammy, you say you're seventeen, but sometimes I think you're ageless."

She went back to the salad patch and her hoeing. "I'm not ageless. I've got an age and it's going on eighteen. It's old enough." She shot him a quick glance, tossing back her hair. He was leaning against the hackberry trunk now, staring up into the pale-green leaves as if he was figuring out the kind of lacy pattern they made against the sky.

"Old enough for what?" he asked, humoring her the way Grandpa did sometimes.

"To know what's what," she said and began to hoe fast and furiously. After a minute she said, "Grandpa's going to fix it so's I can go to school and catch up on learning."

Pete still leaned against the tree trunk. Now the teasing tone was gone from his voice. "You've already learned a lot, Tammy— a lot they skipped in my school."

Tammy stood still, leaning on the hoe handle, feeling herself fill up and brim over with pleasure. After that, a humbleness came over her. "Not books," she said. "Excepting the Bible. Grandpa taught me that. And Grandma taught me common sense real quick because she knew she was going to die and she couldn't take her time to it." Tammy drew a long breath and added, "I just know about living and dying and getting borned—that's all I know. I don't know about loving, excepting the Bible kind of loving your neighbor and the Lord thy God. But I figger I could learn." She gave him a quick look to see how he took that.

Pete smiled his slow, twisted smile and his eyes were bright. Was it just with laughter, was it with thinking how a man would go about teaching a girl such a thing? Tammy could not tell which it was. When she looked back again, his face had sobered. "Out here on the river with only the woods and the water," he said, "I could almost believe there's nothing more than living and dying and getting born—and loving. But, actually it is much more complicated than that. People, custom, money—the whole setup."

Tammy hoed in silence for a while. If Pete would only stop thinking so much about things, he wouldn't worry. She would have to know more than she did, to understand his worrying. "I need book learning," she said aloud.

"You could read books and catch up with things."

"Could I, Pete?"

"Sure you could."

"Would I learn all the worrisome things, too?"

"Perhaps."

Everything Pete said she saved up and pondered and treasured. She made a collection of scenes and small moments. Like the time he went into her room, stepping around her pallet laid on the floor so Grandpa could have the bed. He looked through the books she had on top of the packing cases, stood on end to hold her clothes. "How about this?" he asked, taking up the volume of Shakespeare that had lost its back.

"Can't make head nor tail of it."

Then, sitting on the edge of the bed, he read her some aloud and, goshamighty, who could have known it had a sound like that to it, a kind of music to the words! Pete told her how a play was played on a stage, and then she saw it was an act, like Eddy's and Gladys' act, only different. She would read *Hamlet* after Pete left, and make sense of it if it killed her.

Then there was the last day, suddenly come, the day before the one he had set on to leave. All the day had a going-away feel. Toward evening Tammy took him for a walk, to try out his strength. They went up the bluff and down into the hollow and on to the bayou. Tammy made him stand on the beech log and see the cypress knees, how they had a carved and fluted look, rising from black still water like turrets from sunken castles. She showed him the spring and the rise where there were bricks in a heap where a house once was, and chinaberry trees grown from seeds of trees that somebody must have planted long ago, so that the far past was tied onto the present by a brick and a chinaberry tree.

She found some yellow chinaberries and pinched off the soft part to let him see the seed had a fine carving to it and a soft place through it that a thorn could poke clean. "You can string them on a string and dip them in dye. They look like something you might buy in a store and pay money for," she told him.

Then they went round by the other side of the rise where the yellow jessamine was all in bloom, spread out over the underbrush, rising up to the trees so it was like sunshine pouring down out of the sky and settling there. Tammy picked a load of it to take back to the graveyard. On the way there she took Pete to the high point, the rocky lookout that looked over the whirlpool. That gave him a start, all right, seeing the brown water whirling and the great bend of the river he had come down.

"So that's the place," Pete said, staring down at it. "A mile across, I'd say, and the water going round and round—"

Tammy pointed to where the foam made a lacy trail across the current. "About there's where we found you, on the big log."

"I might be there yet," Pete said.

"Well, you ain't." Tammy waved her hand toward the bend in the river and the level Louisiana land, laid out like a map on the other side. "Look how high we are. Grandpa says the pilots on the boats long ago used to set their course by this high point. They called it 'the rock,' and it used to be whitish before it got worn down and covered over with bushes and things. They could see it at night." She spread her yellow jessamine out on the grass and sat down. "I like to come here. Makes me think of the place the devil took the Lord and showed him all the world. You better set and rest your legs."

Pete sat down beside her, cross-legged, his eyes on the circling water far below. "I'll tell you one of Grandpa's tales," Tammy said, wanting to take his mind from whatever it was on. "It's about a settler coming down the river on a flatboat with all his family and belongings, looking for good land to settle on. It was a moonlight night and he took a notion to float all night instead of tying up, like he mostly did. Well, coming along with the current, he looked up and he seen a house on the bluff all lighted up with music and dancing and he said, 'This sure is a dancing country.' After a while he come on another house and it was all lighted up with folks having a merriment, and he said, 'This is the dancingest country I ever hear tell of,' and after a while there was another house and it was lighted from top to toe and there was more music and partying and he said, 'This here is the outdancingest country in the world.' But when daylight come, he seen he'd got caught in the whirlpool down yonder and he'd been going by the same house over and over again all night long."

Pete laughed. "Sounds possible." Then his mind went back into its own way of thinking, like something caught in a groove. "It looks as if I ought to do something special with a life that's been saved as many times as mine has—when there were so many that were not saved."

Tammy didn't answer. She pulled a blade of grass and chewed on it in silence, letting him think aloud.

"All the time I was away from home I was so sure I had everything settled. But now I'm back, I'm about as unsettled as anyone can be."

"What was it you were planning to do?"

"I was going back into the bank. I'd worked there one summer —I'd worked on a newspaper too, the advertising end. Everything was going to be fine—just the way it always was, only better."

"What would you do in a bank?"

"Oh, I'd count up money, pay it out—all that kind of thing. At first, anyway."

"That don't seem to have much of a muchness to it, don't seem to be getting anywhere."

Pete turned and looked at her. "I guess you don't understand how things are."

"I know, Pete. But look, you wouldn't be making anything in a bank. The most fun is making something, like this cedar necklace you carved—it gives you satisfaction."

"Yes. But in a bank I'd be making money."

"Money—money's sort of secondhand. It's like wearing gloves. Oh, hell's bells, I don't know anything about it, Pete. I'm just talking."

Pete said, "The trouble is that when you come back everything has changed. You try to plan something and it fizzes. It makes you wonder what it's all about, what life's for. . . ." He pulled a blade of grass and chewed on it.

"Goshamighty, Pete, life—life's for living, ain't it? To see what it's like to grow up, to get some kind of a living somehow, and make things, and have children and get middle-aged and old, and come at last to dying. That's a real mystery to find out about, saved up for the end. Why you don't need any reason for life but living." Then suddenly she burst out laughing, and when Pete looked around at her in wonder she said, "Here we set like a couple of billy goats chewing grass. Come on, the sun's fixing to go down and I want you to see the graveyard before it gets too late to read the stones. Besides, Grandpa'd give me a whipping for sure if I stayed out so I didn't get back before dark."

There were only a few stones in the little old graveyard on the brink of the bluff. They were old and crumbling and long forgotten even by those who had set them up. The big live oak with gray moss hanging down was all that grieved over them now. It shaded them and kept back the underbrush by its shade, letting only the grass grow, and the harmless gray and green lichens. Tammy went first to the unmarked grave that was only a low mound under the pointed cedar tree. She spread her yellow jessamine over it with tenderness. "This here's Grandma. Grandpa says when he gets some more cash money he is going to put up a stone for her that'll last a hundred years and she can lie safe under the carving of her name. The poor floaters over yonder haven't got any names." She pointed to the row of wooden markers with UNKNOWN and the dates painted on them in greent paint. "They seem sadder than the rest. Not because they're any deader but because they haven't any names. How can they be called on the Great Day if they have no names?"

"I don't doubt they'll be given back their names any time they have need for them," Pete said. He walked around with his hands in his pants pockets looking at the stones.

"Anyway, being buried up here so high, they've got the jump on most—they'll have a head start on their way to heaven when the Last trumpet sounds."

Pete was studying the stone top of the one grave that was above ground, a little stone house that said it was Celeste who died on Christmas Day in the year of our Lord 1831. "They're all built up like this in New Orleans," he said.

"Are they afeard of being covered up?"

Pete shook his head. "The ground's low. Dig and you strike water."

"H-m, that's funny. There's a sight of places in the world, isn't there? All different. I'd sure like to see them all." She went to a small leaning stone and knelt beside it, fingering out the worn lettering. "Listen to this one, Pete. It makes a poem. Listen:

> "Serve the Lord while yet there's time;
> Your sickness may be short as mine.
> Serve the Lord while yet ye may,
> For no man knows his dying day.

"Give you a creepy feeling, doesn't it? Like life was liable to give out on you any minute and you'd better get what you can while it's going on." She looked away, out over the river to where the sky was red and gold with sunset. The water was bright as the sky and the low green shore was all that kept one from going into the other. The gray moss hung down across the sunset with an airiness delicate as foam. The shadows of oak and cedar were lying down across the grass and the graves. They stretched themselves, settling for the night.

Tammy felt a lonesomeness come over her, sharp as an aching tooth. Tomorrow Pete would be gone. She wanted to hold back time, but there wasn't any way of doing that, any more than you could hold back the river. She stood, looking out, as Pete was looking, over water and sky. "Couldn't anybody but Joshua hold back the sun. Grandpa keeps trying to figger out how he done it. He says science hasn't got far enough along yet to give him a clue, but he keeps ahoping it will some day."

Pete put one arm across her shoulders. "Tammy," he said, "I don't know how you do it, but you . . . you restore my soul."

She turned her head away so he wouldn't see the quick tears that came in her eyes. Her fingers found the cedar chain that hung round her neck where Pete had put it. Soon that would be all she had. "I'll sure miss you, Pete," she said.

All the time from then till next morning had an unreal feeling to it. It was like a sound and its echo coming both together, confusing. It was as if the space between a staying and a going was neither here nor there, but just a heavy in-between time to be lived through. An endurance, that's what it was.

Next morning Tammy dished up the grits and eggs and got out the white-flour biscuits from the oven and called, "Breakfast, Pete." The edges of the words were sharp, they cut into her because they would not be said again.

Pete came in from his washing at the water shelf outside. He had a glow in his cheeks now and his eyes were not hollow the way they were when he came. He folded his long legs under the table and after Grandpa had asked the blessing, he said again what he had said before—that he could never repay their kindness, and if there was ever anything he could do for either one of them . . .

Tammy had poured their coffee and now she went out on deck to breathe the air because a kind of weight had come into her breast. Far off in the swamp there was a wood thrush calling, pure as pain. Tammy made up her mind—she wasn't going to walk to the edge of the swamp with Pete. She didn't want to scatter her good-by through the swamp, trailing it out. She wanted to hold it fast here all together. Grandpa had said he was walking part way along the path, and he could show Pete the way.

Then Pete came out and she put her small brown hand in his and said good-by and he said the same to her. Then he followed Grandpa across the plank and up the bluff, turning at the top to look back and wave. It was a good good-by. Tammy thought, standing straight and firm by the rail; it had been said with dignity, and nothing told that should be hid.

5.

THE Mississippi kept on rising. Far to the north the snows had begun to melt. Rains came, rivers were filling up—the Chippewa, the Red Cedar, the Missouri, the Ohio, the Big Black, the Yazoo and many another. They poured brown water into the Mississippi that stretched itself lazily to receive them all. The shanty boat rose too. It floated now amid the tops of half-drowned trees. The full-leaved willows, caught by the current, were bent all the same way as if blown by a constant, ghostly wind. They trembled at the sides of the *Ellen B.* and the bigger branches scraped and complained at the stern.

The morning sun poured down the slope of the bluff in a waterfall of bright warmth. It drenched the paintless deck and Tammy, sitting on a box plucking a fat hen, wiped the sweat from her forehead with the back of her hand. She put the softest of the hen feathers in the feather bag to make a pillow, when she got enough. The old hen would make a good gumbo. Too old to lay, all she did was set on the empty nest. Plumb mad about setting, she was.

Tammy stopped now and then to look out over the bright river. Away in midstream the water went stumbling over itself to get where it was going. She wished she was going somewhere, too. Ever since Pete left—it was only ten days and nights ago—she'd had a restlessness inside her, wanting to go somewhere, wanting something to happen. She had scrubbed the *Ellen B.* from stem to stern, she had kept herself busy every minute, but nothing eased her missing of Pete. She was one bereft. Grandpa had promised she could have some clothes and go to school in the fall, but that was a long time off. She hadn't told Grandpa how she'd been fish-

52

ing for Cap'n Joe, sending the money off by him to get her a dress she'd seen a picture of in one of the newspapers he brought by. It had come yesterday and she'd spent most of the day just trying it on. It had a silky brown skirt, kind of tight, but they must be wearing them that way, she thought, and a pink satin top, and it sure looked nice. She would put it on if Pete came sometime, as he had promised. He had said he would come when he got all his little plants set out of the hotbeds and into the cold frames. The man he had trusted with them had moved away and he was having trouble getting work done, but he would come when he could. He had promised, in a letter that came by Cap'n Joe, along with the coffee and side meat.

Tammy was in the kitchen with the gumbo cooking on the back of the stove and the smell of it going halfway up to Vicksburg, mighty near, when she heard the sputter and throb of a motorboat. The sounds came from down-river somewhere near the mouth of the bayou. She ran out on deck to see, but there was only the warm sun on the river, a tugboat far away rounding the upper bend, and over the flat Louisiana land, a curve of buzzards drifting down and around, lower and lower in ease and languor.

Then the boat came into view through the willows and Tammy's hands tightened on the rail. Three men were in the boat and one of them was Grandpa, the skiff bouncing along empty behind. Grandpa sat bent over, in the bow, elbows on knees and his old felt hat pulled low over his eyes. It was strange to see him sitting like that, not talking when he had company to talk to. They all should have been talking, shouting out words above the noise of the motor.

There was a great stillness when the engine was cut off and the boat came around to stop alongside. The younger of the two men said, "Half an hour, Deadwood, and no fooling, mind you."

Tammy jumped to give Grandpa a hand aboard. He said, "I mind what you told me. No need to keep asaying it."

"You sick, Grandpa?" Tammy whispered.

He straightened up, waving her to silence. "I've give my word, haven't I?" He stood stiff, looking down with scorn into the faces of the two men.

"Okay, okay," the man said, handing him the rope to the skiff. Then the motor spit and coughed and the boat shot away toward the middle of the river. There it came to rest, the motor going just hard enough to hold it still against the current. It was like a buzzard sitting on a limb, waiting, waiting. Tammy stared at it, feeling a cold wind run along her spine. Grandpa made the skiff fast, saying no word, so at last she had to ask, "What is it, Grandpa, what—?"

"Tammy, child," he said, slow, keeping his eyes on the gray splintery planks of the deck, "they've caught up with me."

One hand rose to her throat. All the old pain and terror she had felt for Eddy that morning long ago came back to her, multiplied a hundredfold. "All account of me——" she began and a choking stopped her from speaking any more.

"Now, now, child, no need to take on about it. 'Tain't as if I'd done a crime. I'm willing to take moral responsibility for what I've done. Each man according to his conscience, when laws quit making sense—that's my rule. I had need of money and I hit on this way to make it, that's all. Needn't hang your head about it."

"Yes, Grandpa." Her voice was a whisper, but she straightened her shoulders.

"Now come on inside and hark to me because my time is short." He went in and sat down, leaning his arms on the table. Tammy sat opposite him with her heart beating so hard it came nigh shaking the table. She felt trembly inside, like the lantern that hung from the ceiling, shaking with the strong spring current.

"Don't you fret about me, honey." His voice came more natural and easy now he was out of sight of the men and the motorboat. "I'll have time for prayer and meditation, and it may be that I am meant to carry the Word into prisons—the Lord moves in mysterious ways, don't forget that."

"I won't, Grandpa."

"And another thing—they can put me in jail, but I'm a free spirit. Can't nobody but the good Lord take that away from me. Besides, like as not the dryness away from the river will ease my rheumatism."

"Yes, Grandpa." She drew a long breath and some of the tight went out of the back of her neck.

"John Bunyan spent a time in jail. So did Martin Luther and many another, account of his moral convictions. It ain't no disgrace. Might be I'd get time to write me a book about science and religion. I got plenty ideas."

"Yes, Grandpa." Some of the scare went out of her now. It wasn't like it was with Eddy. Grandpa hadn't done a murder. "I'll sure miss you, but I'll look after everything till you come home."

Grandpa shook his head. "You can't stay here alone, child. Wouldn't be right, a young girl like you. You must set out quick as you can, whilst the sun's still high, and go to Pete's house. We had a good talk about things afore he left and he made me promise if anything happened to me that I'd send you to his house—though to tell the truth I was thinking more of my dying than getting took up, and so was he."

"Goshamighty," Tammy breathed, "that would be something, to go to Pete's house! It sure would." She dwelt on the thought with wonder.

"I got confidence in Pete," Grandpa went on, "and his folks is all right. I made some inquiry and I know. That's the place for you. Now hand me down my Bible."

Tammy reached it down for him from the shelf, her hands so shaky she almost dropped it. Why—not two hours ago she was awishing something would happen. Plenty had happened now.

Grandpa opened up the Bible and got out a map drawn in pencil with names and numbers of roads. "Pete made this so's you would make no mistake in the road."

"He told me it—I already got it by heart, Grandpa."

"Well, you take this anyway, so's you don't get lost. You can hitch your way—only mind they're good people you get in the car with."

Tammy nodded, her head dizzy with the dividing of her thoughts. Her mind was a fire, fresh-kindled with the heavy smoke amourning for Grandpa's going to jail, and the quick bright flames leaping for herself and her going. "I'll be careful, Grandpa. Don't you worry about me."

"Get me a safety pin now and a scrap of stout cloth." He bent down by slow degrees and took off his shoe. By the time she had what he wanted, he'd taken some money from the inside of it. He made a little bag of the cloth and showed her how to sew it and to fasten it with the pin inside her dress, with the bills hidden away. "One more thing I want you to know, honey. I got a little money put away for you. I tell you so's you can get it if you need it. It's too much to be carrying round. You mind the tomb that's above-ground?" He beckoned her close so he could whisper.

"You mean Celeste that died on Christmas Day?"

"That's it. I dug me a little hiding place down under the head of it. In a tin can. I got the reward moneys there. But don't you touch it less'n you need it bad."

"All right, Grandpa."

"Now you go call the men to come in. I see you got plenty for company."

"To dinner?" Tammy drew back. She shook back her hair and her eyes flashed. "No, no, Grandpa! I'd sooner give them pizen than my good gumbo when they're waiting to take you to jail. Oh, no, not if they's starving."

"That's enough of that," Grandpa said, sharp and quick. "What does the Bible say about your enemies? Besides, they's only doing their duty like I was doing mine, making corn liquor in the swamp. You go this minute and call them in and be ashamed of yourself for grudging them a meal."

Tammy went with bowed head. She beckoned and halloed, and men came in. But she wouldn't sit down with them. Nobody could make her do that and she reckoned Grandpa knew better than to try. She served them and then she went to her room to pack her a gunny sack of clothes to take with her. She put in three cotton dresses and her shoes and the new dress, folded carefully so it wouldn't wrinkle, and she put in her little box of paint that Gladys had given her long ago. Somehow she'd manage to fix up and change to her nice dress before she got there, so as not to shame Pete. Then she went in and kept filling up the men's plates with gumbo because the fat one 'lowed he'd never eaten better, and the other one stowed it away like he was starving. She couldn't swallow a bite herself—it would stick in her throat for sure, so she busied herself making the kitchen neat for leaving.

Grandpa talked along like always. It was a wonder how he could do it. He didn't eat too hearty—Tammy couldn't help but notice that. When they'd finished, afore they could say a word, he opened the Bible and read the Ninety-first Psalm. They fidgeted a bit, but they couldn't be disrespectful to the Bible, no more than they could do a thing but get down on their knees when Grandpa said, "Let us pray." Tammy, kneeling by the wood box, thought that if Grandpa had a mind to, he could keep them all day on their knees, because who would dare interrupt anybody talking to God?

Grandpa was strong on praying, and he never prayed better. When he got to working up to the finish, you'd have thought God was bending down with his ear right on the edge of the bluff or even atop the stovepipe. "O Lord," he prayed, with his voice rising and falling the way it did when he got going good, "forgive us our sins, and we're a sinful lot! Wipe out the meanness out of our souls, O Lord, for we're powerful mean, some of us more than others! Let us feel brotherly love amongst us, knowing some sin one way and some another, each according to his lights. And if an old man, nigh on to fourscore years and soon cut off, if an old man that's spent his life laboring in the vineyard of the Lord, has gone and let his foot slip in the trampling out of the grapes, don't hold it against him, Lord! Be mindful of how the sinfulness of the sin depends on the spirit what you goes and does it in, and recollect in the judging at that final bar that stands above all earthly courts, recollect, O Lord, how the water was once changed into wine, the only difference between then and now being some fool law they made up in Jackson! Now go with us, Lord, in all our ways, however devious they may be, and some of them are mighty devious, especially them that take away the God-given freedom from another human soul and put a free spirit behind prison bars! Forgive them, Lord, and let the sin they do be writ lightly in the book of deeds and misdoings! Amen."

One man kept his chin tucked down in the khaki collar of his shirt and never said a word as he got to his feet and shuffled toward the door. The other one, the fat one with three plates of good gumbo in him, had a redness over his face and neck and he had to swallow his feelings before he spoke.

"It sure goes against the grain with me, Brother Dinwoodie, running you in like this, you being a preacher and all," he said.

"You got to do your bounden duty, brother," Grandpa told him, gathering up what things he wanted to take with him and not forgetting his Bible. "I'd be a poor preacher if I asked you to do other than your duty."

Tammy, emptying the pot and kettle and turning them upside down so they wouldn't rust, felt an easing spread through her. She'd begun to feel better when Grandpa read about not being afraid, and the angels having charge over thee, and now she was filling plumb up with comfort. Nobody was going to hurt Grandpa, no matter where they took him. Bars couldn't jail a free spirit. And look how humble and apologizing he'd got these men in no time at all—hell's bells, they'd be waiting on him before they got to town! And for a fact, they were offering to help him nail up the *Ellen B.* right now.

It was strange, having everything get dark as the board blinds closed across the windows. When she took a last look around her room she could not see herself in the blurred little mirror on the wall. All the things in her room and in the kitchen, as she went through, were wrapped in a noontime darkness, like a package covered up and put away.

Nan could just go wild, Grandpa said. This time of year she'd find plenty to eat, and the same with the chickens. He lengthened the hawser where it was tied round the hackberry tree so that with the going-down of the river the Ellen B. would not be left aground or hung up or anything. Tammy measured the length of time he figgered on being gone by the length of rope he let out. It would be a long time.

Grandpa put a padlock on the door, he gave Tammy one key and put the other in his pocket. Then he kissed her good-by and she held tight onto him for a moment, feeling his cheek wet against hers, feeling all hollow inside herself with the strangeness of what was happening.

"Now take your sack and get ashore, honey."

Tammy did as he said and she went as far as the hackberry tree before she looked back. They were helping Grandpa down into the motorboat, giving him a hand while the engine roared loud, champing to go. Grandpa was going to be all right and she didn't know what-for she had to have such a choky feeling in her throat. It was maybe just leaving everything she was used to. She turned then and went on up the bluff, blinking hard and shifting the sack on her shoulder so her shoes and her hairbrush wouldn't dig into her back. She'd put on her shoes afore she got there, when she changed her clothes.

At the top of the bluff she stopped for one last look, waving to Grandpa, far out on the river, going downstream. He waved back and she went on down the long slope on the other side. Nan came bounding out of the bushes and followed as far as the log across the bayou. The bayou water was nigh to the beech log now, pushing inland, spreading out in all the low places with a steady current. Maybe Nan was afeard of it. Anyway, she just stood there looking across with a lost, sad look in her eyes, as if she knew she was being left. Then she started nibbling at some tender leaves and Tammy tiptoed easy round the turn in the path and got away from her.

6.

THE path through the swamp was no more than a vague notion of a path, for Grandpa was the only one who ever went along it. In the low places where the water had backed up from the bayou, Tammy had to find a log to cross over by. Other places she could jump. The leaves made a roof to the swamp, green and cool. Grapevines rose to the tops of tall bay trees and came down again. Once Tammy stopped to swing where the vine looped low at the edge of black water. It was just right for a swing. She held tight with both hands, sitting in the loop. She walked 'way back and took a quick run forward, lifting her feet. Out she swung, over the still deep water, far, far out. Looking down, she saw below her the wavering line where a moccasin moved, frightened by her shadow. She went out again, stiffening her legs and leaning back to look up and see the leaves spread out like lace to dry on the roof of the swamp. Oh, it was a fair world here in the cool, damp swamp and she'd miss the sight and smell of it when she got out on the dry, warm land! She jumped down then, caught up her sack and ran a way to make up for the time she had lost.

At the edge of the swamp, Tammy stood in the shade of a tall magnolia tree and looked up and down the road. It was hot and dusty with the sun shining straight down upon it. Not a car in sight. Well, it wouldn't hurt to walk a way. Might work some of the excitement out of her. She shifted her sack and was mounting the bank where the road was built up against the backing-up of the bayou, when she heard the thud of hoofs and Nan came bounding to her side.

Oh, what a bother! "Go home, go home," Tammy cried, fanning her skirt and stamping her foot. But Nan would go only a little way, then stand and look as if bewildered, wondering why this day she was scolded instead of praised for her faithful following. Every time Tammy started off, she came slowly after her.

"Oh, Nan, why do you do so?" Tammy cried, close to tears with pure vexation. "I wish I'd never spent weeks training you to follow like a dog!" She caught up a little stick and struck at her, but Nan only planted her feet firm and turned dark, reproachful eyes. Tammy threw down the stick and gave up. Why not take her along? There was land enough, Pete had said, and it would save her from arriving empty-handed, like a beggar. She bent and scratched Nan between the ears and petted her, begging her pardon for the scolding. "Come along then, and mind your manners."

It was good, having company along the lonely road. Nan trotted at her heels, stopping only occasionally for a nibble of grass and then bounding to catch up. Now and then, when a car went by, coming or going, Tammy stood off the road to look at it, waiting for the dust to settle before she went on. Once a shiny black car with boxes piled high on the back seat slowed down and the driver leaned out. "Want a ride?" he called.

"I'd be much obliged." Tammy ran to get in. With her hand on the door, she turned. "Here, Nan, hurry up! Come quick, we're going to get a ride."

The man said, "Hey, I don't want any damn goat in my car! What do you have to have a goat for?"

Tammy drew back. "It's my goat and a mighty nice one, too, I'd have you know!"

"You can have her, sister." He drove on with a jerk and a whirl of dust.

The next car that slowed down had an old man and an old woman in it, nice-looking folks and gentle-spoken. But they said with dismay, when Nan came alongside, "Oh, dear, no, not the goat. Sorry." And off they went, too.

At first it did not trouble Tammy that Nan kept her from catching a ride. She had all the long afternoon to get where she was going, and Pete had said it was not far. She was a good walker, and walking she had time to savor being out in the world. She felt like all the younger sons in the fairy stories Grandma used to tell; she was like Dick Whittington with his cat—only she had a goat. She was a free spirit roaming; she was a pilgrim on a pilgrimage.

When she came out on the paved highway, the cars went by faster and faster. They made the progress of her steps small and slow and she began to have the feeling that she was going round and round on a treadmill, getting nowhere. The earth had a stillness to it, a fixity. It gave her a queer sensation of helplessness, of being bound. The earth was not like the river, that kept going and changing all the time. Pete had been wrong, saying it wasn't far to his place. He must have been measuring distance by the measure of a car's speed and power, not by the placing of one foot before the other and the creeping of the shadows across the road as the sun went down. Her feet began to hurt from the stones of the gravel at the road's edge. She wished she had four feet like Nan to spread her weight on.

It was getting on toward first dark and she had left the highway by the sign that was marked on her map, when an open truck went by. Steam was pouring from its engine and the motor labored at its task. On the hill ahead, it sputtered and gave up altogether. A man and a woman were on the high front seat and children sat in the open back part.

A little boy with a bucket in his hand jumped down from the truck and came running down the hill toward Tammy. He gave a shy glance, stared at Nan a second, then went leaping down the bank to where a little stream ran between muddy sides. Coming back with the brimming bucket, he fell in beside her.

"Where you bound for?" he asked. But when she began to tell him how far she'd come and how far she was going, he broke in to say, "If you think that's a fur piece, we're riding furtherer than that. Way up to Tishomingo."

"Tishomingo—it has a far sound."

"Mammy's got word her ma's sick and got a doctor, fixing to die, and she better hurry if she aims to see her afore she's laid out to be buried. We're going to ride all night."

When they came abreast of the truck, Tammy stopped to watch how the man watered his engine, giving it small drinks to gulp and choke on. He looked round at her and said, "Gotta go slow or she'll bust wide open and then where'd we be?"

The little boy was back in the truck, whispering to his mother. "Sure she can, if she's a mind to. I'll ax her." She leaned down and called to Tammy, "Want to ride, miss? You look plumb tuckered out."

"I wisht I could. I sure do wish I could. But I got my little goat and——"

"That's all right. The chillen is adying to play with her. Pa, help the little thing in."

Tammy felt at home with them. Landfolk, but they were like shanty-boat people, goodhearted and kindly. She showed them her map and they figgered they knew just where to let her off. They shared their supper with her while the engine cooled and rested and Tammy milked some milk into a tin cup for the children. There wasn't much to eat so Tammy ate sparingly, hungry though she was. There wasn't much milk either because Nan was tired, or maybe she just just held it up, feeling strange.

When the truck started on again at last, Tammy caught tight to the side and clung fast. The children laughed and asked if she hadn't ever been in a truck before. She shook her head, afeard her teeth would shake out if she opened her mouth. The headlights cut out a path from the darkness that had come on thick now, and the wind of their going blew her hair straight out behind her. It was a wonder it didn't blow clean off and leave her bald-headed. It made her recollect what Grandpa had read this morning about the terror that flieth by night. This was it, all right. But the Bible said not to be afraid. She tried not to be afraid, and just trying gave her an easing through her tight muscles.

The children stretched out on the old quilts on the bottom of the truck, giggling together, with Nan pulled down to lie beside them. They didn't even look round to see the lighted-up town. Tammy tried to see it but they went through so fast there was just a flash of lights and a swish of other cars and a blasting of horns, and then they were out on the dark road again. Tammy lay down beside the children but whenever she started to doze, she woke with a jerk and a jump.

Then the truck's stopping roused her. They'd come to a fork in the road and the man said, "Here's the sign where you turn off." He got out and helped her down, and Nan too, past the sleeping children. He gave her a piece of rope to fasten round Nan's neck so she wouldn't stray in the dark.

"Like as not you'll catch another ride afore long," the woman called down with kindness, when Tammy thanked them for the lift.

"It don't look like you got far to go now, judging by your map," the man told her.

Tammy looked after the truck till its red back light was lost in the night. She'd never know if they got there in time for the woman to see her ma—and they'd never know if she got to Pete's place. Nothing left of their meeting but the feel of kindness done and kindness taken.

No cars were traveling by the fork Tammy took, and the road was doubly lonesome for her having had company a little way. Oh, but she was glad now that Nan had come along! Her little feet made a cheerful, homey sound on the hard-packed road. After a while there came a lightening of the sky and a late, lopsided moon began to rise over an open field. It was like having an old friend come out to journey with her. But nothing could shorten the distance that seemed to stretch endlessly ahead, nor could anything ease the growing weariness of body and limb, or lighten the load over her shoulder. She might have been picking up stones and adding them to her sack, the way it got heavier and heavier.

Then there were voices ahead and wide laughter, with no boundaries to it. The words too had no edges, blending one with the other. At the curve of the road ahead, shapes appeared, shapes with no faces. It was a fearsome sight, but Tammy went on, bold-seeming for all her panic within. Then suddenly she knew why there were no faces—there were Negroes coming toward her, their faces merging with the night.

"Good evening," she said as they came abreast.

They had hushed their noise as if in wonder at seeing her alone on the road with a goat in the middle of the night, or maybe past the middle for all she knew. "Evenin', ma'am," the women said, and the men's greeting was a deeper rumble, but all full of courtesy and respect. Tammy knew little of Negroes, having seen them only in the distance, darkening the decks of passing boats. She had heard their mellow singing as a barge went by. She knew only that they were humans too, and she was glad to see them in the road. She wanted to delay their going. "Is it far to the Brent place, called Brenton Hall?"

" 'Tain't fur, ma'am."

"Three-four mile, maybe."

"It's a right smart of a way."

"Mought be six mile or more, I dunno."

They passed out of hearing and the stillness seemed greater now, the small cabins set back from the road more than ever withdrawn into sleep and secrecy. Tammy wavered to and fro across the road with weariness and the knowledge that it might be six miles more she had to go. She didn't know how she would make it, for there beyond the shadowy hollow ahead was another slope rising to a yet higher hill. It was these ups and downs that made the aching in her legs. The moon was blinding in her face as she went down into the hollow. She could just make out two men loitering there as if they didn't know which way to go. She could hear their voices, arguing.

"You dassent."

"I dass anything."

"You's drunk, man. Come on."

"Lemme alone, you."

All of a sudden Nan took a crazy streak, bucking and pulling on the rope, trying to run. Tammy had just got her straightened out when they came on the men in the hollow. "Good evening," Tammy said as she had said before.

One man mumbled something, the other came closer to her. "You a white lady?"

"I'm white, all right. But I'm no lady like a lady that lives in a house, if that's what you mean."

"What is you?"

"Oh." Tammy laughed, because she was silly-tired and she didn't rightly know what she was. "I'm a free spirit roaming the earth, that's what I am."

"Oh, Lordy Lord!" the other man said. " 'Tain't no human."

But the man close by her, walking beside her, said breathless and quick, "You got money?"

"Sure I got money."

"Gimme it. Hear me? Gimme." He pressed closer to her so she would have been edged off the side of the road but for Nan pulling hard on the rope.

"I got need of it myself," Tammy said with indignation. "If you want money, go work for it. That's what man's had to do ever since he got turned out of the garden of Eden. You got to make money in the sweat of your face, so get along with you."

Nan gave a jump as lights came over the hill, and when Tammy looked round, the men were ducking into the bushes by the side of the road. The car slowed a little, then shot on up the slope and away. "Goshamighty," Tammy said, "I like to have fell among thieves!"

She had topped the hill and headed down the other long slope when a car came up behind her. It slowed and stopped and she heard a woman saying, "I told you she was white."

A man put his head out the window. "Are you all right?" There was uneasiness in his tone.

"I'm all right," Tammy said with wonder. "Just about walked my legs off, that's all."

"They didn't bother you, those Negroes back there?" He had an urgency in his tone, and the woman said, quick and sharp, "Did they lay hands on you?"

"No," Tammy said. "Just wanting money. But I wouldn't give it up. They got no right to it."

The man and the woman spoke together in low tones. "Where you going this time of night, all alone on the road?"

"I'm going to the Brent place, Mr. Peter Brent's house named Brenton Hall, and I'm not alone. I got my little goat here."

"Better take her in," the woman said.

The man got out and opened the back door of the car. "Do you have to take that goat along?"

"Yes, I got to," Tammy said.

"Then get it in and get yourself in."

"I'd sure be obliged." Tammy sank back on the cushioned seat, feeling it springy and fine beneath her. Nan leaned against her knee, trembling with the swift motion of the car. It didn't seem like a minute till the headlights lighted up a white gate with a beech tree standing tall each side of it. "Yonder must be it," Tammy cried, remembering Pete's words.

The car headed into the drive and stopped. Tammy got out, and pulled Nan after her and thanked them kindly. The woman sounded cross when she spoke. "You ought not to be out so late on the road, you just make trouble."

Tammy shut the door. "I didn't aim to be a trouble to anybody. It was you all asked me to ride. I told you I was much obliged."

"That's not the sort of trouble she means, little girl." The man's tone was kinder. "But just the same, you better stay home nights after this." He backed the car out and it went off down the road again.

They acted as if they had something on their minds, Tammy thought, watching the taillights go twinkling down the road. They acted as if they thought those men might have kilt her. And so they might, for a fact. She'd have been afeard herself it she hadn't been so mad at the idea of anybody's taking Grandpa's good money.

Then turning, she forgot all about it, seeing the long tree-black lane winding in from the gate, seeing the lights of a house set far back from the road. The sight of it heartened her mightily, and excitement wiped out everything else from her mind. She got in back of some bushes and peeled off her travel-soiled dress, shivering a little as she opened her bag and felt for the slick feel of satin. It was elegant under her fingers and she drew it on with pride. One of the buttons came off in her hands—oh, but she was lucky it didn't fall in the grass and be lost. She dropped it in her sack and found her brush and the little jar of face paint. It was a pity she didn't have a looking glass to put it on by, but she did the best she could by feel. When it came to putting on her shoes, she had no luck at all. Her feet were swollen and sore and wouldn't go in. "Hell's bells," she said and stuffed them back into the sack. Maybe folks wouldn't notice in the nighttime, and there was her new dress to take their eyes off her feet and Pete's cedar chain to be observed as well. She took up Nan's rope and shouldered her bundle and started up the long, curving drive.

7.

THERE was music coming from the house. It had a hard, dry beat, overlaid with trumpet wailings that shrilled out, crying in a disorderly kind of order. The sounds streamed forth with light from open door and long window, going farther than the light, leaping amid the shadows like something savage escaping into the night, baying the lopsided moon and dying in the far fields across the road. If it was a party Pete was having, what manner of dancing would be danced to such music as this? It was the kind of music that anybody named Barbara would like, Tammy thought, and felt her high excitement curdle.

She moved slowly to the curve of the drive and saw the shape of the house, how the roof came down low, holding in the porch, and how the trees stood away from it. Two chimneys went up, black and threatening, into the moon-bright sky. It was a big house. Too big. There were two rooms and a hallway on the front. The porch ran around the corner and extended along the side. She had a feeling of other rooms behind those that were visible. There was no telling how far the house went away at the back. Tammy stopped where the drive divided, one part going on to the side and the shapes of parked cars, while the other swept past the front steps to circle a flower bed and return. Red roses were blooming in the flower bed where the hall light fell.

The look of the place overwhelmed her; she felt small and alien. Pete hadn't said it was all so . . . so elegant. How could she walk right up the front steps and across the gallery and go in by the bright door and speak out into strange faces that would be like the faces of the people on the packet boat long ago? She was too weary to stand up under cold eyes that would fasten on her there in the doorway, dumb and lonely. She felt homesickness gnawing at her innards, and the strangeness of sight and sound was near to turning her stomach.

Holding Nan close to her side, taking some small comfort from her warm familiar flank, Tammy went round to the side porch that was darker because that door was closed. She could see chairs there and potted plants on a stand. A tub of ferns was at each side of the steps. The feathery leaves rose up tall and dripped down in a fountain of fronds to the floor. Tammy slid her sack from her aching shoulder to the bottom step. She tied Nan's rope to the neck of the sack so that she could not follow. Now, if she looked through the window for a little, the strangeness might wear off and it might be that Pete would pass near. She could call to him so he would come out and welcome her and tell her where she might lie down and sleep, for truly she had need of it such as she had never felt in her life before.

Her ears ached with the music as she tiptoed across the porch. It came through the open window, harsh and loud so that she almost had to press against its pushing. It was not welcoming music. She passed between the back of the flower stand and the wall and came on the window from the side. She bent with care and looked in through delicate, gauzy curtains. They put a mist over the scene, setting it away, back of a cloud, out of the world. Tammy's eyes, blinking at the brightness, went searching for Pete among the moving figures. He was not there, though it could be that he was in the hallway, where some were dancing. "O God, please let him be there!" she whispered and pressed closer.

What a sight it was, this dancing! Some leaped and whirled and shook, some just clung together, scarce astir at all. The room itself was fine and big, with all its elegant furnishings pushed back against the walls to make room for the frolic. There were delicate, carved chairs, too slim to sit on, surely. The sofas were covered with velvety stuff, and there were shelves cleverly contrived, one above the other. They held rare objects—colored glass and small figures. There were pictures on the walls, gold-framed. Tammy had never so much as heard tell of such a room as this.

But it was the people she came back to with most amazement, especially the girls. The men were properly clad, with coats and fried shirts with collars and ties, as was fitting for a dance, the girls were not dressed up at all. Most of them were barelegged. One wore short white pants, no more than drawers, really, piped in blue at the seams, and a little blue jacket so short it left her plumb naked in a circle round her waist. Goshamighty, you'd think she'd be ashamed to show her skin like that! Her yellow hair was in two tight plaits that stood off stiffly. Her round dreaming face was snuggled into her partner's shoulder.

Another girl had on a two-piece dress with real pretty red braid on it, but what was it made of—could it be pillow ticking? Pillow ticking! Now that was something to put on your back! One girl wore a man's shirt with the shirttail out. You'd think somebody would tell her her shirttail was out. She had on blue jeans rolled halfway to her knees. Another swished around in full, flowered skirt that might have been made from a scrap of window curtaining. She had a white blouse to top it, so thin that you could make out her underbody plain as anything. What's more, she was barefoot and her toenails were painted red as blood. But maybe going half naked was like what Grandpa said about sin—it all depended on the spirit what you went and did it in. Eve. Take Eve, now. She went without so much as a fig leaf, and that was all right, so long as her mind was innocent.

Beyond this room and the hallway there was another wide opening to another room. It was all in darkness except for one lamp on a table, sending down a tent of light on a gray-haired man with spectacles in dark rims. Tammy could see him when the dancers in the hall moved out of the way. He was sprawled in a big chair, taking his ease, reading a book. The light shut him away from the crowd and the noise. He could have been all alone, the way he kept his nose in the book. He had a look of Pete in his length and the bony look of his hands and in the long shape of his head. Must be it was Pete's father.

All of a sudden the music stopped in the middle of a measure. The silence was sweet and easing as a poultice on a sore spot. Tammy could hear Nan munching contentedly behind her and she heard a rooster crow 'way out back somewhere. Then the dancers cried out, complaining.

"Do we have to, Mrs. Brent?"

"We've practiced enough!"

"That old thing again!"

"I bet the other groups aren't half as good as we are."

Then a high, commanding voice put them to silence. "Please, now, just once more and I'll be satisfied. I mean this to be the best dancing they've had at any Rebel Ball since the Natchez Pilgrimage began. Peter, put on the record, will you?"

Peter was there, then, Tammy thought, relief sweeping through her, and that was maybe his mother telling them all what to do. Peter had said she kept herself busy running things. That was all he had said about her. Tammy leaned forward, peering through the window. There she was, quick-moving, like her speech, with dainty, small features and hair that was red-brown, like her eyes. It was set in waves all over so that it seemed to have no ends. She had on a brown dress with white buttons down the front, and underneath, her shape had a solid look as if it might feel hard to the touch. With her small, neat head and her trim, quick body, she put Tammy in mind of a bird. A little brown bossy wren, she thought.

The girl with the bare waist wailed, "Oh, Mrs. Brent, Ernie hasn't come yet. I haven't any partner."

"Professor Brent will take Ernie's place. Come, Joel, be Tina's partner." Her voice penetrated the older man's bright cone of silence and brought him slowly to his feet. He came in, book in hand. His spectacles hung by one hook from his ear, dangling across the leathery folds of his jaw. "Right over there, dear," Mrs. Brent said. "Lay your book down, put your glasses where they won't get broken."

Without a word, Professor Brent crossed the room to lay his book, open, face down, on the table beside the window, glasses on top of it. Tammy was looking through the window trying to read the title—*East . . . West . . .* what was it?—when the music began and everything was changed as if by magic.

It was slow music, dainty and high-stepping, tinkling like bells. It suited the room. It wrought a change on the dancers so that now they moved with grace, making small curtsies and pauses, moving with decorum in all they did. Those who were in the hall came into view, and Pete was among them. Tammy put one hand over her lips to keep from crying out to him in the midst of the dance. She put the other hand over her heart lest its pounding be heard above the sound of the music.

Pete was tall and strange in a dark coat. He was smiling a little as if he took pleasure in this dance out of another age. He smiled down at his partner, and Tammy's lips drew as if she'd bit into a green persimmon. She was more shut out and alone than ever, for that must be Barbara with him, her dark eyes flashing as she advanced to meet him again in the change of the measure. Her face had a peeled look, perhaps because her brows were so thin and fine and curved. Her skin was almost too perfect, bloodless as a white eggshell. The only color she had was in her full red lips and the tips of her fingernails. She was long-limbed, silken-legged, shapely all over. Tammy drew a long breath. No wonder Peter had laughed at the idea of her being a barbarian. She had a polished look. She was shining and civilized, and her hair was smooth as brown metal.

Mrs. Brent kept calling out directions: "Faster there, Ted!" and "Make your curtsy deeper, Roberta!" and "Watch that turn, Deedy!" and "Spin her around, Jack!" She had her bright brown eyes on everyone all at the same time.

The warm air of the room came out through the window and, as Barbara passed close by, Tammy got a whiff of the perfumery she wore. It was stronger-smelling than any flower; it was like . . . like laburnum and myrrh, that were meant to be holy, and whoever went smelling of them would be cut off from his people. On a human it was a wicked smell. Pete—for a moment he was near, and Tammy put out one hand, reaching for his coattail.

Then she drew back, pinned against the wall by light that shot across the porch and swept over the cars parked at the side. Tammy stood pressed against the wall, watching through the potted plants while the car came quickly in by the drive to stop with a grinding, sudden sound. A man leaped out, flinging the car door shut behind him. He jumped clean over a bush that got in his way and ran toward the steps of the side porch. Tammy stood motionless, hoping he would not see her, wishing now that she had called to Pete when he came past the window. She did not want to be caught like a thief.

Just as the man reached the steps, Nan rose up, planting her forefeet on the step. He swerved aside and took the steps two at a time. On the porch he stopped and lifted both hands to his head. He gave it a shake, saying, "Jeepers, I'm seeing things again." Then he went in by the door, pulling it shut quickly as if to shut out the sight of Nan.

Tammy drew a deep breath and peered back into the room where everyone was shouting, "Hi, Ernie!" and "Here's old Ernie at last!" The blonde girl with the pigtails rushed up to him and flung her arms around his neck. "Darling Ernie, where have you been?"

Ernie took her by the bare waist, lifted her up and set her aside without so much as looking at her, the way one would set a frolicsome puppy out of the way. "This place is full of goats," he said with solemnity, nodding his head toward the porch. "Jam-packed full of them, all over the yard and the steps."

Everyone laughed. "Pink goats, Ernie?"

Professor Brent's bony hand reached across the table and took up his book. He eased himself through the crowd and went back to his chair in the far room. Mrs. Brent cried, "Music, please! Just this once more. Positions, now!"

Tammy leaned back against the wall and closed her eyes. Sleepiness came on her without warning, dulling all her senses. She'd go to sleep standing there if she didn't look out. She moved along the wall and stood for a minute facing the closed door. It was a wide door with a doorknob. She lifted one hand to knock but drew it back. Mrs. Brent might be mad if she broke in on the dancing practice. She moved to the steps, sat down there, leaning against the post, feeling the fern fronds tickle the side of her neck. She was lifting one hand up to scratch, when her body drooped and sleep came over her, deep and dark.

A long time later her ears awoke, hearing voices that came from all sides, into her sleep.

"Pete's little goat girl, I bet you."

"Not such a little girl—look at that dress—my aching back!"

"Shut up, Ernie, you've got an evil mind."

"Doesn't look like any little innocent such as he——" The whisper died away.

"Well, it's a live goat anyway—I'm not stewed."

"Oh, gosh—Mrs. Brent's red japonicas——"

Tammy struggled to get her eyes open. Lights were shining down on her from the ceiling, blinding bright. The first thing she made out was Nan at the foot of the steps, a red flower in her mouth, the petals drifting downward as she munched.

"I'll say it's a real goat—whew, what a smell!"

That was Barbara, saying that. A fury came over Tammy. She sprang up, Barbara's wicked smell offending her nose. "A clean goat doesn't smell——" she sniffed the air—"no more than a clean human."

Ernie laughed. "That's telling you, Barb, old girl." He leaned toward her, breathing deep. "Breath of the East, out of the harem to you——"

"Shut up, Ernie."

Then Tammy saw how all their eyes fastened on her like search-lights on a boat on the river, and her flash of anger dissolved under their gaze. She hoped they thought her dress was pretty, she hoped she hadn't spoken out too free. "My little goat's been on the road all day," she said with humility, "and so have I."

Barbara said, "It's Tammy, isn't it," and there was kindness in her tone. "You look all in—hey, you dopes, call Pete."

"Pete! Hey, Pete! Come out here," they called and some ran in to get him.

"I'm plumb tuckered out, for a fact," Tammy said, feeling the strength ooze out of her knees as she spoke.

Then Pete came through the door and crossed quickly to her with long strides. "Tammy!" He caught her by the shoulders with both his hands. "Your grandfather——"

Tammy nodded, unable to speak for a moment. "They came and got him, Pete, and took him away. He told me . . . you said . . . I could come. . . ." Her legs were past supporting her any more. Pete caught her in his arms before she went down. In the dizziness that almost drowned her, she heard a confusion of voices.

"What in the world, Peter? The child from the river?"

"Yes, Mother, it's Tammy. Where shall I put her?"

"Her grandfather——"

"Yes."

"Aunt Renie's little room—that will be best."

"I'll get her undressed, Mrs. Brent. I'll help you." That was Barbara.

Pete was carrying her a long way. His mother kept on saying things: "I didn't realize . . . why, she's a grown girl. . . . Oh, dear, her face . . . that dreadful——"

Then the bed came up to meet her and Tammy opened her eyes

on a light that hung down from the ceiling. It was blinding-bright and she had to blink and squint and close her eyes again.

Pete said, "Why isn't there a shade on this light?"

"Your Aunt Renie does what she likes with this room, Peter."

There was a rattle of china and the sound of pouring water. Then a wet cloth went over Tammy's face, making her gasp. Barbara was saying, "There, there, that'll make you feel better."

Tammy tried to sit up. "I'm all right." But the dizziness came over her again. "Nan——" She tried to say Nan must be hungry.

Pete said, "I'll see to Nan. You just sleep now."

Tammy closed her eyes. Other voices came to her. "I wonder if she has anything fit to sleep in."

"There's her bundle."

"It might be infested. Oh, dear——"

"Maybe there's a gown of Aunt Renie's in here—yes, this'll do."

Then somehow sleep came over Tammy, deep and dark and soft. She let herself sink down into it gratefully, caring no more what anyone said or did.

8.

THE green shades stained the light and subdued it so that Tammy slept on past the next morning's sunrise. She awoke hearing the distant cackle of hens, familiar yet strange and too far away. Where was she? Oh—at Pete's house, in the little room, the one they called Aunt Renie's little room. But it was larger than both rooms on the *Ellen B.*, and the ceiling was high, dwarfing the wooden-posted bed on which she lay, making the chairs and table and bureau seem small.

The bed quivered with her breathing and when she rose on one elbow the better to look around it bounded to her movement as an echo to a call. "The outspringingest bed I ever felt," Tammy whispered in wonder. She felt the bleached smooth sheets with her fingers, she passed one hand over the blanket and studied the bedspread that was thrown down over the foot of the bed. It had a design of minarets and trees of strange shapes and a Persian border new to her eyes.

The walls of the room were plastered white and climbing up the plaster were painted morning-glories blooming, pink and blue. Small kittens played hide-and-seek among them. In every corner was painted a toadstool, oversize, that a little naked angel might perch on it, wearing a peaked hat and blowing a horn that was shaped like a morning-glory.

Tammy's wide eyes moved on to her own reflection in the mirror on the opposite wall. She was a tousle-haired stranger to herself in the blue nightgown they had put on her. It was sleeveless and low cut. It'd sure give Grandpa a start, if he could see her like this. She gave a deep sigh for Grandpa and hoped his aching joints

79

were eased this morning and wished that he too might be awakening amid flowers and angels. Suddenly, words came back to her from last night when she had been too travel-weary to gather their meaning—"anything fit to sleep in . . . her bundle . . . infested——"

Infested—it sounded like a dirty word. Pete's mother had used it. "I got no lice in my clothes," she said with indignation. Then, not seeing her new dress anywhere, she bounded out of bed, feeling a great concern for it. She found it at last in a heap behind her sack on the floor. "No way to treat a body's best dress," she said, "no way at all." She caught it up and smoothed it as best she could and laid it with care across a chair.

After that she tucked the tail of Miss Renie's long nightgown under her arm and made a slow circuit of the room, feeling the smooth wood of the chairs, letting her fingers play around the fine knobs of the bureau drawers, even pulling a little on the knobs to see in what manner the bureau drawers went in and out. When she came to the table she found tubes of paint there and a palette and slender brushes standing in a can of turpentine. A half-finished painting lay face up, showing Johnny-jump-ups and white eardrops in a blue bowl with a kitten curled beside it. "Somebody's sure plumb mad about cats," Tammy said and went on to the window.

She pulled aside one shade and looked out. The early sun shone slantwise between great tree trunks, setting gray moss aglow and throwing far shadows on the smooth-cut grass. Everything was trimmed and tidy beyond all believing, and all the great yard was shut in by a green hedge, squared off at the top like a wall. It was all tamed and set. How could she ever get used to it when she had the habit of the wild running river and the swamp?

She let the shade fall back into place and the room all at once seemed dark. Last night there had been a light. She studied the bare bulb that hung from the ceiling and discovered the button that turned it on and off. No matches, no oil, no chimney to clean nor wick to trim; just a twist of the fingers was all it required. It was a miracle, like the bush that burned with fire and was not consumed.

After a while she left off working with it and set about getting dressed. It was a bother not to be able to throw the wash water into the river and be done with it, but she supposed living on the land was bound to have some inconveniences to it. She hoped she was doing everything right—all the pieces had lovely pink roses on them and were far too fine for the lowly uses to which she must put them.

When she had on her clean undergarments, she slipped her fresh red-and-white checkered dress over her head. In this elegant room, so completely furnished, it seemed dull and faded as never before. She could see it down to the waist in the looking glass— she could see how it hung loose from her shoulders, shapeless and awkward. Maybe it was not good to see too much of one's self, she sighed.

But it was a wonderful looking glass. It was no hardship at all to stand before it and brush her hair a hundred strokes the way Grandma said a girl should do. She turned this way and that to see herself from every angle. Then she got out her little jar of face paint and put a round bright spot on each cheek. It gave her a gay look, though her eyes kept right on being gray and serious under their dark, straight brows. Gray was perhaps a serious color, so they could not change no matter how merry she might be. She leaned close to the mirror. "That's me, that one in there. I'm pretty," she whispered. Then she drew back, still looking, grown uncertain. "Maybe—I don't know. It might be."

She found the hand mirror lying on the bureau and she knew there was a way to see oneself sideways. She searched the angles till she found her profile and she laughed aloud to see it. Who could have known that her nose was so straight, that her chin went out in a little point? She could look all day and still be surprised.

At last she laid the mirror down and made up her bed, pausing to examine the headboard that was made of some dark fine wood and carved with wild roses, like the Cherokee rose. There was still no sound from the rest of the house, although the sun must be well up by now. She wanted to go and see Nan, but perhaps it would not do to go until invited. Besides, it might be that her door opened into someone else's room and she would not like to burst in on a stranger. So she sat down in the little straight chair by the door, hands folded in her lap. She waited a long time.

Then a step came. It paused outside the door. Someone coughed and said, "Hist!"

Tammy jumped up. "Hist," she said.

The doorknob rattled. "Can I come in?"

Tammy opened the door. It was the one they had called Ernie, a cup of steaming black coffee in his hand. He held it out to her and grinned. "To wake you up. An old Southern custom."

"I am awake, but I'd sure like to have it." Ernie was about the prettiest man she had ever seen. He had a smooth-cheeked, shining look. His blue eyes were laughing and his light-brown hair was curly enough to satisfy any girl. Only right now there was a black smudge across one cheek. Tammy wondered if she ought to tell him about it.

He was looking past her at the walls of the room. "Jeepers," he said and came all the way in, "Miss Renie went all out on this, didn't she?"

"Went out?"

"Um-m." With his head cocked to one side and his hands in his trousers pockets, he walked around the room, studying the toadstools, scowling at the angels. "I mean, she really went to town."

"Maybe so—I haven't seen her." Tammy sat on the edge of the bed, watching him.

Ernie turned, blinking his eyes. "You're cute, do you know it?"

Tammy shook her head.

Ernie laughed and waved a hand toward the walls. "What have we here? A human mind, turned wrong side out. If we only knew the meaning of it—how a psychiatrist would love it! Everything means something, something means anything, everything means anything—all that sort of thing. And lurid, I bet. A frustrated soul, maybe. Or is she just poking fun at the universe? Knowing Miss Renie, I wouldn't put it past her—say, don't give me that solemn, listening look. Nobody ever pays any attention to little Ernie."

"I will pay attention to you."

Ernie sat down beside her on the bed. "And I'm going to pay attention to you, little one. But def. Pete said you were rare, but I didn't believe him." He sang the words over like a song, "I didn't believe him. Rare and tender and garnished with mushrooms and morning glories." He laughed at her amazed look, and the bed bounced with his laughter.

"I reckon this is the bouncingest bed in the world," Tammy said. "It's as good as a joggling board."

"And what's a joggling board?"

"I never seen one, but I've heard tell. It's like a bench only it's so long you can jounce it."

"What would one use it for?"

"For courting."

"Not putting ideas into my head, are you, little one?"

"No," Tammy said. "You can use it to joggle a baby to sleep on, too."

"A sort of before-and-after board—say, that's clever, do you get it?"

"Yes." Tammy sipped her coffee, unsmiling.

"I'll be darned if I know whether you do or you don't. But anyway, you'd better drink that coffee down. It's all you'll get for a while. Pete made it at crack of dawn, before he went out." He crossed the room to the looking glass.

"Pete has gone away?" Tammy lowered her coffee cup and her heart sank too.

"Only to the fields to plant and plow. Heaven knows why—

just one of his quaint ideas about how to run a plantation."

"Quaint?" she puzzled. "You mean he doesn't know how to run a plantation?"

"Oh, he'll make out—if he ever settles down and makes up his mind to it."

Tammy pondered that for a minute, sipping the rest of her coffee. "Do—do you live here?"

"Me? Lord, no!" He leaned toward the mirror now, discovering the smudge on his cheek. "Sure messed up my face, poking up that kitchen fire." He took a handkerchief from his pocket and scrubbed his cheek as he spoke. "No wonder my charm failed me. But thank heaven I don't live here, honey child. You couldn't hire me to live in such a state of rural inconvenience." He nodded in the direction of the washstand.

"Yes, on the river you can throw it right out. But you must have stayed all night," she persisted, trying to get it straight.

"Got to arguing with Pete and by the time we were through, it was late—or I was too soused—to drive back to town. Should have known better. Can't argue with a man who sees both sides of a question. Regular Hamlet, he is. Thinks too much. All clean now?" He turned for inspection.

"Yes. Only it was Cassius who thought too much."

"Holy smoke—Pete didn't say—I mean, he didn't mention your being personally acquainted with W. Shakespeare."

"But I'm not. How could I be? It says in the front of the book that he died in 1616."

Ernie thrust his hands in his pants pockets and just looked at her for a while. "All this, and the literal mind! Imagine having the courage to look on life bare, with no veil of foolery between. Tell me, how-come you know your Shakespeare so?"

"A boy that went to school—long time ago when we were tied up alongside folks—he got mad and threw it at me. Then Pete saw it and he . . . he seemed to think a lot of it. So after he left I tried to figger it out."

Ernie grinned. "I see. Pete. So that's how it is. You'd even read Shakespeare for him. That tall, dark and handsome guy is always getting my gals away from me." He turned back to the mirror and straightened his tie. "You're cute as a mule, do you know it?"

He sure liked to look at himself, Tammy thought, and said, "A mule? There's nothing cute about a mule."

"Just a manner of speaking, my love. Means I like you. And speaking of mules, I'm hungry enough to eat one. That Osia!"

"Who is Osia?"

"Miss Renie's cook—when so inclined."

"You mean there's a cook that comes and cooks?"

"Yep. Why not?" He turned and looked at her.

"But isn't Pete's mother here? And Miss Renie?"

"Sure, but—— Oh, I get you. Why have a cook, with two able-bodied women in the house? You've got something there. But Mrs. B. has a headache this morning and Miss Renie never gets out of bed till she smells something cooking on the stove. I just made the rounds with coffee to cheer them in their long wait—Ernie, mother's little helper, that's me."

"It was kind of you." Tammy finished her coffee.

"Say—" he whirled on her so quickly she nearly dropped the cup—"you don't happen to be personally acquainted with a wood stove, do you?"

Tammy had to laugh. "You talk the roundaboutest talk! But I can cook on a wood stove, if that's what you mean."

Ernie caught her by the wrist. "Come with me, baby, and I'll lead you to it."

He took her quickly through a little cross passage to a long ell gallery, giving her no time to look around as she would have liked. She only saw the porch was long and pillared and railed with lacy iron-work, with a table and chairs against the rail. She had a glimpse of an open wooden stairway that went up to more rooms on the floor above, and of iron steps going down to a brick-walked garden. "Biggest house that ever I've seen," she said, skipping to keep up with him.

"Clear out the junk, put in four or five bathrooms, a furnace, a modern kitchen, and it might be livable. Ten thousand would make a start on it. Come on, you can look when I'm not starving." He hustled her through the last door at the end of the porch. "There's a good fire going, thanks to little Ernie. Now do your stuff. Fried for me, sunny side up."

Tammy stood in the middle of the kitchen, lost in admiration. "It's sunny side every side with the sun coming in those two big windows." She drew a long breath. "Hell's bells, it wouldn't cramp you to cook for a regiment in a room like this!" There was a long pine table. There were several chairs, one of them with a seat that seemed to think it was a bed. It had springs in it, too. She could see them hanging down underneath.

"One of Miss Renie's little inspirations—to keep the cook contented when the cash to pay her with runs low," Ernie explained, following her gaze. "It would take Miss Renie to put a chaise longue in the kitchen."

Tammy tucked the name of the chair away in one corner of her mind and went on looking around. The wall beside the stove was hung with stewpans and skillets and egg beaters and spoons, and things such as she had never seen before. There were open shelves with all manner of dishes, flowered and plain and scalloped and straight; glasses, too, beyond counting. There was a real sink and the stove had four holes to cook on at the same time, and there was a shiny white box that mystified her. She had seen a picture——
"Oh, but it's a wonder, this kitchen!" she breathed.

"It's a wonder all right." Ernie sat down suddenly as if his legs had given out under him. "But I don't believe I mean what you mean, or do you really mean it?"

Tammy had no time to puzzle out his talk. She could not wait any longer to get started cooking on such a fine stove. She ran to the sink table and caught up the bucket. "Where do you go for water?"

"You don't go, sugar. It arrives! See?" He came over to the sink table and took hold of a handle. He pumped it up and down and after a moment water gushed forth. "There. Man over Nature and all that."

Tammy put out her hand and let the clear cool water run through her fingers, then she set the bucket to catch it. "However does it get here when there's no river to pump it from?"

"Cistern under the floor. Rain water runs off the roof into it. Some system of gutters, I suppose. A great luxury when installed some eighty-odd years ago. Very odd years, if you ask me."

"And I have to walk half a mile for water like this," Tammy marveled. "Stop—it's wasting. Now where's the food to cook?"

"Right here, sister." Ernie kept his eyes on her as he crossed the room to the tall white box. "I wouldn't miss this for a pretty," he said and flung open the door with a flourish.

Tammy gave a little gasp. "Just like the picture in the magazine Cap'n Joe brought me!" She stood there, barely breathing, feeling the cool air pour forth, hearing the low buzz, admiring the racks and shelves. "It's a dream come true," she whispered. "Oh, I had no notion Pete lived in such . . . such elegance!"

"Don't be taken in by the glamorous past, honey child. The place is really on the rocks. If it wasn't for the Pilgrimage money, Lord knows how they'd get the taxes paid."

Tammy turned from the refrigerator to see if he was joking, but he had no laughter in his blue eyes now. "How could a pilgrimage make money?"

"Admission fees, my child, like to the zoo, the circus and the county fair. It's big business for Natchez and all the country parts around, such as this. People come in droves from every state in the union to see these old places and go to the Rebel Ball and such."

"What is that?"

"Old-time dances—like we were practicing on last night."

Tammy's eyes went back to the refrigerator. "This must have cost a pile of money."

Ernie rested one arm on the top of the refrigerator door and regarded her with bright laughing eyes. "Miss Renie's responsible for this little job. Sacrificed the crown jewels to get it, and did Mrs. B. raise a stink!"

"You mean she didn't like it?"

"Exactly, little one. Though I believe the place belongs to Miss Renie—this little jewel of a house, this ante-bellum plantation home, reeking with history and glamour, as they say in the Pilgrimage pamphlets. The Brents just visit now and then. Mrs. B. just lives for the Pilgrimage." He put on an air and made his voice high-toned, "Yes, the ancestral home, five generations under this roof. Note the fan over the door." He dropped his voice. "But don't note how the door is warped, and pray don't observe how the roof leaks."

"Does the roof leak?"

"Like a sieve, sister."

It troubled her, that the roof leaked. The *Ellen B.* had no leak. "Why doesn't Pete mend it?"

"Pete mend a roof? Child, he works with his brain, that lad. Except when he's carving out things that satisfy his artistic cravings—like the bed in your room."

"Oh! Pete carved that?" It filled her with pleasure that she had slept on a bed that Pete had made.

"But meanwhile, honey child, I starve, and the cold escapes. That's bacon in the paper at the left and behold the eggs in a blue bowl."

Tammy took them out, turning from the refrigerator with reluctance. "I just love it," she said.

Ernie got out the milk and butter and leaned against the door to close it. The handle clicked shut without his even touching it. "You know what?"

"What?"

"Nothing would give me more pure delight than to show you the Seven Wonders of the World. Only at the moment, I slowly starve. If you could just convert these to eatable shape——"

"It would pleasure me," Tammy cried gaily and set to work.

"It'll sure pleasure me to watch you do it." Ernie grinned and sat down by the window.

Tammy was proud that she knew how to cook the eggs and bacon and make fresh coffee and toast from the boughten bread that was all sliced and ready. When the two plates were served and she was sitting down at the table with Ernie, she said, "I haven't had a meal since I left the *Ellen B*. I'm about stove in."

Then Ernie wanted to know about the *Ellen B*. and about everything else she had seen or done in all her born days. She told him between quick bites. "Listen," he said at last, pushing his plate aside and leaning across the table toward her. "I've got to go now, but don't forget me. We've got a date. I'm going to show you the world—not to mention the flesh and the devil."

"What do you mean?"

"I mean I'm going to take you to see things—like the refrigerator, only better. In short, to town, to the shops and shows and hot spots and everything. How about it?"

"Oh, Ernie, I've always wanted to see things."

"I'm your man. I will take you up into a high place and show you all the world."

Tammy shook her head, sobering. "Not that. That's what the devil did."

Ernie leaned back straightening his tie. "And the devil's what I am among the ladies, little one."

Tammy laughed. "You are the beatingest!"

"We're going to have fun, more fun than a barrel of monkeys. But right now it's back to the salt mines for me." He stood, looking down at her, smiling.

"You work in a salt mine?"

Ernie grinned. "Yes, only they call it a real-estate office. And just you wait till you see that house I'm about to pick up on a little deal I've got on. Latest gadgets, everything. Even Barb will open her eyes at that."

"You have a house?"

"Not yet but soon—and so farewell."

"You have to go?"

"That's the general idea. Got to make a living. But I'll give you a ring. So long for now."

"So long," Tammy repeated. "It will seem . . . so long . . . till I see you again."

Ernie wheeled in the doorway. He came back quickly and put his hands on her shoulders. "Get me straight, sugar. I'm just out for a good time, that's all. I saw enough of the sober side of life in the war. All I want is to make money and have fun. See? Nix on the serious."

"You don't have to be serious, Ernie. I like you funny."

"My Lord!" Ernie gave her a little shake. "I really don't want to seduce you."

"It would be an accident if you did, I'm sure," Tammy said with earnestness.

Ernie stepped back and looked at her, his head cocked to one side. "I was never so baffled by woman before." Then he was gone.

Tammy sat smiling to herself. Woman—he had called her a woman. She wished Pete could see she was a woman growed.

9.

TAMMY was still in the kitchen when she heard steps on the ell porch. She went to the door and saw Pete's father sitting there at the table close by the rail. His book was open before him, his head bent over it, showing how his hair was thin on top. Tammy did not know whether to say good morning, or what to do.

After a minute he seemed to feel that someone was near. "Breakfast, please, Osia," he said without looking up.

Tammy started to speak, then she thought she would just fix his plate for him and see what happened. When she set it before him, he turned his head slowly. He lifted his brows, letting his glasses slip down on his nose so he could look over them. "Oh—I thought you were Osia. Tammy, isn't it?" He untwined his long legs and stood, holding out his hand. "How do you do?"

"I do very well, thank you. Osia didn't come and so I fixed breakfast."

"I see. Well now, that's nice of you, going to all that trouble. You are certainly an early riser." His voice was deep and his words came one at a time with slowness and importance.

"I've been up for hours, and it's no trouble cooking in such a wonderful kitchen with the bacon all sliced and the bread ready-made and the refrigerator cooling everything."

"I see," he said again, but he didn't look as if he saw very much. "I was . . . er . . . sorry to hear about your . . . er . . . grandfather."

"Yes," Tammy said with a sigh, "I sure miss him. I thought about him when I woke and wished he could be waking amongst flowers and angels. But that's not likely."

91

"You . . . don't think he's . . . among angels?"

"Not where he's gone. But you'd better eat whilst it's hot. I'll fetch your coffee." She got some for herself while she was about it and brought both cups out to the porch table, thinking what a luxury it was, having a room to cook in and all this long gallery for an eating place. There was no river to look at, but there were flowers blooming in the garden, and beyond the far fence she could make out the young peas and cabbages and maybe turnip greens growing. She was just about to sit down when Professor Brent came to the back of her chair and took hold of it. "That . . . that there's your place——" she began.

"No, no. Just you sit."

Turning an uneasy eye on him, Tammy sat, and felt the chair slide in under her as she went down. Did he think she was too weakly to hitch it in for herself? Or was it just a kind of manners new to her? "I'm much obliged," she said. "It was real mannerly of you."

"What's that?" He went back to his own place and sat down.

"I say I'm much obliged for your helping me sit on the chair."

"Oh. Yes—that is, you're welcome. May I take this opportunity of saying how grateful we are for all you and your grandfather did for Pete?"

Tammy nodded. "You may take it."

"Er . . . take what?"

"The opportunity. It pleasured us, having Pete," she added with a smile.

Professor Brent took a few bites, keeping his eyes on her. "Aren't you having anything but coffee?"

"I ate with Ernie. It's too bad he had to go to the mines. He—he's more fun than a barrel of monkeys."

"Indeed?" Professor Brent looked at her around the corner of his glasses, his brows drawn.

"Though, come to think of it, the monkeys might be rather uncomfortable, packed into a barrel." She held up her hand and studied it. "This is the ring finger, isn't it?"

"I believe so."

"Ernie said he would give me a ring."

Professor Brent cleared his throat with a sound like a bark. "It is highly possible that the . . . the type of fun provided by Ernie may not . . . be altogether desirable in its . . . er . . . ultimate consequences. If you will pardon my saying so."

"I will pardon you." Between his manners and his words, Tammy thought, he had a hard time saying anything, and she was not quite sure what he was saying now. "You mean you think the fun might be of a carnal nature?"

Professor Brent laid down his knife and fork, then he took them up again. "Well, to be frank . . . er . . . yes."

"No, he just wants to show me things—he said he wanted to show me the world, the flesh and the devil. But that was just a manner of speaking. He said he didn't want to seduce me."

"Oh." Professor Brent waited a few minutes, then he finished what was on his plate, studying Tammy all the while. "You don't go to the movies?"

"No."

"You don't read the current magazines?"

"No."

"You have not been associated with young people here and there?"

"No."

"And yet you are infected with the frankness of speech rampant among the realists, current among all the younger generation. A curious phenomenon . . . as if there were something . . . in the air, the time, causing it. I wonder . . . my colleagues in the psychology department . . . it might be an interesting study. . . ."

Tammy waited for him to continue, hoping something understandable would come out of it. When he said nothing more, she ventured hesitantly, "Professor Brent?"

"Er . . . yes?"

"I was thinking that if you would just speak it out when you think learned things, I might maybe get a start on learning by just listening. If you were simple and not too mannered."

"You would like some learning?"

"I sure would. Only I don't know just where to begin."

"H'm, that is a question. I should inquire of the professor of education, perhaps. Personally I should begin with mathematics and perhaps some of the simpler phases of physical phenomena." He was silent.

"What special things do you teach?" Tammy asked after a bit. "Physics."

She considered the word, seeking something familiar in the sound of it. "External or internal?"

"External—if one must call it one or the other."

"Like liniment? Or . . . or a poultice?"

Professor Brent blinked, and spelled it out for her. "Not to be mistaken for physic, meaning medicine, though the sound is similar."

"Oh, I mistook it. Then what is it?"

"To put it simply . . . as you . . . er . . . very sensibly suggest . . . it is the science of matter, the study of material objects."

"Science. Grandpa is always talking about science."

"Indeed? There are many fields of science, of course."

"Who puts them all together and makes sense of them? I mean who finds out what they mean?"

"The philosophers try to do that. Though even there, or perhaps I should say most of all there, you would encounter a considerable measure of confusion. Of course some of us go into the implications of higher mathematics, of theoretic physics, but even there——" He shook his head doubtfully.

"Is no one unconfused? Is no one sure?"

"No one to my knowledge," Professor Brent said after some consideration. "Perhaps there is some surety in the past, in what has happened. But the past is too often mere hearsay, myth or fable. Actually nothing is sure, speaking absolutely. A straight line is no longer the shortest distance. Two and two do not necessarily make four. Perhaps from time to time there is an illusion of surety—in experimentally verified mathematical physics, say. And yet as long as there are increases in empirical knowledge, will there not be continual changes in man's conception of the theoretic component?"

Tammy seized on the two words that had meaning for her. "Continual changes," she repeated. "Then there doesn't seem to be much solid ground to stand on." She leaned back in her chair considering the complex and uncertain nature of scientific things. Yet surely there was the sun shining on the great oak beyond the side drive, there was the plowed field yonder, stretching to the horizon and the blue sky bending down to meet it. There were people everywhere who had a living and a dying coming to them, who suffered and loved and hated and rejoiced. Those were sure things. And Grandpa was sure about a great many things. "Grandpa says there is a scientific explanation for everything."

"Indeed?"

"Yes. Take Methuselah, for instance. Grandpa says his living nine hundred sixty-nine years was account of something in his food, and if the doctors keep on figgering, they will find it's some new kind of stuff they just haven't noticed yet."

"Ahum-mm. An interesting theory."

Tammy drew a long breath and filled up with pride that Grandpa had said something a learned man would think well of. "He says that ever since Adam ate of the tree of knowledge, humans have had to reason out every little thing. They ain't been satisfied by faith any more since then. They're just bound to figger it all out for themselves. Maybe that's how-come they're mixed up. Oh, I could preach a fair sermon myself on that." Tammy smiled.

"But in finding out these things man has increased his convenience and his physical comfort . . . yet mentally, spiritually——"

"There's more confusion out in the world than I thought for," Tammy said.

"Yes." Professor Brent drew the word out on a long sigh. Then he went away into his own mind and was silent.

Tammy considered his mind. It was likely overgrown with words so he might have a hard time making his way about in it, just as he had a hard time getting anywhere, on account of his manners bogging him down. After a little she slipped out to the kitchen with his dishes. She was washing them when she heard a high-toned quick voice from the gallery. Mrs. Brent had decided to get up.

"Just a cup of coffee and some toast, Osia," she called.

Professor Brent said, "Osia isn't here. That's Tammy."

"Tammy? In the kitchen? Well, that's one worry off my mind."

"I wouldn't be too sure. This is a most unusual case."

Tammy went to the door and wished Mrs. Brent good morning. "I'll bring your toast and coffee."

Mrs. Brent smiled briefly, showing her false even teeth. They clicked a little as she spoke, as if reminding her in the midst of her ordering that she could not order everything. "Dry toast, please. You really are making yourself useful, aren't you?"

"Grandpa told me to," Tammy said and waited to see Professor Brent push in Mrs. Brent's chair. He got it in all right, so she hurried back to the stove. With her mind on making the toast dry, she heard only snatches of the talk on the gallery, gathering the fact that Mrs. Brent was not pleased with Ernie and thought something a shocking situation. She was likely a woman easily shocked, Tammy thought. Then there was the sound of heels clicking loudly down the length of the porch, and a woman's voice, deep and dramatic-sounding, saying, "Where is the little girl? Is she up yet?"

Mrs. Brent said, "She's in the kitchen. But please, Aunt Renie——"

She was already in the kitchen door, a tall, thin-faced old woman, quick-moving and quick-spoken. "So this is Tammy!" she cried. Her dress was curiously flowered and stiff; it looked iced or waxed. She kept her thin, high-beaked nose tilted as if to hold on her rimless glasses. Curled around her neck like a fur piece was a large black cat. "I'm Miss Renie, Pete's great-aunt." She put out her bony hand and advanced to meet Tammy, her black eyes dancing, her face lighting up.

Tammy set the coffeepot down to shake hands. "Howdy," she said. The cat drew back and said, *"Hssst,"* and fluffed himself.

"Behave, Picasso. Stop clawing my batik." She spoke her words in little bunches as if she were plucking them off a tree. "Do you like cats?"

"I sure do. I had a little kitten once long ago, but it died."

"I have seven, besides Picasso. Have to keep them in the barn while Ena—that's Mrs. B.—is here. She hates them." Miss Renie bent over the stove sniffing with her thin bony nose. "Eggs? Bacon? You?"

Tammy nodded.

"Superb!" Her dress crackled as she whirled to a shelf and took down a plate. "Put it here. I love to eat but I hate cooking. Never pass the kitchen stove that I don't kick it. I'd spit in the sink if it was sanitary. One more piece of bacon. Picasso adores it." Suddenly she set the plate down on the top of the stove and bent closer to Tammy, blinking her quick black eyes. "What's that you've got on your face?"

Tammy lifted one hand to her cheek, wondering if she had a smudge like Ernie's.

"Paint?"

"Y-yes."

"Rub it off. It's not for you. Here, take this dish towel. Osia can wash it."

Tammy lifted the cloth to her cheek with reluctance. "I . . . I thought it looked nice."

"Rub hard. That's it. Don't want to look like a tart, do you?"

"A . . . a what?"

"Call a spade a spade. Don't tell me you don't understand."

Tammy shook her head. "Not unless it's a little pie."

"It's a . . . a strange woman, that's what it is."

"Oh—that lieth in wait at the corner and leadeth the young men astray? No, I didn't want to look like one of those." She scrubbed furiously.

Miss Renie sighed. "It used to be easy to shock people. It was my one recreation for forty years. Nowadays they just go me one better. I may as well give up. I'm just too old." She took up her plate again.

"Don't say you're too old, Miss Renie. Grandpa says you don't begin to live till you're past seventy. Then's when you're free."

Miss Renie, heading for the door, plate in hand, looked back over her shoulder, peering around the cat. All she lacked was a broomstick. "Free?" she demanded.

"Yes," Tammy said, taking up Mrs. Brent's plate and the coffee-pot. "First, you have to mind your parents, then you have to set a good example for your children. But when you're seventy you can do as you please. Also," Tammy added, following her to the porch, "you are free of all desires of the flesh."

Miss Renie laughed. She stopped Professor Brent with a wave of her hand. "I'm already down, Joel."

Mrs. Brent said, "What on earth are you talking about?"

"Sin," Miss Renie replied with relish. "I'm not as old as I thought I was. Still have a taste for it." The cat leaped to the chair beside her and sat there like a human being, so Tammy, not wanting to disturb him, sat down on the top step.

Mrs. Brent tried to take a bite of her toast and laid it down with a shake of her head. "I just can't chew."

"Soak it," Miss Renie said.

"Is it your teeth?" Tammy asked with sympathy.

Mrs. Brent looked at her a minute before she answered. "Yes." It sounded like the cat's hiss.

"Grandpa had a time when he first got his store teeth."

Miss Renie chuckled. "Did he ever get so he could chew right?"

"Aunt Renie, please, I'm trying to eat."

"And I'm only trying to be helpful. Go on, Tammy."

"He got onto it. Said it was just a trick, like spitting accurate or anything else you had to learn." Tammy clasped her hands around her knees and rocked back and forth. Miss Renie made her feel easy, in spite of Professor and Mrs. Brent. "Grandma had all her teeth drawed the day she was twenty-four and never took them out except to wash them. That was how-come she could bite the burglar."

Miss Renie choked on her coffee. "How-came she had to bite the burglar—be quiet, Ena, I want to hear. Go on, Tammy."

"The burglar come creeping in the night, come right aboard the *Ellen B.* Grandma felt his hand go under her pillow. That's what woke her. She turned her head real slow and bit him in the arm. He hollered like all-get-out and ran. Grandma said it just showed what you could do if you kept your head."

"And your teeth in your head." Miss Renie laughed. "Did they catch the burglar?"

"They did so. Picked up a man with a bite in his arm and sent for Grandma to come to town. But she said, shucks, she didn't have time to go to town and see if her teeth fit: she was busy putting up blackberry juice. She put them in a paper bag and sent them in by Grandpa. They fit all right and the man got sent up for I don't know how long, and—— Oh, here comes Pete!"

Tammy ran down the walk toward the gate. Pete was smiling, his dark hair was tousled and his shirt collar open. This was Pete as she knew him on the *Ellen B.*, not the strange Pete in fine clothes as he was last night. But just before she reached him, she stopped and put out her hand with dignity.

Pete asked how she was and how she had slept and they walked side by side along the brick walk between the sweet olive trees and across the wide bricked space where the walk opened into a little square with flowers on all sides.

On the gallery Miss Renie was saying, "Why didn't you walk right in on them? I would have."

"You!" Mrs. Brent said with indignation. "I have a sense of delicacy. Before breakfast, too."

"Don't confuse the issue, Ena. It's as moral before as after and personally I think you are hipped on the subject. Ought to be psychoanalyzed."

"If you please——" Professor Brent protested. Then they all looked around, coming out of their huddle, as Pete and Tammy mounted the steps.

Tammy said, "Pete, you sit down and I'll get your breakfast time your pa gets your chair under you." She ran to the kitchen, glad she knew how Pete liked his eggs, glad she could show him how quickly she had learned her way about in such a strange and wonderful kitchen. When she came to the porch again with his plate and coffee, Mrs. Brent was speaking.

"Unfeeling, I call it. Not a sign of proper grief——" She broke off at sight of Tammy and no one spoke for a minute.

Tammy said, "I never knew such a stretched-out breakfast as you all have." No one said anything so she added, "But I like it," and sat down on the steps. They all looked at her with serious eyes.

Then Pete said, "Tammy, I do want to hear about your grandfather. I wish you could have let me know."

"There wasn't time, Pete, or anything anybody could do. It all happened so fast. Then I came right on here like he told me."

"He wasn't sick long?"

"Sick? He wasn't sick at all. He'd been in the swamp all morning. And he wasn't upset about it, Pete, though I was, of course. He said it was the Lord's will and no need of kicking against the pricks."

"That must be a comfort to you." Miss Renie slipped a bite of bacon to Picasso.

"It is. And what's more of a comfort is thinking he won't be suffering any more with aches and pains in his joints. Maybe."

"Maybe!" Mrs. Brent said with a little nervous jump.

"Well, we couldn't be sure, but he thought the dry warm air might ease him."

Professor Brent said, "Fundamentalism, of an extraordinary sort."

"No, it's the rheumatism Grandpa has."

Pete laid down his knife and fork and spoke sharply. "Tammy, what are you talking about? Where did they take your grandfather?"

"I don't know exactly, Pete. He said he would write when he got settled." They all looked so startled she knew something was wrong. Then Mrs. Brent's words came back to her: ". . . no proper feeling, no grief." She looked from one face to the other. "Did you think he was dead?"

"Yes, Tammy," Pete said. "You told me they came and took him away, so naturally——"

Tammy laughed right out. "That would tickle Grandpa, for sure."

Miss Renie was the only one who laughed. "And if it isn't the nether regions, do tell us where he is to be—in dry warm air?"

"In . . . in jail."

There was silence for a moment, then Miss Renie choked. "Ena, your face——"

"I see nothing amusing in the situation. It's dreadful, shocking."

"Mother——" Pete began.

Tammy stood quickly, serious now, too, her gray eyes flashing and her chin high. "Excuse me, Mrs. Brent, but it isn't shocking. Grandpa wouldn't do anything shocking. It was just a matter of personal freedom—and some fool law they made up in Jackson about corn liquor."

"Jail—corn liquor—what a position that puts me in—me, the corresponding secretary of the W.C.—and the Pilgrimage coming —— Oh, my head!"

"Wait a minute, Mother," Pete said, "You don't——"

Tammy broke in. "I reckon you're thinking you don't want to have anybody round that's kin to anybody in jail. So . . . so I'll say thank you for the night's lodging and the breakfast and I'll get my bag and be going along." She turned from them and went along the porch toward the back hall door and the passageway. She held herself proud and hoped they wouldn't see the hurt and fury that was inside her.

Pete came running after her. "Tammy, no! Wait——" He caught her, one arm around her shoulder, but she stiffened away from him. "It isn't like that, Tammy, please. It's quite all right for your Grandpa to be in jail—I mean, we were just startled, having thought he was dead. Of course you are going to stay. Come on, I want to show you the land and my tomatoes—and there's Nan waiting to be milked. Truly, we want you."

Tammy let him turn her about and lead her back to the table. She stood there, facing them, looking from one to the other. "Is it true—that you want me to stay?"

"Of course, child," Miss Renie cried. "And when your grandfather gets out of jail, he'll be welcome, too." She turned on Mrs. Brent who had let out a little gasp at this. "The house is still mine, Ena, and so is the plantation, and it won't be Pete's till I die and I'm feeling very healthy indeed right now. I shall invite whom I please."

"I have never disputed your right to the house, Aunt Renie. It was only when you started selling off family heirlooms to buy such things as refrigerators, wholly out of key with the period of the house, that I was in duty bound to protest and——"

"Let's not go into that again." Professor Brent's deep voice drowned her out. He turned to Tammy. "We shall always be greatly in your debt, Tammy, and it is only right that you should stay here as long as you care to."

"I wouldn't want to be just a . . . a debt——" Tammy began.

"No indeed," Miss Renie cried, "the place already has debts aplenty."

Pete said, "Mother——"

"Yes, yes, you must stay, Tammy, of course. I'm not saying you shouldn't. Only I feel the responsibility of a young girl and her conduct more keenly than some others here seem to. Entertaining young men in the bedroom before breakfast—I cannot let that pass without a word no matter whose house this is."

"What do you mean?" Pete demanded.

"Ernie with coffee, that's all," Miss Renie put in.

Tammy turned from Mrs. Brent to Miss Renie. "I reckon you were right about the paint I had on my face. Seems like she has mistook me for the whore of Babylon or something. But if I was I'd have the decency to close the door, like Grandma said."

Mrs. Brent said, "Oh, my head—such language!"

"It's in the Bible, I believe," Professor Brent said.

"Not everything in the Bible is suitable for polite conversation and you know it, Joel."

"Isn't it?" Tammy puzzled. Then she turned to Pete. "When I I was on the *Ellen B.*, seemed like I had everything figgered out, how it was. But out in the world . . . I . . . it's all mixed up. I can't make folks out."

"Who can?" Miss Renie cried. "But you'll get onto it—more's the pity."

"Will I?" Tammy asked with a sigh. Then she said, "Pete, if you'll get me a bucket or something, I reckon I'd better go milk Nan."

As they went down the path, she looked back toward the ell gallery. They were all in a kind of a huddle, leaning together, and she thought that if they weren't Pete's folks she'd be bound they was framing mischief, for sure.

10.

PETE took her past the kitchen garden to the field where his cold frames lay, open to the morning sun, their white covers thrown back like discarded shawls. The plants stood in orderly rows, thrusting up their tender leaves with trembling eagerness.

"Look at them!" Tammy cried. "I never seen so many in all my days." She bent over, resting her hands on her knees, studying the plants in the first cold frame. "Seems like they're fair itching to grow for you, Pete."

"Hope so," Pete said. "The fertilizer and all this just about cleaned me out. They've got to do well."

Tammy straightened up in time to catch the grim look on his face and a little shiver went through her. He mustn't count on it so. Nothing was as uncertain as growing things. You couldn't set your heart on them, you could only hope. To cover her dismay, she waved a hand at the green rows on the far side of the level field. "What's all that, Pete?"

Pete relaxed and smiled. "That's my little gamble of the season —more tomato plants, some extra ones, set out much too soon, of course. I'm taking a chance on the weather, just to see. If they should survive, I'd be ahead of everybody and get the top price. And more than that, I'd take it as a sign that I——" He broke off and added, "It is the damnedest thing, how you have to depend on the weather. They need a little shower right now."

As they started back, Pete pointing the way toward the barnyard gate, Tammy looked up at the cloudless pale-blue sky. She hoped the Lord would keep it in mind, how the weather ought to be for

Pete's planting. Then she said, "Pete, I can't figger it out, the way you talk poor, when you've got all this." The sweep of her arm included field and barnyard and woods beyond and the house rising gray and chimneyed above the tall shrubs of the garden.

Pete shook his head. "The land's washed out, full of gullies, and it's just hilly enough so that even if I had machinery——" He shook his head. "The day of the mule and the plow is over, I can see that. Most of the small farms with level fields are going into big combines that can have the best modern equipment. But it's a tough time for the little man with a place like this."

Tammy stopped in her tracks. "Why, Pete! Ain't nothing little about you. Or this place either. It's so big it fair takes my breath away. There must be no end of ways to make money here. You got to just try out this and that."

"Well——" Pete smiled, holding the barnyard gate open for her ——"I'm trying tomatoes."

Tammy looked back toward the field. "I hope you set them out in the dark of the moon."

"Come to think of it——" Pete laughed, as if the thought cheered him——"I believe I did."

In the barn lot, back of the carriage house, a few hens were scratching by the feed troughs. The cow had gone to pasture, Pete said, the mules to the field, but the smell of them lingered on the mild morning air. Nan stood there, looking lost and lonely and Tammy dropped down on her knees and gave her a hug because it seemed a long time since they had parted the night before.

It was good to be milking again, familiar and restoring after all the excitement of new places and new people. They came crowding in upon her thoughts as she milked. She had widened her world in this brief space of time and, in widening it, had somehow diminished herself. It was going to be hard, she thought, to keep herself whole and all together in the midst of people who came trailing their strange, mixed-up lives around them, who came wrapped in their notions, concealed behind their manners. How could she ever get to know them truly or find her way among them without bewilderment? Only Pete—she was beginning to know him, now she saw him in the midst of his life. She felt her hope and her longing go out to him—just the way he was feeling about his tomatoes, and about as risky a business, too.

The milk stream played on the bottom of the bucket and it filled slowly. Pete came back from somewhere in the barn, bringing a box for her to sit on, though she did very well just squatting. He sat on his heels and leaned back against the feed trough, looking far away toward the woods beyond the field. Since he was not noticing, Tammy could look at him all she would, satisfying the hunger she had had for the sight of him. Why should he have this dear familiarity to her? Maybe it was because she had nursed and tended his body, had watched his strength return after weakness, helped him take his first steps. He was her child to whom she had given life.

Her eyes dwelt on the firm, bony line of his jaw, the shape of his head, the way his hair grew on his forehead. She thought she would never get tired of seeing Pete's face, not even if it grew old and lined, his mouth sunk in with the loss of his teeth, his hair white, or gone, maybe, like Grandpa's.

Pete turned to her now. "Did you have any trouble finding the way here, Tammy?"

Then she told him, first about how the men came for Grandpa, how Nan followed and then how long and wearisome was the way. "I didn't have the least notion you lived in such a place as this, Pete. It made me afeard to come right in, amidst all those people, too. I felt strange to them and to the steps and the glass in the windows and the doorknob on the door and everything. That's how-come I just sat down and leaned against the post and went to sleep."

Pete nodded. "It's too big—too big to paint or to keep up the way it should be kept. I don't know what I'm going to do, Tammy. Not even after all this time. I just keep on going from day to day."

"You mustn't lose heart about the farming, Pete, when you ain't more than just started on it."

"The truth is, it seems to lack purpose, somehow, as well as money. I can't figure out what would be the best crops to raise, if I do go in for it. Meanwhile I'm just putting the other fields in cover crops, trying to improve the soil. You see, it's all so different from the way I thought it would be."

"How'd you think it would be?"

"Like it was when I was a boy on vacations here with Aunt Renie, when she had a man managing the place and lots of tenants and an air of plenty. I didn't realize then how she had to scrimp along. That was the life I was looking forward to—riding out early to see how the crops were growing, living independent of however the world went." He bowed his head and ran his long fingers through his hair. "But with only two men left on the place, and one of them old Prater——" He fell silent.

"Pete?" Tammy said after a little.

"Yes?"

"Don't you reckon you better change your notion to fit . . . however things are . . . now?"

"You mean, give up this idea, go in town on a job—like Barbara has been saying? And a lot of what she says makes sense, I'm telling you. Or do like my father says and go back for another degree, or——"

"No, no, Pete." Tammy gave Nan a slap to send her out of the way. She stood and came quickly to him, the pail in her hand. "You've got everything here, Pete. You're rich. What do you have to be afeard of? And why do you have to do what other people say? Why do you have to listen to them?"

"God, I've been listening to other people all my life. Every one of them saying something different." Pete stared before him, his eyes dark and resentful.

"But Pete—hell's bells, didn't you ever in your life decide anything for yourself?"

Pete was silent as if searching his life. "Of course. In the war.

If I'd stopped to wait for orders in some of those tight spots I wouldn't be here now."

Tammy, studying him, remembered something he had said aboard the *Ellen B.* "You had peace in the middle of the war. That was what you said."

"It seemed simpler there, somehow."

Tammy laughed. "I ain't been here but overnight, Pete, but already I see how unsimple people are. You just got to pay them no mind."

"If I could just be sure———"

"Were you sure of things in the middle of the war?"

"Sure? I wasn't even sure of being alive the next minute. I didn't expect to be sure when I went into it."

"Then, lookahere, Pete. You're expecting too much of peace and just ordinary living. There ain't any way you can make it foolproof sure. You can't stave off trouble or dying, even if you are in the middle of peace."

Pete stood. "Tammy, you do say the damnedest surprising things sometimes. How do you do it?"

Tammy laughed. "Grandpa's got a sermon about all that—I been hearing it all my life. And how he ends it up is by saying you can't expect to manage everything yourself. You've got to leave something to the Lord."

"I envy those that can do it," Pete said. "Do you?"

"Mostly, I do, Pete, but it ain't always easy. Grandpa says mankind's took over too much lately. Says folks used to leave the Last Day and the end of the world in the Lord's hands, but now they've took it over themselves, with the atom bomb. That's how-come everyone's so uneasy. They don't trust each other like they used to trust the Lord."

Pete laughed, and yet he was serious too. He gave her hair a tweak. "I'm glad you're around, Tammy. Everything looks better when you're here. I've been needing you."

Tammy's eyes fell. Warmth and happiness spread through her.

She loved this moment here with Pete, the smell of the barn lot in her nose and warm sun shining down on her head. There was a line in the Bible that said, My heart awakened . . . my bowels yearned for him. That was how she felt. But Pete? She looked up at him and saw that he was still considering his problems. So she put her mind to work, searching out his concern. "Where did all the tenants go?" she asked, stepping back from him.

"To town to work in the factory, or down the road to the new milk-canning place."

"Do they can milk into cans there, Pete?"

"Yes."

"Then you better just raise cows. They'll be needing milk to can for sure, they're bound to."

Pete laughed. "That's what the county agent's been telling me. Only I don't know enough about it. I'd have to go to Ag College and study cattle raising. Here I've been all over the place consulting experts, Tammy, and you toss me the same advice right off the bat."

"It's just common sense, Pete."

"The trouble is—" he looked down at the ground, kicking at a lump of dirt with the toe of his shoe—"Barbara's got some funny notion about it, thinks she'd lose caste or something, living on a dairy farm—a small one, like this would be. I guess she can't see herself milking when the hands don't show up."

"Cows are easier to milk than goats, Pete. I bet I could milk a sight of cows."

"I'll bet you could." At a sound from the barn he looked around quickly and called, "Who's that? Hey, you Roots, come on around here. What you doing?"

The little brown boy who had dodged around the corner of the shed when he saw them, came back now, hurriedly wiping his nose on a ragged shirt sleeve. "Ain't doin nothin, suh."

"Where's your pappy this morning?"

"He home."

Pete turned to Tammy. "I was just going down to his house to see why he isn't out working this morning. Want to come? Roots can take the milk up to the house."

Tammy held out the pail and Roots took it from her, his eyes on the ground. "What-for you been crying, Roots?" she asked softly.

He caught his breath in a little gulp. "Pappy say I got to tell Miss Renie. Tell her I can't have no more drawing lessons."

Pete had turned away, but he looked back now. "What's that? No more lessons? Why not?"

The boy bent his head. "Don't know, suh."

Pete looked down at him scowling. "Well, you get on up to the house with that milk and I'll see your pa. Come on, Tammy."

Tammy caught up with him, taking a skip to keep even with his long strides. "He knows something, but he's afraid to tell, Pete."

"Yes, and I'm afraid to find it out. His father is my only real worker. If he is going to quit me or anything——"

They crossed the lot to the rail gate on the far side, Nan following close at their heels. Tammy shooed her back when Pete unfastened the chain that held the gate shut. But he said, "Oh, let her come."

In single file they went along the fence line at the edge of the field. Rows of young oats, tender and sparse as yet, stretched away to a wall of woods. From the woods a line of trees, like a green arm curved through the hollow of the pasture ahead. Tammy followed it with her eyes, thinking there would be running water there. That would be good for cattle raising.

At the corner of the field where blackberry bushes dropped their pure-white petals, they passed through a zigzag gate, too small for cattle and just the size for Nan to wriggle through. Then a hard-beaten path led across an open, sunny space toward a little gray cabin that held two chinaberry trees, like green umbrellas, before its face. The chimney at this end was stoutly built of stick and mud. Blue wood smoke rose straight and tall in the still air, like Jacob's ladder set on the earth and the top of it reaching to heaven. Tammy stood motionless, seeing it. "Must be this is the gate to heaven," she said, as Jacob had.

"Why do you say that?"

"It is a beautiful house, the color of rain. There must be all of three rooms, and the tin roof's sound above it. There could be geraniums at the windows and curtains hung, fresh and clean. It is such a house as I have dreamed of, set well on solid ground."

Pete stood looking at her, saying no word.

"The front room for living and cooking, one to sleep in and one to put the children in. Ground for a garden and space for chickens. Who could want more than that?"

"Food, shelter, love, companionship, children, chickens and maybe a goat or two. Is all the world crazy, or are you, Tammy— and me, listening to you, almost believing?" Then he laughed and said, "Come, let's see if we can convince Steve that this is the *summum bonum.*"

"What's a *summum bonum?*"

"The highest good. Latin." He rapped on the floor of the cluttered porch and called, "Halloo!"

A slim dark young woman with a baby in her arms stood in the open door. "Mornin', Mr. Pete," she said, unsmiling. Her dark eyes flicked uneasily toward the sacks of clothes, the kitchen pots and pans strung on a rope and lying in a heap at the end of the porch.

"Looks as if you were about to clear out, Lena," Pete said.

The woman joggled the baby in her arms, not answering, letting its cry cover her silence.

"What's it all about?"

Lena came out on the porch. She spoke in a wshiper. "It's Steve, suh. Been on another jag. Now he's got the notion of moving to town."

"Where is he now?"

"Round tother side the house. He'da had us gone fore now only his ma been over here since day, argyfying with him."

"Osia's got sense. You can't go anywhere with that sick baby." He went slowly around the corner of the house.

"Hey, you Steve," Lena called above the baby's rising wail. Then as Tammy moved nearer and stopped at the foot of the steps, Nan at her heels, she said, "I heard you talking about this-here house. Did you mean that, what you said?"

"I sure did. You're lucky, having such a house."

Lena joggled the baby to silence. "It suits me. I wisht Steve could'a heerd how you talked about it."

Tammy mounted the steps and looked down into the baby's wrinkled dark face. "What's his name?"

"I name him Karo, account of he was so sweet. That was before I got a rising and my milk give out. He ain't been sweet lately."

"Karo. That's pretty. What do you feed him?"

"Miss Renie been giving me cow's milk."

"Let me hold him." The feel of him in her arms as she rocked him to quiet with the motion of her body carried her back to long ago when other shanty boats were beside them, people and babies. It carried her back beyond that into time before she remembered, and it took her forward into all time to come. "He's too light," she said after a while, "he doesn't weigh anything."

"Yassum, it's cause he don't get no use of his food. No more'n get it down than he throws it up."

"I wonder if goat's milk would suit him better. Grandma saved a baby's life once with goat's milk. Want to try? I didn't strip Nan anywhere dry."

"I'm that worried I'd try anything."

"Got a bottle and a nipple?"

When Lena was gone into the house, Tammy heard Pete talking back of the house somewhere. Another voice answered him: "It looks like I got the going-away blues, Mr. Pete. Restless. Feel like I got to go."

Tammy's dark brows drew together. That voice—or did all Negroes talk alike? Lena came back with the bottle and Tammy sat down on the step, calling Nan to her, pushing her around. The two little children came out now and watched with wide solemn eyes as the stream of warm milk went into the bottle. Tammy studied them with quick glances in the midst of her milking. They were the color of the river in high-water time, a pleasing color—if one did not look for it to be white. She smiled at them, feeling relaxed and easy. Lena and the children rested her. They were not cluttered round with . . . with notions the way the others were, up at Pete's house.

Pete's voice came to her again. She held it in her ears and treasured it. He spoke to this man with understanding, saying, "That's the way I've been feeling myself, Steve, ever since I got out of the service. Had to go way out West before I could get it out of my system. But of course I didn't have a wife and children to think about."

Tammy held up the bottle, measuring the milk with her eye. "That's enough for him the first time. Give it to him quick whilst it's warm."

They bent over the baby, watching. He pushed aside the nipple once or twice with his pink tongue, then he began to draw on it. He made little smacking sounds. As the milk went down in the bottle his eyelids drooped and when it was almost gone, he slept. Lena let out a long sigh. "He ain't never took it so well, Must be the Lord sont you for sure, ma'am."

"If you'd be good to her, I'd lend you Nan. Then you could milk him some milk whenever he's hungry. But now you'd better lay him on his stomach on the bed for a while." She turned to the two children. "You can pat her now if you like. Her name is Nan. Will you be good to her?" They nodded, speechless.

Pete came around the corner of the house, followed by a lean

Negro in khaki clothes the color of his skin. He looked around quickly as Nan moved away from the children along the porch, her little hoofs clicking sharply on the boards of the floor. His eyes widened, showing a circle of white around the dark centers. His face took on a grayish tinge, as his glance shot across to Tammy. His feet shuffled quickly as if they would carry him away, yet he did not move, some strange paralysis holding him rigid. Beads of sweat came on his forehead.

Tammy knew him now, for sure. Pete was across the yard, examining the well. Lena was in the house with the baby. "Never mind," Tammy said.

Then Lena came out. "Steve, the baby done drank the goat's milk good, and she say she'll loan us the goat to feed him."

"L-loan . . . her goat . . . to feed my baby?" Steve's voice was hoarse. His eyes kept coming back to Tammy.

"Sure I will," Tammy said. "Just treat her nice. I'll come down to see her some time, so she won't pine for me."

Steve, after a quick glance at Pete, wiped his forehead with trembling fingers and turned away from them. "Reckon I's kind of drunk last night when I . . . got so sot on going. Reckon I didn't know what I was doing."

"Okay, Steve," Pete said. "You can get on down to the lower forty now and finish that piece of fencing. Prater's got things started but he's needing some help. I see your well's holding out all right."

Steve started to speak and gave it up. Then he set out across the yard in a long loping stride. Tammy looked at Pete to see if he had noticed anything. She didn't think he had, but it was hard to tell about Pete.

"Well, thank the Lord, Mr. Pete." They all turned as a tall dark woman came round the corner of the house. "I heerd what he say and you done work a miracle for sure."

"Morning, Osia," Pete said. "Steve's all right. Just restless, as he says. You coming up to the house?"

"Yassuh, I been trying to get there, but Steve—I been here since day argyfying with him. Four boys I got, and two girls and three dead and Steve the only one ever give me trouble. He sure make up for all the rest."

"He's a good worker. He'll be all right. Come on, Tammy, let's go."

"When he work," Osia muttered. Then she added, "Tell Miss Renie I'll be up there in a minute."

Pete looked back as Nan jumped down from the porch to follow, and Lena caught her. "You better take that rope you have your pots tied with and fasten her up for a while."

Tammy walked on, not wanting to see Nan trying to follow. Pete overtook her at the zigzag gate and even before he spoke she knew he had not missed anything that passed between her and Steve.

"Where had you seen Steve, Tammy?" His tone was quiet, yet there was something disturbing in it.

Tammy stood by the gate, feeling the warm ground under her bare feet, steadying herself on the solid ground. "I saw him when I was coming, on the big road." She went on through the gate and along the path beside the hedgerow.

"There was more to it than that."

The words hung in the air like a question. "Nothing that mattered, Pete," Tammy said, not looking around.

His hands fastened on her shoulders, stopping her, turning her to face him. "Tammy, you don't understand these things." His voice was sharp and strange in her ears. "Tell me just what happened. I must know."

"I will tell you. He spoke to me, I spoke to him, and he went on." She studied Pete, wondering what had come over him. It was something from outside himself; it was the same thing she had sensed in that couple in the car, an urgency and a fear.

"There's more to it than that." Pete looked away across the field in the direction Steve had gone. "I'll get it out of him."

"No." The word seemed to startle him. It came out crisp like Grandma's speech, and it stopped Pete short. "What has come over you, Pete?"

Pete drew a long breath. "You've lived on the river all your life, Tammy. You don't know—it isn't what one Negro does or says. It's what another one might do."

"Do you punish one man for what another might do?"

Pete turned away with impatience, then his face grew troubled "That wouldn't be right, of course. Only——"

"Why are you so afeard, Pete?"

Pete studied her a long moment. She could see him coming back to himself from being someone else. "Is it fear?" He ran his fingers through his hair, shaking his head. "I don't know. It's more complex than that. It's partly my desire to protect you— from this or any harm."

"You can't let yourself be like that, Pete. It was because I was not afeard last night that I could stand up to Steve and tell him to get on about his business."

"What was it he wanted of you?" Pete was still worried but the other strange quality was gone from his voice.

"He asked for money. He was a little drunk. I told him to go work for his own money, what I had was mine."

"And he went?"

"Yes."

"God!" Pete said. Then they went on in silence till they came to the garden gate. He looked down at her as his hands reached for the latch. "Thank the Lord you were not afraid, Tammy." Then he said, as they went on together, "You . . . you bring me back to myself somehow, Tammy. You—I'm grateful to you."

Tammy glanced up at him and looked away. "You're welcome, Pete," she said with a sigh. She went up the steps with a sadness folding round her like a cloak. Pete liked to talk to her, he liked the things she said, but that was all. His heart was not awakened to her, his bowels did not yearn for her.

11.

THE ways of people puzzled Tammy, what they did and why. She set her mind to figure them out, questioning one or another of the household. But there were times when a strangeness came over her, holding her back, troubling her in a way that was new to her. Then she saw herself through their eyes—shabby, alien and unknowing, lowly. She saw that her manner of talking was not like theirs and she tried to improve her speech. Miss Renie, hearing her catch back an "ain't," began to help her with such things.

But even with fine clothes and proper speech Tammy was afeard she would not ever blend with the world here. Her way of thinking was too different. It must be that her life on the river had marked her and set a great gulf between her and these people. Only with Pete, when she was alone with him, walking out to see how his tomatoes grew, then she took heart. Pete did not look down on her from a high place. He turned to her for help and encouragement.

Pete answered all her questions with patience, though sometimes he just laughed and said, "Well, Tammy, that makes me wonder, too."

Mrs. Brent was quickly upset. "That's just the way it is, Tammy," she would say with sharpness. Or "Everyone does. It's customary." And if Tammy asked why, she only said, "Oh, dear —my head, and there's so much to see to."

Then Tammy would say, "I'm sorry. What do you want me to do now?"

For Brenton Hall was being put in order for the Pilgrimage,

117

when people would be coming from everywhere to see such places as this. From the outside, where Pete worked with old Prater, raking the lawn and drive, clearing out the flower beds, the house had an open-eyed look of surprise, with all its shutters flung wide. Inside it was agitated by all manner of activity. Osia was mopping, Steve was carrying out rugs to sweep, Miss Renie was tacking her batiks on the passageway walls, getting out paintings to hang on the ell porch. Mrs. Brent, with her head tied in an old brown scarf, was all over the place, directing, inspecting.

Tammy polished the long dining-room table where they never ate, the chairs and the sideboard. She labored over the intricacies of whatnots and small carved seats and mirror frames. It was a wonder to her, how many things had been contrived for ornament alone. It troubled her that there were so many more chairs and sofas than they could ever sit in, more dishes than could be eaten from. What was the good of having more than could be used? It would take a body all day every day, just to keep them properly clean. Miss Renie seemed to feel the same way about it, for she had said at breakfast, "It's a waste of time, all this cleaning up. If you'd just leave the blinds shut, Ena, the way they stay the rest of the year, nobody could see the dust."

Mrs. Brent had bristled at that. "Aunt Renie, I don't care how you keep house the rest of the year, but Pilgrimage time is my responsibility and I'm going to have the place clean if it kills me. I won't have people going away from here talking the way they do after going through some of those old houses down in Natchez."

"To hear you, Ena, the pilgrims will be climbing the bookshelves to spy out cobwebs, crawling under the beds——"

"They do just about that and you know it, Aunt Renie. Now I don't ask you to do a thing——"

"Just as well you don't." Miss Renie set down her coffee cup with a little bang.

"I'll see to it all. What you don't realize is that there will be important people coming from all over the country, as well as our friends. The reputation of the South is at stake. We have a responsibility to our position, to tradition, to the past and——"

"Needn't tell me anything about responsibility to the past," Miss Renie said, her black eyes snapping. "I've spent my whole life looking after the past. First Pa and Ma—not that I begrudged them—and then Aunt Tessie, though she didn't live long, poor soul. Just wanted to come and die at the old place and naturally here was Renie with nothing to do but take care of her. Not that I wasn't willing——"

Professor Brent slipped away then, his book under his arm. Pete had already gone. Osia came to the door and said, "Want I should clear off now or start scrubbing?"

Mrs. Brent began, "Clear this——"

Miss Renie went right on, "It just meant I had to give up my painting once more. My life has been one of sacrifice, start to finish and I've had about enough."

Tammy, stroking Picasso who sat in her lap, said, "What was it you were all the time wanting to do, Miss Renie?"

Miss Renie gave her a black look. "Go to New Orleans and have a studio in the French Quarter and live an unfrustrated Bohemian life."

"You haven't anybody to take care of now. Why don't you go?"

"Now? I'm too old."

"You're still aliving, ain't you?" Tammy said.

"Not ain't—are you not. Yes, I'm living but that's about all. Though I might do it—if I had the money."

"Money—why, you could get a sight of money for this house and all these things——"

Mrs. Brent groaned and lifted one hand to her head.

"Now that's an idea." Miss Renie gave Mrs. Brent a wicked glance, caught up Picasso and swept away toward the back hall door.

"Oh, Tammy——" Mrs. Brent sighed—"Tammy, please. Don't go putting notions in her head. She has enough without—— Oh, dear, I sometimes wonder why I go through with this every year. Nobody co-operates. Singlehanded——" She broke off abruptly.

"Don't you get any pleasure out of it?"

"Well, it is a satisfaction just to be busy."

"No matter what you're busy at?"

"Yes, yes." She sipped her coffee in quick little sips. "It keeps you from thinking."

Tammy's lips parted in surprise. It would be awful not to think—unless you had nothing but bad things to think about. "What is it you don't want to think about?"

Mrs. Brent's reddish-brown eyes fastened on the blue distance beyond the garden and the green field. "About getting sick and old and . . . and dying, and about my two little babies who died." Her voice went off in a whisper with the last words.

Tammy drew a long breath. Two little ones like Lena's, not brown, but pink and white. Not getting better but worse. And Mrs. Brent all the time busy to keep from thinking about dying, being afeard of dying. "Looks like that would take the scare off it—looks like a body would be ashamed to be afeard of doing what two little ones by theirselves already gone and done."

"Yes, yes, that is true, isn't it." She spoke so softly it was hard to hear her. Then she came back to herself with a little jerk, gathered herself together again. "This isn't getting anything done. Those rooms must be ready for the roomers." She turned on Tammy sharply. "You ask why I do all this. It's for Peter, of course."

"For Pete!"

"Certainly." Mrs. Brent sat up straight. "One must maintain a certain position in the world, or else the next generation has to start all over again, building it up. That wouldn't be right."

"What is . . . position?"

"It's what you've acquired through generations, what you're born to."

"But how can you lose what you're born to? I should think you couldn't lose that. It's like the color of your eyes and——"

"Oh, Tammy, you just don't understand."

The eagerness went out of Tammy's eyes and her shoulders drooped. Here it was again, the thing that haunted her, that made her see she could have no real place in Pete's life. She was only here for a little while by chance, and Mrs. Brent was always reminding her that she was one apart and below. Yet, if one could lose position, it did look as if one might gain it. She looked up, wanting to ask whether if maybe one learned grammar and manners and the ways of people, if then maybe——

But Mrs. Brent pushed aside her coffee cup and said with decision, "Position is what people think of you, the impression you make on them. Really, it's money that counts most nowadays, more even than family. Peter must marry well and have money and nice things and . . . and security. He mustn't have to skimp along on nothing the way I've had to do all my life."

"Oh." Tammy was silent, her eyes fastened on Mrs. Brent. Then she asked, "Does Barbara . . . have money?"

"No——" Mrs. Brent sighed——"but she knows the value of it, and of course her family is one of the oldest in the country. And she has wealthy kin——her cousin Alfred Bissle, for instance, with no heirs and . . . Oh——" She stood abruptly. "Nobody will get anything done if I sit here all day trying to—— Come, Tammy. I'll get you some dustcloths."

Tammy was perched now on the tall stepladder, taking out books, dusting them, putting them back. She had just run into a whole nest of medical books and she stopped to look at pictures and read a little here and there. It was a surprise, how much people's insides looked like chickens'. She bent over a picture. "I declare, that's funny, that is."

"What is funny?" Professor Brent looked up from his reading over by the window.

"I was just seeing here how they study folks before they're born. They can't cut up humans to look at through a microscope, so what animals you reckon they use?"

"Oh, you've found Uncle Ezra's medical books, have you? Well, I am not an embryologist. What animal is it?"

"But what you reckon?" Tammy persisted. It did her good knowing something that a professor did not know.

"I have no idea."

"Pigs!" Tammy could hold back her laughter no longer. "I'll have to tell Grandpa about that. I bet he could preach a sermon on that."

"No doubt. By the way, didn't you have a letter from your grandfather yesterday?"

"Oh, yes. I've got it right here." She touched the front of her dress.

"How is he?"

"He says his health and his whereabouts are both comfortable and he hopes I'm the same and to write him in care of the Forestville jail. He preaches the Word but it's stony ground, except for the jailor's wife who is a godly woman and makes very good pies." Tammy clapped two books together and the dust floated out on the air to reach the sunlight coming in by the western windows. "Sure is plenty of dust here," she said. "If I was the Lord I reckon I could nigh on to make a man out of it. Made out of the dust off books, it would likely be a learned man, too."

Mrs. Brent spoke from the door. "If you'd give over thinking so much of men, you'd get through with that dusting sooner."

"It ain't thinking of men that delays me," Tammy said. "It's their insides that slows me down. I was just reading a minute ago about guts—a human's is around thirty feet long. You wouldn't think——"

"Tammy, please, must you use that word? Really, it isn't nice."

Tammy looked down at her gravely. "People talk about their hearts all the time—and their insides too. So why——"

"It's not at all the same." Mrs. Brent came in and sank down in the black leather chair by the west window. She leaned back her head and closed her eyes.

"I'm sorry, Mrs. Brent. I'll try not to say it. It's just got me kind of wild, being turned loose amongst so many books. If Grandpa stays in jail long enough I'll read them for sure. How long did it take you?"

"Take me?" Mrs. Brent opened one eye and looked up at Tammy. "Why, I haven't read them. Oh, some, of course, but nobody reads all the books they have."

"You mean folks own books and don't read them?"

"Certainly. They are often bought purely for decorative purposes. And really I don't know anything that gives a room more of an air." She looked around the room now with satisfaction and sneezed in the midst of it. "Joel, you shouldn't sit in here with all this dust."

Professor Brent went on reading. Tammy said, "He likely don't notice it. A man's got more hair in his nose than a woman. He don't breathe it like we do."

Mrs. Brent sat up straight. "Tammy, I want to ask you to do something for me. You may think it is—well, fussy. But the Pilgrimage is coming and important people. You will be helping Osia keep the punch bowl filled, but some of the people may speak to you. Now you . . . you say things that upset people, Tammy, unexpected things. I'm not saying there's any harm in it—sometimes you are very understanding. But I don't want people upset. People have been living in a certain way, with certain ideas about what's proper, for a long time, and when you question them it's— well, it's disconcerting."

"Doesn't anybody else ever question them?"

"Maybe so, Tammy, but nice people don't."

"Oh."

"Will you just try your best not to talk too much? That's all I ask of you."

Tammy stood motionless with the duster in her hand, her eyes on the floor. Mrs. Brent was ashamed to have her around with the Pilgrimage coming, ashamed of how she talked. Not just her grammar that Miss Renie was trying to correct, but the things she said. Mrs. Brent likely thought she wasn't good enough even just to stay in the house. Tammy went to dusting fast and furiously. If it was Mrs. Brent's house, she wouldn't stay a minute.

She moved the ladder along, having finished one section of the bookcase. Mounting to the top, she felt a sadness come in place of her anger. Pete's mother, this was, ashamed of her. From the top of the ladder Tammy looked down on her as she leaned back in the chair resting with her eyes closed. She seemed little and defenseless there, just a small human, trying to forget, trying to have things the way she thought was right. Suddenly Tammy was sorry for her, sorry for all people everywhere trying to have something they couldn't get. I'm that way, too, Tammy thought, trying to have something I can't have.

"I'll try not to talk too much, Mrs. Brent," she said.

"All right, Tammy." Mrs. Brent spoke with mildness, not opening her eyes.

"Actually, my dear," Professor Brent said, "Tammy has a most interesting and unusual mind. I have been thinking of consulting some of my colleagues as to the best method of education. It seems to me that we have here, in a way, a blank, a virgin page—John Locke's idea——"

"Please, Joel, I am just trying to get through the present emergency as best I can."

Tammy, dusting the top shelf and trying to figure out how her mind could be a blank, had come on the head and shoulders of a man, done in white plaster but thick with dust. She took it in her hands and turned it round and round with wonder. "I been itching to get my hands on this. Is it your pa, Mrs. Brent?"

Mrs. Brent threw up her hands in a gesture of despair. "Of

course not, Tammy, that's Shakespeare. You'd better take it out to the kitchen and use a damp cloth. The dust is an inch thick."

Tammy, coming down with the bust cradled in her arms, laughed to herself. "Next time Ernie asks if I'm personally acquainted with W. Shakespeare, I'll say, 'Well, I gave him a bath one time.' You couldn't be much more acquainted with a man than that, could you?"

"I'm sure I wouldn't know. Now who is that?" Mrs. Brent rose and went to the back hall where a bell was ringing.

Tammy stopped in the hall doorway to see what made the bell ring. Mrs. Brent was holding something to her ear and she spoke toward a little black trumpet that came out from a small box on the wall. Mrs. Brent said, "Hello, hello, hello," with impatience.

"Goshamighty," Tammy breathed, "it's a telephone!" It must be a newfangled one because it was not like the one in the catalogue that you could buy a fancy-dressed doll to cover, nor yet like the one in the toy department that was all in one piece. There had been a time when she wanted that toy phone more than anything. She had thought that if she had it she could sit on the deck of the *Ellen B.* and talk to anybody in all the world. She still ached a little when she thought how she had wanted it.

Mrs. Brent turned around in the middle of a sentence. "Tammy, will you please go on—it makes me nervous having you there listening to every word."

Tammy shook her head. "I wasn't listening——"

"Wasn't listening—why! Wait a minute, Louise, I have to——" She turned back to Tammy. "What were you doing if you weren't listening?"

"I was just thinking how funny it looked seeing somebody standing there talking at the wall."

"Well, no matter, run along." She turned back to the phone. "Sorry, Louise, I had to stop. . . . Yes, it is very—— Really, you have no idea. I'm so upset sometimes. . . . Nonsense, there's nothing romantic about it and there won't be if I can help it. But do tell me now, who are you going to send me? No more women, I hope—not after the one we had last time."

Tammy went to the kitchen and got a damp cloth to wash Shakespeare with, thinking Mrs. Brent ought to talk lower if she didn't want to be heard, for her high excited voice carried words all the way to the kitchen.

"Yes, I could have the room ready tonight. Who is he? You mean Barbara's New York cousin Alfred Bissle? . . . That is wonderful. I've always wanted him and Peter to meet. . . . I know, but it might work out that he would have an opening in his office. . . . He does? Oh, Louise, I do appreciate your sending him here. And who is the other one? . . . you mean the artist, the one who had those pictures in the magazine and the articles. . . . Fernan? . . . Aunt Renie will be out of her head. . . ."

Tammy rinsed out the washcloth and hung it up. She was glad there were people coming to stay in some of the empty rooms in Pete's house, because it did seem a shame to have so many empty and not being used.

With Shakespeare in her arms she started along the ell porch, but Mrs. Brent was still talking, so she set him on the table beside the railing and went down the steps to the garden. She got tired of the house sometimes. She had to get out where the sky was overhead and the sun was shining. Besides, she wanted to see Pete. She could not get along without seeing Pete now and then.

Steve was by the side drive with a rug spread out, sweeping it with long slow sweeps of the broom. He gave her a startled look, the way he always did when she first came on him. "Mornin', Miss Tammy," he said, turning from her.

Tammy stopped on the grass. "You don't have to be afeard of me, Steve."

"No'm . . . I just . . . no'm, I reckon not." He stood, looking down, as if embarrassed by her presence.

"How is Karo?"

"He's just doin' fine, ma'am. Getting fat. That goat's milk sure done wonders." Now he was at ease again.

"And how's Nan?"

"She doin' good, Miss Tammy. The chillen makes a pet of her. They's crazy 'bout that goat."

"I'm coming down to see her when I get time." Tammy went on around toward the front of the house, looking for Pete. Old Prater was on his knees among the roses in the circle and she stopped to talk to him for a minute. He was a bent, slow Negro with a dark face, crisscrossed with lines. His eyes were pale and vague with age. His old felt hat had lost its band and around the crown there were perpendicular slits, as if he had cut them with a knife. When she had inquired about how his rheumatism was this morning, Tammy said, "Why do you have holes cut in your hat?"

He sat back on his heels. "Well, ma'am, when you gits old, it do you good to air your brains. Seem like they circulate better when they ain't so confined."

"I reckon that's why Grandpa's always pushing his hat back," Tammy said. Then she caught sight of Pete coming from the other side of the house, and went to meet him. "I'm dusting the books," she said.

"Are you? Seems to me you're out walking in the sunshine."

Tammy laughed. "What are you doing?"

"Oh, I'm raking, tying up roses, odd jobs. It's good to be doing something." He looked excited and happy.

"That's what you need, I reckon, Pete—something to be working at, something to be working for—like the Pilgrimage right now."

Pete looked past her, his lips making a twisted line. "At least it keeps me from thinking. It's a drug, all this activity. When it's over—well, then I'll have to settle things." He gave himself a shake, waved one hand toward the front gallery where rose vines were all neatly tied in place, curling round the gray pillars. "See, it almost makes you not notice the house hasn't seen a paintbrush in the last twenty years. How do you like it?"

"It's beautiful, Pete. Only I'm not quite broken in to seeing things all tied up and trim. It's so different from the swamp and the river where it all goes free. Pete——"

"What?"

"You wouldn't like being all tied up in an office, would you?"

Pete looked at the trees and the lawn and all the blooming things. "No, I really wouldn't. But what makes you——"

Tammy smiled. "I just wanted to know." She turned quickly and ran toward the front gallery. "Got to get back to my dusting," she called with a wave of her hand.

In the library Mrs. Brent was sitting on a low stool beside Professor Brent's chair. "Mr. Bissle is a very important person," she was saying. "He has this big advertising business in New York, and Louise says that he told her he needs another man to train for the Atlanta office. You've just got to exert yourself, Joel."

"Exert myself?" Professor Brent said, his eyes following Tammy as she crossed and mounted the ladder with Shakespeare in her arms.

"Yes, yes, Joel. Talk about things he's interested in and be entertaining—and tactful with Peter so he won't get obstinate the way he's been ever since he got back from that plane crash and the river. Joel, it means so much."

"Does it, my dear?" Professor Brent's voice was gentle. "It's just that I have this new course next term and my mind is on that."

"Well, get your mind off it, then. This is more important. It's Peter's whole life."

Professor Brent drew a long breath. "I can't make him out since he got home from the Pacific. He seems to have lost all power of decision. It's as if he were waiting for something to happen to drive him ahead—another war, maybe. I don't know. It looks as if the whole world is just sitting waiting."

"Oh, Joel, don't go talking about the world. I've got enough on my hands without that."

"That's just the trouble. Nobody is taking the large view, the overall picture. This book———" He tapped the book open on the arm of his chair.

"Joel, please stop thinking about your new course and put your mind on this. Peter has to be pushed in the right direction, that's all."

"Right?" Professor Brent was leaning back in his chair staring up at the ceiling. "A relative term. What is right for one nation does not seem right to another. That's the cause of all the confusion and conflict and———"

"Listen Joel," Mrs. Brent broke in, "we may not know the absolute right, but we know right enough to go by, and Peter———"

Professor Brent sat up in his chair and looked at her over his glasses. Tammy thought he was fixing to shake her for sure because she wouldn't let him say his say out. "Now that's an idea. Right enough to go by—I must make note of that." He began to write in the margin of his book. "No need to agree on the finer points, just find the common ground of what's right enough to go by."

Mrs. Brent drew a long sigh. "If you'd only listen to me. These tomatoes now, that Peter's thinking he'll make a fortune on, gambling his last cent on them—oh, I get so impatient with him sometimes. He must go into something that's certain and sure."

Tammy put a handful of books back on the shelf. "It beats me how everybody keeps looking for something sure. How can anything in the world be sure? I reckon even an office can close up." Then as Mrs. Brent looked up, she added, "Besides, Pete doesn't want to work in any office."

"What do you mean?" Her words came so sharp and quick that Tammy, coming down the ladder, almost tripped on the sound of them.

"That's what he said."

"Do you mean that you told him about Mr. Bissle and——"

Tammy shook her head. "I didn't tell him anything. I just asked him."

"Well, don't ever repeat anything you hear, especially over the telephone."

"Oh. I'm sorry, Mrs. Brent. I won't." Looked like she was always having to say she was sorry.

Mrs. Brent rose. "I must see that Osia finishes cleaning his room, gets out the linen. He's coming after supper, Louise said. Now Joel, you will be nice to him."

"Yes, yes, of course, my dear."

"The other one, the artist, no matter about him. Besides, he won't get here for several days, but he's paying for the whole time of the Pilgrimage, so it doesn't matter."

Tammy almost let a book fall, and her little gasp made Mrs. Brent pause in the doorway. "You mean they pay, like boarders?"

"Certainly, Tammy."

"Then why don't Pete make a business of boarders? Lots of folks would be wanting to board in such a place as this, and——"

"Boarders!" Mrs. Brent dropped the word like she'd got hold of something dirty by mistake. "We've never done such a thing as that."

"Well, hell's bells," Tammy said under her breath as Mrs. Brent went on, "can't anybody do anything but what they already done before?" She didn't think Professor Brent heard her but after a little he spoke without looking up from his book.

"There has to be a first time for everything, Tammy. You're quite right. Though whether it's the hen or the egg that starts it——" His voice trailed away into silence.

Tammy went on with her dusting, not seeing what chickens had to do with it, except that they would be good to feed boarders on. Now and then she stopped to look inside a book and try to get an idea of what it was about. She could hear Mrs. Brent on the ell porch telling Miss Renie about the other roomer that was coming and Miss Renie saying his name over and over, "Fernan, coming here! Oh, my God, after all these years something is going to happen! Mahomet to the mountain—— Fernan, here!"

Tammy took out a large dark book and dusted it. Bacon, it said on the back. She opened it and turned the pages. A phrase caught her eye: "the idols of the market place." She read a page or two, then put the book back and went on dusting. Too many long words—but the phrase stayed with her. What were the idols of the market place? Things bought and sold. That was the kind of barbarian Barbara was, worshiping the idols of the market place. Just as she had thought that day on the boat when Pete first told about her. "I was right all the time," she said.

Professor Brent looked up from his reading, but before he could speak, the telephone bell began to ring. Reluctantly he rose and went to the hall. Mrs. Brent called from somewhere at the back, "I'm coming," and Professor Brent after a word or two at the phone called, "It's not for you." He came back to the library. "For you, Tammy, the phone."

Tammy dropped the dustcloth. "Must be Grandpa," she whispered, beginning to tremble. "Must be he's dead or something."

"He wouldn't be calling if he were dead," Professor Brent told her.

"For all you know, there's telephones in heaven," Tammy said and went to the hall. The ear part hung down, swinging back and forth. She put it to her ear and listened, but there was no sound at all. As she stood there waiting, Barbara appeared in the front door, with a small satchel in her hand. She was a picture out of a book. She wore a wide black hat and a black-and-white striped dress with red buttons and shoes, red as her lips.

"Hi, there, where's everybody?" Then as Mrs. Brent came through the back hall door, she added, "I brought my costume for the Pilgrimage. Cousin Al here yet?"

"Not yet." Mrs. Brent gave Tammy a curious glance and went on, drawing Barbara into the library.

Tammy wished the phone would say something, but there was still no sound. She could hear Mrs. Brent saying, "Well, just stay and have supper with us, Barbara. Peter can run you home later. Mr. Bissle will be here tonight and I've so much to talk over with you."

Then Pete came hurrying in the front door, not even noticing Tammy. "Hi, Barb, thought I heard you. Ernie bring you out?"

"No," Barbara said, "I picked up a ride with one of the boys from the office."

Tammy changed ears on the phone but there was still no sound. Only a faint far buzzing. She thought whoever was wanting to talk to her must be a long long way off, it was taking so long for his voice to reach her.

Mrs. Brent came out of the library, pulling Professor Brent by the sleeve and saying something about fixing a screen. "You want me to fix a screen?"

Mrs. Brent whispered, "No, but can't you leave them alone in there? Don't you see? Come on."

"What's the matter, Tammy? Has the phone gone dead?" he stopped to ask.

"It hasn't spoken yet. Oh—now——" A voice in her ear was saying, "Tammy, Tammy, that you Tammy?"

She nodded to Professor Brent. "It's atalking now."

"Say, is that you, Tammy?" the voice said.

"Yes, it's me."

Professor Brent said, "You'd better turn around and speak into the phone."

"Damn it, I can't hear you," the voice shouted.

"It says it can't hear me," Tammy told Professor Brent.

Professor Brent turned her around and pushed her closer. "Try that, now."

"Hey, Tammy, this is Ernie."

"Oh," Tammy breathed. "It ain't Grandpa dead or alive. It's Ernie."

Ernie said, "Say, who are you talking to? Who else is horning into this?"

"Professor Brent."

"Yes, Tammy?" He turned in the back hall doorway. "Something I can do for you?"

Ernie said, "Well, tell the old goat to leave you alone. I want your ear for a minute."

Tammy shook her head, looking at Professor Brent. "He isn't an old goat. Hasn't even got whiskers like Grandpa."

"Jeepers," Ernie said, "I hope he didn't hear that."

"No," Tammy told him, "he's going down the ell porch, talking about manners and this generation."

"Come closer, I can't hear you."

"Where are you?"

"I'm in town."

"Then I can't, less'n I walk and I reckon it's a right far piece."

Ernie laughed and the sound hit her ear so she nearly dropped the phone. "Say, sugar, how about it, will you be ready time I get there?"

"Ready for what?"

"To see the sights, paint the town, see the world."

"Oh—right now?"

"Soon as I can get there."

"Oh, Ernie, that would be wonderful. I'll be ready in a minute."

"Good. See you soon, 'By." There was a little click, then just a faint humming and no more talk.

Tammy waited a moment, holding the phone to her ear. It was like being connected with all the world, being part of everything miles away, everywhere. Slowly she hung the receiver in place. Then it came over her—Ernie was going to take her to town! She ran to her room to brush her hair and put on her shoes and her new dress. But when she got it on and looked at herself in the looking glass, she saw that it wasn't a good dress after all. Not like Barbara's. It was tight in the wrong places, the seam was splitting at the side. She took it off with sadness and put on her old faded blue. It was baggy, it was shabby and old, but it made no pretense. Maybe a belt would help. She found a piece of string and tied it round her waist. That was better. But there wasn't much use, she could never look as beautiful as Barbara. Then she went back to the library. She could finish dusting the books before Ernie got here if she hurried.

Peter and Barbara were sitting on the far side of the library, Pete on the low stool, facing her. Barbara was saying, "Of course, Pete, for vacations and the Pilgrimage it's wonderful. But for regular living—I think you're crazy. I grew up with cows and chickens and nobody could hire me to go back to such." She looked up. "Hi, Tammy."

Tammy said howdy. Her lips parted to tell them that she was going to town with Ernie, then she remembered Mrs. Brent had said don't ever repeat anything you heard on the phone.

Barbara lifted one shoulder as she turned back to Pete, and it was like someone closing a door. Tammy stood motionless. She was shut out, alone, and the way Pete was looking at Barbara as if he'd been hungering for the sight of her—that was what barred the door fast against her. She turned away, took up the dustcloths and got to work, feeling a weight in her breast like a heavy hand, pushing. Barbara hadn't passed her over so at first. She had studied her aplenty whilst she was thinking there might have been something between her and Pete on the river. But now she had set her aside and forgotten her. That was worse than being looked down on. It made her into nothing.

She went to the far shelves, away from them. She made a noise with her dusting, clapping books together to send the dust flying so she would not hear what they were saying. She could close a door as well as Barbara could. But once she heard Pete say, "Just how much have you been seeing of him, if you don't mind saying?" and

Barbara answered, "Oh, you know how he is—always underfoot."

Then after a little Barbara's voice rose. "Sure, Pete, I know you could. Like my brother did one year on the Copiah place. But then the next three years he didn't get his money back on the fertilizer. You can't tell me anything about raising truck."

Tammy took a quick glance at Pete and the look on his face made her want to cry out against Barbara and what she was doing. She listened a minute longer and then she could stand it no more. "No, no," she cried so sharp and quick they both turned startled faces. "You hadn't ought to be doing that, discouraging the heart out of anybody that's just trying this and that, to see. Most of all, anybody's got to believe there's a way. It's not believing there's a way that makes people afeard."

Barbara laughed. "You ought to show Tammy your ribbons some time, Pete. Then she would know you couldn't be—'afeard,' as she says."

"Afeard is a good word," Tammy said hotly. "Words are supposed to be to say things with, aren't they? I reckon you know what I mean when I say it, don't you?"

Barbara gave her a cross look, but before she could speak, Pete said, "Sure, it's a fine word. Good old English, like lots of Tammy's expressions." He rose. "Come on, Barb, I want you to take a look at my tomatoes."

Tammy saw her put out a hand to Pete, as if she couldn't get up from the chair without help, and she knew all at once that it wasn't a word she and Barbara had been fighting over, it was Pete. Barbara knew it, too, for all she made out that Tammy was nothing at all. They'd just been talking double talk, and she was tired of it. With her handful of books pressed close to her breast, her eyes flashing, she said, "There's a sight of other things a body could do besides raising tomatoes on a fine place like this, if they just had a mind to. Like taking boarders, and raising cattle and milking the cows and—oh, no end of things."

"Boarders?" Barbara laughed as she let Pete pull her to her

feet, and then kept hold of his hand longer than she needed. "I can see people coming to board where there's no hot water, no plumbing, no heat——"

"But there's so much else," Tammy broke in. "All these here books and the fine furniture and the electric lights and the refrigerator. Must be plenty of people would be able to see what an elegant place it is."

"Guess it's all in the point view," Pete said, giving her his slow smile.

They had passed through the door when Barbara spoke, careless of who might overhear. "Easy to see how she feels about you, Pete, and Brenton Hall as well."

"What? Oh, nonsense, she's just a child."

"Child of nature, and that kind's dangerous." Barbara laughed. "Not that I blame her. Feel the same way myself, except when you get these fool ideas. Honestly, Pete——" Her voice was lost as they went on down the hall.

Slowly Tammy unclenched her hands and bent and picked up the books that had slipped to the floor. Easy to see, was it? The words left her stripped and raw. Only Pete hadn't believed them. She was just a child to him. Tammy leaned her forehead against the bookcase, her eyes stung by sharp tears. She did not hear Professor Brent until he spoke.

"Anything wrong, Tammy?" he asked with concern.

She shook her head and blinked her eyes dry. Then feeling him standing there, silent but kindly, she whirled on him. "Tell me true——" she choked and went on——"could it be that anybody that didn't know how to talk proper and wanted to terribly could learn the words so people wouldn't think they was . . . was funny?"

Professor Brent rested one foot on the lowest step of the ladder and leaned over, elbow on knee. "I know they could," he said with earnestness. "That's one of the things that can be learned. But there's one thing cannot be learned."

"Wh-what's that? I might as well know."

"That is—to have something worth saying, to have some ideas to put into words. That's a thousand times more important. That's what you have, Tammy."

"You reckon?" She stared at him with parted lips.

"Reckon?" He straightened up. "I know." Then as he was going to his chair by the far window, he stopped and sniffed the air. "Nothing subtle about that scent, is there? Which one is it, I wonder? Naughty or Nice, or Dither—such names they have nowadays."

"I don't know what she calls it," Tammy said, fanning the air with her dustcloth, "but it sure stinks. Hangs on like a spirit, ha'nting some place when the body's gone."

Professor Brent sat down. "Does a spirit hang on?"

Tammy studied him a moment. He was just talking to cheer her. A goodhearted man, he was. "I reckon it could," she told him. "Grandpa always says anything could be."

"H'm." Professor Brent laid his book face down on the arm of his chair as if he didn't really want to read it. "He is always trying to reconcile science and religion, you say—has he any scientific explanation of the idea of the resurrection of the dead, I wonder?"

"Yes, he's got that figgered out," Tammy said, glad to take her mind off Pete and Barbara, walking out together, maybe holding hands under the trees. "It's the Last Trump that does it. Gabriel's horn." She dusted briskly as she talked.

"Indeed? And how?" He slid down in the chair with his legs stretched long before him and looked up at Tammy from over his glasses.

"He got the idea from a Chautauqua lecture he heard one time. The man said you couldn't destroy anything, according to science."

"The indestructibility of matter—yes, go on."

"And he said if you played the right sound on a fiddle you'd make a bell ring or a glass answer as if you had struck it with a spoon."

"Sympathetic vibration, yes."

"Well, he figgers it this-a-way—I've heard him explain it many's the time. He says when Gabriel blows his horn, he will blow all the sounds there be and for every human critter there is a sound that makes his scattered parts ring back and rise up and draw together just the way they used to be. That's how they rise."

"That theory offers food for thought, certainly. Science has made clear many phenomena as puzzling as any possible resurrection of the dead could be. Eventually everything will be explained. We have only scratched the surface so far."

"Then what?"

Professor Brent blinked. "I don't know that I have given much thought to that. It is rather remote."

"Grandpa says when humans have got it all figgered out, they will see that ain't the point."

"Oh?" Professor Brent sat up. He took off his glasses and polished them with his handkerchief. "That is a rather disturbing thought—to a scientist. What is it then, if it's not the point?"

"It's the beside-the-point."

"And what's the point?"

"Oh, just what the Lord's been telling us all along, I reckon—to suffer long and be kind."

"I see—not the exploration of the nature of matter but the development of man's spiritual nature."

Tammy nodded. "Grandpa says humans have got the serpent by the wrong end."

Professor Brent got up and began walking back and forth. "Why did I ever agree to give this new course? Just because I know physics, why must I be supposed to lecture about its implications? Why am I supposed to know about what the world is doing with the results of research? Economics, international relations, human relations, war, peace—what have I got to do with them? All I want is to be left alone in my laboratory."

Tammy studied him as he walked back and forth. He wasn't really talking to her, he was only speaking out the things that had been worrying him, the new things he had to teach at his school.

"It must be," she said after a while, "must be you've come out to a kind of end, in your figgering. I reckon it might be the atom bomb is a kind of end, and what upsets you is finding out it ain't the point—like Grandpa says. There's still all these other things that ain't settled yet."

He didn't seem to be listening. "It used to be that a man was safe in his laboratory. A scientist could just dig in and enjoy himself, doing what he liked to do. Now he's got to know philosophy, government, politics, religion, people—the whole thing's come tumbling down on his head. And this course—why did I ever say I would give it?" He went and sat down in his big chair at the end of the room. "It's all very disturbing," he said, and took up his book with a little groan and settled down to it.

Tammy finished dusting in silence. Now she had upset Professor Brent, and just when he had been trying to hope her up. It was like Mrs. Brent said—she upset everybody. "I didn't mean to," she said, laying the dustcloths neatly over the lower steps of the stepladder. But Professor Brent didn't seem to hear, so she went slowly out, through the front door, and down the steps. Pete and Barbara were nowhere to be seen. She walked across the yard and looked toward the field. They weren't there, either. Barbara'd have him off somewhere alone, where she could walk close to him and hold his hand.

Tammy went on beside the kitchen-garden fence till she came to the corner where she could look over at Pete's tomatoes in the cold frames, and at the others, the brave venturing ones, already set in the open. They were all beautiful in the warm afternoon sun. She hoped the Lord would keep a close eye on them and let them grow, even if it set Barbara up to get the money. She wanted it to be a sign to Pete that he could make out right here. That was the important thing. She reckoned it didn't matter so much about herself, though it would be a powerful pleasant thing if the Lord could arrange things. She left it at that and turned away, somehow eased in her heart, now she had put it up to the Lord. Then she went on down the drive to the gate to wait for Ernie.

12.

ERNIE'S car tore along in a fury of speed. It went faster than the truck had gone the night of Tammy's journey to Pete's house. A cloud of dust whirled up like a cyclone and when they slowed on a curve, the dust enveloped them. The car had sides but no top and there was no getting away from the wind. Tammy sat with her hands clasped tight in her lap and her lips pressed close together. Her hair that she had brushed with such care blew back with their going, the wind tore her breath away. It blew her head empty and scattered her wits with its wildness.

On the wide paved road cars came toward them and flashed by, sucking in the air like creatures hungry for breath. She could see the going faces as they passed, strangers' faces, all wiped out and emptied-seeming or else taut and strained with speed, like people fleeing from the noise of fear. Such a power of people, too, all going hell-bent to get somewheres they weren't, each one at the wheel holding his life in slippery fingers and in the near moment of passing, holding her and Ernie's too, that they had no right to. One little turn the wrong way and they'd all pile into kingdom come, strangers ending up close kin in their speedy riddance. It was a fearsome thing to think on.

It was a new feeling, this being hurled forward by a force outside herself, by a power that was trapped yonder in the front of the car; throbbing and roaring. She felt like something turned loose from the hold of the earth; she knew now how it must be with the suns and the stars in the sky, going their courses as the Lord had set them on their way. The earth was stirring, too, in its circling path. Only the Lord had luckily contrived things so that

140

it seemed to be at rest, hung upon nothing, like the Bible said. Otherwise how could one endure its motion through the firmament?

The green fields flashed by, the hills carried them up and down. Then Ernie looked round at her for the first time. Quickly he stopped the car at the side of the road. "Say, are you carsick?"

Tammy let out her breath. She had been holding it for a long time. "Never went so fast in all my born days."

"Good Lord, why didn't you stop me? You poor kid!" He put his arm round her shoulders. "Gosh darn it, I feel like a heel. I was just trying out the motor—had it gone over yesterday. Say, I'm awfully sorry."

"That's all right, Ernie. But it did feel like I had been caused to ride upon the wind. It came nigh to dissolving my substance, for sure."

Ernie laughed. "The way you say things!"

Tammy did not answer. Pete had said she said the damnedest things. She hoped she wasn't too queer-seeming to Pete. It didn't matter about Ernie. Or Barbara or the rest.

"You just lean back and we'll take it easy from now on." Ernie started the car again and held it down to a quieter pace. He turned one of the buttons in front of him and after a minute music poured forth to fill the car and overflow on all sides.

Tammy drew a long breath and relaxed. The music enveloped them. It seemed to bear them along upon itself, keeping them safe from all harm. It swept up and down with a dip and a rise to match the way the road ran. It washed over her, sweet and pure enough to wash away the bitter taste she got when she remembered how Barbara was walking now with Pete.

"Hawaiian music—like it?" Ernie asked.

"Hawaiian! Did Pete hear it like this when he was there?"

Ernie gave her a reproachful glance. "Pete! Does everything have to remind you of Pete?"

"Yes." Tammy leaned back against the red-leathered cushioned seat. "This is like riding in Elijah's chariot of fire—it's like going up to heaven in a whirlwind."

Ernie laughed. "I'm not aiming at heaven just yet, sugar, only at Fairville, population 1650. See the sign. Pop. 1650, it says."

Tammy sat bolt upright now, turning her head this way and that, trying to see both sides at once. There were houses set close together with green lawns before and between and flowers blooming. "Goshamighty, but you could send word clean through the town, one end to the other just by word of mouth, this house to the next." Cars were coming and going and people were walking on a special walk made to keep their feet from dust and mud. "It's a beautiful city," she sighed.

"That should make the chamber of commerce take heart, if they could only hear it." He slowed the car to let her look the better, pointing out the sights till they came to where the filling stations began and the stores filled all the spaces. Then he turned into an open place with the nose of the car pointing toward a big sign that said, ZEEKER'S DRUGS. Another sign said, HAVE A COKE.

"How about a soda?" Ernie said and flung the car door open. He came round and opened Tammy's door for her.

"Soda?" That was what Grandpa took when he'd et too free, but it might be that coming so fast was enough to give a body need of soda or something. Her own innards were kind of disquieted for a fact, but not that bad. "You got gas, Ernie?" she asked as they crossed the paved walk.

He glanced back at the car. "Gas? Sure thing. Filled up." He opened the door of the store and they went in.

It was a longish room with high stools at one side against a high table and, in the middle, rows of round tables with little spindly chairs where people sat eating. There were glass-enclosed places after the manner of cupboards with pretties spread out to be looked at—clocks and silver spoons and rings in a velvet tray and gold watches, elegant beyond words. On top were things like toothbrushes, hairbrushes and jars of beautifying mixtures and bottles of perfumery, maybe even suchlike as Barbara smelled of. "Where are the drugs, Ernie?"

"To the back. We'll walk around and see them too." Ernie was patient with her wanting to see everything. He was truly kind, besides being so nice-looking she felt a pride at being seen beside him and remembered to smooth down her hair with her hands.

It was a wonder, how many bottles there were! It must be that living in towns made people sickly. And likely they ate too much, she thought, seeing how many sat eating now when it was not any mealtime but just the middle of the evening with the sun still high in the sky.

"Let's sit here." Ernie pulled out a chair for her at one of the little tables. "I could do with a hot dog and soda. How about it?"

"For me? No soda, thank you. My stomach's all right."

Ernie blinked. Then a girl in a green dress with a little white apron came and said, "What's yours?" She paid Tammy's "Howdy," no mind at all.

"Couple of hot dogs, one without. And two chocolate sodas." As the girl went away, he added, "You'll like this kind of soda, Tammy."

After she had thought about it a minute, Tammy said, "I reckon there's lots of things I ain't—I mean, that I'm not rightly acquainted with." Her eyes fell. "There'd be some as would laugh at me."

Ernie leaned toward her across the table. "If there's ever anybody laughs at you, just let me at him."

He looked so fierce that Tammy had to laugh, and now he laughed too. "That's right, don't let's get serious. We're out for fun, sugar."

"Seems almost like you're afeard of getting serious."

Ernie pushed a curly fair lock from his forehead. "Might be," he said, closing up.

Tammy studied him, considering how he kept running around having fun. He was like somebody dog-paddling to keep afloat.

It might even be that he had a heaviness in his heart, but what it was she could not figger out. "Looks like everybody's afeard of something."

"Does it?"

Tammy nodded. "Even Mrs. Brent. Keeps her plucking at everything round about her."

"Not Mrs. Brent. Most people are scared of her."

"It's dying she's scairt of."

"My Lord!"

"And Professor Brent's afeard, too. Of coming out of his laboratory and seeing the world. He's a fox, dug himself a hole."

"And me?"

But Tammy looked away and would not tell him. If he did have a continual sorrow in him, he would not like to know it was not hid.

"Say, did you ever eat a hot dog?" Ernie asked, his blue eyes dancing.

"No, nor a cold one either."

"Think you can?"

"I can if you can." She looked down at the plate the girl had set before her. There was a long roll with a store-boughten sausage in it. Maybe she could eat it if she didn't think about dogs too much. She could wash it down with the soda.

"With, here—without, there," Ernie said.

The girl seemed to know what he meant, for she changed the plates, giving Ernie the one she had put down before Tammy.

"Straws, please" Ernie said.

"Seems like you speak with foreign tongues, Ernie. Only it's regular words, not Latin or anything."

"What words?"

"With, without, straws—you can't eat straws."

"Watch." He took up the long thin papers from the table, opened them and there were the straws, all hollow. Then he showed Tammy how to suck up the soda.

It was a wonder how good it tasted through a straw. "This here alone would be worth the trip, Ernie, drinking like this, and seeing how they wrap up the straws. That's something fine. The man that thought that up was smart."

"Tickled with a straw," Ernie said. "Never knew what that meant till now."

Tammy reckoned that he thought it too small a thing. But it wasn't too small to pleasure a body. She ate in silence now, letting her ears take in the sound of voices, letting the feel of people soak into her. She hadn't been amongst so many since long ago when Grandpa used to preach of a Sunday to the shanty folk. Those she had known. These were strange to her; they pressed in on her with their strangeness.

"What are you thinking, Tammy?" Ernie asked.

"People. How it would be to live all the time in their midst, like this. Seems it would rub the edges off, living so, making one like to another. All leaves on the same tree."

"Hm-m." Ernie drank the last of his soda, his eyes upon her as if she was as much a wonder to him as all the sights she was wondering at.

As they left, Tammy watched how he paid for their eating, and when they were outside, she said, "That cost too much, Ernie. Why, you could get a big sack of meal for that much money—and some side meat too. I wouldn't have let you if I'd knowed."

"It was worth it, sugar. But this is the first time a woman ever complained to me about my spending money on her."

"Must be you've been going out pleasuring with the horseleach's daughters."

"With the who?"

"It's in the Bible. They was always crying, 'Give, give.' Don't you know the Bible?"

"Had Freshman Bible. Got 65 in it. That's all I know."

"Well, anyway, you're too free with your money, Ernie. Look! You left two bits on the table. I saved it for you. Like as not you'd never have missed it even."

"Well, I'll be—!" He held it in his hand, staring at it. Then he put it in his pocket and stood with patience while Tammy examined the things in the drugstore window.

Tammy was reading the sign, THIS WEEK'S SPECIAL—SICK-ROOM SUPPLIES. Spread out on little racks and shelves were all manner of interesting things. There was a white tray with legs, a rubber sheet, a bottle marked RUBBING ALCOHOL HALF PRICE. There was a red-dish bag with a hose to it, a flat rubber bag, a big white thing with curved sides. "Whatever is that, Ernie?"

"What? Oh, that. Well, to put it delicately—— No, there isn't any way to put it delicately." But he told her just the same.

"My, that would have been nice to have when Grandma was down sick abed and couldn't get up. What a lot of inventions and contraptions for the easing of the way of living! You could get so taken up with them you wouldn't think about anything else. . . . I reckon some do," she added, thinking of Barbara.

"Seen it all, sugar? There's yet more on Fairville's Great White Way. Two blocks of it at least."

The sidewalks were thronged with people, some dressed in style, some shabby. "Saturday," Ernie explained. "They come in from the country."

It was hard to see everything all at the same time, but Tammy tried. Once she dodged through the crowd to stand amazed at the edge of the walk. "Whatever can this be, Ernie?" she cried. "It's got colors running round like a rainbow in a cage."

Ernie followed her, laughing. "I'm having fun, Tammy."

"Oh, so am I. But what is it?"

He put on a voice like Professor Brent's. "You see here the traditional sign of the haircutter, the mustache trimmer, the dispenser of news, gossip and hair tonic. The tonsorial artist. In short, the barber."

"It's a curious notion."

"What? Having the hair cut?"

"No. Having this to mean haircutting." Then, when Ernie explained how the barber used to be a surgeon and a bloodletter, she said with admiration, "I reckon you know about everything, Ernie."

Ernie straightened his tie. "Well, almost."

"Look quick." She turned him around to see. "Is that a hat?"

"You mean the bunch of roses on her ear? Yes, that's the name it goes by."

"And the other one, right behind her—looks like a thistle with the prickers pulled out. How can she see where she's going, the way it sets on her head?"

"Don't ask me to explain women's hats."

"Looks like they've got a far piece from the meaning of a hat because rightly it's something to keep off the sun. They've got off the point, like Grandpa says the world has." They edged their way across the walk again toward the store windows, Tammy searching the faces of people. They were all strange to her, unseen by her before. "All their lives have been going on all these years and me not knowing, nor being known," she puzzled. "What do they come to town for, Ernie?"

"To look at each other, to buy things."

"Work all week so's they can come to spend it on Saturday?"

"That's the idea."

"It don't seem sensible."

"What should they be doing?"

"I don't know, Ernie, but something more than this—playing or singing or working at something different."

"You've got a funny head on you, woman."

"Professor Brent says it's a virgin page."

"He does, does he? The old goat. You've got him eating out of your hand all right."

Tammy shook her head. "He just wants to educate me."

"Better let me do that. I—I don't know what it is about you, honey child. Must be you're just so darn cute."

"Cute? That's something I never aimed to be, but——" She

stopped short, catching his arm, and cried, "Goshamighty, what's she doing there plumb naked?"

"Who? Where?"

"Yonder in the store window!" Then she saw it was no live creature, just a big doll, a false figger.

"Yes," Ernie said, "this is Clarke's Emporium. Ladies' Ready-to-Wear. See, here comes a man to put another dress on the dummy."

They stood and watched while he stepped amid gloves and stockings to put a blue-flowered silky dress on the naked shape. "I declare," Tammy said, "I've seen so many wonders I reckon I couldn't be much more amazed if it had been a live one in there."

"I'd have been amazed myself at that," Ernie chuckled.

"You know," Tammy said, "it would be a good thing may-be——"

"What?"

"Not if they really went naked, all the people in the world, but if they just remembered they were naked under their clothes. Might make them less apt to be warring all the time."

Ernie watched her instead of the window. "Now how did you get to thinking that?"

"It would make them know every minute that they weren't anything but blood and bones and flesh and purely mortal. They'd see how pitiful humans are and tender under their clothes."

"Jeepers," Ernie said as they moved on down the street. He took her arm as they crossed to the other side and started back. "That little head of yours——"

"Plumb full of notions. I know!" Tammy laughed. "That's what Grandpa's always saying." They came now to a line of people moving slowly toward a large doorway plastered with pictures of men on horseback shooting guns. "What are they going there for?"

"Regular Saturday show. Western. Want to see it?"

"A moving picture? Oh, Ernie, would it cost a lot?"

"Not too much. Let's go in."

It was dark inside and the people were talking. It was not until they were seated that Tammy could look to the front and see the words that flashed and changed, the pictures that came and went. There was a room with elegant furnishings—"Hunt's for Fine Furniture. Try Our Easy Time Payments. Why Wait When You Can Enjoy Our Sleeping Princess Inner Springs Now? A Small Down Payment." On and on it went: "Leave Your Films with Us. Twenty-four-hour Service." . . . "When Clothes Are Dirty Ring Seven Thirty. It Pays to Look Smart. Try Our Glamour Girl Permanent." . . . "For That Sweater-Girl Line See Our New Up-Cups."

Tammy turned and found Ernie watching her. "If you did everything they told you to, you wouldn't have time for anything else. Why do the people talk all the time? I can't half take it all in."

"This is just the ads. Same thing every week. The real show isn't on yet."

"It's awfully exciting."

Ernie put his arm across the back of the seat behind her. "You're what's exciting."

"Am I, Ernie?"

"You bet."

Then a hush came over the crowd. "Is this it, Ernie?" Tammy whispered.

"This is it, and I don't believe I mean what you mean, sister." His arm came round her shoulder and he drew her close.

Tammy watched the changing screen, but it was mostly names, on and off. She stirred under Ernie's arm, drew away. "Set over yonder way more, Ernie. I got to keep my mind on this."

Ernie said, "When I build a theater, the seats won't have any of these old arms on them."

"Why not?"

"Cramp my courting."

"Are you courting?"

"In a way, yes."

"Is that what people do in movies?"

"Take a look around you, little one. You'll see."

Tammy looked. There were couples with their arms around each other, for a fact, and right in front of her, two were kissing like they'd forgot to quit. "They ain't looking at the picture. You'd think they might better go home and go to bed."

Ernie choked and coughed till a lady behind them tapped him on the shoulder and said, "Here, son, have a cough drop."

Then a man on a horse went galloping across a wide-open land, and shooting began. Tammy sat on the edge of her seat, barely breathing from then to the end. She was still in a maze when they came out into the bright lights of the street, pushing their way against the second-show crowd. Then all at once she caught Ernie's arm. "It's dark, Ernie! We ought to have been home afore this. I never thought—I was just thinking would the man get there in time to save the girl."

"Why, the evening's young, sugar. Just nine o'clock——"

"I don't care. I don't go by clocks. Where's the car? Oh, Ernie, please!"

He was looking at her with a puzzled look. "First time I ever took anybody home before midnight. What's your hurry?" But he lengthened his stride to keep up with her.

"Grandpa'd give me a beating for sure if he knowed I'd stayed after dark, Ernie. I've just got to get back."

"Okay, baby, but it's a record for little Ernie."

The car went quickly through the dark, the lights seeming to lay down the road before it. Their music was flung out into the night and they trailed a backwash of song. They went without a care for those who had to walk, but when they passed a slow, plodding figure, Tammy looked after it, remembering how the road felt underfoot and how slowly one went, just putting one foot before the other. Her mind was filled with the story she had just seen in the movie. She thought it might be enlarging to the mind to see into the lives of the cowboys and the girl and the turmoil they lived amidst. But they didn't hardly seem like real humans, when you considered it. Who was the girl's pa and ma, and where were they? She was just sprung up, like. None of the people had roots to them, they were tumbleweeds blowing in the wind. Folks in a big hustle-bustle, that was all. And all the time you sat watching, your own life wasn't getting any mind paid to it at all. It was just slipping off from you in the movie-dark.

Tammy looked round to Ernie to tell him what she had been thinking. Then it seemed ungrateful to say such things, so instead she asked. "Do you live with your folks, Ernie?"

"Haven't got any. The woman that gets me won't have in-law trouble." He hummed along with the music for a minute, then added, "All my family ever did for me was leave me a little scrap of no-count land down below Bogue Chitto. At least it's been no-count——" He broke off to whistle along with the music.

It was a wonder, Tammy thought, how people had land and didn't think much of it. Then her thoughts went on to Pete.

They turned in the gate at last and saw the lights of Pete's house streaming out to meet them. The black trees of the drive swished past and they drew up at the side with a grating of gravel and a grinding of brakes.

"There you are, my pretty. Have a good time?"

"Oh, Ernie, the best time in the world. Thank you." She was about to jump out of the car when his hand on her arm stopped her.

"Wait a minute. You don't get off that easy." He pulled her closer. "Just one kiss for Ernie."

Tammy drew back. "Not in the dark, Ernie. It would not be seemly."

"My Lord!" Ernie said and let her go.

Then his door was jerked open and Pete said, with fury in his tone, "Ernie, get out."

He got out so slowly that Tammy had time to come around the car before he shut the door and faced Pete.

"I heard you, Ernie."

"Say, what's eating you? Didn't you hear the answer I got?"

"I heard that too." Pete looked around. "Just go on, please, Tammy," he said, and turned back to Ernie.

"If it's account of me you're mad at Ernie, I ain't agoing," Tammy said. But neither of them paid her any mind.

"What's eating you, Pete?" Ernie had a scowl that sat oddly on his smooth brow.

"I don't like it, your taking Tammy off this way without a word. You knew what you were doing, even if she didn't."

"Come out of it, Pete." Ernie put his hands in his pants pockets and rocked back and forth. "This isn't the Victorian Era—or is it? I don't see any reason why I have to account to you for anything I do—or tell you where I've been. Tammy's O.K. and you know it."

"I'll tell you, Pete——" Tammy began.

Ernie said, "He isn't talking about you, Tammy. He just thinks he is."

"Certainly I am. I didn't know where she was. I feel a responsibility and——"

"Aw, get wise to yourself, Pete. You've been hearing things, and not about Tammy, either. Now suppose you listen to me. I stepped aside for you once—not that you asked me to, but—well, I just did. But I'm not doing it any more and you may as well know it. Just because you are standing still, marking time, getting all your psychological knots untied, you needn't think the rest of us are going to twiddle our thumbs forever."

"I see," Pete said. "Now I really begin to see." He was silent for a little, then he looked up and the anger was gone from his voice. "That's fair enough warning, Ernie. We've been friends a long time. We'll keep on the same way, shall we?"

Tammy turned away unnoticed. What they were saying had

nothing to do with her. She had only set it off, like a spark to a pile of fat pine. They had been talking about something that was underneath their words—as she and Barbara had wrestled under the surface of what they were saying in the library. Goshamighty, she thought, stumbling along the gravel drive toward the front steps, living out in the world was enough to drive a body loony! There was so much under the surface, all tangled up. She was plumb wore out with it.

13.

As she neared the front gallery, Tammy heard voices and through the darkness made out dim figures sitting there. She heard Mrs. Brent's bright telephone voice and Barbara breaking in with light laughter. There was a strange man there, between Professor Brent and Miss Renie in her rocking chair that squeaked. The strange man's speech was clipped and sheared and he was asking how much on an average they took in at a Pilgrimage, and what proportion of the money went to the people who opened their homes.

But all that had nothing to do with Tammy. She sank down miserably on the bottom step, trying to keep herself from the light that streamed from the hall. When Pete got through with Ernie he'd remember to be mad with her because she had stayed out so late, long after dark. When he got through with Ernie he would come and tell her what he thought of her. It would be worse than any beating Grandpa ever gave her. That only made her bottom ache.

All of a sudden she realized someone was speaking to her from up on the gallery. "Didn't you hear, Tammy? Mr. Bissle is here, our roomer from New York. I want him to meet you." Miss Renie's tone was the bright false one she used when she was tormenting Mrs. Brent.

"Oh." Tammy stood. "Howdy," she said and nodded her head toward the large dim figure beside Miss Renie.

"And is this the daughter of the house?" Mr. Bissle asked.

For a moment no one spoke and so Tammy answered, "No. Oh no, Mr. Bissle. I'm just staying here while Grandpa's in jail."

Mrs. Brent drew in her breath as if someone had hit her. Barbara's laugh rang out. "That's a good one. That's the best yet. Oh, Cousin Al, you ought to hear some of the——" She broke off abruptly as Pete came into the light at the foot of the steps.

Ernie had started his car, but stopped it at the sound of Barbara's laughter. "Hey, that you, Barb?" he called. "Want to ride back to town with me?"

"Wait a minute, Ernie." Barbara ran down the steps as Pete sat down, not saying anything, across their width from Tammy.

"Why don't you just spend the night, Barbara?" Mrs. Brent said. "Tomorrow's Sunday and you don't have to go to the office. And maybe your cousin will have dinner with us. Our house is inadequately staffed, Mr. Bissle, but Osia's chicken dumplings are quite famous."

"Thank you, I——"

Pete said, "Sure, Barb, what's the rush? I'll tell Ernie." He got to his feet.

But Barbara, calling back over her shoulder, "That will be wonderful, Mrs. Brent," waved Pete down again. "I'll tell Ernie myself. I want to ask him to phone home for me and say I won't be there. It'll save me a toll call." Her heels crunched quickly through the gravel toward the car at the turn of the drive.

Mr. Bissle gave a pleased little grunt. "Glad to see that at least one of the younger generation has some regard for saving."

"Oh," Mrs. Brent cried in her bright company voice, "we all think Barbara's quite wonderful. She has worked up to a splendid position in the Savings and Loan—five girls under her, isn't it, Pete?"

"I believe so, Mother," Pete said.

Mrs. Brent waited a moment as if she were hoping he would say something more and when he didn't she went on: "The brother's family—wife and three children I think it is—have been quite a burden but I believe he has come round to taking some sort of job now, and that eases the financial burden for her. Barbara has done so much——"

Tammy leaned forward, shutting her ears to the talk and searching the shadows beneath the first oak of the drive to see what Barbara was doing. The car was there, turned so that it hid Barbara and Ernie from those on the porch, but Tammy could see. They were standing on the other side of the car, close together, moving closer. Goshamighty, Tammy thought, that woman is a deep ditch and a narrow pit, and she don't care who falls in! Just got to be kissing somebody all the time.

Miss Renie spoke from the porch. "Everybody says how good Barbara has been, looking after her worthless brother and his family. But personally I think they'd have managed if Barbara had just tended her own business and left them alone. I don't believe in sacrifice or———"

"Now, Aunt Renie." Mrs. Brent broke in. "You don't understand this———"

But Mr. Bissle said, "You're quite right. Better to let people stand on their own feet. Trouble with the world today is that nobody wants to work. Now take me—I never had anybody helping me and I haven't done so badly."

Mrs. Brent said, "Of course, Mr. Bissle. Exactly. All your cousins are so proud of you and your great success in the financial world. My son Peter has always admired your career from afar. He was connected with the advertising business before the war and doing so well."

Ernie's car door slammed, and Barbara's quick laugh rang out. "You've got a one-track mind, Ernie. So long for now, and thanks just the same."

Mr. Bissle said, "Healthy laugh, she's got. There's nothing like being healthy. For my age I'm a remarkably healthy man. You know what I attribute it to?"

Mrs. Brent sighed faintly. "What, Mr. Bissle?"

"Two baths daily, winter and summer."

Miss Renie made a little choking sound, and Professor Brent said hastily, "The ancient Romans had a rather interesting water system."

Tammy edged along the step till she came to Pete. She couldn't wait any longer. She had to find out before Barbara came back. "You mad with me for staying after dark, Pete?" she whispered.

"Of course not, Tammy. Only I didn't know where you were and I was worried. And I'd have taken you to town myself if I'd known you wanted to go."

"Would you, Pete?"

"Sure. Now tomorrow—how'd you like to drive down and see your grandfather?"

"Oh, Pete, that would be wonderful."

He stood as Barbara approached. "We'll take the day to it."

Barbara waved him down again and sat between him and Tammy, her back turned to Tammy. "It's lovely here on the steps looking out into the moonlight. We ought to take a walk, Pete." She moved closer to him and they went on talking together softly.

On the gallery Mr. Bissle was saying, "Didn't have any idea they took baths in those days. Matter of fact I don't know much about history, and tell the truth I never missed it. All they teach you in schools is facts."

"Indeed?" Professor Brent's tone was chilly.

"Well, I declare," Tammy said. "Here I been worrying about getting myself an education and maybe it ain't necessary at all."

"One man's opinion, Tammy——" Professor Brent began.

"I'm not saying anything against it, Professor. That's the way you make your living, and it's all right if you want to do it that way. Of course you'd make more money as a bricklayer, now wouldn't you?"

"Well, yes, but——"

"The world pays in proportion to how valuable a thing is. If I was a young man starting out, I'd go into plumbing."

"Oh, dear," Mrs. Brent said. "But you—you didn't go into plumbing, you went into advertising, Mr. Bissle."

"Yes, and I haven't done too badly. I've managed to keep comfortable."

"I should say so," Mrs. Brent murmured.

Miss Renie asked, "Are you just on vacation now, Mr. Bissle?"

"Well, yes and no. Brought plenty of work along. I'm looking around for a place to retire to in a few years."

"Would you like a place in Mississippi?" Miss Renie leaned forward, her rocking chair creaking.

"Aunt Renie, please!" Mrs. Brent's voice was distressed.

"I'm looking around. Florida's full of robbers."

Mrs. Brent said, "Peter was there for some of his training."

"Oh? What branch were you in?"

"Submarine service," Peter said.

"You didn't get much out of that that would help you get a start in the world, did you? Just ribbons, I bet."

"Oh, Mr. Bissle, you should see Peter's. And his citations——"

Pete shifted uncomfortably and Barbara leaned closer to him. "I'll break it up. Oh, Mrs. Brent, where is Tammy?"

"What's that? Tammy? Why, she's right behind you."

"Oh——" Barbara looked around—"so she is. Stupid of me. I wanted to ask where you went, Tammy, and what you saw."

"I seen a sight of things," Tammy said. She clasped her hands around her knees and rocked back and forth on the step, not missing how Barbara had turned the talk and how she was looking to her to keep it turned. "I seen——"

"Saw," Miss Renie corrected.

"Saw. I saw a plenty—all the city, with houses so close together it's a wonder folks can breathe, and stores and people so thick they was bumping into each other, buying things. All the signs and the movies too, and the radio between the music was telling them to buy this and that and they was doing it fast as ever they could."

"Ah, advertising—that's what does it," Mr. Bissle said.

"But if you bought everything they told you to buy, it would take a million dollars, I reckon."

"Made you want to buy, didn't it?" Mr. Bissle said, rubbing his hands together. "Pretty good for business, I'd say."

"No. It's wicked. It makes people into barbarians that worship the idols of the market place. I read about it in a book, dusting."

Barbara laughed and Pete said, "What book, Tammy?"

"It said Bacon on the outside, and that's the kind of barbarian I was telling you about on the *Ellen B.*"

"Oh!" Pete said.

"Sounds like nonsense to me," Mr. Bissle said. "Barbarian—why, you've got it backward. That's civilization—mass production, nation-wide advertising."

Mrs. Brent broke in before Tammy could speak. "Ernie had no business taking Tammy all the way to Jackson. He drives too fast."

"He didn't take me to Jackson. It was Fairville we went to."

"I didn't realize there was another large city in this state," Mr. Bissle said, distracted from his argument.

"Oh, yes," Tammy told him quickly. "Pop. sixteen fifty."

"Sixteen fifty?"

"It means there's that many population," Tammy said, pleased at knowing something he didn't. "That's what the sign said. It's a big place all right."

"What else did you do besides look at people?" Barbara asked, choking on the question.

Tammy studied her a moment, seeing there was some other reason, under her words, for all this asking. But she was tired of hidden meaning, she was plumb sick of double talk. "I'll tell you," she began.

"Skip it, Barb." Pete spoke out of the side of his mouth.

"But I really want to know, Pete."

"Like hell you do," Pete muttered.

"Well—" Tammy looked across at her thoughtfully—"Ernie bought me some dog meat. It didn't taste bad but I kept thinking about dogs and how they wag their tails at you so friendly. It cost a lot, too. At the drugstore."

Mr. Bissle said, "Is the meat shortage so——"

Barbara laughed. "Oh, Cousin Al, it was a hot dog, of course. Go on, Tammy."

"Ernie took me to the movies, too. There was a lot of courting going on there."

"Thought they had a Western on Saturdays," Pete said.

"It was real people courting, Pete. Ernie said that was what they did at the movies. The picture was a lot of men riding and chasing each other, and there was a girl. She danced on top of the table where they was all sitting drinking. Didn't have much clothes on, but more'n the naked one in the store window."

"What do you mean, Tammy?" Miss Renie asked.

"In the store window. It was a false figger and they put a dress on her whilst we was watching. I saw a sight of things in the store windows—hats and dresses and ways to do your hair, and many inventions that would be a mighty convenience. Like the bedpan and——"

"Well!" Mrs. Brent interrupted. "I'm sure you saw enough to tire you out. You really should go to bed, Tammy."

"But I'm not——"

"Just turn on the back hall light as you go through, please, and I'll put it out later."

Tammy stood, her heart pounding hard, her eyes blazing down at Barbara. She knew now what Barbara had been doing—holding her up to scorn, mocking, like the children that ran after Elisha shouting, Go up, thou bald head. "Oh, I wisht I could call the she-bears out of the wood," she cried.

Mrs. Brent said, "What on earth, Tammy? Are you out of your head?"

"But of course," Miss Renie cried. "The she-bears that tare the forty-two children for Elisha."

"Yes," Tammy said, with a gulp. "It used to be I thought he was being purely cruel, but now I see he was mightily provoked."

"In any case," Mrs. Brent said with severity, "there are some things we just don't talk about."

Pete sprang up and came to Tammy as she stood in the light from the hall, saying, "Sorry, Mother, but you're wrong. Tammy was asked to tell what she saw. You——" He put one arm round her shoulder. "Don't mind, Tammy."

"Aw, Pete, don't take it so seriously, for heaven's sake." That was Barbara, trying to make up to him, seeing she'd gone too far. "I was just——"

"I know what you were doing." Pete's voice was cold.

"Well, my goodness——" Barbara turned toward the others—"you know how Pete hates to have anybody talking about his medals. I was only trying to turn the conversation."

Tammy looked up at him, feeling his arm across her shoulder, comforting and kind. Her anger melted; she felt a sorrowfulness enter into her bones. Pete was kind, kind as he would be to any odd, lost one, blundering and ignorant. "Must be I talk too free," she said.

Barbara had risen. "Forget it, Pete. I'm sorry. Come on, let's take a walk—it's a gorgeous night."

Tammy moved from Pete's arm. "I will go to bed." She turned and went in by the open front door, walking with dignity to hide the ache inside of her.

In her room she undressed slowly, not turning on the electricity, but moving by the light of the moon. When she lay down on her bed, she tried to stop thinking about Barbara. She had a sight of other things to think about—all she had seen and heard in town, and there was Mr. Bissle who did not believe in education. That was really something to puzzle over. And tomorrow—tomorrow Pete was going to take her to see Grandpa! But just the same her mind kept worrying at Barbara, like a dog with a bone.

After a while she heard voices on the ell porch. Professor Brent saying, "These stairs are rather steep but if you'll just follow me. Your room is right up here, Mr. Bissle. Coolest room in the house."

There were more steps and talking, but all far away. Then the house grew quiet. Tammy turned and tossed and could not get to sleep. It must be the moonlight, she thought. She got up and sat in the low chair by the window. Under the trees the shadows were black and motionless. In the open places the moonlight was still on the grass, not leaping and dancing as it was on the river. After a while Tammy leaned forward, catching her breath. Two people were coming through the gap in the far hedge. They moved closer together, they stopped in the shadow—Barbara lifting her face and Pete bending down.

"Goshamighty," Tammy breathed, "that there is the outkiss-ingest woman! Her lips drop honey. But I bet her end is bitter as wormwood." She stood up, hands clenched at her sides. "One like that's got no right to Pete. She ain't good enough." Then she turned away and climbed into her bed. She could not bear to watch them walking back toward the house, moving close to-gether in the moonlight. The real trouble was, Pete wanted Bar-bara. He was caught by her beauty, he was snared by her shapely limbs and her fair speech. "I reckon I've got a body, too," she said and hid her face in the pillow.

14.

IT WAS a bright day early in the morning, warm and full of a Sabbath feel, as if the earth had memories of the Seventh Day, its finished birthday, and wrapped a holy stillness about itself, remembering. The morning came to Tammy lying in the carved bed in Miss Renie's little room. She opened her eyes and took in the light and savored the stillness. It rebuked her for her anger of the night before. Be still, the morning said to her, and fret not thyself, the sun is risen.

Tammy stretched herself under the sheet and pushed back her dark hair from her face and let her hands, like another's, move from her throat down over the gentle mounds of her breasts, along the smallness of her waist and the firm outcurving of her thighs. Amid the confusion and the diverse stirrings of strangers, she was yet one, whole and discreetly contained within herself, her soul bound pleasantly by her body. Yes, like she was thinking last night, she had a body too. But it would shame her to use it to entice a man. "This is me," she whispered, "me out in the world, but still me." Being herself was what held her back from being wily and cunning in the ways of the flesh. And yet, she reckoned, there might be ways you could put a man in mind of it, in seemly fashion. Else how had women been making out all these years?

This was the day Pete was going to take her to see Grandpa. All at once she was filled with strength and resolution, and the day stretched ahead of her, rich and filled with promise. She rose and the smell of the morning drew her to the window, the sparks of dew invited her. She dressed quickly and went out by the small passageway and the ell porch, her bare feet making no sound. The bricks of the garden walk were cool and smooth as water, the sweet shrub by the path had been breathing sweetness all night long and now the dew on every leaf was scented. Gather it up in a bottle, Tammy thought, and there would be perfumery fit to sell in a drugstore.

When she came from the little house back of the kitchen behind its decent screen of vines, the loose plank walk rattling under her light step, she stopped to look up at Pete's house. It was really two houses, the ell being the first built and complete in itself. Then later the front part had been set up at right angles to it. Now the morning sun was behind the ell and the green tops of oak trees showed above its roof that was still black with the night's dew. It looked cool and gray and beautiful with the two galleries one above the other and both laced with black iron railings. No wonder people came from far to look and admire.

There was a stirring of pans in the kitchen, the creak of the coffee grinder. Osia had come. She was cooking breakfast. The rest of the house was shuttered and sleeping, holding those who slept.

Pete's father and mother were in the big bedroom back of the library in the front part of the house. Mrs. Brent would be still from her buzzing, her perpetual beating about. She was all day like a busy bug, a lightning bug, cupped around by her life. Sleep would have to pierce her sharp as a pin, holding her against her will—sleep that was cousin to the thing she feared. Professor Brent would be lying beside her with his long feet making a finish to his length. All his long words would be folded within his mind and his manners would be keeping him well to his side of the bed.

Tammy came through the gate and latched it behind her, looking up again at the house. Miss Renie was in the other big room across the passageway from Tammy's, with the tester overhead and Picasso curled at her feet. Maybe she was dreaming, going in her dreams to all the far places she had never got to in her waking. Barbara was in the downstairs ell room, next to Tammy. She would be smiling in her sleep, with her smooth cheek snuggled low and her arms around a pillow, snuggling into it, dreaming maybe of a couch that was perfumed with myrrh and aloes and cinnamon.

Pete—Tammy's lips shaped to a smile. She knew how Pete slept from how he lay when he was sick on the *Ellen B.*—one hand flung out and one drawn close against his breast, holding in with one hand and giving with the other; his lips relaxed to show the sweetness he kept strictly hidden within himself. She let her mind rest tenderly on Pete as she moved between the sweet olive trees. Their fragrance came to her shyly. It was not bold like the sweet shrub, it was delicate and fine. It was less than air but it was more penetrating. It surrounded her, it passed through her, as if all her body breathed it in. It was like her thinking of Pete, for that was of her body too.

In the big upstairs ell room beside Pete's room, was Mr. Bissle, making a high mound with his stomach under the bedclothes, keeping his head stiff and cautious on the pillow, even in sleep. He would not be one to dream. Nothing so fragile and fair as a dream could come through the thick white dome of his bald head.

That was all the house held. Her eyes fell on the bed of corn-flowers and verbena against the house wall. Old Prater had worked hard to weed it but he hadn't finished this part. Maybe she could do it before breakfast while everyone was sleeping.

She had a big heap of grass and weeds on the walk beside her when she heard a shuffling step on the upper ell porch. It couldn't be Pete—he would never walk like that. She sat back on her heels and looked up. It was Mr. Bissle in a blue-and-white-striped robe not wide enough to meet around his middle. It showed his sleeping suit that was made of pale-blue silky stuff. He looked as if his mamma had forgotten he was grown and had dressed him in baby blue. He was a bald-headed baby, got out of his crib too soon in the morning.

He had come to Pete's door now. He opened it softly, looked

in, closed it again. Then he went the length of the porch to the last door, to the room that was to be Mr. Fernan's, and did the same. Then he came down the stairs, placing one foot carefully and the other beside it till he got to the bottom. Then he stood, looking as if he wanted to go somewhere and didn't know where.

"It's out younder back of the kitchen, by the plank walk," Tammy called, and bent quickly to her weeding again.

"Humph," he grunted and scuffed his slippers down the steps and along the walk, not looking her way. When he came back Tammy did not turn. It was more seemly not to, considering where he had been. But his shuffling steps halted by the flower bed, so she said, "Good morning, Mr. Bissle."

He scowled down at her as if he had the sun in his eyes, though the sun had not yet come over the house. "Outrageous," he rasped. "Didn't they know who I am? Didn't they know I'd have to have a private bath?"

Tammy sat back on her heels, lifting her head. "I wouldn't be alooking. Nor anybody else." Her eyes went over his shape. "Wouldn't anybody want to see you. Besides you could keep your door shut."

"I'm not inviting anybody to see me." He looked up at the house as if he would like to shake it. "Five dollars a night and they don't give me a bath."

"Can't you wash yourself?"

"Who said anything about washing? I simply expect the ordinary conveniences of civilization, that's all. Especially when I pay for them. It's incredible. Not a tub in the place, I suppose, not a——" He looked fit to be tied.

"Miss Renie has a little foot tub she soaks her feet in. I could slip in and get you that, if you——"

"A foot tub! A tin foot tub, no doubt. My Lord, how do you expect a man of my size to get himself into a foot tub!"

"Oh," Tammy said. "It's more than just washing yourself

clean? You want to get all the way under. Like the Baptists. Total immersion."

"That's the idea."

"Then there ain't a thing in the world to do about it, less'n you go to the river, and that's a right far piece."

Mr. Bissle grunted and went over to sit on the steps. "The quaint charm of the Old South, ante-bellum atmosphere," he grumbled. "I've got work to do. I've got to be comfortable, I tell you. My baths—two a day. . . . What was that woman thinking about, sending me to a place like this?"

"Maybe she was thinking about what Mrs. Brent told her."

"And what did Mrs. Brent tell her? I'd like to know."

"She told her that being here you'd likely come to know how wonderful Pete is and get a notion of giving him a job in your business."

"Well, I can tell you right now I have no notion of giving any-body anything." He reached in the pocket of his striped robe and got out a crumpled pack of cigarettes and a match. He scratched the match on the steps with a sweep of his hand. "And was I right last night when I said a young man had better take up plumbing! I recommend it to the young man of the house." And having said that and drawn on his cigarette, he seemed to feel better. "Just how wonderful is this Pete?"

Tammy took a long breath. "He is the most wonderful there is."

"H'm. So that's how you feel about it."

"Yes." She flung back her head and looked at him squarely.

"I thought my little cousin Barbara had a mortgage on that prop-erty."

"She wants him, if that's what you mean. She wants him for richer but not for poorer. She doesn't want him unless he has a good job and can buy her everything in the world."

He nodded. "Barbara's got a good head on her. Runs in the

family. She knows how to look after number one. That's what
you've got to do in this world."

"But she isn't going to get Pete." Tammy went back to her
weeding.

"Why not?"

"Two reasons, the way I figger it."

"What are they?"

Tammy moved along the path to a new patch of grass. "One is:
you ain't going to give him a big job because you're mad about not
having a bathtub big enough to put yourself in whole."

"Nonsense. That's another matter. I wouldn't let a thing like
that influence me." He puffed a minute. "Matter of fact I need
a new man." He scowled off into the distance, maybe seeing his
need and where it was. Then he added, "And Barbara'd make a
smart wife for him. She'd push him. Nice-looking fellow, with
some advertising experience, in a small way, of course. But he
needs push."

"Barbara isn't going to push him."

"Why not?"

"Because I ain't going to let her."

"You?" He gave her a queer look.

"Me." Tammy sat back on her heels again and looked at him.
"I don't know myself how I'll manage it, but I'm agoing to. She
ain't got the least notion of how to love one man and no other."

"Love," Mr. Bissle said with scorn. "Love's a disease."

"Didn't you never love a woman?"

"Not me. A man travels faster if he travels alone."

Tammy looked at him a long minute. "It's a curious thing, to
see a man alone," she said. "Alone, with nothing maybe but a
bathtub."

"Humph." He stood. "Haven't got a bath. No room service
either I suppose."

"Room service?"

"Breakfast sent up, that sort of thing."

"Oh, yes, you can have that. When do you want it?"

"Half an hour." Then he mounted the steps and the stairs to his room, not looking back.

Tammy finished the weeding and went into the kitchen to wash her hands. Osia had breakfast ready on the stove and she was sitting at the kitchen table drinking her coffee. "That-there man, look like he's a big man from way off, way he talk. How-come he has to wash hisself so much?"

"Because he's so big, I reckon," Tammy said, going to the stove to pour herself some coffee. "He's put all he's got into himself. That's why. It's puffed him up in mind and body. He don't believe in learning." She sat down across the table from Osia. "And he don't believe in love."

"Now that's something, ain't it? A big man like that, come in a car as big as a house only it got white-rim wheels on it, and don't believe in learning." Osia got up and went to the stove. "Is he going to get his clothes on and eat now?"

"He wants it in his room." Tammy sat drinking her coffee and watching Osia put the long griddle to heat and move with confidence among her many pots and pans. "Osia?" Tammy leaned her elbows on the table and rested her chin on her clasped hands. "Osia."

"Yassum?" Osia turned her dark head and looked at Tammy over her shoulder. She was a thin, tall woman, slow moving, with a kind of grace in her moving, as if a drumbeat out of distant time and place had set the rhythm of her step.

"Osia, why is it, when I sit down, you get up?"

Osia turned her dark glance away. "There is a lot of things, Miss Tammy, that you don't seem to know nothing about."

"I know I don't. I'm always puzzling. But this—is it a kind of manners that goes with cooking?"

"No, ma'am." It seemed for a while as if she was not going to

say any more than that. She poured batter on the griddle in six
neat circles. Then she said with bitterness, "It's a kind of manners
that goes with the color of your skin."

"That's a funny thing. It don't seem to make sense. There are
so many manners that don't make sense. Like Professor Brent
getting himself up and putting a chair under, if you're a woman,
and not, if you're a man. That might go back to the lords and
ladies days, like it was in *The Idylls of the King*. But this-
here——"

"This-here goes back to slavery days, Miss Tammy. That's what
it goes back to."

"That was long ago, too. Do you reckon it will wear off in
time?"

"Not in my time." Osia got a tray from the shelf and spread a
white napkin on it.

"Is it worrying to you?"

"No'm. I'm used to it. It don't worry me so much, but it worry
my chillen. I declare, you sure do think of the beatingest things,
Miss Tammy." Osia shook her head. "Look like you come on
the world with a fresh mind. Ain't cluttered up."

"That's what Professor Brent says. It's a blank and he wants
to write on it, only he doesn't know what, yet."

"You better do your own writing, Miss Tammy. Don't let nobody fool with your brain. Now I got to get these-here cakes up
yonder whilst they's good and hot." She set the plate on the tray.

"I'll take it up," Tammy said, rising. "You cook me some.
They smell powerful good. What's in them?"

"Just cold light bread and sody, eggs and buttermilk and a
speck of salt. Flour and some butter, too. That's all. Hey, you
Roots, come in here!"

Roots came in from the pantry, a pencil and pad in his hand.
Tammy said, "Hello, Roots. You been drawing?"

"Yassum." He stood with eyes on the floor.

"He's all the time drawing." Osia got down a cup and saucer

for Mr. Bissle. "He ain't content with drawing just what Miss Renie tell him. He draw the beatingest things."

"What you got there?"

Shyly Roots held out his drawing pad. Osia gave it a quick glance and she had to set down the coffeepot, she got to laughing so. "You sure got that one to the life. That's Mr. Bissle to the life. Just how he look from here." She turned back to the stove, wiping her eyes. "Lawdamussy, it just about kill me some time, what that child draw."

Tammy studied the drawing. It had no more than a dozen lines to it, but every line meant something. A curved line and a circle with a round head on top—that was the shape of Mr. Bissle from the back, for sure. One hand held a cigarette and the smoke curled over his head. "What's he sitting on?" She pointed to the rounded line on which he perched.

Roots turned his head, as if he wasn't going to answer. Then he said, "I heard you all talking about a tub. That there's one big tub, big as the world."

"That ought to hold him." Tammy smiled. "But why did you put one star up in the sky?"

"I heerd you saying something about a man being alone."

"But I don't see why . . . a star——"

"Ain't nothing make you feel so lonesome as a star, Miss Tammy. 'Specially just one."

"That's right," Tammy agreed. "It does make you lonesome." She held out the drawing to him.

He shook his head. "You can have it."

"I'd love to keep it. Here Osia, give me the tray. I'll take it." She folded the sheet over and took the tray from Osia. "He sure ought to be pleased with this breakfast."

On the upper ell porch she held the tray in one hand and rapped on Mr. Bissle's door. "Here's your breakfast, Mr. Bissle."

"Come in, come in."

He was sitting in bed with pillows behind him and pictures and printed papers and written papers all around him. He looked like some kind of bald-headed bluebird that had been making himself a nest of papers. "Just set it there." He waved to the small table beside the head of the bed, looking up. "Forgot to tell you I never take anything but dry toast and coffee. What's that I smell?"

"Battercakes and sausage and molasses and coffee."

"Battercakes!" He hiked himself up higher in the bed and looked around. "H'm." He reached over and took a cake in his fingers. The butter dripped on the sheet. "Indigestible, raw inside, poisonous to the liver." He sniffed it, took a bite, and a look of wonder went over his face. "Suppose I'll have to eat them, now you've got them here." He took up the tray and balanced it on his stomach. Roots's picture fluttered to the floor. "What's that? The bill?"

"N-not exactly." Tammy stooped to pick it up.

"Well, give it to me. May as well know the worst right off." He put another battercake in his mouth.

"I . . . you may not like it. You aren't really so . . . though you're nigh onto it."

He took it from her, stared at it. He turned it this way and that, twisting his face to one side and then the other. "Lord, that's an idea! Who did this?" he roared.

"It . . . it was Roots. But he——"

"Who on earth is Roots?"

"Just a little boy. He didn't mean——"

"Just a little boy, eh?" He half closed his eyes and a crafty look came over his face.

"Just a little black boy," Tammy said.

"Oho! A little black boy, eh? Better yet. Give me my pants."

Tammy looked around the room. His pants were folded neatly over a chair by the other wall. She went slowly to the chair and took them up. Then she started for the door, carrying them carefully over her arm.

"Hey, what are you doing?" he demanded with his mouth full of battercakes and sausage.

"I'm not agoing to give them to you. He didn't mean no harm by that picture. I'm agoing to take them downstairs and keep them till you get out of the notion of beating him."

Mr. Bissle choked down his mouthful. "I'm not going to beat anybody. I'm going to get a quarter out of my pocket and buy the picture. Now give me my pants!"

"Oh!" Tammy stared at him. "You like it?"

Mrs. Brent's distressed voice came up from the lower porch. "Tammy! Tammy! Come down at once. What on earth are you doing in Mr. Bissle's room?"

"Yes, Mrs. Brent, I——"

"Sure I like it. It's perfect," Mr. Bissle said. "Just what I've been looking for—ten men working on ideas and here a little black boy—— But you needn't tell him that. A quarter's plenty." He looked up at the ceiling and smiled. He was like a fat baby in a crib. "This place brings me luck. Bath or no bath, I guess I'll stay."

"Tammy, are you coming?" Mrs. Brent sounded wild.

"Just a minute, Mrs. Brent. I'm coming soon as I give Mr. Bissle his pants."

"O Lord!" Mrs. Brent's moan came from down below. "Will I have to—you see, Joel, I just can't take the responsibility for what happens. And Mr. Bissle—of all people——" Her voice died away.

Mr. Bissle wiped his fingers on some of the papers that were scattered over the bed. He reached in his pants pocked and brought out a handful of change. "You're witness to the fact that I've bought it. It's mine, and all the rights and privileges."

"Are you coming, Tammy? Or will I have to . . . to send Professor Brent up?" Mrs. Brent sounded as though she couldn't wait any longer.

"I'm coming just as soon as he gives me a quarter, Mrs. Brent," Tammy called back.

Mr. Bissle selected three nickels and a dime and held them out, counting them into her hand. "Looks like more that way."

Tammy took the money and stood a moment, uncertain. "What you want of that picture, Mr. Bissle?"

"I'll show you." He found a red pencil and resting the drawing on the brief case across his knee he printed "ON TOP OF THE WORLD." Below that he added "WITH A HUBBA."

"What's a hubba?"

"New cigarette we're launching." He held the drawing out before him and admired it. "You'll see it on every billboard in the country, in every magazine. Swell. That's really pretty swell." Then he looked down at his empty plate. "Lord, I ate all those cakes without thinking what I was doing!"

Tammy turned in the doorway. "You want some hot water and soda?"

"No, just bring me some more. I'll die happy."

Tammy came down the stairs with Mr. Bissle's empty tray in one hand and the money jingling in the other. Professor and Mrs. Brent sat at the porch table, breakfast untouched before them. Tammy was hurrying on toward the kitchen when Mrs. Brent straightened up from leaning her head on her hand and said, "Tammy!"

Tammy stopped short and looked around.

"Tammy," Mrs. Brent said in a choked voice, clicking her teeth, "this is too much. I cannot—— Where did you get that money?"

"Mr. Bissle," Tammy said. "And you don't need to be worrying. He is in an awful good mood now. He says he can die happy, and it's give him an appetite. He wants some more battercakes, 'though he doesn't usually eat anything but dry toast."

Professor Brent said, "Let Osia take him the pancakes. You come here."

"All right, Professor Brent. Just a minute. He wants more battercakes, Osia," she said, going on into the kitchen. "Gosh-amighty, Osia, I never knowed anybody could make money that easy. Roots, lookahere—twenty-five cents!"

Mrs. Brent was talking in little gasps. "Before the servants! Joel, this time you must do something. And Mr. Bissle, you'll have to order him out. Oh, why did this have to happen?"

Tammy could hear what she was saying but she couldn't give it her mind yet. She put the money on the kitchen table beside Roots. "He bought your picture, Roots," she cried. "He liked it. He paid you twenty-five cents for it, look!"

Roots grinned, speechless. Osia said, "Now ain't that some-thing!" Then she caught sight of Professor Brent standing in the doorway and added hurriedly, "Yessuh, Professor Brent, I'm bringing your coffee right now."

Professor Brent went back to the table on the porch. "I sup-pose you heard that, my dear? I cannot understand why it is that you always expect the worst."

"Because it's the worst that usually happens. Oh, Joel, I don't know what to think. There was that other time—with Ernie—before breakfast, too."

"Tammy, come eat your breakfast," Professor Brent said as she came from the kitchen.

Tammy ate in silence, looking from one to the other, wondering what the trouble was. Miss Renie came out with Picasso as usual. Tammy said good morning and went on trying to puzzle things out. Osia carried another plate of cakes upstairs and came back.

"Why so serious and silent, Tammy?" Miss Renie asked in the middle of her breakfast.

"I'm just figgering something out," Tammy said, her eyes on Mrs. Brent. She was remembering how Mrs. Brent had called and called her to come down from upstairs, and yet there was nothing she was in a hurry to tell her. Then she remembered her last words, in that shocked tone, "Ernie—and before breakfast too." That was what she had said. Suddenly it was all clear to Tammy. She laid down her knife and fork and leaned forward, fixing Mrs. Brent with her serious gray eyes. "Mrs. Brent, did you think that Mr. Bissle and I were——"

"Oh Tammy, please——" Mrs. Brent glanced nervously toward the stairs and Mr. Bissle's feet as he began to take the steps one at a time.

"I haven't got on any face paint this morning and you shouldn't have. Besides, I wouldn't have picked Mr. Bissle out if I'd been alooking around."

"Oh, my," Mrs. Renie cried, "don't tell me I got up so late I missed all the fun!"

"Aunt Renie," Professor Brent said, "your use of the word fun in this connection shows a paucity of vocabulary that appalls me." He took off his glasses and began polishing them on his napkin.

Tammy was not to be turned aside. "But, Mrs. Brent, really, did you——"

Mrs. Brent was fidgeting in her chair. She spoke in a hasty aside, keeping a watch on Mr. Bissle's slow descent of the stairs. "Tammy, I—well, it was a most compromising situation . . . what was I to think. . . . Anybody would have——"

"You ought to be ashamed," Tammy said, and added, "If I ever get into anybody's bed, I'll come straightway and tell you. I promise you that."

"Oh, dear me, Tammy, please be quiet."

"I'll be quiet, but I'll tell you and——"

Mrs. Brent cried, "Oh, Mr. Bissle, here you are! Do come have a second breakfast with us." Then Barbara came out, and Pete came down the stairs.

Mr. Bissle beamed on everyone. "Good morning, good morning!" He shook one finger at Mrs. Brent, saying, "Not another thing, thanks. Have to look out for the liver, you know." He turned to Barbara. "How's my little cousin this morning? Stunning as always." He planted a kiss on her cheek. "Don't tell me we aren't kissing cousins, because I know better."

Barbara laughed. "How about a stroll in the garden, Cousin Al, before I have coffee? I want to see that new car of yours."

"Sure thing. I want you to see that little job. Lovely day, isn't it," he added as they went down the steps. "Fine old ante-bellum place—the real thing."

Pete looked after them rather darkly in spite of the glance Barbara flung him over her shoulder as she went. Then he kissed the top of his mother's hair, nodded to Tammy and said, "Sunday morning and Osia's battercakes—that's worth getting up for. And we've got a fine day, Tammy." His eyes sought the far field where it was a fine day for growing things, too.

Tammy nodded and filled up with happiness. He hadn't forgotten.

After a little Barbara came back. "It's a swell car." She took the chair Pete placed for her. "Cousin Al's polishing off the rear end that wouldn't go in—it's so long. It's even got a vase for flowers. It's big enough to hang pictures in. Wouldn't I love a car like that!"

Miss Renie said, "I have a small canvas he might like. It's the one of Rosa Bonheur's six kittens and the garden toad."

"I'm afraid Mr. Bissle's taste doesn't run to kittens, Aunt Renie." Pete smiled.

"Or toads," Professor Brent said. "Not unless he's promoting frogs' legs, in which case he would prefer a bathing beauty poised for a dive into the frog pond, saying to the old bullfrog on the bank, 'I just adore frogs' legs.'"

"And he'd reply, 'It's mutual, sister.'" Pete laughed. "We ought to go into advertising, Dad. Between us we'd amount to something special."

Mrs. Brent said, "Don't joke about serious things, Peter. I wonder if we had better have hot rolls or spoon bread for dinner. Of course there will be dumplings with the chickens."

Miss Renie turned on her quickly. "Are you planning to have chicken for dinner?"

"Certainly. I thought you heard me last night when I invited Mr. Bissle."

Miss Renie rose hastily, setting Picasso on her shoulder. "You didn't give me much time to prepare them, Ena." She called kitchenward, "Osia, send Roots along with the bucket of scraps for the chickens."

Tammy said, "Miss Renie, I could clean the chickens for you."

"Heavens," Miss Renie turned on the steps, "you don't think I'm going to clean chickens, do you?"

"But you said, prepare them. Don't you take their innards out before you cook them?"

"I'm not thinking of their innards," Miss Renie snapped, sweeping on down the steps. "I go to prepare their immortal souls."

"Goshamighty!" Tammy breathed.

"Well said, Tammy," Professor Brent said.

Miss Renie stopped on the walk. "I have to have a little fun." She went a few steps more and turned again. "You don't want me to be a frustrated old maid like some of these you read about that drown themselves in the rain barrel, do you?"

"No, indeed, Aunt Renie. Have fun," Pete called, and Professor Brent said at the same time, "I should say not—it would contaminate the drinking water."

Miss Renie gave a snort and went on. Tammy looked from one to the other. "What was she talking about?"

Professor Brent explained. "Aunt Renie, Tammy, believes in the transmigration of souls. She goes now to tell the chickens that two chicken souls, or three, perhaps, will shortly ascend to some higher form of life—such as the pig or the goat. Though if their conduct in the poultry world has not been of noble sort, it is possible that they descend to earthworm or roach."

Tammy listened, openmouthed. "That would sure make a sight

of souls. Would every crawling thing have a soul—like a red bug or a louse?"

Barbara laughed and turned to talk to Pete, on the other side of her.

"Oh, dear, Joel," Mrs. Brent sighed. "Must we go into all this? I am trying to plan dinner and——"

"Just a word more, Ena. This is really an interesting idea and one cherished by many people of great intelligence. Part of Tammy's education. Yes, Tammy, even bacteria and the yeasts may have souls. And if so, why should the vegetable world go soulless?" He looked over the garden and beyond the fence to where onions and lettuce made green rows against the earth. "There would be a progression there, too, perhaps, from turnip to more spiritual parsley. Who knows?"

Barbara was talking to Pete in a low tone, but Pete was not really listening, Tammy thought. She could tell by the laughter in his eyes as he looked from his father to her and back again. Tammy said, "But on judgment day there'd be an awful mix-up, with such a power of bodies for one soul."

"That is a contingency for which I am personally unprepared," Professor Brent said.

Pete laughed aloud and Barbara looked annoyed. "Excuse me, Barbara, I——" Pete began.

Tammy leaned forward, hooking her bare feet around the legs of her chair. "Would they work up to humans, maybe?"

"Human beings are generally considered a higher form, though there are times when I have my doubts."

"And what would humans go on to?"

"There we enter the speculative realm, if we have ever been out of it. The evolution of man——"

"Please, Joel." Mrs. Brent passed one hand across her brow. "I can't think when you are talking."

Tammy leaned back in her chair and put a final question. "Is it thinking about their souls that makes Miss Renie so fond of cats?"

Professor Brent looked at her over his glasses. "She expects to become a cat in her next incarnation."

Barbara turned to Mrs. Brent. "I know you are going to have a wonderful dinner, Mrs. Brent, but I've just been trying to tell Pete that Cousin Al wants to take him and me to Jackson to that new eating place with the French name. It would give them a good chance to get acquainted, I thought."

Mrs. Brent brightened. "Now that's an idea."

Pete said, "I am going to take Tammy to see her Grandpa today. You come with us, Barbara. Another day Mr. Bissle can———"

"There won't be another day, Pete. You know I'm taking afternoons off these next two weeks so as to come help receive the pilgrims. I won't have any time. But say, why can't we go by and drop Tammy at the jail and pick her up on the way home? Here comes Cousin Al. I'll tell him."

Pete shook his head. "It's too far and besides . . . well, that isn't the way I planned it."

"Too far, nonsense! In a car like that? We can go around through Longhaven—with New York plates—that'll be swell. Everybody will open their eyes."

Mrs. Brent nodded her approval. "Of course you'll go." Then she called to Mr. Bissle, "Come right in and join us. We linger at table Sunday mornings."

"But I———" Pete began.

"Oh, Pete, don't be stuffy. Cousin Al wants to show us a good time—and does he know how!" She smiled around at Mr. Bissle as he came to stand behind her chair, one hand on her shoulder.

"Peter, please," Mrs. Brent said in a hasty aside. "I don't know what's come over you. You never used to be so———"

Tammy saw the tense set look come into Pete's face and she turned away, her head bowed. He wanted to go with Barbara. She could not keep him back from what he wanted to do. "I could give you back your promise, Pete," she said in a small voice.

"That settles it." Barbara leaned back, smiling, triumphant.
Tammy flung around. She stiffened. "But I ain't agoing to."

"Why, Tammy—" Mrs. Brent began.

Pete ignored them both. "Thanks for the invitation, Mr. Bissle,
but I have already promised to take Tammy to see her grandfather
today."

Barbara shrugged and Mr. Bissle nodded. "That's okay by me."
He gave Pete a shrewd look. "Like to see a man stick by his guns.
Barbara'll show me the country, and I'll show her how it feels to
ride in a real car for a change."

15.

PETE'S car was not like Mr. Bissle's, nor yet like Ernie's either. It was a jolty car without a top and it rattled and bumped along the road. It had no music. But Tammy thought that a fair enough arrangement, for with Pete there was no need of vases full of flowers, nor music. To be near him was a song singing, though now the song ran in a minor key, subdued, because Pete had a silent spell on him. Glancing at him now and then, she could almost see into his thinking, feel his sharp disappointment. Well, she sighed, watching the fields and green woods go by, this ought to show her. What was the use having him away with her, all to herself, if his mind and heart stayed behind?

She kept her silence, hoping the distance would thin out his thoughts of Barbara who liked better to go off with New York plates and white-rimmed wheels than to ride with him. Barbara had made up to him at the last, coming out to the car, laying her lovely white arm along its window, talking and laughing while Tammy ran to the kitchen to get the lunch Osia had packed in a shoe box. She waved good-by and said, "See you tomorrow," as they left, but she had put a pucker in Pete's mind like a green persimmon in the mouth. Maybe after a while it would get washed out.

The road was not the same road Ernie had taken. It held the morning sun behind them and it went with many turnings where it was going. There was no dust on the trees that bordered it, for the traffic was light. The new green leaves shone like water where the sun fell, and the oak tassels were gold. They passed a hollow where bush honeysuckle bloomed on either bank. It was delicate and rosy, like a sunrise cloud strayed off from the sky, to hide itself and lie low till tomorrow's dawn. Tammy looked to one side and the other, and was glad Pete was not taking her to towns.

He followed her glance now, seeing what she saw—cattle grazing on a grassy slope. "I always like to see cows on a hill like that."

"Reckon you'd like to have cattle on a thousand hills, wouldn't you, Pete?"

"A fat chance I've got of having any, except Aunt Renie's moth-eaten old Jersey."

"But Pete——" She shook her head. "I can't understand it, your talking so poor and down, when you've got so much. Even a car."

"Such as it is." He laughed.

"Runs, don't it? And Brenton Hall—it's an elegant place."

"I'll tell you how it is, Tammy." It seemed to ease him to be saying it out. "It's not just that the place is shabby and needs repairs, it's the actual lack of cash. It's the way you have to have money to get it back into running condition. Aunt Renie has been selling off the timber all these years to pay taxes, to keep herself from starving. Oh, I could get a job in town. I could probably get a good job with Mr. Bissle. I'm not so dumb that I don't see that's what my mother and Barbara are wangling for. Maybe I'm just a fool, but——" he turned the car aside to miss a hard-shell turtle crossing the road—"let's skip it, shall we? Maybe I'll clean up on tomatoes. And anyway I'd like to have one day off, free from thinking about anything but just what's here and now."

"That's what I been wanting you to do, Pete."

He leaned back in his seat and let his hands lie loose on the wheel. They rode in silence, but now it was different. A kind of peace had come over him and the silence was sweet. After a while he slowed the car. "Know where you are, Tammy?" He stopped on the side of the road in the shade of a magnolia tree.

Tammy, looking ahead, saw a bridge. "The bayou bridge," she

whispered. At the side of the road was a path leading back past the magnolia, dipping down into the cool shade of the swamp. Tammy could see no more because a mist came into her eyes. "Pete——" Her voice broke.

"We'll take our lunch and picnic on the *Ellen B.*," Pete said. "That's what I was planning all along. You can leave your shoes in the car."

Tammy led the way along the path, skipping, running, whirling to be sure Pete was behind her still. The full foliage spread a canopy against the sky, the air was cool and damp. The spring water, when they stopped to sample it, was pure and cold as ever.

"It's a wonder," Tammy said, "how it all goes on just the same, how you can go away and come back and find it all here."

They crossed the log over the bayou's still black water, mounted the long slope and came out at last on the top of the bluff. The river danced and sparkled under the noon sun. The *Ellen B.* was snuggled safe among the green willows, below the bluff. Tammy ran helter-skelter down the bank and a hen flew up cackling madly, scattering chicks to right and left. "It's the old Dominicker," Tammy cried, stopping, panting. "Stole a nest and got her a brood. She's a smart one, she is."

Pete pulled on the hawser and drew in the *Ellen B.* and Tammy leaped across, not waiting for the gangplank. She danced the round of the deck and came back as Pete stepped aboard. "I'm fair wild," she said. "I could kiss the deck and hug the stovepipe. I could lie down and die of pure pleasure."

"You're right," Pete said. "It's good to get back. I'm going to sit down and just look at the river. But I ought to have told you we were coming here, so you could have brought your key."

"I've got it, Pete, pinned in the front of my dress with the money Grandpa gave me. I keep it on all the time."

Pete sat with his back against the shanty wall, his eyes on the water, and Tammy unlocked the door and went in. It was musty-smelling and dark inside, strange and familiar both. Tammy walked slowly around the kitchen, touching table, stove and each small thing, letting her fingers know that she was home. There was nothing missing but Grandpa, and she was going to see him soon. She caught up the water bucket and went out to Pete. He had such a look of content on his face that she told him to sit and rest while she went back to the spring for cool water. Goshamighty, but it was good to be with her own again!

Back from the spring, she found that Pete had brought out Grandma's chair to the deck and was studying it. "I would like to make some chairs like this. If I'd thought to bring a tape measure, I could get the size."

"Why don't we take it back with us, Pete? It'd sure make me feel at home, having Grandma's chair to sit in when I get a lonesome feeling."

"Good idea. It'll go in the back of the car."

They picnicked on deck, under the shade of the little tin roof that made a porch, not talking much, not needing to talk. When Pete said it was time to go, Tammy said they must go by to see Grandma's grave before they left.

It was quiet in the little graveyard atop the bluff, no breath of air stirring the moss, no tremble in the cedar's branches save when a thrush whirred out, startled by their coming. The grass was green and tall on Grandma's grave, and Tammy thought that if she could look out of Heaven and see Pete sitting down in her rocking chair, she would be pleased to have him here. Tammy sat on the ground at his feet, her hands clasped around her knees and looked out over the wide bright water and the low-lying far Louisiana shore. "Peaceful, ain't it?" she said.

He was silent a long time, then he said, "Why can't I feel like this all the time? Is it the river—or is it you?" He looked down at her, smiling a little.

Tammy hid her face against her knees. After a while she said, "I know how it is with you, Pete. You feel for people—that's why they can pull you this way and that. And when you love them—

and you can't go their way—it hurts you. See yonder driftwood out in the river?"

"I see it."

"You're kind of like that, Pete, with the current pulling one way and the eddy going another. You're caught in the ways of the water."

"Am I driftwood?"

"Till you come out of puzzling and take up your life, I reckon that's what you are, Pete." She turned, trying to read his face to see if he was mad with her for speaking it out.

But he couldn't be, for after a moment he said, "You see, Tammy, I've been feeling I ought to find something special, something . . . big. Because this is three times now that my life has been saved, when others weren't. It makes me stop and think. That's what I've been doing—just thinking. Twice in the war, and once here, it's happened."

"Seems like the Lord has a reason—is that what you mean?"

"That's one way of putting it, yes."

"Seems like you ought to do something important?"

Pete nodded.

Tammy chewed on a grass stem. "Out in the world there is a lot of people, and just a few of them do really big things. I reckon, if they're good things, the Lord told them what to do."

"Nobody's told me anything to do." Pete smiled down at her ruefully.

"Then maybe, Pete, maybe——"

"Maybe what?"

"Maybe what you do isn't so important as how you do it. That depends on how you are, inside yourself. That's how you can be big as the biggest. It's how you come out even with them."

Pete leaned down and tweaked her hair. "You're a funny one Tammy—so wise and yet——"

Tammy rose, turning her head away to hide the sudden trembling of her lips. When Pete spoke that way—— Oh, that wasn't the way she wanted him to feel about her! "I'm not so funny as you think," she said in a choked, small voice. And then, to cover it, she added quickly, "I've got a longing for the sight of Grandpa. It's seeing the river and all, I reckon. And it might be far to where he is."

"Of course, Tammy." He got up quickly. "I've just been thinking about myself. I think about myself entirely too much." He took one arm of the chair and Tammy the other, and so they went slowly down the glen and across the bayou and back to the road and the car.

After they had driven away beyond the bridge, they came out into a paved highway. Pete's car went as fast as Ernie's now, but the rattle in its bones, the creak in its joints, made a noise that drowned out all talk. They topped a rise and Pete shouted, "This is Forestville ahead."

A church steeple and some chimneys rose from a sea of green treetops, a gray water tower with the town's name on it stood higher yet. They sped down the slope and turned into the main street of the town, passing houses and lawns and people and cars. "You know where the jail is, Pete?" Tammy called above the noise of the car. She thought it might be a place of high walls and barred windows and great iron gates.

Pete slowed close by the side of the road. "I'll soon find out." He called to a man walking on the green grass in front of a house, "Say, can you tell me where the jail is?"

"What's the matter, Bud? Going to give yourself up?" He sauntered to the side of the car.

Pete laughed. "Just looking up a friend."

"Well, we got the nicest little jail in the county. Go to the blinker and turn right. You'll see the jail on the far corner two blocks down. Ivy all over it. You can't miss it."

Pete thanked him and they drove on, coming soon to a green lawn and an ivy-covered building set back from the street. The bars were twined with ivy. "It really is a pretty jail," Tammy said. "I thought he was just fooling. You reckon they'll let us see Grandpa?"

"Sure they will," Pete said.

They mounted three steps and went in by an open door. There was a bare long hall and at the left, a room with the door ajar. "I'd better see the jailer," Pete said.

The room was empty. There was only a bench and a chair with no legs where legs ought to be, though coming down from the center of the seat was an iron piece that ended in legs. It sat before a desk with several empty soft-drink bottles and some papers on it.

"Now that's a curious thing," Tammy said. "A jail and nobody keeping it and nobody kept."

"But there must be. Come on, let's see." Pete drew her with him down the hall. They passed a stairway and went on to a closed door at the end. Pete tried the handle and it turned.

"Listen," Tammy whispered. "Don't you hear? It's Grandpa and he's apreaching. That's his preaching voice. Open it easy."

Pete swung the door gently on its hinges. There was a little passageway and then a barred gate through which they could see into the middle of the jail. It was a courtyard, with barred balconies all around, upstairs and down, with all the gates swung wide and the people of the jail come down to hear Grandpa. He was off to the side, standing on a big goods box and preaching for all he was worth. The sound of his voice rose now and filled the high space overhead and came nigh to shaking the walls.

"He's agoing great," Tammy whispered, almost choking on the words because it was so good to see him. They stood back a little, watching and listening.

". . . and here I be," Grandpa was shouting, "here I be, a voice come out of the wilderness, a cry come forth from the swamp, a holler off the riverbank, and apreaching on the text, 'The great day of His wrath has come and who shall be able to stand?' And I'm nigh on to the end of my sermon, so keep yourselves harking and hold your peace."

"He's seen us," Tammy said. "He's asaying that to us."

Pete nodded and Grandpa went on, "For I'm atelling you that there's many a man that walks the earth, free to come and go, who's jailed up as much as any of you, and all by reason of this fear that's come upon him. He's bound and gagged and plumb hog-tied with the fears of civilization. Not that I'm agin civilization, but it's got off on the wrong foot and brought the world to a pretty pass. Man's so afeard that all he talks about is security."

Pete folded his arms and leaned against the wall, listening. It did Tammy good to see how he was listening to Grandpa.

"Now there's two kinds of knowledge come to man," Grandpa went on. "One's here—" he tapped the Bible in his hand—"and one's by way of man's figgering in his mind. They call that reason, and in these latter days it has led to science. But the Good Book calls it eating of the tree of knowledge.

"Now I come up out of the swamps and out from my sojourn on the river waters, and I look around at mankind and I see he's done cast aside the Word and taken up altogether with reason. Now the Lord let man eat of the tree, and we got a right to seek knowledge. But in these times it's led us astray, it's set us lopsided instead of upright and that's how-come we're nigh onto the second fall of man. The great day of His wrath hath come and who shall be able to stand?

"Man's give himself colic with eating too much of one fruit of the tree of knowledge and too little of another. He's unbalanced his diet and come near unbalancing his mind. It's no wonder he's apalsied with fear. He's et too free of science and too sparingly of brotherly love. He's got inflammation of the liver from too high living and too low thinking, and the softness of his comforts has give him softening of the brain. The kind of gas he's got on his stomach is a deadly and explosive kind, because it comes from the atom bomb. He's got water on the knee from lack of bending it, and now his head's asplitting with a headache like nobody's business, since he split the atom apart.

"I tell you, man is in a sorry state and it looks like the Lord's about give up on him and said, Just go on and blow yourself up, you dern fool. Yessir, there ain't but one hope left for man, and that's to see with his reasoning mind how he's got off his feed, and how he'd better search out the good fruit growing on the tree of knowledge. He's got to purge himself of the pizens of hate and envy and greed. He's got to eat of the bread of humility and drink deep of the milk of human kindness."

He mopped his forehead with his handkerchief and there was a little stirring among the men who sat listening. A few looked around toward Tammy and Pete, but mostly they waited for Grandpa to go on.

"Now I been listening to you all." Grandpa searched their faces with his narrowed blue eyes. "I been harkening and holding converse with one and another. This man says, 'I had hard luck.' Another says, 'I growed up in bad circumstances,' and another says, 'It ain't my fault, it's the system of government that done me wrong.' And another sets back and says he's the common man and this-here's the age of the common man and if he don't get his share, he's going to take it. I tell you it ain't nobody but himself's responsible for a man's being low-down and mean and common. And a man that goes around whining and putting the blame on somethin' outside himself ain't fit to be called a man. He's done lost his human dignity and how in this day of wrath is he going to be able to stand? I tell you can't nobody outside yourself make you secure. You got to start inside and work out, and when you stand on your own feet, then the Lord is your right hand, pointing out the way; then the Lord is your shield and your buckler, of whom shall ye be afraid?

"You tell me you got things pressing in on you, this side and that side. You say you're about fit to be tied, with it all. Well, I tell you that's all right. When the pressure gets too high like the steam in the boiler, it'll find the way out. It won't be far off either.

The way is always close to hand, only many's the time a man's too big a fool to see what's in front of his nose."

Grandpa changed his tone and Tammy whispered, "He's awinding up now." Pete nodded.

"You needn't think the atom bomb's new. The Lord's been knowing about it all along. Next time I'm going to preach to you on Sodom, Gomorrah and the atom bomb. Now let us pray."

There was a rustling and a stirring as the men bowed their heads. "Lord," Grandpa said, "let us go back into our places, into our small locked cells, with no fear in our hearts but the fear of the Lord that makes us strong and free, that gives us back our human dignity and sets us firm on the unshaken firmament! Amen."

"I reckon he's done now," Tammy whispered.

But Grandpa was not quite done yet. "Now," he said, "let every man shake the hand of the man on his right before he goes, because brotherly love has got to begin sometime and it might as well be now."

Pete took Tammy's hand, smiling down at her. Grandpa stood still and waited till the men had shaken hands and passed in orderly line, going back each one through his open gate and closing it behind him. Grandpa did not go into any cell. With his Bible under his arm, he came toward them, unlocked the big gate with a key from his pocket. He shut it behind him and, blinking, took Tammy in his arms. He shook Pete's hand hard to make up for not having any words for a moment. Then he said, "Let's come into the front office and let me sit down and look at you. I'm fair weak in my knees for joy."

"You don't seem to be shut-up and closed in, Grandpa. How can that be?" Tammy marveled.

"It looks to me as if you're the jailer," Pete said.

"Well—" Grandpa sat down in the chair before the desk and turned to show how it turned, and so that he might see them sitting side by side on the bench—"in a manner of speaking, I am the jailer. The real one, a mighty nice fellow, likes to get out for a drive with his folks on a Sunday and he's got into the way of leaving me in charge whilst he's away. We have our service and it gives the men something to think about when they have to go back into their cells. Yessir, they tell me that they often ponder on the things I preach about. Makes me feel that the Lord does indeed move in a mysterious way, his wonders to perform."

"And how's your rheumatism, Grandpa?"

While Grandpa was telling about his rheumatism, Pete got up and began walking around the room, looking at the bars across the window, coming back to the desk behind Grandpa and then just walking about, eyes on the floor. He might be listening with one ear, Tammy thought, but the other was sure attending to something else. When Grandpa finished, saying, "I'm that spry, honey, you'd think my joints was greased," Pete said he was mighty glad to hear it. Then he said he thought he'd better get some gas for the car and that he'd be back in a little.

Tammy looked after him uneasily. Grandpa kept on talking but she couldn't take her mind off Pete for a minute.

"Looks like he's kind of edgy and wound-up," Grandpa said at last.

"Yes," Tammy said on a long breath.

"Likely as not my sermon got him to thinking. It takes a man that way sometimes when he's troubled in his mind."

"That's what he is, Grandpa."

"Well, honey, just give him time. Pete's a man got power. You can feel it. And like I was saying, when the pressure gets too high to bear, he'll find a way, and likely close to hand."

"You reckon, Grandpa?"

He nodded. "I ain't got a doubt of it. Now you tell me what-all you been doing, child."

"Me?" Tammy smiled. "I feel like I been on a long journey

out into the world, a pilgrimage, finding out about things and inventions and people in the midst of them."

"If you've found out all about people, you're doing well, honey."

"I've found out a little. The trouble is—" she leaned forward, clasping her hands tight around her knees—"people, they got so many notions and ways and cunning devices so they say one thing and underneath they're saying another. They got as many layers to them as an onion."

Grandpa nodded. "You're learning, child." Then, hearing Pete's step in the hall, he said, "You got a lot to be thankful for, having such a good place to stay." He turned to Pete. "I hope she's been making herself useful."

"She has indeed." He smiled at Tammy and sat down on the bench beside her.

Grandpa studied him awhile. "It's kind of you to be looking out for her so well. It's much appreciated, I tell you. Does your aunt that lives with you take to her?"

"She does that. Aunt Renie really needs somebody in the house with her, especially after the next two weeks when my father and mother will be going back to town."

"I see," Grandpa said. "I see."

"Now, Mr. Dinwoodie," Pete said, "I believe I might be able to use some influence about getting you out of here. My father, and some friends of his . . ." He hesitated.

Grandpa looked from him to Tammy and then out the high window, and after a moment he shook his head. "I thank you just the same, Pete. But I don't believe in the shortening of judgment nor the easing of the penance. Not that I got my judgment yet. Case won't be called till next week or so. But the way I feel, the Lord's put me here for a purpose and I mean to fulfill it. Besides, my rheumatism is easing something miraculous, and they feed me fine. I got every convenience, not to say luxury, and I wouldn't turn a hand to budge out of the place—unless you're getting tired of Tammy here."

"That's impossible," Pete said. "Why, Tammy—she's like a little sister to me. You don't know what a help she is."

Grandpa nodded slowly. "I see," he said with a kind of sadness in his tone. "I see. Well, it's all in the Lord's hands."

Then Peter said they'd better go. Clouds were blowing up. "Looks as if there might be something brewing in the weather line, it's got so muggy all of a sudden."

As they drove away, Tammy looked back at the vine-covered jail set back on its green lawn. "It sure is a pretty jail, Pete. And you know, it looks to me like Grandpa's mighty pleased with it."

"Well, he didn't seem too anxious to be bailed out or pardoned, that's a fact."

"Looked to me like he was holding back the real reason, the way he stopped a minute before he answered you. Maybe——"

"Maybe what?"

"Nothing," Tammy said, keeping her thought to herself. "But he's got a long head on him, Grandpa has."

16.

AFTER the tramp through the swamp, after the long drive, Tammy slept hard and deep. Once in the night the sound of rain roused her just enough to think of Pete's tomatoes, drinking it thirstily. It was much later that she was vaguely aware of hurrying steps overhead. But it was the knocking that brought her sharply awake to fling the night from her, lips parting to call that she was coming.

The knocking was not at the door. It was a sparse, strange tapping at the windowpane, a scratching and whispering along the outside wall of the house, on leaf and earth. Cool clean air came to her, rarely pure. Tammy sprang out of bed and ran to the open window. The sound was everywhere, a thousand footfalls in the thin dark. "Goshamighty!" Tammy cried as the strokes on the windowpane grew louder and white balls danced on the sill. "Pete's tomatoes!" The hail stones bounded on the grass, catching the faint morning light. They were quickly driven by the wind into small white drifts and eddies. They struck everywhere, cruel and hard. A rain of leaves fell with them, severed from the oak. No small green tender thing could live through their terrible cutting.

Tammy tore off her gown, snatched up her dress, diving into it, buttoning it as she stumbled through the dark room, across the passageway and down the ell gallery. In the garden her foot slipped on a heap of hailstones, but she caught herself and ran on, not feeling the cold underfoot, knowing only that the fall had ceased as suddenly as it had come.

In the kitchen garden, the lettuce was flat, the beans were stripped and beaten, but she gave them only a glance as she ran down the muddy row. Ahead—she strained her eyes to see—the plants that Pete had put out early stood no longer brave and fine. There was only a muddied green carpet where they had been. In a moment, in a twinkling, they had been cut down. But the cold frames —surely that was what they were for, to guard the young plants. That was why the cloth cover was spread each night and fastened down. Tammy stopped short before the nearest one. Beaten and torn, thin cloth trembled along the sides of the frame and hail lay in heaps, weighing down, muddying the rest of it amid the crushed green of the plants. She dropped on her knees and began scooping away the hail, flinging it furiously aside.

"No use, Tammy. They're done for."

She sprang to her feet and saw Pete sitting on a stump at the edge of the field, bent over, elbows on knees, as if he too were crushed and beaten down by the hail. She caught her breath in a sob and looked up at the brightening sky and the innocent pink of sunrise clouds. "Oh, Pete," she cried, "why did it have to come like this, why—?"

"It just did." Pete's voice was as flat and hopeless as the little green things. He came to her and patted her shoulder. "Never mind, Tammy. I'm slow at figuring things out, but this is plain enough for even me to understand." He drew a long breath. "In a way it's a relief, to get it all settled."

"No, no, Pete." She turned and bent to jerk away the broken cloth, flinging the strips aside. "There must be some left. There's bound to be. See." But there were only a pitiful few, standing close against the boards of the frame, tucked away in the corners. She ran to the next cold frame, whispering under her breath, saying, "O God, let there be some! He's got to have some." The hope was a raw ache inside her. Pete followed and watched as here too she snatched away the cover.

Maybe there were a few more here, but pitifully few that had survived. Tammy straightened slowly, hands limp at her sides.

She had thought to hearten him and she had only shown him how complete his ruin was. Her breath caught in a dry sob and she began to shiver, the chill of the early morning going through her sharp and merciless. Then she felt Pete's arms around her, felt him draw her close, and with her face hid against him, she got out the choking words, "I wanted you to have them. I wanted you to have all the tomatoes in the world!"

He stroked her hair. "Bless you, Tammy." The bleak stricken tone had gone from his voice. "You're cold," he said with tenderness.

In the midst of her shivering, she felt the warmth of his body against her, spreading through her, purely sweet and keener than the hurt, dissolving it. Must be the Lord had arranged a man and woman so, that they could find comfort in their misery, strength to go on. Strength? She felt it, pouring into her. She flung back her head, caught Pete by the shoulder and shook him hard. "Don't give up, Pete! You got to fight back. Don't you see—when the Lord slaps you down, you got to rise up. That's the only way you can sass Him back." She flung away from him and dropping to her knees began gathering up the best of the plants, handing them up to him. "Here—come on, take them, set them out. The field's all ready and waiting. They'll grow, they got to grow."

"By heavens, Tammy," Pete said, taking the handful she held out to him and moving toward the furrowed line, "you'd put heart into a turnip."

"I ain't considering turnips; it's tomatoes I'm heartening." She filled her skirt with plants and ran ahead of him, bending to lay them spaced along the row for his setting-out. Some of them wouldn't know the difference, others might weather the beating they had had. They were going to have a chance to live. "If they've got any guts, they'll make out," Tammy called back over her shoulder as she went ahead with another lapful. And again, bending to set down a plant, moving on and bending again, she shouted, "The sun's coming to warm them." And starting a new row, she stood with her feet planted far apart, straddling it, and called to him how she'd heard tell that hail did wonders for the ground, and he'd better make his stakes stout to hold a mighty crop.

After a while old Prater came, shaking his head and mumbling about how the Lord giveth and the Lord taketh away. But after a moment he shuffled over to another one of the cold frames and began sorting out the broken plants from the whole. Then Steve and Lena, knowing untold the urgency, joined them, and they worked all together, drawn close by disaster, to salvage what they could before the warm sun should wither the plants.

When Tammy straightened once to rest her back, she looked round and saw how they were strung out in a row across the field under the wide pale sky. "Seems like it's a line, a long line, Pete, going back beyond the time of knowing, a line of all the people ever wrestled with the earth, to get a living from it. I can nigh on to make them out behind us yonder, Pete. You don't feel so odd and lone and weak when you know you're one of a line."

Pete looked at her with a kind of wonder in his face, then bent again doggedly to his task, and they all worked on while the sun mounted higher in the sky. At last he said, looking the field over, "It's more than I hoped for." Turning to Tammy he told her she'd done enough, she'd better get back to the house because after all the Pilgrimage would begin today. He put his hands on his hips and looked at her and smiled, and that was better than any spoken thanks could be.

The Pilgrimage, Tammy thought, going past the sweet olive trees and along the brick walk to the ell steps. She'd plumb forgot that this was the day when people would stroll through the yard and the gardens and come through the house to look and hear its story and the manner of its living these hundred years and more. This was the day—she had to keep telling herself as she washed and put on fresh clean clothes—the day when all things were to be spread out for strangers, come from far parts, to read and marvel at. Even this little room, which she must remember to make neat and straight, would have people walking through it because of Miss Renie's painting on the walls. It was one of the wonders of the Pilgrimage and once had had a piece in the paper about it.

She rinsed out her muddy dress and hung it out of sight behind Miss Renie's painting rack. Then she went toward the sound of voices in the back hall.

"Oh, there you are at last, Tammy," Mrs. Brent cried. "I called and called you but you didn't come."

Miss Renie, coming down the hall with a painting in each hand, said, "She's been out helping with the tomatoes. Have you forgotten already that the hail wiped out——"

"I haven't forgotten anything, Aunt Renie—how could I when I've had nobody to help around the house all morning? There's no use trying to gather up spilt milk and it may be all for the best in the long run, sorry as I am." She turned to Tammy again. "It's not a girl's place to be out in the field working alongside Negroes. I should think you'd have more pride than that."

"I was proud to be aworking with them, helping Pete." Tammy's eyes flashed.

Miss Renie, going on to the porch, let out a wicked chuckle, the way she always did when anybody stood up to Mrs. Brent. Like night before last when Pete insisted on her promising not to put ribbons across the doorways to keep the pilgrims outside—like it was a museum, he said. He had made her agree to serve ice water to them too, and Mrs. Brent had given in meek as anything.

Now she just said, "Oh, dear me," and brushed a lock of her reddish-brown hair with the back of her hand and sighed heavily. "Oh, Tammy, if you'd just help me and not talk! This rug—take hold and help turn it, so the hole will be under the sofa."

Miss Renie came back with two more paintings which she carried on into the front parlor, murmuring something about having to get the light right so when Mr. Fernan saw them——

Tammy had just got the rug to Mrs. Brent's liking when there was a wrenching sound in the parlor and a crash. When they rushed one behind the other to see what had happened, Miss Renie turned around with impatience. "Nothing's wrong, Ena. I'm just trying to get this shutter open to let in some light from that side and——"

"Aunt Renie, please. Will you leave that shutter closed?"

"Dear me," Miss Renie said. "After all the to-do about having them open, now you——"

"It's just this, Aunt Renie," Mrs. Brent said and the way she was holding on to her temper made Tammy feel for her. "Those curtains went to ribbons when Steve shook them, and I can't have people seeing—— Oh, don't you know if things look too shabby, we'll be taken off the Pilgrimage list and then where'll the tax money come from?"

Miss Renie went on looking at her paintings, shifting them this way and that, saying nothing. After a moment Mrs. Brent turned to Tammy and said in her usual tone, "You did the books so nicely in the library, Tammy. But the chairs and the table are still to be dusted."

"I'll do them right now, Mrs. Brent," Tammy said and ran for the dustcloths. But even hurrying so, she heard Mrs. Brent say, "That girl—sometimes she is so provoking, and then again——"

In the library Professor Brent was reading as usual. It was a wonder, Tammy thought, how everything was going on just the same, as if there'd been no hail come out of the sky at daybreak. He said now, "I suppose all the fuss and feathers are proceeding as per schedule, Tammy?"

"There's plenty of proceeding going on. Looks like Miss Renie will be changing pictures right up to the last minute, account of Mr. Fernan's coming."

"Mr. Fernan, yes. I hope for all our sakes that he comes up to expectations." He opened his book, but Tammy, trying to get the dust from the carved legs of the table beside him, noticed that he did not turn any pages. After a minute he laid the book on the arm of the chair. His fingers rapped on it with a worried little tapping sound. "Tammy," he said, "how did he take it?"

She knew what he meant, and she saw now how it was that Mrs. Brent had been so vinegary. They were both worried sick. "He's taking it all right."

Professor Brent drew a long breath. "I hope so. You don't know what we've been through, Tammy. I don't mean just this tomato disaster, but ever since he got home from the war, so taut and tense, with this terrible indecision."

Tammy sat back on her heels and looked up at him in wonder. "I seen it in Pete, but I didn't know you all did."

Professor Brent got up and began walking back and forth, hands clasped behind his back. "Of course we knew he was in the plane crash . . . though we didn't hear till after he was recovering from pneumonia and perfectly safe. Then we didn't know what to do. He'd said so . . . so violently that he wanted to get away, by himself, go west. He hadn't let us know about the accident, so I said we must wait. But his mother . . . I hope I never have to go through another such time."

"I didn't know," Tammy murmured.

"That's why . . . this hail . . . I'm so concerned to know——"

"He's taking it all right, I reckon," Tammy said again, wishing there was more she could tell him. "I think it might be it will help him make up his mind."

He turned on her quickly, whipping off his glasses to study her. "You think so?"

Tammy nodded. "He just said, well, that settled it."

"If it does, I'd be glad of the hail, much as he needs the money. It doesn't matter really what he decides on. Though his mother . . . has ideas, and I think he ought to take advantage of the government help and go back for another degree."

"Grandpa says he's got power. Says it's dammed up, but when the strain gets more than he can bear, it'll find the way. All ready to hand, he said it would be."

"What did he mean by that?"

"I don't know exactly. Grandpa has a way of going on from this to that, and might be he was talking more about the world and how it is confused and afraid and how when it is fit to blow up, then it'll see the way that's been under its nose all the time."

"Well," Professor Brent said, "patience—we'll have to wait and see." He came back to his chair as Mrs. Brent bustled in with two bowls of red japonicas.

"These were down underneath the leaves and escaped the hail." She tried them on the table, then on the mantel and again on the table. "I cannot get my mind on what I am doing," she complained. "Osia's being so difficult about wearing a bandanna. I don't know what I'm going to do with her. If I hadn't been right there she would have burned a hole in Barbara's dress. She just stood there with the iron resting on the front of the blouse."

"Why is it necessary for Osia to press Barbara's dress?" Professor Brent inquired.

"Barbara will get here at the last minute, Joel, you know that, and she'll have no time. I have to see to everything. Are you nearly through, Tammy?"

"In a minute," Tammy said.

Miss Renie came to the door with a picture in her hand. "Roots is so talented. I would like to put this one in a prominent place."

"Please, Aunt Renie—it is out of key with the period."

"It should be in a place of honor, but I will consent to having it up there with Shakespeare, if you feel that way about it. Tammy, will you run up the ladder and set it there?"

"It is sure a curious one," Tammy said, when she had placed the picture to Miss Renie's liking. "It's a pity you can't tell what it is."

"Perfectly clear," Miss Renie said. "Symbolic, and really interesting. He calls it 'Eel Eating Violets.' Remarkable composition."

"Why does the eel eat violets?" Professor Brent asked.

"That's what makes it interesting." Miss Renie stopped looking at the painting and turned her narrowed gaze on Tammy, who was still studying the picture with wonder. "What is Tammy going to wear?"

"Tammy?" Mrs. Brent set down the bowl of roses with a small bang. "Why, she doesn't need to wear anything—I mean, she doesn't have to appear. She will be helping Osia keep the water pitchers filled. That's going to be quite important." She gave Tammy a brief smile.

Miss Renie snorted. "Of course she has to appear. I don't know why this hasn't been thought of sooner. She ought to serve the ice water."

"Peter is going to see to that."

"Pete must be at the front door, Ena. After all, this is to be his house when I go on. It is his place to invite the guests in. I don't know what you are thinking of, Ena."

"Well, Tammy has no costume," Mrs. Brent said with finality. "So it's quite impossible. I won't have my arrangements upset by any last minute makeshifts. It would ruin the artistic effect, Aunt Renie. You should know that."

"Art is truth," Miss Renie said haughtily. "I have a costume for Tammy. One that would fit her very well. Come, Tammy, I'll get it out for you. It probably needs pressing."

"Aunt Renie! What are you planning? Oh, haven't I got enough to worry me without——"

"I'm not planning anything, except to have Tammy properly dressed. I have my grandmother's gray dress she wore all the way here when they came by ox team from Virginia."

"Aunt Renie, you wouldn't! That unsightly old thing! That calico fright—and besides I always thought your grandmother came from Virginia in the family barouche, drawn by two blooded horses. Joel, you know—surely you must know how your own grandmother came."

Professor Brent looked up from his book. "My dear, the steps by which historical fact is transmuted into myth are many and varied. It is often difficult to lift the veil of antiquity and separate truth from legend or mark the exact moment when the one passed into the other. There are many classical examples."

"Meanwhile," Miss Renie said, "you come with me, Tammy, and I will find the dress."

Tammy stood hesitating, looking from Miss Renie to Mrs. Brent, undecided which one to mind. "Looks like I'm kind of ground between two wheels," she said and turned her head away so they would not see how terribly she wanted to be dressed like the rest.

Professor Brent settled the matter. "The prospect of seeing you made into hamburger distresses me, Tammy. By all means go with Aunt Renie and get the dress in order for the Pilgrimage. It will be interesting to confront romance and myth with simple fact."

Miss Renie beckoned and Tammy followed before Mrs. Brent regained her power of speech.

In Miss Renie's room, they pulled the little hair trunk that was like Grandma's from under the bed. Miss Renie lifted the lid and took out the dress. It was gray calico with sprigs of pale purple flowers, black-centered, small and scattered far apart. "It's a lovely dress," Tammy whispered and pure delight spread through her.

"Just your size, I'll warrant." Miss Renie held it up to Tammy. It had a plain front with a seam down the middle and it came up to a tiny standing collar. The sleeves were wide at the hand. Miss Renie laid it on the bed with the wide full skirt spread out. The back of the waist had tiny buttons down it.

"There's a white standing collar, sort of a dickey—" Miss Renie rummaged in the trunk till she found it—"a bit yellowed with age, but all the more becoming. It's linen." She laid it down beside the dress. "You must do your hair like the portrait."

"Which one?"

"There in the corner. Ena won't have it in the hall or the parlor with the others. Not glamorous enough. But it's Grandmother Cratcher just the same, and she walked barefoot beside the wagon from Virginia, and her father was murdered on the way by a bandit. She came to the house to sell eggs—that's how my grandfather saw her first, if you want to know the truth."

Tammy studied the portrait. It showed an elderly woman with a wide, flat face. A plain woman with her head held high. "What's that in her hair?"

"Oh, yes, I must find that for you. It's a comb." Miss Renie went to search through the trunk again. "You must do your hair like that—parted in the middle and smoothed back, showing your ears. Let the figure-eight knot start low and come up high, so that when you get the comb in—here it is—the comb will show from the front. See how it's done?"

"Oh, yes, Miss Renie, I know I can do it." Tammy was breathless with excitement.

Miss Renie held up the comb for her to see. "Carved bone. My grandfather made it for her. He could make anything with his hands. Pete takes after him in that." She laid the comb on the bed and it was delicate as gray lace against the creamy spread. "Come in when you're dressed and I'll put it in your hair. Now I suppose I'll have to array myself like the lilies or something. At least my costume is artistic."

"I reckon anything you have is bound to be that."

"Well, I made it myself, batiked my own design—you'll see. Run along now."

"Thank you, Miss Renie," Tammy said, her eyes shining. "I'll go iron the dress now whilst the irons are hot."

"Wait a minute. Take these hairpins for your hair. And here's the sunbonnet that matches the dress. Press it too. Ena will have a tantrum." She chuckled to herself. Tammy could hear her as she went down the hall.

"Osia, Osia," Tammy cried, whirling into the kitchen with the dress held up before her, "I'm agoing to be costumed like the rest of them!"

Osia looked up from the ironing board, standing the iron on its tail. "Reckon you got as good right as any of 'em to be all got up. But it's a kind of plain dress you got there, ain't it?"

Tammy stopped short in her prancing, seeing now the dress Osia had just finished pressing. It lay like a delicate pink cloud across the ironing board. Barbara's dress. It was all ruffles, top to hem, and there wasn't much top to it. Where the sleeves ought to be, there was no more than puffed-up ruffle looping round. It shone and glistened in the light. It must be pure silk for sure. It was the most beautiful dress in the world.

"I'll go spread this-here on the bed in the room Miss Barbara gwine dress herself in, then I'll come iron yourn, Miss Tammy."

Tammy looked down at the dress in her arms. How drab and dull it was, and plain, as even Osia could see! "I'll do it, thank you, Osia," she said soberly.

But as she ironed away on the wide skirt that spread over the ironing board and looped down to the floor, she got back her satisfaction in it. When Osia came, she told her with only a faint, small sigh, "I reckon this-here suits me better'n something fancy. I reckon I ain't a fancy person, and it wouldn't be no use putting on."

"Naw'm," Osia agreed, "you ain't fancy, Miss Tammy. You ain't neither silk nor satin, but you's pure one hundred percent whatever you is. Now you gimme that iron. I done ironed everybody's else's clothes and I don't grudge doing yourn. Besides, seems to me like you ain't had no food in your stomach this day. Even Mr. Pete took a sandwich and some coffee upstairs when he went up to his room a while ago. Umm-mm, pore Mr. Pete! I declare, look like trouble pursue him and seek him out."

Tammy poured herself some coffee and took one of the sandwiches Osia had made and set aside under a damp white napkin. She stood by the door, looking over the kitchen garden to the field. "He'll maybe get his money back on them, won't he, Osia?"

"Yassum, by the look of the field, I reckon he'll do that. I just hope this won't onsettle Steve again. He was counting on them tomatoes, too. Mr. Pete promised him a good share—that's how-come he got him to stay on last time he set his head on going."

With a sigh Tammy set aside her coffee cup and came back to the ironing board. "You sit and rest yourself, Osia. You've done a sight of work today."

"I done that." Osia sat down on the chaise longue and kicked off her shoes. "But what got me down is that there slavetime bandanna Mrs. Brent done brought me to put on my head." She jerked a thumb toward the red kerchief that hung over a chair back.

"It's just that everybody's going back into old times, Osia, dressing up like other days. That's what we're all doing."

"Don't make sense to me."

"It don't make much sense, for a fact, Osia." Tammy ironed on in silence for a while. "On the other hand, it might be good to look back once a year like this and see how far you come. Seems to me you come a long piece since slavery times, Osia. Look how you got all your children up in the world, full of learning and knowing how to get a living, independent and not looking to no-body, and Roots selling a picture to a big New York man."

Osia was silent a long time. Then she said, "Yessum, I reckon I gets your drift." She got up and crossed the room to take up the bandanna and hold it out in her hand, turning it this way and that. "It's a real pretty red," she said, accepting it. She smoothed it out and laid it over the chair. "Now I better get the rest of them sand-wiches made for you all's dinner. Mrs. Brent say everybody got to eat hand to mouth today on account of the folks coming and we ain't got much time, account of the first day being the worst."

Tammy was glad when she could go into her room and shut the door and begin to get ready. The dress lay spread wide across her bed, the bonnet beside it, and the collar a little apart. Her hands trembled with eagerness as she bathed and put on clean under-clothes. She brushed her dark hair till it was smooth and shining.

Then she drew it back, leaving her ears bare. It gave her a start to see how she looked when she got it done. "I never knowed I took so after Grandma," she said. There was something surprising about her ears, too. She couldn't make out what it was. Her eyes looked bigger than they should and her eyebrows straighter and blacker than usual. The knot, starting low on her neck and running up like the portrait's, seemed firm and solid. But she didn't want it dropping down, so she put in another hairpin for luck and turned to get the dress. Now, at last, she was going to be costumed.

The dress went on easy, but it came together by the hardest. She could just hook the hook at the waist in the back. Miss Renie would have to do the buttons. The white collar came up neat around her neck and the gray collar rose part way on that. She sure was closed up, but it might be she was more easy that way than she would be all open, like Barbara was going to be. She went barefooted across the passage to Miss Renie's room, and when she saw Miss Renie she caught her breath. "Miss Renie! You look . . . you look like the Queen of Sheba! Only I reckon she never had a dress like that."

Miss Renie turned from the harp-shaped mirror above her bureau, her long black-and-gold earrings flashing in the light. Her basque was black as her eyes, with a stiff black ruff standing up behind her neck, after the fashion of a queen. The full black skirt was spread out in a stiff round, held out by hoops to show the border of tortoise-shell cats that walked, life-size and proud, their tails curving this way and that in a kind of rhythm.

"I reckon there never was such a dress in the history of the world," Tammy said.

"There wasn't. Designed it myself." She held out her arms to show the yellow cat on each wide-flowing sleeve. "I have to have a little fun," she added and turned Tammy about to pull her dress up and fasten the buttons in the back.

Tammy held her breath so the buttons would go into their holes. "I better not eat with this on," she said.

"You have to expect to make some sacrifice for beauty. Now turn around and let me see you." She stood back with her hands clasped before her and her eyes half closed.

Tammy turned all the way around, and Miss Renie said nothing, so she turned again. It must be the dress made her mighty plain, or surely she would say something.

"Your lines. I never would have suspected it in those baggy things you've been wearing. Your ears, too—never cover them again. Oh, yes, the comb." She found it on the bed and placed it just above the knot of Tammy's dark hair. It felt like a hat sitting there, with its teeth clamped onto her head. "Now," Miss Renie said, "a little lipstick—not too much. Hold your mouth still. Do your lips so." Again Miss Renie stepped back and looked at her. "Amazing."

"Do I look . . . all right?"

"Here, see yourself." She drew her to the mirror. "What do you think?"

"It . . . it is a stranger! It is a picture of somebody else." She lifted her hands, moving them to make sure of herself. "No, it's me." Her eyes followed the line of the waist down and she put her arms quickly over her breast, turning away.

"What's the matter?"

"I never seen my figger so plain out to be seen. Is it . . . is it decent?"

Miss Renie laughed. "It's charming."

Tammy turned to her again. "Do I look growed?"

"You definitely look grown. Grown is the word."

"Am I—" her voice sank, but she had to know—"am I pretty?"

Miss Renie gave a terrible snort. "Pretty! Don't insult yourself. You have great distinction. That is much better. Pretty indeed! You have dignity." Miss Renie went to her bureau drawer and got out a gold necklace and fastened it around her long thin neck. It hung down in a tasseled square, black-figured like the earrings.

Tammy stood motionless, thinking about Pete. Would he like distinction? Would he like dignity? Then she heard Barbara's laugh and her quick steps running through the hall toward the room where her beautiful dress was waiting. "I'll be dressed in a minute, Pete, in no time flat." And Pete answered, "It would be a miracle—but you almost make me believe in miracles."

Then Barbara said, "I suppose the hail got your tomatoes the way it did everybody else's around here."

"Yep. They're about done for."

"Well—" Tammy could almost see her shrug her shoulders as she said it—"luckily there are other things you can do in the world."

"So I'm beginning to see."

Then her quick steps went on. Except for missing the money, Tammy thought, she was likely pleased.

Miss Renie said, "You must have a breastpin for the front of your dress." She searched in the drawer and brought one out. It was made of black hair, finely plaited and set behind glass and bound with a silver band. Three little hair pendants hung down, silver-wrapped, like three black tears. "My grandmother Cratcher's pin, made of her father's hair. Fine as a woman's. You need no more ornament than this." She pinned it at Tammy's throat. "It is a mourning pin."

Tammy shook her head. "No. I would not wish to mourn. I've done enough of that already this day."

"Nonsense, don't be superstitious. The mourning's run out of it before this and there's only the love left in it, the silver and the black hair."

"Truly?"

"Yes. You can sing 'Black Is the Color of My Truelove's Hair.' "

"I can sing it. And my truelove's hair *is* black," Tammy said with gravity.

"Then you'd better go make hay while the sun shines. Go on out and let . . . let them see you. Find out just what Ena wants you to do. And speaking of Ena, here's the sunbonnet. Just carry it in your hand. No shoes, remember. This is going to be good."

Tammy went out by the passageway and turned into the hall. It was empty. So was the parlor, but the long mirror gave back her reflection, slender, whole and strange to her eyes, save for the look of Grandma. She went out by the big front door, her long skirts limp around her legs, and came to the front gallery. Pete was not there. Old Prater was down by the front gate. She could see his white coat through the shrubbery. Then she turned and found Pete standing in the doorway, watching her.

"Tammy," he said with wonder in his tone. His eyes had a light in them as they went over her and came back to her face.

She stood straight and proud, her hands at her sides, one hand holding her bonnet and swinging it by the strings. Pete liked the way she looked. She knew it without his saying another word and, knowing it, she had a liveliness come over her, possessing her, showing her how she might turn his mind to merriment so he would forget his loss for a while. "I come from Virginny," she said, "walking all the way, alongside the wagon, ox-drawn. I been sleeping on the ground by night and walking all the day. I come to the great house to sell fresh eggs, atoting them in my bonnet and singing, 'Black Is the Color of My Truelove's Hair.' "

"Come in," Pete said with a bow, falling in with her play. "We have need of eggs. And would you like to see the great house and what's in it, and how fine a man can live with slaves to wait on him?"

"It would pleasure me, sir, for sure," she said and put her hand in the crook of his arm when he offered it.

They came into the hall, laughing over their pretending, and

Tammy heard Professor Brent saying, "Did you hear that, Ena? Sounds authentic."

Mrs. Brent said, "Yes, I heard, but, Joel, please, will you slide that ladder back into the corner where it belongs? I don't want it here for people to trip on."

Pete, keeping to his pretending, took Tammy on a tour of the parlors, pointing out the mirrors and the carving on the sofas and the carpet under their feet. He led her to the dining room and let her see how people ate in elegance off dishes thin enough to see through, with flowers and birds painted on them. He showed her the sideboard and the silver teapot and pitcher and sugar bowl set on a silver tray. Then he took her across the hall to the library.

Mrs. Brent was still there, her golden-brown net skirts so wide they came near to filling the room. Her arms and shoulders were bare and her hair, caught up on the top of her head, fell in a cascade of curls. She was standing as close to Professor Brent as she could get with her hoops and she was saying, "And truly, Joel, are you sure you wouldn't notice my teeth?"

He bent and put a kiss on her bare shoulder. "You'll always be young and fair to me, Ena."

Pete turned to Tammy, still on his arm. "They aren't born yet, Susannah, but they don't know it."

Mrs. Brent whirled her skirts around. "Tammy——" Then she was struck dumb by the sight of her.

"Great-grandmother Cratcher, just come from Virginny to take the Pilgrimage," Pete said.

Mrs. Brent blinked her red-brown eyes. "Why . . . why . . . that dress doesn't look as disgraceful as I thought."

"Grandmother Cratcher never looked as handsome as this," Professor Brent said, "or the artist should have been slain for slander, painting her the way he did. I have——"

"Hush, Joel, I almost had an idea." Mrs. Brent cocked her head on one side and studied Tammy.

But he went on just the same: "I have often wondered why my

grandfather fell for her, as we say on the campus. Now I know. She had not the face to launch a thousand ships, but oh, her form divine!"

"Really, Joel! It's the dress. It's quaint, and actually charming."

"You mean Tammy's charming," Pete said.

Mrs. Brent seemed to notice him now for the first time. "Peter, will you please go and call to Barbara to hurry. The cars will be coming in a minute. Come, Tammy, I want to show you what you are to do. Joel, the ladder . . ."

On the ell porch, Mrs. Brent looked at the goatskin hickory chair that had come from the *Ellen B.* "That isn't right here. It will be in the way. Peter, come take it down into the garden. Put it on the brick walk on the path at the side. No, the other side—under the dining-room window."

Miss Renie came out in her wide black-and-gold gown. She waved a hand toward the garden square where a cut-glass bowl and glasses were set on a lace-covered table. "Ridiculous, Ena, having that fine lace and glass bowl. Spoils the picture. I'm amazed at you. Tammy should be dipping ice water from the old brassbound tub, dipping it out with a gourd dipper, into the earthenware cups."

For once Mrs. Brent took a suggestion. She called everyone to come quick and make the change. She even found an old red-checkered cloth with a fringe, to cover the table. Then she told Tammy how to dip and serve and where to stand on the walk. She was hurrying back along the ell porch as the sound of the first cars came from the drive, when all at once she whirled about, clapped her hands and cried, "I've got a wonderful idea."

"You haven't time for another," Miss Renie told her, straightening one of the pictures on the porch wall.

"But it's this—for Tammy." She tripped back to the top of the steps. "Listen, Tammy, I heard you talking a while ago, pretending you were somebody else. I want you to keep on being old time. Just talk naturally and you will be. Pretend you play the part of a woman out of long ago. Do you understand?"

"Be Grandmother Cratcher, that's who," Miss Renie said.

"No, no, it isn't necessary to call names—people aren't interested in that kind of thing. Just play a part, or make people think you're playing a part. Don't you understand?" She was terribly eager.

Tammy nodded. "That will be easy. I won't be shy of folks, pretending I'm someone else."

Mrs. Brent drew a long breath of relief. "An inspiration. Don't you see, Aunt Renie?" she added, hurrying toward the hall. "It will cover up grammar, everything. Really I do think I'm clever." She rapped on Barbara's door as she passed, calling, "Time, Barbara. Do hurry."

"Ena's mother was frightened by a cyclone," Miss Renie said, walking back and forth on the long gallery. "Just think, Fernan may be among those coming in the gate right now! Oh, be still, my heart."

Then Barbara came out and stood a moment for Miss Renie and Tammy to admire her. She was a dream, a vision, beautiful beyond words, Tammy thought, staring openmouthed. Barbara smiled. Her rose-pink dress ruffled into a tiny waist; it ruffled out in tier on tier, spreading wide over the hoops. Her bare arms, her white shoulders, the line of her throat—it made Tammy ache to see how lovely her body was. Barbara laughed and dropped a curtsy and Miss Renie said, "You'll pop out in the front, if you don't watch yourself."

"I'll watch," Barbara called back laughing, as she swept away toward the back hall door, her skirts jouncing, her ruffles rippling and her head high.

Tammy drew a long sigh, thinking that now Barbara was going into the front hall where Pete would see her. Then Miss Renie came to the head of the steps. "There's more art in truth than in fiction—don't ever forget that, Tammy."

Tammy shook her head. She did not want art, she just wanted Pete.

17.

TAMMY stood in the shady side garden where the brick walk widened to a square, and waited for the first pilgrims, her heart beating hard and fast. She was costumed, she was a part of the Pilgrimage, she had something important to do, and Mrs. Brent had taken back what she'd told her yesterday about not talking to anyone. With the gourd dipper she scooped up water and poured it over the block of ice in the brassbound tub, cooling it. The cups stood ready on the table, arranged neatly on the red-and-white checkered cloth with fringe hanging down low on the table legs.

She could hear the roll of cars on the drive, the slamming of car doors. Some of the guests were already in the house and more were coming every minute for Pete to welcome in by the big front door. The murmur of their talk was like the sound of bees in a blossoming locust tree. Barbara's gay voice drifted out through the dining-room windows and Tammy caught snatches of her talk—"The silver was the old judge's gift to his bride. . . . The plates came from Paris and match the dinner service in the cabinet. . . ."

Now and then Mrs. Brent's high-pitched company voice could be heard in the parlor. "Yes, the fifth generation under this roof. . . . You are now in the main part of the house, built in 1832. . . . Note the carving, done by a slave artist. . . . The furniture . . ."

Suddenly panic came over Tammy. Everyone else had something to tell. Mrs. Brent had told her how to talk, but nobody had told her what to say. Goshamighty, what could she do? She gathered her long skirts and threw them over her arm as she tore up the step to find Miss Renie. Barefoot and noiseless she sped along the ell gallery toward the back hall door. She was turning into the pass-

215

ageway when she saw Ernie alone in the hall, just outside the dining-room door. Something in his face stopped her short. What could he be looking at with that steady, serious gaze, with that longing in his eyes?

Tammy tiptoed into the hall without a sound, looked where he was looking, and saw Barbara in her lovely rose dress, lovelier than ever in the candlelit dining room. She stood by the long sideboard, showing off the silver and the dishes and herself. Tammy drew a sigh as Ernie's sadness spread out and enveloped her. She began to understand now the things that had been beneath his words that night when he and Pete had talked beside the car. It was Barbara they were fighting over, really. But Ernie didn't have a chance and, knowing that, she felt a kinship with him. The weight of his longing and her own lay heavy on her as she went through the batik-hung passageway to Miss Renie's door.

Miss Renie sat in the low rocker beside the window with her black-and-gold skirts spread like a tent around her. She was bowed over with her head in her hands so that all Tammy could see was the top of her head and the black ruff rising up at the back of her neck. "Miss Renie," she cried, "what's the matter?"

Miss Renie straightened up, showing a tragic face. She stood with dignity, took a lacy handkerchief from her bosom and wiped her eyes. "I'm not a fool," she said. "Why pretend? I know they're no good—my paintings. Now Fernan——"

"Has he come already?"

"Last night, but he went off early this morning. I saw him going, not stopping to look at my paintings as he passed. But he will, and oh, they're horrible botches——" She turned her dark eyes on Tammy. "Did you want something?" she asked with gentleness.

"I'm sorry, Miss Renie." She felt weighted and leaden from seeing the inner layers of people. Oh, when she first came to Brenton Hall she had thought them all diverse and devious enough, but she had just been walking on the surface then. Now she began to know so much that it filled her with a sadness and a pity for human beings everywhere. Then she remembered what she had come for. "I don't know what to say to people, Miss Renie, when they come to drink the ice water."

"Invent." She turned to the mirror and began to powder her nose before the looking glass. "That's what they're doing in there, with only a grain of truth to go on. So why can't you? Take Grandmother Cratcher's story and add on to it."

"You mean I could make up things, or tell one of Grandpa's old stories?"

"By all means. Just the thought of hearing one of your grandfather's tales restores my sanity. Now run back to your place. They'll be swarming out in a minute."

"Thank you, Miss Renie," Tammy cried, excitement sweeping through her. "I think your paintings are beautiful." She ran back quickly to the still empty gallery, down the steps. •

Then Ernie came out. "Hi, honey child—whew!" He whistled. "Say, you—jeepers!" He stood speechless, staring down at her.

"You like me? I'm costumed."

"And how! You're a slick chick if I ever saw one. Who'd have thought—jeepers! I'm knocked for a loop." He came down the steps, and Tammy, imitating Barbara, made him a curtsy and then filled a cup with ice water for him. "You know what, sugar?" he said.

"What?"

"I'd like to see you all diked out in glad rags as of the current season. I tell you what. If—" he bent down and rapped on the table leg—"if this one very special ship of mine comes in, we'll go to town and I'll rig you out in the latest. How about it?"

"You mean—buy me some clothes?"

"Exactly, little one."

"That would be wonderful, Ernie."

He set his empty cup down. "Too bad it's only water, and I've got to beat it. Just dashed out to look the scene over. So long."

"So long, Ernie," she said and watched him hurry away toward his car. Maybe if she had fine clothes, like Barbara—— Then, turning, she saw the pilgrims coming through the back hall door and Miss Renie there, leading them down the passageway to see the batiks on the wall and her room with the big bed and the harp-shaped mirror and everything.

Tammy could not keep still because of the excitement that filled her. She walked back and forth and then moved to the foot of the steps, just looking. My, but there was a sight of people coming, all dressed up in hats and flowered dresses, the men with coats and ties and carrying their hats in their hands! They put her in mind of the Pilgrimage boat she saw long ago on the river, when the people looked down and called her quaint. She was quaint, for a fact, now.

It was a funny thing, she thought all at once, how she was seeing Pilgrimage people again after so long. It made a kind of pattern out of living, as if happenings came back in a loop or a curve to where they'd been before, like the earth going round the sun and the circle of the year. The old grandmother Cratcher had come like this, walking in with her fresh eggs to sell, and she'd married the son of the big house and lived her life like a lady. And now here she was, Tambrey Tyree, come off the river—would that happening be like to happen again? She didn't know, how could she tell? Especially when there was Barbara in the dining room with a rose-colored dress showing her fair white arms, and cut so low across the front she'd pop out if she wasn't careful. She likely thought that would entice a man, and likely it would.

Miss Renie was drawing the crowd after her down the ell porch now, speaking with majesty and elegance, as was fitting. "The timbers here are chestnut, hand-hewn," she was saying, "and there's not a nail in the building. These are some of my later paintings. Those down by the kitchen door were done by a little Negro boy on the place, a pupil of mine, whose people have been in the family for generations. His grandmother is there in the kitchen doorway with the red bandanna on her head . . . the sixth generation to serve as cook. His paintings are most original."

The people began coming down the steps now, and Tammy advanced to meet them. She made a little curtsy and said, "Would you care for a drink to cool your throat, ma'am? Would you like to wet your whistle, sir?"

"Listen to her," they said, "all in character."

"Look at that dress, and the comb."

"That's the real thing."

"And barefoot, as I live."

They talked her over as if she were one of Miss Renie's pictures and didn't have ears to hear. Then they gathered closer round the table, accepting the cups she gave, saying, How lovely the garden is, and cool; saying, Look at the size of the sweet olive trees and smell how sweet they are. Then one of them said, "Could you tell us the history of the dress you have on?"

"It was made in Virginny," Tammy said, her tongue loosened all at once. "My mammy sewed it for me with a needle and a fine thread. She made it for the journey acrost the land. She sewed it strong for lasting because it was a far way to come." She turned to some newcomers and curtsied again. "Would you care for a drink to cool your throat, sir? Would you like to wet your whistle, ma'am?"

"Tell us some more," the people said. "Tell us about your journey from Virginia."

"It was a far piece." Tammy ladled out the ice water right and left. "And full of peril. We come awalking with the wagon creaking loud under what worldly goods we had, and the oxen moving slow. We come over the mountings and down by the Trace, Mammy and Pappy and me and one crawling babe that had to be toted, and some odd-size sisters—two or three. That's how we come." She stopped to wave to Osia to bring more clean cups and take the used ones away.

"She's good, do you know it?" said a redheaded young man with a row of pencils in his left top pocket. He came edging in closer and the man that was with him said, "You might get a feature out of that, Mike. I'll look around for Fernan while you're here." Then he went around toward the front of the house.

"What happened on the way?" a lady asked, chopping her words in a way that was foreign to Tammy's ears.

"A sight of things happened," Tammy said, "and some of them powerful strange. My pappy was a musical man and he had him a old board fiddle, strung with the hairs from a horse's tail. He played it with a curving bow, likewise made of the same. It made the varmints peaceable and the wildcats purr. It drawed the birds down out of the trees; they flew along singing before and behind. That was what brought the trouble on us, that was what got us grief." Tammy broke off as more people came down the steps. "Would you care for a drink to cool your throat, sir?"

A murmur went roundabout. "Don't stop. What was the trouble?" they asked. The redheaded man had a notebook out of his pocket and he looked up from what he was writing. "You can't leave it there. Come on, sister—give."

Tammy's eyes went from one face to another. "You ain't aweary of listening?"

"Lord, no!" the redheaded man said. "How could the birds make you trouble?"

"This is how," Tammy said, clasping her hands and looking round at the listening crowd. "There was a robber in that country went by a musical name. He played a harp like an angel, and they called him Little Harp. Now he noted the birds was leaving him, the mockingbird and the jay. He observed the loss of the little brown thrush and even the sparrow. And then he was bereft of them all. Only thing left was the buzzards and a mean little peckerwood bird. When it lit out to leave him, he followed it through the swamps. He come to edge of the Trace where all the birds was aroosting, while my pappy slept. It were the middle of the night by then and the campfire burning low."

Some new people came round the corner of the house from looking through the garden. They were talking amongst themselves, but the crowd around Tammy hushed them down. "She's telling a story," they said. "Be still and listen," they whispered.

So Tammy went on, "We lay on the blanket sleeping, Mammy and Pappy and me, and a crawling babe and some odd-size sisters —two or three. Now Pappy had buried his bag of gold in a little dug hole, under his sleeping head, and his horsehair fiddle was lying beside him with a night wind blowing on it, making a ghost of a tune."

Tammy stopped and looked around to see how they all were taking it. They were taking it all right. One man was sitting in Grandma's chair, but not rocking, with his eyes half closed, but not sleeping—the way Miss Renie looked at a picture, his head cocked to one side.

"Get on with the story, sister," the redheaded man said.

Tammy got on with it. "So Little Harp knowed then that the peckerwood had led him aright. He raised his hatchet and brought it down and slew my pappy sleeping, by splitting his head in two. The hatchet went down into the ground and clinked on the bag of gold. That's how Little Harp stole our treasure, how he stole the fiddle away and left us all aweeping because our pappy was dead. Mammy cut off a lock of my pappy's hair and she wove it for a keepsake. She made three tears of his fine black hair, all bound with a silver cord, and she worked a year for a Natchez silversmith for fashioning this breastpin I wear. Now ain't that enough to tell you?"

She looked round at them, and thought it was a wonder they listened so hard to one of Grandpa's old tales he was always telling about the old days.

A talking went through the crowd and a little girl said in a high thin voice, "Is she true? Is she a ghost come back?"

Everyone laughed, and the white-haired lady in the prim black hat said, "How did you get along when you came to this country?"

"By the hardest," Tammy said. "But a rich man up the road a piece, he lent us a cabin made of logs, dirt-floored, and he lent us a scrap of stumpy land, so Mammy made out by nipping and tucking and selling eggs when she had them to spare."

"But how did you ever come to live in this fine house?" a young girl in a blue-flowered dress wanted to know.

"That was the best of all," Tammy said. "It was nigh on to being a miracle for sure." She stepped back from the table, her hands clasped together as she saw herself, set back into other years. "I come up the driveway out yonder, with the fresh eggs stowed in my bonnet and my bonnet hanging over my arm. I come singing up the driveway with the live oaks on either hand."

"What were you singing?" the little girl asked.

"I was singing, 'Black Is the Color of My Truelove's Hair.' When I got to the gallery yonder——"

"Sing it," somebody said and the other cried, "Sing it—go on, let's hear how it goes."

Tammy moved away, down the walk, to give herself room, then she came toward the ell steps slowly, swinging her bonnet and singing as she came. The people fell back to let her pass. When she came to the iron steps, she mounted them halfway and turned at the close of a line. "That's how I come asinging up to the great house door. 'Will you buy fresh eggs this morning?' I asked of the young man there. He took me by the hand and said, 'I'll take the eggs and the bonnet. I'll take the gown and what's in it,' and he kissed me then and there. So he made me into a fine lady and carved this comb for my hair."

Of a sudden Tammy stopped short. She saw Pete standing in the garden beside the sweet shrub bush. He must have been hearing her foolishment and her pretending. She felt the color come into her cheeks, thinking how she might have put a notion in his head. But all the folks were still waiting, so she had to make a finish to her talking. "That's how I come to the great house, and how I lived here till I died."

There was a great clapping of hands and talking as she came back to her table and took up the gourd. Then the main body of the crowd moved on through the garden and Pete came and stood by her side.

"That was like a song. Every word of it," he said, with wonder in his tone.

"It's just an old story Grandpa told me, added onto what Miss Renie said."

"Will you do it each day for the pilgrims?"

"If you want, Pete." She looked up at him smiling because he seemed so proud and pleased.

"So your truelove's hair is black, is it?"

"Yes."

His eyes smiled, but all he said was "I've got to get back to the front door now. There's another bunch coming."

Tammy watched him out of sight, then she helped Osia with the cups. Osia said, "I heerd you, Miss Tammy. You got a gift."

"Have I, Osia?" She was still in a daze because of the look on Pete's face. Then she saw the redheaded man coming toward her from the drive.

"That was a sharp skit all right. How about answering a few questions for me?" he said.

"I don't know much," Tammy said, "but I'll answer what I can. What manner of thing do you want to know?"

"Where'd you pick up your material?"

Tammy shook her head. "I didn't pick up anything."

"Aw, please. Where'd you get your story?"

"Oh, that. From Grandpa mostly, and what Miss Renie told me about her grandmother."

"And the technique?"

Tammy shook her head.

"Not talking, eh?" He gave her a curious look. "Are you telling your name? I'll find out, but if you don't want me to use it——"

"Do you mean my real name or——"

He grinned. "I'd like your stage name, too."

"I haven't but one name. It's Tambrey Tyree."

He looked puzzled so she spelled it for him. "Thanks," he said. "You a relative of the Brents?"

"No. Oh, no."

"Visiting, for the Pilgrimage?"

"No. That is, I'm just staying here."

"Oh, I see. One of the Pilgrimage roomers, like Fernan."

"No. I'm just staying while Grandpa's in jail."

"Jail! Say, what are you giving me, the run-around?"

"I'm not giving you anything."

"Are you telling me! But would you please just answer a few questions for me? After all, I got to make a living." He grinned at her. "Now, where do you live?"

"On the *Ellen B.*"

His friend came up and stood listening. He helped himself to ice water and watched Tammy over the rim of his cup.

"What's the *Ellen B.?*"

"It's a boat."

The redheaded man ran his fingers through his hair. "Is this straight?"

"No," Tammy said, "you've rumpled it all up."

He turned to his friend. "Am I baffled! She says she's staying here while her grandfather's in jail." He turned back to Tammy. "Would you mind telling me who your grandfather is?"

"No."

"See—she won't talk."

"I didn't say I wouldn't talk. I said I wouldn't mind telling you. My grandfather is John Dinwoodie. Brother Dinwoodie. But some folks call him Old Deadwood on account of his getting the bodies out of the river."

The two men looked at each other. "Say, that rings a bell. Was he the man that rescued Pete Brent after the plane crash?"

"Yes, we done it together. Got him off the log in the night."
Tammy drew a breath of relief because now their questions began
to make sense. She told them all about it, and how Grandpa came
to be in jail. They were real interested, she thought, and they
thanked her several times.

"Now if we could just get a few shots——"
But the other man interrupted. "I got some beauts while the
show was on." Then they thanked her again and went away.

Tammy thought she would sit and get her breath while waiting
for the next group of people to come. She started for Grandma's
rocking chair and saw it was occupied. The same man she had seen
earlier was still sitting there. Then Mr. Bissle came down the steps.

"Congratulations," he said, beaming. "You ought to go to
Hollywood."

"Where might that be?"

"Good Lord, you're joking! You mean you don't know?"

"There's a sight of things I don't know, Mr. Bissle."

"It's where they make the movies. All the big actors are out
there. It . . . it's——" He gave up.

"Grandpa doesn't hold with play acting."

"Lord!" Mr. Bissle said again. He hiked up his pants and went
along the garden path, shaking his head.

Tammy went to the steps and sat down. For a little while she
and the man in Grandma's rocking chair were the only people in
the garden. He sat without moving, his feet on the footrest, a pencil and a small book in his hand. He wore no coat, his shirt was
open at the neck and his gray hair was uncombed.

"Tammy—is that your name?" He called it Tam-mee.

"Tammy is my name," she said.

"Do you mind that I made the sketches?" He tapped the little
book in his hand.

"Sketches?"

"The small pictures. You permit?"

"Me? Of me?"

"Yes." His small dark eyes watched her, unblinking.

"Pictures, like Miss Renie makes pictures?"

"Do you mean those on the wall?"

"Yes."

"Heaven forbid!" A lock of gray hair fell across his forehead as he shook his head.

Tammy studied him gravely. "You don't like her pictures?"

"They are——" He shivered.

"And you would tell her that if she showed them to you?"

"So help me, I will."

"Then I will not let you make pictures of me."

"Do you know who I am?"

"No, but I think you are Mr. Fernan, maybe." He did not look like a great man. His skin had a curdled look, like cheese; his face was wide and flat. But she had never seen a great man, so he might be one after all.

"Yes, I am Fernan. Do you still refuse?"

"Yes."

"Do you want me to lie about those paintings?"

"No. But you could be kind about it."

"My business is to paint, not to go through life saying things that are not true." His speech went up and down like the speech of those who came from the French-speaking parts.

"It is a little thing to do. Miss Renie is kind."

He shrugged his shoulders. "I will, for you, do what I can."

"Then you may make my picture. But why do you want it?"

"It is a long time that I have been looking for one face and one form. Now I find the two together. I make a great painting, to cover one large wall, many figures, showing the building of this country and what has gone into it and how the country is now. One woman I want in the center, a pioneer woman, looking forward now, as she has always looked forward and seeing clearly. I find her here by chance, after all my looking.

"Me?" Tammy asked with wonder.

"You."

"It would be a great honor to be so painted, by a man whose renown is in the streets."

"Yes."

Tammy leaned over, elbows on knees, chin in hand. He could not have seen Barbara or he would not be wanting her to be in his picture. She had better tell him. "There is someone you haven't seen—in there."

"You speak of the one in the dining room?"

"Yes," Tammy said with sadness, "wearing a dress like a morning cloud the sun has shone on before the sun comes up. But she is a barbarian at heart."

"Why do you say that?"

"It is the meaning of her name."

"I do not wish to paint a barbarian. And your name—has it a meaning?"

"Immortal is the meaning of my name."

For the first time he smiled. "I am very pleased with you. Now tell me something of these other people in this house where I am to stay."

"There is Miss Renie, who paints."

"Yes, what of her? Besides her painting."

"She thinks she will be a cat when she dies. She does good and reviles it, and she works hard at staying sane."

"Who else?"

"Mrs. Brent. She is in the parlor in a red-brown dress."

"I know how she looks, for I came first through the house. What is she like, really within? That is what I would know."

"A bug in a bottle. She finds consolation in . . . in making arrangements. She is a respectable woman and quickly shocked."

"And the Mr. Brent? In the library, without doubt?"

"Professor Brent. He is a man of quick mental parts, but his words weigh him down and delay him. He knows the science of matter. That's what he teaches in a college."

"And the young man? He who welcomes those who come?"

"Pete. Pete——" She was silent, trying to think how to tell about Pete, trying to separate thought of him from feeling. "How can I say?" she said at last. "I see him only with my heart."

Mr. Fernan smiled again. "I shall have great pleasure in painting you. But now, here they come, the thirsty ones. Will you sing for me while you give them to drink?"

"Sing?" Tammy looked back over her shoulder to him as she hurried to get into her place again.

"But yes. Have you no more songs?"

"I can sing a sight of songs—'Lord Lovel He Stood at His Castle Gate' and 'Make Me a Cambric Shirt' and 'One Saturday Night as We Set Sail' and 'Last Night I Dreamed of My True-love'."

"Then sing them for me, please. Begin with 'Cambric Shirt.' I like that name for a song."

As the people came down the steps, she began filling the cups and singing at the same time:

> "Make me a cambric shirt
> Without a stich of needlework,
> And you shall be a true lover of mine,
> Rosemary and thyme.
>
> "And wash it in yanders well
> Where water never flowed and rain never fell.
> And hang it on yanders thorn
> That never bloomed nor blossomed since Adam
> was born."

She sang it through many verses, her voice thrown back and echoed by the house, so that it rang out clear and true. Mr. Fernan nodded his pleasure and the people clapped. So she went on to another and another song, through all the afternoon.

18.

ONE day followed the other in the Pilgrimage and each was like the other in the way it took up everyone's time and attention, and in the way the crowds came swarming in to hear Tammy's songs and the story she told of her bonnet and gown. There was just one wonderful difference. Every day after the first, when she came singing to the steps with the bonnet swinging on her arm, Pete was there. When she looked up at him, he took her hand and bent and kissed her, according to her words. Then she put an end to her story, saying, "That's how I come to the great house, and how I lived here till I died."

What Pete was thinking inside himself, she did not know. It seemed as if he had somehow, for the time of the Pilgrimage, fled into the past, like it might be a city of refuge in the land of Canaan. But for Tammy every day went up to one high point, as she mounted the steps to meet him. All the days of her life gathered themselves together and waited for that moment, then added it and mounted higher. Pete did his part in dumb show, putting out his hand at the right time, bending to give her the kiss, waiting for the final word of the story, then walking with her down the steps while people clapped and laughed. First he kissed her on the forehead, then on her cheek, and Tammy thought that if the Pilgrimage would only last long enough, he might make it all the way to her lips.

Mrs. Brent had come to the ell gallery the second day. Tammy had seen her there behind the rose vine watching, amazement on her face. Tammy didn't know how she looked when Pete kissed her because when that happened she knew nothing else in the world. But when Pete was hurrying away toward the front door to receive other guests, she heard his mother say, "Really, Peter, is that necessary?"

And Pete had answered, "No, Mother, but it's fun—and people seem to like it." Then all Mrs. Brent's friends went crowding around her on the porch, saying nice things and congratulating her. She put off her sour look and bowed and smiled and said, Yes, she had thought they would like it, and Yes, it was one of her best inspirations.

It was the newspaper a few days later that really upset her. Every morning there was a great cleaning to be done because of the passing of many feet over the carpets and because of the dust that seemed to create itself each day anew. Pete worked in the yard and the garden with old Prater helping, for people were untidy, throwing papers and trash that had to be gathered up before the new day's guests arrived. This morning Tammy was sweeping the front gallery. Mrs. Brent was among the roses, gathering fresh bouquets for the vases when Pete came up from the drive with the morning's mail and the newspaper.

"See this, Mother," he said, stopping by the circular rose bed below the steps and holding the open paper out for her to look at. "Good picture, isn't it?"

"How on earth——" Mrs. Brent began. "Why, I didn't know this was going on!" She stood with her arms full of roses, staring at the paper. "Why wasn't I called out to see to it? And of course, Barbara should have been in the picture. Really——"

Tammy went on sweeping, but when she heard her name, she stopped in wonder, listening.

"Is it all about Tammy?" Mrs. Brent said.

"Mostly," Pete told her. "Except this about her grandfather."

"Her grandfather!" Mrs. Brent leaned over the paper. "Oh, dear me, why did they have to——"

Tammy came slowly down the steps, the broom clutched tight in her hands. Something was wrong, something had happened to

Grandpa. She stood frozen at the foot of the steps while Pete and his mother read on, her heart pounding.

"It's outrageous! They should be sued for putting such things in print. And who told them? Tammy, of course!" She turned and caught sight of her standing there. "Oh, Tammy, why did you? I told you not to talk. I begged you not to and here——" She made a gesture of despair and turned away. "It's too late now."

"Wh-what is it?" Tammy faltered. "I . . . I wasn't going to talk, but then you told me to. You said——"

"It's all right, Tammy," Pete said. "It's only the truth, and very interesting, at that."

"If you'd only called me, Tammy. If you had only let me know the reporters were here, I could have managed everything."

"I didn't know . . . I haven't seen any . . . but what is it? Has something happened to Grandpa?" She came up to Pete quickly. "Please tell me."

"Your grandpa's all right." He turned on his mother. "You can't blame Tammy, Mother. Mike could get information out of a stone. I saw him here the first day of the Pilgrimage."

"Mike?" That was what the redheaded man was called, Tammy remembered.

"There," Mrs. Brent said with indignation. "She knows all right. Oh, I might have known!" She went off with her roses, snapping the scissors at the empty air.

"See, Tammy," Pete said, holding the paper out for her. "Not a bad picture of you."

"Me?" Tammy turned troubled eyes from Mrs. Brent, disappearing around the corner of the house, and looked at the newspaper. "Goshamighty!" she whispered, seeing herself standing on the ell gallery steps, the lacy black ironwork making a frame for her. "I never seen myself in a picture before in all my born days."

Pete laughed. "You probably didn't even know when he took it, did you?"

Tammy shook her head. Then her eyes ran down the page.

"There's printing about me, too," she said in wonder. She read with haste, skipping in her excitement. ". . . original touch to the usual Pilgrimage routine . . . charming sketch given by Miss Tambrey Tyree in the gardens of Brenton Hall . . . authentic costume belonging to the Brent family . . . family tradition and river folklore . . . romantic story back of her presence . . . granddaughter of John Dinwoodie . . . daring river rescue of Peter Brent after plane crash below Vicksburg . . . Old Deadwood, as he is known on the river . . . now an inmate of the Forestville jail . . . claims to be victim of a court 'unfavorable to human freedom' . . . especially with reference to the making and selling of corn liquor . . . preaches daily to his fellow prisoners . . ."

"I reckon that-there is what your ma don't like," Tammy said with a sigh. "That-there about the jail and corn liquor. What gets me is how they knew all that."

"Did you talk a while with Mike? The redheaded chap?"

Tammy nodded. "He asked me a sight of questions, but how was I going to know?"

"Of course you couldn't. Never mind Mother; she'll get over it when she sees the crowds this will bring."

"You mean people will read it and come?"

"Sure they will."

Tammy looked toward the corner of the house where Mrs. Brent had disappeared. "I reckon I'd better just shut my mouth and act like I'm dumb the rest of the time."

"You can't do that, Tammy. Why, you're the best part of the Pilgrimage."

"Am I, Pete?"

He looked down at her smiling. "Of course you are."

Then Osia called from the front door, "Miss Tammy? Miss Tammy? That there Mr. Fern, he want you to come set while he draws your picture."

"Tell him I'll be there soon as I finish sweeping the steps."

Miss Renie came out on the gallery. "Tammy, run quick! He

wants you. Never mind the steps, for heaven's sake! What are you thinking about? Give me the broom."

Pete stood watching as Tammy ran up the steps, handing Miss Renie the broom as she passed. Miss Renie began to sweep in long strokes, flinging the broom as high as her head each time. "I never expected to see you sweeping, Aunt Renie," he said.

"You never expected to see the world's greatest artist on the back gallery either, did you?" Miss Renie snapped.

"Is he really the world's greatest?" Tammy called back over her shoulder.

"He's the world's greatest that we ever had on the back gallery, I can promise you that." She gave a final flip of the broom and hurried back into the house, saying, "I've got to go and watch."

Tammy sat on the ell steps, holding herself stiff, her face set and still. Mr. Fernan was in Grandpa's chair on the brick wall in front of her, drawing pad and pencil in hand. "But no," he said looking up, "it is not necessary that you stop breathing for me. Relax—" he smiled—"and talk to me."

"You mean I don't have to be still."

"Not that still."

Tammy drew a long breath and leaned back, resting her elbows on the step above her. "I just seen myself in the paper, Mr. Fernan. I never seen my life and my name put down in print before."

"No? It happens often to one." He glanced up to the gallery where Miss Renie was sitting, sheltered by the vines, but near enough to see and hear. "Me also, the young man has put through a series of questions. I escaped him for several days but he caught me on the walk yesterday."

"Maybe I should not be so puffed up," Tammy said.

Mr. Fernan nodded gravely, looking at Tammy and back to his busy pencil. "The first time it happens, one is apt to be puffed up."

"The young man led me on. It's maybe a way he has learned."

Miss Renie rested her arms on the iron railing and peered down at Mr. Fernan's drawing. Though she had fairly gone wild at the thought of his coming, she was hushed by his presence. A kind of awe seemed to have come on her and she had even avoided him as he went to and from his room in the ell. This was the first time Tammy had seen her come near him.

Mr. Fernan paid her no mind but went on talking with Tammy as he worked. "I see that you make a study of people. Each day when they come, the pilgrims, as you say, I watch you, how you watch them."

Tammy said, "I have to, to catch up, because I have no learning and I've lived all my remembering life away from people." Then she told him how when she was on her way here she had pretended she was a pilgrim on a pilgrimage and then when she got here the Pilgrimage had come to her. "It is a wonder how many kinds of people there be, coming from all parts and talking strange ways. But they all have two eyes and two ears and members alike one to the other. They breathe this same air and smell the sweet olive all in the same manner. And they have a living and a dying and a begetting in between."

Mr. Fernan nodded. "It is the common ground to all, that of which you speak. One of the great aims of art is to make apparent this common ground, to show this large likeness by way of the small, and so pass into the region beyond time."

"Beyond time," Tammy repeated. "I reckon I been living outside of time all my born days. Not just account of having no clocks to mark its passing but because——" She paused, trying to find the words.

"Because," Miss Renie said all at once, "because you have been concerned with the fundamentals of living, the universals."

"Exactly." Mr. Fernan looked directly at her for the first time. "It is in her face. It is what I have been seeking. Here I find it at the moment when I give up looking and come for vacation. *Le bon Dieu* has sent me." He was silent, working steadily, his feet planted on the footrest.

Miss Renie could make no answer. Her hands were locked tightly together and she sat stiff and tense, breathing quickly.

"Another thing I have found—it is your little pupil, Miss Renie, the little black boy you call Roots. You have taught him well, not too much."

Miss Renie's hand rose to her throat. Her black eyes were fixed on him now with a fierce bright light.

"Some of his drawings—the charcoal, I think of now—they go back farther yet, beyond even the fundamentals of which we have spoken. They are the thing before it becomes the thing, the thought before it is conceived."

"But Roots said that," Tammy cried. "About the one that looks like something coming out of a mist. He said 'That's something before it gets here.' And about another one, with a far line like the rim of the sky or the end of the sea and with only a near small curve at the front, he said 'That is me and the . . . the bigness.' "

"Exactly." Mr. Fernan turned to Miss Renie. "Your pupil will go far, Miss Renie. It should satisfy you that you have put the brush in such a hand. It is enough to have lived for that alone."

Miss Renie bowed her head and hid her face in her hands.

"Continue in the same manner," Mr. Fernan went on. "Give him the simple arrangements for line and perspective and balance, and for the rest, let him be free."

Tammy brought her hands together silently. Mr. Fernan had been kind after all. This was better than talking of Miss Renie's paintings. Miss Renie knew her own work was nothing to talk about.

Then Mr. Fernan added, his eyes on Tammy: "This, too, I can say in all truth. I like your batiks very much, Miss Renie—that gown you wear for the pilgrims, the hanging of the gryphon and the papyrus plants, the one of figures dancing in the woods. They have a softness of texture and color, a vagueness of outline. Nice, very nice, indeed."

Miss Renie's hands, pressed close against her cheeks, could not hide the radiance of her face. She made a little choking sound but no word came.

Mrs. Brent came down the gallery with a basket of red japonicas and some glass bowls. She set them on the table beside Miss Renie, looked at her and said, "What on earth's the matter, Aunt Renie? You look as if you'd been struck by lightning."

"I have," Miss Renie said in a whisper. "Be still, can't you?"

"Why should I be still? What's going on?"

"Don't you see? Mr. Fernan is drawing Tammy."

"Tammy? Why in the world should he draw her?" She had dropped her voice but Tammy could hear just the same.

"Because she has beautiful lines."

"The idea! She's very odd-looking, that's all. Why can't he wait and do Barbara? Tammy's had enough publicity."

Tammy said, in answer to Mr. Fernan's lifted brows, "She doesn't like it because I told them and they put it in the paper, about Grandpa's being in jail. It looks like everything I do is wrong."

A sadness settled over her. Every time she got her hopes up that she was not so different from people, something came along to take her down and set her in a lowly place. Likely enough it was just because she was odd-looking that Mr. Fernan wanted to draw her.

19.

THE time of the Pilgrimage was passing. Tammy tried to delay its going, but the tighter she held to each moment, the faster it slipped through her fingers. It was a hurrying, pressed and filled-up time, and yet with all that was happening, there was something more for which she waited and which did not come. Pete had said that morning in the field, that it was a relief to get it all settled. Yet he didn't act like one who had settled on anything. In the mornings and other times when the Pilgrimage was not carrying him away into the past, he seemed more withdrawn than ever, though maybe with one difference. There was a set look to his jaw. He was maybe thinking then of the life ahead of him, Tammy reflected, of the long days in an office that seemed stale and unprofitable to him, for all the money there might be.

Barbara had a kind of triumph round her all the time. In her lovely rose ruffled dress, she was fair as the moon, an army with banners, taking Pete like a city. Tammy turned away from the sight of her sometimes, when she was laughing and talking with him, and calling, "Oh, Cousin Al, come here—I want you to hear this," making up to Mr. Bissle like he was a bundle of myrrh.

Other times, in the morning when she was helping clean, Tammy would call to Pete as he passed by. She would say, "I been out to look at the tomatoes. They're sure doing fine." Or again she would say, "You know, Pete, cattle is one thing hail don't cut down in a moment. And once you get a start of cattle, they multiply and increase, give them time."

Another day when she was waiting for Mr. Fernan and Pete stopped by the steps for a moment, she told him something she had been thinking about the night before. "Pete?" she began with such earnestness that he laid down the sketch he had been turning this way and that to see if it really favored her.

"What, Tammy?" He had the gentle way, the kindly look in his dark eyes, that always made her heart melt and her bones as water.

"Pete, I been thinking. What you need is a little money to start you a herd of cattle."

"I've been thinking that for some time, Tammy."

"Well, I got money you could have."

"You? What do you mean, Tammy?"

"Grandpa give it to me. He said, use it if I needed. It's hid in a tin can, under the head of Celeste that died on Christmas day and——"

"Celeste?" Pete puzzled.

"You know, in the graveyard. The grave above ground. It's right there, buried. I been thinking if it ain't used I'll be like the man that digged in the earth and hid his talent."

"Tammy," Pete said, shaking his head, "would you do that for me?"

"Sure I would, Pete. You could pay it back if you wanted. You could pay it back with . . . with usury."

Then Mr. Fernan came and Pete just smiled and shook his head and said, "Thanks just the same, Tammy. I won't forget that."

Another morning when she was posing again, he came from the front of the house with a newspaper in his hand. "Hey, Tammy, look here," he said. "Your grandpa's in the paper again."

"Goshamighty," Tammy said, "what's happened now?"

"He's all right. It just seems that the good ladies of Forestville have decided it's a shame to have so godly a man in jail. May I interrupt a minute, Mr. Fernan?"

Mr. Fernan laid aside his pencil and studied his drawing. "Time she was having a little rest. We have been hard at it."

Pete dropped down on the steps beside Tammy and opened the paper for her to see. She read the headline: OLD DEADWOOD RE-

FUSES TO LEAVE JAIL. She turned to Pete. "Now what does that mean? How could he be leaving when they put him in there by law?"

"There's more about it down here," Pete pointed out. "The ladies persuaded the judge to dismiss the case."

Tammy bent over the paper, reading the fine print. "On being told that he was to be released from jail today, Old Deadwood, self-styled prophet of the penitentiary, berated the judge for his leniency, declaring that he will not be a party to such inconsistency on the part of the law. 'I ain't got a notion of leaving till my time is up,' he said. 'Trouble with this country is it's too wishy-washy and this-here is just another instance of it. Let the judge stand his ground. I mean to stand mine.' A number of prominent citizens have recently been attending the services at the jail, and we have it on good authority that Judge Derryberry expects to be one of those in attendance next Sunday. 'Thirty years on the bench,' he is reported to have remarked, 'and this is something new to me.' Old Deadwood has already announced his text, 'Unstable as water, thou shalt not excel,' and he hopes the judge will be present."

"Well, I declare," Tammy said. "Grandpa has always been itching to get after shilly-shallying in high places. Looks like he's going to do it."

Mr. Fernan said, "It is something to which I look forward, meeting your grandfather, Tammy. He is a man after my heart."

"He is an original character, if there ever was one," Pete told him. "These years on the river he has done a great deal of thinking, and his ideas are worth hearing." He turned to Tammy. "One thing I'm glad of: that he isn't coming to take you back to the *Ellen B.* You can't possibly leave with all these swarms of people coming especially to see you."

"Do they come to see me?" Tammy asked with wonder.

"Of course." Pete rose. "I'll tell you something else. The committee had been talking about taking Brenton Hall off the Pilgrimage list. They do that sometimes, if a place isn't kept up. But

you've done more for it than two coats of paint and a new roof."
At the foot of the steps, he turned and looked at Tammy as she
took her pose again. "We couldn't let you go, anyway, Tammy."

It was something to think about and treasure and remember,
Pete's saying that. All the rest of the morning she kept hearing
how he had said it. "We couldn't let you go, Tammy." It made a
kind of song in her heart.

But by dinnertime clouds were blowing across the sky, darkening the earth and threatening rain every minute. There could be no
ice water in the garden today. Everything had to be inside, and the
rain, beginning soon after the hour of the Pilgrimage, kept many
people away. Pete did not come out to do his part because she did
not do hers. There was no room on the rain-spattered porch. It
was cool and nobody cared for ice water to drink. So Tammy could
sing naught but sad songs this day, because of missing Pete and
their play acting, and because she could see how Barbara came
often from the dining room to stay with Pete in the front hall.
Tammy could hear her laughing and talking with Pete there and
welcoming those who came, as if she asked them into her own
home.

Tammy was singing about Lady Nancy Belle whose lover came
too late and found her in the churchyard, when she heard the sound
of a truck in the driveway. Grandpa was climbing down from the
truck; he was coming through the drizzling rain across the garden
toward the ell steps. He was coming to take her home to the *Ellen
B.,* she thought, and in the midst of her singing the tears came
slowly down her cheeks. Standing, waiting for him to come up the
steps, she finished the song and thought it was lucky it was sad,
because then maybe the people standing around would think her
tears a part of her pretending. They were clapping for her when
Grandpa got to the top of the steps and gave her a great hug. Then
he held her at arms length. "Hell's bells, honey, I never knowed
before how much you favored your grandma!"

"Do I, Grandpa?" She wiped her tears away with the back of

her hand. "It was Miss Renie fixed me up like this. And Mrs. Brent give me the notion of acting out the story. Only today, the rain come."

"I read about you in the paper, child, and it sure made me proud."

"I been reading about you, Grandpa. Are you . . . free?"

"Well, in a way, honey, except for myself keeping me to it, according to my principles and disregarding that slipshod judge. I got a chance to ride to Fairhaven with a man coming this way, and so I says I'd just come by to see how you was doing."

"And you didn't come to take me back to the *Ellen B.?*" she cried, feeling like dancing and singing all at once in spite of the rain.

Grandpa shook his head. "It don't look like the time is yet come for that, honey. There's still work for Old Deadwood in the vineyard of the Lord. My sentence ain't yet fulfilled and I don't figger on cutting it short."

Tammy drew a deep breath of relief. Then, the people being mostly gone, she led him to where Mr. Fernan sat in Grandma's chair that was set inside, near the kitchen door today. Mr. Fernan told how he was making the pictures of her so she could be in his great painting.

"I make the quick sketches," he said, holding out his drawing for Grandpa to see and marvel at, because it was so like her. "She is to be the central figure." Then he went on to tell how the painting would be in a great building in New York and how it was to show the past and the present too, and the discoveries of science and the state of the world and how people today were in a confusion, looking back always with fear and longing to the past.

"Yessir, that's the truth about present-day people," Grandpa said, sitting on the iron rail where the drip from the eaves fell on the back of his hat and rolled off in a little shower to the ground. "They put me in mind of the goofus bird, for a fact."

"What does the . . . the goofus bird do?" Mr. Fernan asked.

"It flies backwards all the time," Grandpa said. "It don't give a durn where it's going; all it cares about is where it's been."

"Exactly," Mr. Fernan nodded. "I shall have a goofus bird in my painting, if you can tell me how it looks."

"Well," Grandpa pushed his hat still farther back on his head so he could scratch and think, "now you mention it, I don't know as I ever seen one to know it. But I imagine it's a kind of heavy-bodied, long-necked bird, something like a cross between a crane and a wild duck, with a touch of pelican throwed in just for meanness."

Mr. Fernan rubbed his hands together with pleasure. "I can see it plainly. It is what I need—just back of Tammy I shall place it, and above, against the sky. Very good indeed. I am grateful to you for the idea."

Tammy stood in her long calico dress, her hands clasped before her, looking to one and then the other as they talked. She was proud of Grandpa as he went on to talk about how he was trying to gather up the best out of the past, to save its faith and its willingness to venture without fear. He told of how he tried to give folks things to believe in and to go on. "We got to have a new religion and a new philosophy built on what parts of the Bible will fit in with the findings of man's reasoning mind in a scientific way," he said. "We got to throw out the parts of all our religions that don't make sense in the light of this day and hang onto the rest—and that's a plenty, I tell you. That's what I'm apreaching, because that's what I come to believe during my sojourn on the river and my meditations in the swamp."

Tammy laughed. "Sounds like you's fixing to preach Mr. Fernan a sermon, Grandpa."

Grandpa said, "No, I ain't got the time today, much as I'd like to."

"I'd like to hear it," Mr. Fernan said. "What church do you serve, Mr. Dinwoodie?"

"No church at all, sir. The churches don't take to me, because I got no education excepting the Bible and common sense and what I pick up here and there and think up in my mind. And I don't

hold with churches because they done got too filled up with hocus-
pocus and too emptied of the true teachings of the Lord."

Mr. Fernan nodded, agreeing, and Grandpa added, "Looks like
you and me is fermenting the same barrel of mash, sir. Seems like
there's some hope for the world when two folks like us, going in
by different bungs, come out the same spigot."

Then Pete joined them and welcomed Grandpa and begged him
to stay for a visit. "We'd be so glad to have you," he said.

"And I'd be proud to stay in this mighty fine place you got here.
Yessir, the Lord's done set you down in a wide place, Pete. But I
got to go along now. Maybe toward the end of the week I'll come
up and make you a little visit, the Lord willing." He spat a mouthful of tobacco juice down on the flower bed and shook Pete's hand
and Mr. Fernan's. "I just run by to see how my little girl was
doing."

"She's doing all right," Mr. Fernan said.

"That's good; that sounds mighty fine to me," Grandpa said,
giving her a good-by hug. "I ain't doing so bad myself, honey," he
added. "They tell me that if I want to be assistant jailer any time,
the job is mine."

"Why, Grandpa! But the *Ellen B.*—and me——"

Grandpa chuckled and shook the water from his hat brim.
"Don't you worry, child. I got my eye on you all the time. Just
you keep on like you're doing, and I'll be seeing you soon." He
bowed again to Mr. Fernan and looked from Pete to Tammy and
back again. "It's all in the Lord's hands. He ain't failed me yet."
And having said that, he went away through the gray evening.

Tammy, watching him go, thought again as she had the day at
the jail, that Grandpa had a long head on him, there was no two
ways about it. She looked round to Pete to see if he knew what
Grandpa was leaving in the Lord's hands, but Pete was looking
toward the hall doorway where Barbara stood. Tammy's heart
sank, for Barbara was beautiful beyond words as she came toward
them with a shine in her eyes and warmth and a glow to her bare

arms and shoulders and the pure swell of her bosom above the rose-colored dress. Pete moved to meet her. Pete was like a summer bug, drawn to the light.

Barbara swished her rose skirts past Tammy and came up to Mr. Fernan who was still sitting in Grandma's chair. "I'm Barbara Cray, Mr. Fernan, and you don't know me from Adam, but I know you, of course."

Mr. Fernan would have risen but that she waved him down again. "Yes, Mam'selle?"

"I was wondering if you would like to go in with us to see the dress rehearsal of the Rebel Ball. We've been working on the dances in little groups for weeks and now it's really something. And if you want to make some sketches of the dancers, this night would be better than later when the big crowds will be there. It's awfully artistic." She smiled down at him, tilting her head to one side and showing a dimple in her cheek.

Tammy, watching her, knew that she was wanting Mr. Fernan to draw her picture. Likely, Mrs. Brent had not mentioned how she had asked Mr. Fernan yesterday to make a sketch of Barbara, and how he had said no thank you, it was an ordinary type and he preferred something more subtle and rare. Mrs. Brent had been furious.

"Thank you so much," Mr. Fernan began now with a slow inclination that was like a bow. "It is so kind of you."

"Then you can ride in with Pete and me, and Pete can bring you back."

Pete said, "I'll be delighted."

"So very kind," Mr. Fernan went on as if there had been no interruption, "but I do not believe it would interest me."

"You mean . . . you don't want to go?" Barbara stared at him, her mouth open in surprise.

"Exactly, thank you," Mr. Fernan said. "You have, I think, too much of the past here. One grows weary of it. On all sides I hear it said, 'My grandfather was old Judge Soso; my great-uncle,

Colonel Soso. . . . A thousand slaves we had. The great balls—we duplicate one for you so that you may come into our dream of the past.' No, I have too much. You do not look enough to the present and to the future."

Barbara looked set back for a second, then she waved to Mr. Bissle who was coming in from the drive and said, "Oh, some of us are old-fashioned and all, Mr. Fernan, but when it comes to living, we're as up-to-date as the next. You ought to see our country club at Longhaven if that's the kind of thing you want. All modernistic, and as smart a crowd as you would find anywhere and a hot jazz band. And if you want to see an up-to-date house you ought to see the one Ernie has just bought. At least I think he's closed the deal."

"Ernie has bought a house?" Pete's tone was incredulous.

"Sure he has—that white modernistic job on the country club road. Every gadget and convenience——" She broke off to welcome Mr. Bissle. "Hey, Cousin Al, come here. Mr. Fernan is sick of antiques, he wants something modernistic, and I want you to convince him we've got that, too. Didn't you say our country club is as swell as any in New York?"

"Sure it is," Mr. Bissle agreed, shaking the rain from his hat. "Air-conditioned and everything. Swell joint."

Barbara slid her hand through his arm. "What's more, you liked the Rebel Ball too, didn't you?"

"Now that's really something," Mr. Bissle said. "Hollywood could take notes on how that's put on. What you need though, Barbara, is some decent advertising—mass-psychology appeal, that sort of thing. 'See the Ante-Bellum Belle! Who Put the l'Amour into Glamour'—all that kind of thing."

"Oh, Cousin Al, you'd really put us on the map. Heavens, I've got to dash and change." Barbara picked up her skirts and ran along the porch toward her room. "I'll be ready in a minute, Pete," she called back over her shoulder.

"Okay, Barbara."

Tammy, seeing his eyes follow her as she hurried along the ell porch, drew a long sigh. This happened every night—Pete drove Barbara in to town, they went to dinner and to the rehearsal, dancing together as she had seen them that first night. She would be glad when the ball was over.

Mr. Fernan was speaking, his sad dark eyes turned on Mr. Bissle. "Twenty years I put in at business. That is how I gained the leisure and the financial independence to become an artist."

"That so?" Mr. Bissle stopped with one foot on the step that led to the upper ell porch.

"But I would not recommend that to a young man. Better to combine the two—a sustenance job, part time, and leisure to pursue some creative art, part time also. That is the ideal. It is also the solution of the economic difficulties of production."

Pete stood motionless looking at Mr. Fernan. After a minute he said, "That interests me very much."

Mr. Bissle asked, "What business were you in, Fernan?"

"Ever hear of the Fernan shoe?"

"Sure thing. Who hasn't. High-class product. Crisp and Pico handle their advertising. It's an account I wouldn't mind having myself. You connected with the business at all now?"

Mr. Fernan shook his head. "I have finished. Did I not tell you?"

Mr. Bissle went on up the steps. "It's a pity."

Tammy stood over against the wall, watching Pete. He seemed to be studying Mr. Fernan with a curious earnestness, but when he moved nearer, Tammy saw that it was Grandma's chair he was looking at.

Mr. Fernan turned to him. "You, too, admire? It is an excellent piece of work. It is a chair of which there should be more."

"A small business—that's what you said, wasn't it?"

Mr. Fernan brought his hands down on the arms of the chair. "Exactly." His sad eyes lighted up. "I see what you think. It is a good idea."

Tammy let out a little gasp. "You mean people would buy chairs like that?"

"Just give them a chance. You have the wood in plenty?"

"Hickory? There's enough for anything."

"And the hides?"

"Well," Pete said, "with a herd of cattle one might manage."

Tammy's hands were pressed against her breast so nobody would hear how her heart was pounding. Pete had found something to do, right here at Brenton Hall. Like Grandpa said, ready to hand. Then she heard what Pete was saying.

"He's really skilled at anything of the sort. Roots, by the way—" he nodded at Roots's paintings on the wall behind Mr. Fernan's head—"Roots is his boy and he has some of the same sort of ability, I imagine. I've been trying to figure out something to keep him on the place. With a lathe——"

"No, no, no," Mr. Fernan broke in. "By hand it must be, with the stroke of the knife blade showing. There are enough people who appreciate true craftsmanship."

Tammy had turned away. All Pete was doing was fixing things for Steve. He would get Steve started, then he would go away himself. Or did he mean that Steve might help him, that he himself—— "Pete——" she began.

Barbara came down the porch in her town dress carrying her suitcase. She broke in as usual, as if no one else in the world had anything to say. "Come on, Pete, while the rain's stopped," she said with impatience. "We're going to be late. Here's my bag. It's such a nuisance to have to carry my costume back and forth." She gave Pete time to do no more than wave good night.

As they went down the walk together, Tammy heard him ask, "Where's Ernie?"

"He went back early. Why? Don't you want to take me?" She sounded cross. "Damn this weather!"

"Of course, Barb, I just——" Then their voices passed out of hearing as they went toward the carriage house and Pete's car.

Tammy watched them, thinking Barbara was likely mad because Mr. Fernan had not wanted to draw her picture. But she had Pete. She should be content, no matter what. Tammy looked around at the long gallery. How dreary and chill it was, for all its fine ironwork, how empty the whole house was without Pete!

The rain began again after supper, and whenever she woke in the night, Tammy heard it beating on the roof and beating against the windowpanes as if it would drown all her hopes. Maybe it was good for Pete's tomatoes, but it was ruination for her. Oh, surely there could be no more rain left in the skies. But there was. All the next day the rain came at intervals, and when the pilgrims arrived, there was still a drizzling. Mrs. Brent was in a state about the mud that was brought in and tracked over the rugs. Tammy was downhearted too, because there would have to be another day for her like yesterday, and no play acting with Pete. There was a crowd in spite of the rain. The porch was filled so there was scarce room to move about in, and it was warm and muggy so that many people came for her drinks of water, and she sang as she served them.

Then toward the end of the afternoon Professor Brent came out to the ell gallery bringing with him some men who, she saw at once, were not like the other pilgrims. She studied them as she sang. They had a manner of importance and dignity and they stood in a row against the wall, not looking at Miss Renie's paintings but watching and listening to her song and arguing among themselves with a low buzzing. Several in the crowd looked around at them, annoyed, and one woman said, "Sh-sh, for shame," but they did not seem to hear. They were no doubt people unaccustomed to being sh-sh-ed by anyone.

When she came to the end of her song, while the crowd was still clapping, Professor Brent brought them nearer and she served them water. They drank without seeming to know what they were drinking, their eyes on her, as if she were some new kind of animal they had never seen before.

"I thought," Professor Brent was saying, "that you would find it interesting, gentlemen, in the light of what I told you of her environment—a sort of challenge to our educational system." He turned to Tammy, his dark eyes twinkling. "Tammy, you may remember I told you I would present to some of my colleagues the question of your education?"

"Yes, Professor Brent," Tammy said, standing very straight and looking gravely from one to the other.

"Well, they came by this afternoon on their round of the Pilgrimage. This is Professor Carley of the English department." He indicated the younger one who looked as if he had been ordered from among the men's suits in the catalogue, he was so perfect, though small size. "And here is Professor Fureau of Education, and Doctor Somer of Psychology."

Tammy said, "Howdy" to each one as his name was called, then as they seemed to be waiting for her to say more, she looked again at the mail-catalogue one. "I can read and write English already," she said.

He smiled, showing his even white teeth that were the falsest-looking real teeth or else the realest-looking false teeth she had ever seen. "There is a little more to it than that," he said, not telling what it was, keeping it secret inside himself. "How did you learn these delightful folk songs?"

"Grandpa used to sing me to sleep with them, and Grandma knew a sight of them, too."

"And how did your grandparents come to know them?"

"Oh, they just come down to them like they come down to me. Old songs, they are, that have been a long time ripening through all the course of time. That's what makes them pure and sweet."

"Um-m." He patted his lips with a blue-bordered handkerchief that matched his eyes and set down his cup so he could put it back right in his front coat pocket with the corner showing.

"It would be rather interesting," Doctor Somer said to Professor Brent, "to try out the free association series on her, to determine her aptitudes, in fact, to give her all the intelligence tests."

"You mean——" Tammy hesitated, then gathered her courage and went on——"you mean you know how to test me to see if I have any sense?"

"Er . . . in a way, yes." He plucked at his brown pointed whiskers, studying her through his thick-lensed spectacles.

"But," Tammy puzzled, "looks like if I didn't have any sense, somebody would have noticed it before now."

Doctor Somer looked annoyed when Professor Brent laughed and said she had plenty of sense. "You, as a man of science, Professor, should be the last to find it amusing that we are applying the scientific method to psychology. I assure you that it is possible to gauge and analyze intelligence in as objective a manner as the chemist uses in his laboratory."

Tammy was shaking her head, remembering how Osia had warned her not to let anybody monkey with her brain. "Seems like I wouldn't like getting my mind tore up and pinned down like that. Besides, how can you? A mind's kind of moving and open, like—like water."

"It's really very simple," Doctor Somer said, his voice losing its sharpness, "and not at all . . . er . . . harmful. Merely a matter of human engineering. Through these aptitude tests we discover the various compartments and at the same time we relate them to the contemporary social configuration."

"Oh," Tammy said. "But—I don't know. Seems it might be better to keep the mind free-flowing."

"That's just what we don't want—all this vagueness." He turned back to Professor Brent. "You see what we must fight against constantly, this notion that the things of the mind cannot be classified scientifically. The focus of consciousness is off center and——"

"Center of what?" Professor Brent interrupted. "You know, Somer, the mere use of scientific terminology——"

While they went on arguing, the other professor held out his cup to Tammy. "May I have some more?"

Tammy dipped up some cool water for him and asked, seeing the others were not noticing her, "Are you the one he said teaches Education?"

"Yes," he said in a kindly tone.

"Then it seems to me like anybody wanting an education wouldn't have to look any further. You could just teach it all to them and be done with it."

Professor Fureau looked pleased. "We cover the field pretty well in our department." He brushed some hairs off his coat collar though it was a wonder where they came from because his head was mostly bald. "Of course, I myself am an exponent of methods."

"Methods?" Tammy puzzled. Pete was coming from the back hall and she beckoned to him to hurry. He could maybe help her to understand.

"Yes," Professor Fureau said, with a nod to Pete as he joined them. "You see we have worked out an approved method for teaching in each of the areas—or I should say, nuclei—of the various subjects, for we are as scientific in Education as they are trying to be in Psychology."

"Looks like Grandpa's right in style, Pete, making the Bible scientific," Tammy said with pride.

"And," Professor Fureau went on, "we are of course making every effort in these days to correlate the subjects with reference to their societal value. Personally, however, being a specialist in methodology, I am occupied mostly with the methods of teaching the various methods."

"Oh," Tammy said. She seemed to have come up to a standstill with him now as she had with Doctor Somer. It was the tongues they spoke in that made them so hard to figger out. And yet now she thought maybe she had a glimmer of what he meant. "Meth-

ods of teaching methods," she repeated. "It's likely arranged the
way it is when you hold up a looking glass in front of another one
and you see yourself looking at yourself looking at yourself——
Goshamighty——" she turned to Pete in dismay—"it's enough to
scare you, how it could go on forever. Maybe I don't want education, Pete. I just want to get taught some learning."

Pete moved closer to her. He looked from her to the professors,
his dark eyes twinkling. But he said nothing at all.

Doctor Somer, who seemed to have argued himself out of argu-
ments for the moment, turned back to Tammy saying, "It would be
interesting to try the tests. I'll see what commitments I have."

Pete said, "I always came out at the bottom on those things. Always got to thinking that maybe some of the answers didn't really
fit any of the questions and that there were actually a lot more pos-
sibilities. Then first thing I knew the time limit was up."

"You are perhaps the too-many-aptitudes person. We run across
that type now and then."

"I reckon," Tammy said, "that to get to be a professor of it, you
must have known every one of the answers right when they gave
you the tests."

"Me?" Doctor Somer blinked behind his thick glasses. "What a
very curious idea. Why, I am one of those who helped standardize
the tests." He glanced at his wrist watch. "This has all been very
interesting I am sure, but——"

They all began to move away except Professor Carley who had
been standing there studying Tammy all the while. She turned to
him now. "Is there anything you want to—to do to me?"

He smiled his secret smile, lifting his brows. "Academically
speaking, no."

"Coming, Carley?" Doctor Somer called with impatience.

"I'll be right there." Again he lowered his voice. "All quite
wacky. Don't bother with them. Thanks for the songs and I'd like
to hear you sing again some time." Then, seeing they had all
turned and were listening, he added, going away, "And about the

problem of your education, to institute actual implementation—"
he gave her a slow wink as he spoke—"I could send you a list of
the hundred ten books———"

Tammy looked after them as they disappeared down the hall.
"Somehow, they all seemed to be more taken up with themselves
than———"

Pete was scowling at Professor Carley's neat back. "Academically, no," he muttered. "Why, the little———"

Tammy said, "Did he mean I could just read some books
and—— What is it, Pete?"

"Oh, let him go. Honestly, my father must have combed the
campus to get that bunch together. Usually there's one out of
three that isn't so . . . so . . ."

"They're all so serious," Tammy said, "and disturbed. I thought,
being so educated, they would be—well, that they would kind of
pleasure in it more."

Pete looked down at her, his face softening, his eyes holding
hers. "Didn't I tell you, Tammy, back on the river, you know the
important things already?"

Before she could speak, Barbara called from the back hall door,
taking him away. But she could not take away this one small magic
moment they had had. The memory of it stayed with Tammy all
the evening, after they had gone to town to the big ball. The way
Pete had looked at her—it warmed and cheered her that night
against the sound of rain falling steadily on the roof. She told the
Lord in her prayers how important it was for the sun to shine next
day. "After tomorrow, Lord," she said, "let it rain a flood if You
like, but tomorrow I'm bound to have the sun and no two ways
about it."

Morning showed her that the Lord had heard for sure. The sun
was shining as it never shone before, and every green leaf and
every blossom seemed washed clean and readied for the coming of
the pilgrims. They came in swarms and droves all through the
warm afternoon, they flocked to the garden for a cool drink of

water, and when she began to tell her story, there were yet others who came straight from the parked cars to hear her before going in to see the house.

When she came up the walk, swinging her sunbonnet and singing "Black Is the Color of My Truelove's Hair," she sang it loud and clear and gaily as never before. And this time when Pete took her hand and bent to kiss her, he found her lips. Then she could speak no more for a moment; she could only stand there with her eyes downcast and the warm color flooding her cheeks.

But Pete spoke up for her and said, "I'll take the eggs and I'll take the bonnet. I'll take the gown and all that's in it."

Then her voice came back and she lifted her head to speak proudly, saying, "That's how I came to the great house, and how I lived here till I died." She dropped Pete's hand quickly and ran back to her table, not looking at him or at anyone, but scooping up the ice water and handing it right and left without a word because her breath came so fast and the pounding in her ears drowned out the chatter and the clapping that was louder and longer than ever before.

20.

THE Pilgrimage was over. The certain, the beautiful past had withdrawn into itself again and there was left only the confused present and the uncertain future. The house had put on its usual air of shuttered quiet, the fine china was stored in the dining-room cabinets, the dead flowers were thrown out, and the dust was once more gathering undisturbed on the books in the library. Brenton Hall could rest in shabby seclusion for another year. It no longer mattered that the parlor carpet was threadbare, that the sofa in the hall had a block of wood in place of one leg.

At dinner on the ell porch Mrs. Brent said, "Well, that's over for another year. One of our most successful seasons. I only hope there'll be enough money handed out to homeowners this year so that we can reshingle the roof and replace the front steps. Really yesterday, with all that crowd, I was afraid they'd give way." She drew a long sigh. "If only Mr. Bissle—from something he said last night I thought——"

Professor Brent said, "I hope I'll have a little quiet next week to finish my outline for the new course."

Miss Renie said, "Thank Heaven the Pilgrimage is over! Now I can dye in peace."

Tammy turned to her in alarm. "You are going to die?"

"Yes, my batik. The one of the woman walking, bowed and resigned, alone under the live oaks with the moss hanging down like widow's weeds. I want Mr. Fernan to see it before he goes. It is symbolic."

"What's it symbolic of, Aunt Renie?" Pete came out of his absorption to ask.

"Of my acceptance of life and death, of my conviction that it is enough that I have taught Roots well. It will show that I have accepted my fate."

"It's good to have it all settled, Aunt Renie." Pete smiled. "After speculations and wonderings, struggle and indecision, it is surely good to have come to some sort of settlement of things."

"You're so understanding, Pete." Miss Renie gave him a sharp glance from her quick black eyes.

The others looked at him hurriedly and away again, trying to hide their watchfulness and as usual not succeeding. But this time, Tammy thought, Pete did not close up and draw back from their anxiety and their eagerness to know and to be reassured. There was something new in his face and manner, a quickening, a resolution. Her heart stopped beating for a moment and began again with hard painful throbs. Was he remembering the last day of the Pilgrimage when he had bent to her on the steps? Or was it something that happened in his long talk with Mr. Bissle last night after everyone had gone to bed? How could she know? How could she wait to know, feeling this tightness in her breast, this wild wondering that possessed her mind?

Pete leaned forward, looking from one to the other, as if he were about to speak. Then a car came into the driveway. He looked around and his face lighted up. "There's Barbara now."

Ernie and Barbara came up the garden walk together, Ernie talking with excitement in his tones, Barbara interrupting, "But Ernie, you old dope, why do you have to be so mysterious about it? Why wait till tonight? Tell me now, for heaven's sake."

Pete went down the steps to meet them. "Hi, Ernie," he said, giving him an affectionate slap on the shoulder. "Come on, Barb. I want to show you what I've been doing in the south woods."

"Oh, Pete—in these shoes? In this——" She looked down at her high-heeled red slippers, her peppermint-striped dress of silk.

"I don't care whether you have on shoes or not," Pete said.

Barbara looked at him in amazement. She said, "Okay, Pete,"

put her hand on his arm and called out in the direction of the porch, "Hey there, I'll see you all later." Then they went off arm in arm by the garden path, toward the lower gate.

Ernie called, "Hurry back, Barb. I've got to be in Jackson before five o'clock." They paid him no mind and he came onto the porch, grumbling. "I like that."

Miss Renie said, "Have some dinner, Ernie. We've just finished, but Osia can bring you a plate."

"Thanks, Miss Renie, but Barb and I stopped at Freddie's joint on the way down. I haven't got much time," he added, looking after Barbara and Pete resentfully. "Barb wanted to pick up her costume and stuff—she's going to have a picture taken next week for that Pilgrimage-calendar thing Mr. Bissle dreamed up. So, as usual I'm just a chauffeur." He sat down on the steps with a sigh. "You all going back to town soon, Mrs. Brent?"

"Yes, Wednesday perhaps. I've so much to catch up with there —a club paper on Trends in American Literature on Friday, and two committee meetings Saturday. It'll be nice to get back into things."

Tammy let the talk flow unheeded around her. She could not have listened if she had tried. She knew now what Pete had made up his mind to—Barbara. It had always been Barbara. Mr. Bissle came down and joined them, sitting at the cleared table in Pete's place. He was talking, but Tammy did not listen till she heard Pete's name.

"Yes, I've got a hunch about that young man. Had a good long talk with him last night—about other things, of course. Always sleep on a hunch, that's my motto. But I may as well tell you now, I can use him in my business. He can get his training in the New York office; then there'll probably be an opening in the Atlanta branch by the time he's ready."

Mrs. Brent could only say, "Oh, Mr. Bissle!" on a long breath.

Professor Brent said, "Well, if it's what Pete wants—I've said all I am going to say to him."

"Of course," Mr. Bissle went on, beaming like a premature Santa Claus, "I must admit that I have it in mind to be helping my little cousin Barbara at the same time. Smart girl, Barbara. She'll fit in all right."

"Yes, yes," Mrs. Brent breathed. "Oh, sometimes, the way things work out—though I shall miss him terribly—it does seem as if there is a design after all. I——"

Miss Renie got up and left the table abruptly, with a kind of snort.

Tammy stood uncertainly, and nobody noticed her. She walked slowly down the steps, and when Ernie caught at her skirt, she struck it free from his hand and went on. She stopped once on the garden path and looked back at the house, Pete's house. Pete's and Barbara's it would be. She might as well go on down to the road and set out now for Forestville and the jail and Grandpa. No use waiting to see them come back from their walk, all shining with happiness. She could not bear that. Walking like someone in a daze, she turned into the driveway, passed Ernie's car and went on under the great oak trees.

Ernie caught up with her, halfway to the gate. "Say, wait a minute." He turned her around and looked at her. "Knocked for a loop! Well, there's two of us. Where you going?"

"To the jail. To Grandpa," she said. The gay light was all gone from Ernie's eyes, he had a stricken look. She marked it in the midst of her own dazed hurt.

"Listen, kid. There's no place for you at the jail." He stood a moment in thought. Then he said, "I've got to go to Jackson. Lord know's I don't want to be here at the rejoicing, not any more than you do. You wait here. I'll step back and pick up my car and tell them you're coming along for the ride." He did not wait for an answer but hurried back toward the house.

Tammy walked slowly on. Ernie, too, she thought. Well, he would take her away for a ride. Maybe when she got away, she could think. Maybe in Ernie's car the wind would blow this haze,

this fogginess from her brain. Then she could take it in, that Pete
was lost to her forever.

The wind blew faster than any she had ever felt, even when a
tempest blew along the river. Black clouds piled up, rain poured
down. But she stayed in her hopeless blur. Ernie was sunk in his
own thoughts. The rain-drenched fields and the woods flew by, the
towns too, without her turning her head to see. They had no interest for her any more.

Then Ernie began to talk. "Damn it all," he said. "Just when
I'm onto something big. Just when things for once were all going
my way. . . . I never gave up till now."

Tammy felt his despair that was like her own. "I saw you look
at Barbara one day. I knew."

He laughed a short laugh, and his voice was bitter. "I've been in
love with Barbara since we were in grammar school together. I'd
have got her too, in spite of everything. Only Pete—he had to
come into the picture, just before he left for overseas. Pete—tall,
dark and handsome. So she ditched me for him. Hell, I said, and
went on into the Army."

They rode in silence, Tammy feeling it a comfort to have Ernie.
It was better than being alone. Without a flicker of interest, she
saw they were coming into a city, weaving in and out of traffic.
Ernie said, "Of course, you were licked from the start, poor kid.
But that doesn't make it any easier."

"Licked from the start," Tammy repeated, hands twisting and
turning in her lap as if they itched to be doing something about it,
as if they upbraided her for being so still and beaten.

The rain had stopped when Ernie turned the car into a sloping
space along the edge of a sidewalk. "Now you just sit here,
Tammy. I'll be back in a little while. Then we'll know whether to
go jump in the lake or—— You wait, hear me?"

"Yes, Ernie, I'll wait."

After he had gone, she began to look around, her wits working
slowly. This was Jackson. Where they made the laws. Where they

made the law that had put Grandpa in jail and sent her to Pete's house. It was a horrible city. She hated all the people in it, hurrying along the walks, looking in the fine store windows, all dressed up in fancy clothes and hat and gloves, with the big buildings going up to the sky. It wearied her to see them.

Then the car door jerked open and Ernie got in beside her. He looked as if lightning had struck him. He looked all on fire and shaken to pieces, too. When he took out a cigarette and lighted it, his hands were shaking. "What is it, Ernie? What on earth——"

He leaned back and laughed. It looked as if he would never get done laughing. He wiped his eyes and blew his nose and said, "Well, it's happened. Now of all times. A day earlier and it might have done some good."

"What are you talking about, Ernie? What's the matter?"

"That little piece of stumpy no-count land, that godforsaken hole down in the country, that place I've been trying to sell for the last ten years to keep from paying the taxes on it." He turned to her. "Oil, baby. That's what. Oil. The well's come in. Black gold. Money, that's what I've got. More money than you ever heard tell of. Ernie's. Too late, but money just the same. And maybe it's never too late for money. How about it? Shall we start celebrating? Drown our sorrow in riotous living?"

"What—what do you mean?"

"Come on, honey child, let's go to it. Here's the town. Let's eat, drink and be merry! Come on." He caught her by the hand and pulled her toward him across the seat, flinging his door wide.

Tammy pulled back, remembering her faded blue dress, her bare feet. "I can't go nowhere, Ernie. I ain't got my shoes, and my hair's all blown."

Ernie looked at her. "True, little one." He seemed to have got his spirits back all in one swoop. "But money! There's nothing money can't do. Say, this is going to be fun. Come on."

He pulled her out of the car and across the walk with people staring at them, stopping to look and point. He walked her through the big glass doors and into a store so large and fine that one could easily get lost in it. He led her quickly to the back, to where there was a wide door in the wall, and a man standing in a little room. Some people were coming out, others going in. Ernie pushed her ahead of him into the room. "Ladies' clothes, please," he said in an ordering tone.

The door closed and they began to move—straight up! Tammy clung to Ernie, feeling her stomach drop down to her toes. No one showed any dismay, so Tammy clamped her lips together and let out no sound after the first gasp. They stopped, the door opened and some got out, some stayed. Again there was the terrible swoop of upward motion. Again they stopped and Ernie led her out to where she could stand on a solid floor. She swallowed and caught her breath. "What are you going to do with me now, Ernie?" She held tight to his arm, waiting for her stomach to get back into place.

"You'll see." He led her across a carpeted open space.

A beautiful lady with gold hair piled high came to meet them. She had on a silky black dress that fitted her shape so that anyone could see where everything was and no doubt about it. "Something for you, sir?" Her eyes were going over Tammy, startled and scornful, long-lashed, blue eyes.

"Yes," Ernie said. "I'd like to sit down and talk."

"This way, please." She led them to some elegant seats and a long velvety sofa.

Ernie sat down and lighted a cigarette, taking his time to it, while Tammy sat on the edge of the seat, tucking her bare feet back as far as she could and looking around in wonder. Beautiful dresses hung in long racks against the wall. False ladies, like the one she had seen when Ernie showed her Fairville, stood motionless, with dresses on them. Real ladies walked about in the wide spaces, all elegant with hats on and gloves, and other ladies, bareheaded, met them and said, "Something for you, madam?"

Ernie tapped his ash on the velvet carpet. "Will you get me the head of the department, please?" he said, cool and commanding.

The tall blonde lady stood a moment, as if she didn't know what to do, looking from Ernie to Tammy and back again. "Certainly." She went off with her nose in the air.

After a while another lady came. She had white hair done in braids on top of her head. "Yes, sir?" she said, her eyes going to Tammy, sweeping over her, down to her bare toes.

Ernie said, "Strip her and start all over. Everything. Give her the works."

"No, Ernie. Ain't nobody going to strip me," Tammy said.

"Then strip yourself, sugar. We're going to outfit you from the skin out. Can you see to it for me?" he asked the lady.

"Certainly, sir. I will send to the other departments for what's needed."

"Ernie," Tammy said, sitting straight and proud. "It ain't decent. I won't do it. All these people around! Your money's put you out of your mind." She shook her head at the tall lady. "I won't do it. It ain't decent."

The lady said, with a wondering look that covered them both and left her still wondering, "I will take you to a little private room where you can undress without being seen."

Ernie gave her a push. "Run on, baby. We can't take all day to this. I'm getting thirsty."

Tammy looked from one to the other. "You mean you want to get me new drawers and . . . and everything?"

"At last you get me." Ernie grinned. "Lord, I thought I was past enjoying life. I thought sorrow's cold hand had chilled my blood beyond all warming. But there's life in the old boy yet. Beat it now, both of you." He leaned back half smiling, drawing on his cigarette.

Tammy followed the lady across the room, the carpet soft under her bare feet. They went through an open doorway and down a narrow passage, past curtained rooms. Tammy peeked into one as they passed and saw a woman nigh onto being plumb naked. They went on till they came to an empty room, curtained off and having many mirrors.

"Here we are," the lady said. "Now let's get that dress off so I can take your size." She measured Tammy with a long tape measure, trying it round her in several places. "You have a nice figure, a perfect fourteen. Now I'll be a few minutes collecting things for you. Just sit down and wait."

But Tammy could not sit down yet. She stood before the center mirror and saw herself three times, coming and going and straight ahead. Then she walked around the little room. There was only one chair and a little shelf in the corner with pins and a small white comb. There was a window, too, looking out on a bare, blank, brick wall. Tammy pressed her face against the pane. It was about a mile down to the ground. She got dizzy, looking so far down. Then she took the comb from the shelf, hoping nobody would mind, and combed the tangles from her hair, standing in front of the looking glasses, seeing how her flour-sack petticoat hung limp around her legs, seeing herself three times over. It would be enough to drive a body crazy, she thought, if she had to look at herself multiplied like this all the time.

Then the lady came back with boxes and, over her arms, a pile of white silky stuff. "Let's get our clothes off now, dearie."

"You going to take yours off, too?"

"Me? Certainly not. What are you talking about?"

"You said our clothes."

"No, no. Here, let me help you." She took hold of the petticoat.

"I can do it."

"Now the . . . er . . . the other garment. . . . Now just step into this little number. One of our newest. It's a panty girdle."

"It ain't got any opening," Tammy said, turning it about.

"Here, put your foot in. Now the other. Pull it up."

"Hell's bells!" Tammy wriggled from side to side. "If I get in here, I ain't ever going to come out again, that's sure."

"Oh, you'll get used to it. There. It's a lovely fit."

"B-but supposing I have to go to the——"

"You can just pull it down," the lady said with impatience. "Now let's try this bra."

"Whereabouts do I put it?"

"I'll show you. Hold out your arms. Now this slip."

"Slip? It's a petticoat, a pretty petticoat for sure." It slithered on like water against her skin, white silk with lace at the top and all around the bottom.

"Now sit down and we'll get our stockings on."

"You already got yours on," Tammy said, and then realized that was just the way the lady talked. Maybe she figgered they were still her stockings till Ernie paid for them. "These-here things are going to cost a sight of money," she said, troubled.

"The gentleman does not wish the cost to enter into our choice. Easy, now. These are our fifty-one gauge, best quality—Night Mist."

"Don't seem much point in putting on anything you can't see. I'm as naked with as without."

"That's why we recommend them so highly." She fastened them up with the snappers that dangled from the girdle. "Now, try these shoes. I think they are the right size. I'll get the other things."

Tammy sat down by the hardest. She was bound round her middle and her hips like a sore finger. She studied the shoes and thought they were mostly heels. "Can't get my foot into any such foolishment as that," she said. But somehow it went in. When she stood she nearly fell over. "Like that pair of stilts Grandpa made me one time. I reckon I can get around on them if I go easy, but I can't go far, that's sure."

The lady was standing there watching, a dress and a bunch of pink flowers in her hand. "Your gentleman friend suggests this little ensemble." She held it up. "It looks better on. Just lift your arms. That's it."

Tammy moved her hands down over her sides, feeling the softness of silk. She looked at herself in the slim, straight gray dress and she shook her head. Pete would not see her. What was the use?

"Don't you like it?"

"Ain't it kind of bare in front?" She pointed to the deep *V*.

"There's a short cape." The lady put it around her shoulders, a gray silk cape lined with rose just the color of the buttons down the front. It fastened at her throat and fell in graceful folds that rippled when she moved. "And now the hat." She set it on Tammy's head and then stepped back, clapping her hands and smiling for the first time. "I wouldn't know you for the same! It's the most amazing thing. Just shows what clothes will do."

Tammy studied herself in the looking glasses, equally amazed. The hat was little more than a circle of pink roses, but beautiful. She was dressed as fine as Barbara ever was, and she looked just as nice—only what good, now, to be so fine? Still, there was no denying that even in the midst of her grief it was a comfort to see how she looked. "I wouldn't know myself, for a fact," she said.

When she got out into the open part of the store, Ernie did not know her either, for a minute. "Jeepers!" He stood blinking at her. "A slick chick, if I ever saw one." He whistled.

"Do you like it?"

"Oh, brother!" Ernie turned to the lady. "Good job. Now give me the bill and I'll make you a check. But be quick. . . . Her things? Oh, just put them in a box and we'll throw them into the car."

Outside, Tammy walked slowly so she would not fall over her shoes, and held herself straight so her hat would not come down over her face. Ernie put her old clothes in the car, and they walked on down the street. People turned to look after her, but they did not look the same sort of looks they had looked before, when Ernie was taking her in. Ernie, walking close beside her, kept his hand on her arm, and he was looking, too.

The walks were wet. Tammy stopped once and said, "Ernie, I'd better take off my shoes and stockings, hadn't I? They'll be ruint."

"No matter, sugar. Let them get wet. I'll buy you more if need be. Holy smoke, don't you realize we're in the money now?" He turned the corner with her and they went in at a wide door, through a hallway hung with paintings like Miss Renie's, only bigger, then to a big room where people sat at tables and men in white coats moved around with trays and dishes of food. There was music coming from somewhere and there were candles burning in tall candlesticks on every table. There were flowers, too.

When they were seated, Tammy said, "Ernie, did it cost five dollars to get in here? I saw you give that man——"

"It'll cost more than that to get out, sugar." He talked to the man in the white coat and gave him more money, and after a while he came back with a package that Ernie put in his pocket and took right out again. It smelled like corn liquor when he poured some into the glasses with ice in them.

"There are ways," Ernie said. "When you've got money, you can have anything. Here's to misery!"

Tammy took a sip and it stung and burned all the way down into her stomach, so she knew it was corn liquor or something akin and went slow on it. But Ernie kept filling up his glass. The music played, and people talked all around them, and strange dishes of food were brought them. Ernie ate and drank and Tammy ate. None of it seemed real. Pete and Barbara—they were far away, together, in another world. The ache stayed inside of Tammy but it was strange to her, like the dress and the hat and the undergarments that held her stiff and straight.

When the dishes were gone and nothing left but cups of coffee, Ernie leaned toward her across the table. "Funny how a broken heart keeps right on beating, isn't it?"

Tammy nodded.

He put one hand over hers where it lay on the white table cover. "Funny how you can still feel, isn't it?"

Again she nodded, her eyes fastened on him, gray and serious.

"Nothing revolting about me, is there, baby?"

"No, Ernie, no. Of course not."

His eyes brightened as his hand moved over her wrist along her arm. "Kind of like it, don't you?"

"Y-yes," she said with wonder, looking down at his hand. "For a fact, it does pleasure me—after a fashion."

He drew back with a sullen look. "What do you mean, after a fashion?"

"I mean——" She considered it for a moment, then her eyes looked past him, seeing the gray morning, the field and the broken tomato plants. She felt Pete's arms around her, his body against hers. "There ain't nothing . . . holy . . . about it."

Ernie filled his glass. "I've been asked to be lots of things to lots of women in my life, but, oh my aching back, nobody ever asked me to be holy!" He drained his glass. "Pete! I suppose he's holy."

Tammy nodded, turning her head aside to hide the quiver of her lips.

Ernie beat on the table with his fist. "What's he got that I haven't got?"

Tammy shook her head. "I don't know, Ernie."

"I'm a man, aren't I?"

"Far as I know, Ernie, you got members and parts like any other."

Ernie leaned back in his chair and laughed aloud. People at other tables turned their heads. A man in a white coat came hurrying over. Ernie straightened up. "Another one like the last," he said to the man.

"But, sir, I'm sorry, but——"

"It's all right. Take it with me."

"Yes, sir." He went away and in a minute came back with a package that he helped Ernie put in his pocket.

"That's the stuff," Ernie said. He lighted a cigarette. Then he leaned one elbow on the table and looked at Tammy. "Something mighty tantalizing about you, honey. That's what I told the lady in the ladies' ready-to-wear. Give me something discreet but tantalizing, I said. You know something, honey shild?" His liquor was beginning to mush up his tongue at the same time it loosened it. "I been thinking about you. Trouble with modern women———" He stopped and puffed on his cigarette. "Always get philo . . . philosophical this stage. Modern women, trouble is, they don't tantalize. They give all, 'fore you get round to asking."

Tammy leaned back in her chair, sadness coming over her. All her finery, all the sweet music and the flickering candles, the elegant silver and the gay company round about, became as dust and ashes.

"Same thing's true of modern litera . . . literashure. Tells all— 'srevolting." He hiccuped. "Excuse me, 'srevolting, I say."

"Yes, Ernie." Tammy smothered a yawn.

"Modern cour'ship all wrong. Miss half the fun." He leaned his arms on the table to steady himself. "Now how's about you and me getting married, honey?"

Tammy's mouth dropped open.

"Don't say 's so sudden. Been working up to it all evening, having won-wonderful time." He gave himself a shake and said quite distinctly, "If you can't have what you want, better take what you can get. Makes sense, doesn't it?"

Tammy nodded slowly. She reckoned it did. But . . . Ernie?

"I got money to burn. Got a house . . . pay for it in the morning, now I got the dough. You'd love it. Push a button and it chews up the garbage. Push another and it puts the cat out. All this and Ernie, too—how can you hesitate, baby?"

Tammy considered it gravely, seeing herself married to Ernie in fine clothes, pushing buttons, moving amid wonders. Then slowly she shook her head. Not even if the house was beamed with cedar and raftered with fir. "I don't think Grandpa would like it, Ernie," she said, thinking to ease his hopes down.

"Goshsakes, I don't want to marry Grandpa! Question is, would you like it?"

All at once weariness came washing over her in a wave. Ernie was drunk and Pete was lost to her forever and she was sick of heart. "Please, Ernie. I just want to go to bed."

He nodded. " 'sall right with me, honey child." He started to rise and sat again suddenly. "Get married in the morning."

Tammy said, "We can talk about it in the morning."

"Okay." He beckoned to a waiter who came and helped him up. "But don't ever say I didn't ask you. Always do the right thing, that's Ernie. This cover it?" he asked the man, giving him a handful of bills.

Outside, it was deep dark, though lights were still burning on the streets. She had stayed out till after dark and then some, Tammy thought, but that didn't matter any more. Nothing mattered. She took Ernie's arm so he could walk straight and they went back to the car. He was a long time getting it unlocked because he couldn't find where to put the key. "Can you make it go, Ernie?"

"Sure I can, sugar. Lemme just put my mind on it. Never get too stewed to run a car. Hotel isn't far."

"We ain't going to any hotel. We're going to Grandpa."

"Funny," Ernie said. "I thought it was a hotel. Must be the old brain's weakening."

"Watch where you're going, Ernie!"

He turned the wheel and they missed the side of the little tunnel they were going through. There were not many cars now, so it did not matter if Ernie's car did not go straight, in the place where it belonged to go. When they got away from the town, everything was dark and wet, with water still running across the road. Sadness stayed with Tammy, and her fine dress did not cheer her. She did not want to talk, and Ernie was silent too, needing all his mind for the running of the car. They had gone a long way when they came to a place where there were boards across the road and he had to stop.

"What does it say, baby?"

Tammy read by the car's light. "Bridge out, it says. D-e-t-o-u-r. What does that mean?"

"It's French. Means get off the road and go around."

The side road was bumpy, and water splashed. They met one truck and the man in it shouted something, but they couldn't tell what. The car slipped and slid in water and mud. After a while there was nothing ahead but water, and Ernie slowed down to look at it. Then he rested his head on the wheel in front of him and slept till Tammy shook him awake. "It's a river, come up," Tammy said. "Can the car go in water?"

"Sure it can. Just take it easy. This car can do anything. Anything. Watch it." He started it up again and they plowed into the water. It was all around them now and by the lights of the car Tammy could see it, yellow and swirling before them.

The engine sputtered, the car stopped. Ernie said, "Well, that's that." He leaned his head forward on his arms and slept. Tammy shook him, but he only muttered something and slept on.

Goshamighty, Tammy thought, what am I going to do? It's a flood, for sure. A flood? She remembered then. She had prayed the Lord to stop the rain for the Pilgrimage and she'd told Him to send a flood the next day, if He'd a mind to. Well, He'd done it all right. Here it was, a judgment on her, and no two ways about it. She studied the water moving across the road. It wasn't stopping, it wasn't going down. The little bush that quivered in the current off to the right—she thought to watch it and know by it, if the water was rising.

The woods on both sides of the car were flooded. There was no sound anywhere, only Ernie's breathing and the soft movement of the water. She tried again to wake him; then she sat still, her hands in her lap. Maybe another car would come and pull them out. But no car came.

I got to do something, Tammy thought at last, seeing the bush was deeper in the water. And me in all this finery! She reached in back, close to the window, and got the box that held her old clothes. She took off hat and dress and slip and shoes and stockings, making a neat roll of them. She put on her old things. She reached down and got Ernie's shoes off, and rolled up his pants legs as high as she could. He was limp as a dishrag, but she shook him and pulled him till he stirred. "We got to get out, Ernie. Wake up!"

"Okay, baby, 's all right," he said, not opening his eyes.

Tammy was afraid to open his door lest he fall out. She had to get out and go around. The water was cold and dark but she held onto the side of the car and edged through. It was up to her knees, and swift. On Ernie's side at last, she got the door open and jerked his feet out into the water. That woke him and he let out a yell.

"Wha's going on? Here, wait. Say, we gotta get outahere!"

"Yes, yes, Ernie, come on."

"Gotta get car keys . . . somebody steal it."

Tammy took them from him and put them in his pocket. But if thieves were coming, she'd better take her new clothes. Holding him upright, she reached in and got the bundle. Then they struggled ahead through the water. It was slippery underfoot, but solid, and they went on by the car lights till they were out of the light and out of the flood and onto the muddy road. "We've got to find a house or something," Tammy said, and urged him on. The cold water had wakened him enough so he could put one foot before the other, and so they staggered along the road. There were fields on each side, or open spaces, and back from the road at last the shape of a house.

Tammy left Ernie on the steps and went up to the door, holding her new clothes cradled in her arms. She knocked and called till a light appeared, moving at the back of the house. After a little a man came to the door, holding the lamp in his hand. "Could you let us in?" Her teeth were chattering so the words had a hard time coming out. "The c-car's stuck in the high water."

Then Ernie stood up, his hair falling over his forehead, his body rocking. Tammy ran back to catch him. "Wanna go to bed," he said. " 's cold out here. You got a drink on you, brother?"

The man stood looking at them and at the bundle in Tammy's arms. Tammy said, "I'd sure be much obliged, if you'd give me a place to put him and——"

"Humph," the man grunted. He had a disgusted look on his face. "Come on in. I can't turn a woman out in the night, but I'd like to. Wonder he didn't drown you both." He led the way inside and back through the hall to a bedroom with a white iron bed and a clean pink spread. He set the lamp down on a table. "There," he said. "Let him sleep it off. The curse of drink—I'm sorry for you, young woman. May the Lord help you." He went out and closed the door.

Ernie got to the bed and fell across it. Well, Tammy thought, looking round at the lamp, the bureau, the bed, this was what came of staying out after dark. She picked up Ernie's feet and put them on the bed, and pulled him about properly. His sock feet made a muddy mark on the clean spread, but she couldn't help that. Then she looked around the room again. There was one straight chair against the wall, so she went and sat down on it, her hands folded in her lap. She sat there a long time. Then gave herself a shake. It ain't sensible, she thought and went to the far side of the bed. She opened up the covers, flinging what she could of one blanket over Ernie. She blew out the light and crawled in beside him.

21.

TAMMY stirred in her sleep. She tried to turn and there was no room. She was dreaming of Pete and she didn't want to wake. She fought against waking, though his voice was cold and hard. "Of course it's my business," he said. Barbara came into the dream, too. "Take it easy, Pete. Be your age. After all——" She laughed.

All at once Tammy was awake, her eyes open, seeing Pete in the doorway and Barbara behind him. She sat up. Ernie rolled over with a groan, and everything came back to her. "Goshamighty!" She sprang out of bed.

Pete paid her no mind. He went to Ernie and shook him. "Get up! Get up, you——"

Ernie sat up. His feet slid to the floor, and he caught his head in his hands. "Oh, my head!"

"Stand up!" Pete said, so quick and sharp a dead man would have got to his feet.

Ernie stood, blinking. "What's the matter? Hi, Barb."

"Get ready!" Pete said. His clenched fist shot forward and caught Ernie on the chin.

Ernie fell back on the bed. Barbara said, "Pete, stop it!"

But Pete bent and pulled him up again. Ernie stood there rocking back and forth, one hand to his jaw. "For crying out loud, Pete——" He made a feeble gesture of striking out, and Pete knocked him down again. This time he fell with a crash to the floor and lay there.

Barbara cried, "You brute!" and dropped down beside Ernie.

273

"You've killed him!" She took Ernie's head in her lap. "Ernie, darling——"

"You can't kill that kind," Pete said. "Come on, Tammy." He turned on his heel and went out without looking at her.

Tammy stood rigid, staring after him. The man who had let her in the night before came to the door. "So that's how it is," he said with disgust. "You weren't married to him."

Tammy shook her head.

"Get out of my house. Might have known no decent woman would have been with that drunk. Get out now! Get going!" He went down the hall toward the porch muttering about folks that pretended, that made out they were married and weren't.

Tammy did not move.

Barbara said, "That fool Pete. Couldn't he see—— Oh, Ernie, I just heard about your oil."

Ernie came to. "Hi, toots, what's the rumpus?"

"That darn fool Pete——"

"Where's Pete?"

"He's gone." She turned to Tammy. "And you get out, too. I'm sick of you both."

Ernie said, his voice a wondering whisper, "You staying with me, Barb?"

"Of course I am, you dope, now and forever, if you want to know." She turned to Tammy again. "Will you get out of here?"

Tammy got. She went through the hall and out onto the porch. On the steps she halted. Pete was standing in the little path that led to the road, waiting for her. But he had heard her; he knew she was there. "Come on," he said through his teeth.

Tammy drew a deep breath, and fury went through her. "I'm not coming."

The man, sitting on the edge of the porch, just watching them, got to his feet now and came around beside her. "Don't you hear him? Get out of here, you——" and he cursed her.

Pete came back in a hurry. "Shut your mouth!" he said.

The man laughed. "Well, you caught her, didn't you, the dirty little——"

Pete drew back his fist and knocked him sprawling. Then he turned to Tammy. "Come on!"

Tammy flung up her head. "You ain't got no right to think things. You——"

Pete cut in on her, his eyes flashing with anger. "I don't want to hear about it. Will you come or will I have to knock you out, too?"

Tammy's hands clenched at her sides. "I ain't coming."

Pete caught her up from the ground and, holding her dangling against his hip, strode down the path.

Tammy stopped struggling. "Let me down," she said, her voice cold and hard as his had been, and quieter. He set her on her feet, and she stood there looking at him. "You'd ought to be ashamed," she said, and walked ahead of him to the car.

They drove without a word, Tammy sitting stiff and angry. When they came up the drive to Brenton Hall and he stopped the car, she turned and looked at him, a long furious look. Then she got out and slammed the car door behind her and walked with dignity across the brick garden path, up the ell steps, and so came at last to her room. She stood there looking round for a minute, lay down on the bed and stared at the ceiling for a long time. She didn't know how long she had been there when the door was flung open and Miss Renie burst in.

"Oh, you here, Tammy?" She had on an apron streaked with yellow, and a lock of hair hung down crazily across one eye. She brushed it back with one yellow-stained hand and said, "Now where is that orange dye?"

Tammy sat up, rubbing her forehead, all in a daze.

"It must be in this bottom drawer," Miss Renie said. She dropped down on her knees by the bureau, jerked the drawer open and began pawing through it. Then she pulled the drawer out and dumped everything on the floor. "I know I've got it somewhere." She went on looking, paying Tammy no mind. "There, thank heaven." She started to get up, but said, "No, I'd better put this stuff back. Ena's mad enough without finding all this on the floor."

"Mrs. Brent . . . is mad?"

"Cried her eyes out all night and now she's got a fearful headache. All she can say is 'Oh, Peter, Peter, I can't bear it!' "

"Pete? She is mad with Pete?"

"Yes, yes," Miss Renie said with impatience, stowing things away with both hands. "Ridiculous, of course. Pete never had a notion of working for that damyankee. Too much sense for that."

"He's not going to . . . to take the job?"

"Of course not. He's going to the Ag college and study cattle raising and come back and raise beef cattle and make cowhide-bottom chairs on the side, as Mr. Fernan says."

"Goshamighty!" Tammy breathed. "And . . . Barbara?"

"Oh, she's not interested—if he asked her to be, which I doubt. Now where's that dye? Oh, I'm sitting on it." She slammed the drawer shut and stood. "The moon has to be orange. I've got the yellow meadow grass waxed in and the streak in the sky and now I've got to do the moon and the little flowers. . . ." She went out talking to herself.

Tammy sat bolt upright, staring before her. "I give up too soon," she whispered. Then she dropped back on the bed, buried her face in the pillow and wept.

The room was dark when she heard steps and Professor Brent's voice saying, "I'll get you a glass of cool water, and call Tammy as I go by."

Tammy sat up in bed and pushed her tousled hair back from her face.

There came a light rap on the door, "Tammy, your Grandpa's here."

"Th-thank you," Tammy said. "I'm acoming." She got up and washed her face. Pete had likely sent word for him to come and get her. Well, he could take her right back to the *Ellen B.* Now.

She choked down a sob as she brushed her hair. Then she packed all her things in the sack she had brought them in.

Walking slowly down the hall with the bag slung over her shoulder, she heard voices on the front gallery. She stopped and leaned against the wall by the parlor door, listening. They were all out there, Miss Renie's rocker creaking as usual. She could hear Grandpa talking away, like always.

"Well, yes, Professor Brent," he was saying, "I've got St. Peter and his record book figgered out, too. Radio give me the idea. Every word spoken on the air could be picked up and recorded, so a human's whole life would be right there, when the time come to judge the quick and the dead."

"That's rather ingenious," Pete said.

Tammy caught her breath. Pete was there, too. She waited, gathering courage to face him and all the rest.

Mrs. Brent was talking along, to Miss Renie, or maybe just to herself, her voice weak and thin. "Well, I just can't ever plan anything any more. Two bombshells in twenty-four hours—it's too much."

"I'm glad Pete is showing some sense at last. That Bissle!" Miss Renie snorted.

"Really a very ordinary person," Mrs. Brent admitted, "but he does have money." She sighed heavily and went on: "And as for Tammy, well, all my friends said how charming, how unusual! She is unusual. I just hope it's for the best."

Tammy leaning against the wall, blinked her eyes and puzzled her head but she couldn't figure out what Mrs. Brent was talking about.

Grandpa said, "Yes, Mrs. Brent, the Lord moves in a mysterious way, His wonders to perform."

"Yes, yes," Mrs. Brent said. "I've just been trying to think of someone I know near the Agricultural school. The housing short-age——"

"Mother," Pete broke in, "aren't you being a bit premature? After all I haven't had a chance, and I wouldn't blame her if——"

"But you know what the housing problem is, Peter."

Grandpa said, "There's the *Ellen B.*, and the college is alongside the river."

Tammy drew a long breath. She didn't know what they were talking about. But the *Ellen B.*—that was where she wanted to go. Right now. She slid her sack to the floor and walked slowly out to the gallery by the big front door. Grandpa came straightway and took her in his arms, and she had to swallow back the lump in her throat. "I want to . . . to go to the *Ellen B.*, Grandpa. I——"

"Of course, honey."

Tammy straightened her shoulders and gathered her strength. "But there's something I got to say to Mrs. Brent because I promised her I would."

"Yes, Tammy?" Mrs. Brent said.

Tammy's eyes sought her in the shadows beyond the square of light from the front hall. "You know I promised you I'd tell you . . . if I ever . . . got into bed with a man and——"

"Oh, Tammy, I never . . . I mean . . ." Her voice sharpened. "What on earth are you trying to say? What——"

"Well," Tammy broke in on her, "I done it." She heard the gasp that seemed to come from all over the porch. Grandpa, who was just sitting down again, said, "Hell's bells, what's all this?" But she went right on just the same. "The car stopped in the flood in the middle of the night coming from Jackson. Ernie was full of corn liquor. I got him out and up to a little farmhouse and onto the top of the bed. I sat in a chair—it wasn't even a rocking chair —for a long time. Then . . . it didn't seem sensible, so I opened up the other side of the bed and crawled in with him and went to sleep. Now I told you and I reckon I better be going because I know what you all think."

Professor Brent said, "I'm sure you handled an awkward situation in an admirable manner, my dear Tammy."

Miss Renie said, "For heaven's sake, if I'd stayed out with a man all night in my day and time, my name would have been mud the rest of my life, even if he'd married me at dawn at the point of a shotgun. But nowadays you just can't shock anybody and there's no use trying."

Mrs. Brent said, "Why, Tammy, I hadn't even noticed you were not at home last night, I was so upset. And as for this—well, you are a most unusual girl, I must say. But if Pete's made up his mind to it, I'll not say a word, because I'm so thankful he's like himself once more. Only I do think we ought to try to correct your grammar before you marry him."

"Hell's bells," Tammy cried, "I ain't going to . . . to . . . marry Pete!"

Mrs. Brent bristled. "And why not, I'd like to know?"

"For one thing, he's mad at me. And for the other——"

"And what's that, pray?"

"He ain't ever asked me."

Pete had crossed the porch as she spoke, coming to where she stood in the light from the hall. He caught her hands in his. "I'm asking you now, Tammy." The chairs all creaked as their occupants leaned forward to listen.

"B-but I thought you . . . thought . . ."

"I was a fool, Tammy. I just went out of my head when I saw you lying there."

"And you ain't mad at me any more?"

"I love you, Tammy."

"Goshamighty! Right out here in front of everybody?"

"In front of the whole world," Pete said, and his lips came down to hers.

Mrs. Brent said with at catch in her voice, "What on earth are you crying about, Aunt Renie?"

"B-because I'm just an old fool and it's the nearest I ever came to a proposal!"

Grandpa said with a contentment in his tone, "Well, looks like the Lord's arranged everything right satisfactory, and I reckon Pete better be finding him a regular preacher so's they can get hitched proper. That is, if Tammy's a mind to."

Pete lifted his head at last, and Tammy looked around through the stars that spun before her eyes and shot sparks through all her innards. "I've a mind to, Grandpa," she said.